Michael Cunningham is the author of the bestselling novel *The Hours*, which won both the Pulitzer Prize and the PEN/Faulkner Award and was adapted into an Academy Award–winning film; *A Home at the End of the World,* also adapted for the screen; and *Specimen Days*. Most recently, he edited *Laws for Creations,* a collection of poetry and prose by Walt Whitman. He lives in New York.

ALSO BY

MICHAEL CUNNINGHAM

A Home at the End of the World

The Hours

Specimen Days

Laws for Creations (ed.)

Additional Praise for *Flesh and Blood*

"*Flesh and Blood* is the real thing—a novel about an American family surviving an American half-century that manages to be terrifically engaging and delicately written and heartfelt at the same time."

—Bruce Barcott, *Seattle Weekly*

"Stunning . . . In precise and beautiful prose, he explores the desire for connection and the knowledge that most of the time we remain adrift."

—*US* magazine

"Reading Michael Cunningham is like putting on see-through glasses. He's got this way of exposing his characters' deepest inclinations and motivations, letting us peer through glass directly into their souls."

—Matthew Gilbert, *The Boston Globe*

"Masterful . . . Crosses emotional and sexual boundaries with rare humanity and art."

—*Mirabella*

"Call *Flesh and Blood* a soap opera for people who value intelligent and subtle writing. . . . The telling has such grace and style that even the most predictable event catches one off guard. This is a superior novel."

—Ronald Reed, *Fort Worth Star-Telegram*

"Without ever glossing over the often irreparable harm people do to those they love, this thoughtful novel reminds us that in the end, the love is more important than the harm."

—Wendy Smith, *The Plain Dealer* (Cleveland)

"Voluptuous . . . this elegiac meditation on anger, mistrust, and loneliness has a ferocious perceptiveness that puts Cunningham on another level as an artist."

—Dwight Garner, *Harper's Bazaar*

"*Flesh and Blood* is nothing short of literary genius."

—Owen Keehnen, *Men's Style*

"The story of Constantine Stassos freshly examines the American immigrant experience and conflict between generations. . . . Thoroughly realized action, vivid character delineation, and the splendid control of language guarantee both the unity and powerful impact of this successful novel."

—*Library Journal*

FLESH

AND

BLOOD

FLESH AND BLOOD

MICHAEL CUNNINGHAM

Picador

Farrar, Straus and Giroux / New York

www.picadorusa.com

Picador® is a U.S. registered trademark and is used by
Farrar, Straus and Giroux under license from Pan Books Limited.

For information on Picador Reading Group Guides,
as well as ordering, please contact Picador.
Phone: 646-307-5629
Fax: 212-253-9627
E-mail: readinggroupguides@picadorusa.com

Library of Congress Cataloging-in-Publication Data

Cunningham, Michael, 1952–
    Flesh and blood / Michael Cunningham.
        p. cm.
    ISBN-13: 978-0-312-42668-2
    ISBN-10: 0-312-42668-2
    I. Title.
PS3553.U484 F57 1995
813'.54—dc20

                                                    94024628

First published in the United States by Farrar, Straus and Giroux

First Picador Edition: May 2007

10 9 8 7 6 5 4 3 2 1

THIS BOOK IS FOR

DONNA LEE &

CRISTINA THORSON

ACKNOWLEDGMENTS

I'd like to thank Joel Conarroe, Ken Corbett, Stacey D'Erasmo, Stephen Kory Friedman, Jonathan Galassi, Gail Hochman, and Anne Rumsey, all of whom read this book in various stages. Also enormously helpful were Evelyn Burkhalter, Marcelle Clements, Dorian Corey, Anne D'Adesky, Paul Elie, Nick Flynn, William Forlenza, Dennis Geiger, Nick Humy, Adam Moss, Angie Xtravaganza, and the members of the House of Xtravaganza, particularly Danny and Hector. The John Simon Guggenheim Memorial Foundation provided deeply appreciated financial support, and on an unseasonably cold morning in Washington Square Park, Larry Kramer generously provided me with the title.

Once an angry man dragged his father along the ground

through his own orchard. "Stop!" cried the groaning old man

at last. "Stop! I did not drag my father beyond this tree."

—GERTRUDE STEIN, *The Making of Americans*

I

CAR

BALLET

1 9 3 5 / Constantine, eight years old, was working in his father's garden and thinking about his own garden, a square of powdered granite he had staked out and combed into rows at the top of his family's land. First he weeded his father's bean rows and then he crawled among the gnarls and snags of his father's vineyard, tying errant tendrils back to the stakes with rough brown cord that was to his mind the exact color and texture of righteous, doomed effort. When his father talked about "working ourselves to death to keep ourselves alive," Constantine imagined this cord, coarse and strong and drab, electric with stray hairs of its own, wrapping the world up into an awkward parcel that would not submit or stay tied, just as the grapevines kept working themselves loose and shooting out at ecstatic, skyward angles. It was one of his jobs to train the vines, and he had come to despise and respect them for their wild insistence. The vines had a secret, tangled life, a slumbering will, but it was he, Constantine, who would suffer if they weren't kept staked and orderly. His father had a merciless eye that could find one bad straw in ten bales of good intentions.

As he worked he thought of his garden, hidden away in the blare of the hilltop sun, three square feet so useless to his father's tightly bound future that they were given over as a toy to Constantine, the youngest. The earth in his garden was little more than a quarter inch of dust caught in a declivity of rock, but he would draw fruit from it by determination and work, the push of his own will. From his mother's kitchen he had spirited dozens of seeds, the odd ones that stuck to the knife or fell on the floor no matter how carefully she checked herself for the sin of waste. His garden lay high on a crown of scorched rock where no one bothered to go; if it produced he could tend the crop without telling anyone. He could wait until harvest time and descend triumphantly, carrying an eggplant or a pepper, perhaps a tomato. He could walk through the autumn dusk to the house where his mother would be laying out supper for his father and brothers. The light would be at his back, hammered and golden. It would cut into the dimness of the kitchen as he threw open the door. His mother and father and brothers would look at him, the runt, of whom so little was expected. When he stood in the vineyard looking down at the world—the ruins of the Papandreous' farm, the Kalamata Company's olive groves, the remote shimmer of town—he thought of climbing the rocks one day to find green shoots pushing through his patch of dust. The priest counseled that miracles were the result of diligence and blind faith. He was faithful.

And he was diligent. Every day he took his ration of water, drank half, and sprinkled half over his seeds. That was easy, but he needed better soil as well. The pants sewn by his mother had no pockets, and it would be impossible to steal handfuls of dirt from his father's garden and climb with them past the goats' shed and across the curving face of the rock without being detected. So he stole the only way he could, by bending over every evening at the end of the workday, as if tying down one last low vine, and filling his mouth with earth. The soil had a heady, fecal taste; a darkness on his tongue that was at once revolting and strangely, dangerously delicious. With his mouth full he made his way up the steep yard to the rocks. There was not much risk, even if he passed his father or one of his brothers. They were used to him not speaking. They believed he was silent because his thoughts were simple. In fact, he kept quiet because he feared mistakes. The world was made of mistakes, a thorny tangle, and no amount of cord, however fastidiously tied, could bind them all down. Punishment waited everywhere. It was wiser not to speak. Every evening he walked in his customary silence past whatever brothers might still be at work among the goats, holding his cheeks in so no one would guess his mouth was full. As he crossed the yard and ascended the rocks he struggled not to swallow but inevitably he did, and some of the dirt sifted down his throat, reinfecting him with its pungent black taste. The dirt was threaded with goat dung, and his eyes watered. Still, by the time he reached the top, there remained a fair-sized ball of wet earth to spit into his palm. Quickly then, fearful that one of his brothers might have followed to tease him, he worked the handful of soil into his miniature garden. It was drenched with his saliva. He massaged it in and thought of his mother, who forgot to look at him because her own life held too many troubles for her to watch. He thought of her carrying food to his ravenous, shouting brothers. He thought of how her face would look as he came through the door one harvest evening. He would stand in the bent, dusty light before his surprised family. Then he would walk up to the table and lay out what he'd brought: a pepper, an eggplant, a tomato.

1 9 4 9 /   "It's some kind of night, isn't it?" Mary said. Constantine couldn't answer. Her courage and beauty, the pale straight-spined fact of her, caught in his throat. He sat on her parents' swing, which creaked, and watched helplessly as she leaned over the porch railing. Her skirt whisked against her legs. The dark New Jersey wind played in her hair.

"Oh, nights like this really get to me," she said. "Will you look at all those stars? I'd like to scoop up big handfuls and sprinkle them over your head."

"Mm," Constantine said, a muffled groan he hoped had signified his pleasure. It was almost six months now, and he still couldn't trust his fortune. He couldn't believe he was dating this magnificent American girl. He had a second life now, inside her head. He worried, almost every moment, that she would realize her mistake.

"You'd look wonderful with stars all over you," she said, but he could tell from her voice that she'd grown tired of her own idea. When her voice dropped and her hands went idly to her hair she'd lost interest in whatever she was saying, although she could keep

6

talking without listening to herself. He'd never known anyone so steadfast and yet so easily bored.

To bring her back he stood up and went to the railing. He looked with her at her parents' small back yard, her father's toolshed, the riot of stars. "You are the one that looks wonderful," he whispered.

"Oh, I'm all right," she said, without turning to him. Her voice maintained its hazy, sleepwalker's quality. "But you're the beauty, and you know it's true. Just the other day a girl at school was asking if it didn't make me nervous, to be seeing a fellow as good-looking as you. She was speaking out in favor of homely boys."

"I am a homely boy," he said.

Now she did turn to face him. He was surprised to see an angry flush on her cheeks.

"Don't fish," she said. "It's unbecoming in a man."

Again, he'd said the wrong thing. He'd thought that by 'homely' she'd meant boys who cared about making a home. Always, he tried to position himself so that he resembled what she wanted most.

"I don't—" he said. "I only mean—"

She nodded, and ran her finger down his shirtfront. "Don't mind me," she said. "I'm a little jumpy tonight, for some reason. All these stars seem to be driving me just slightly crazy."

"Yes," he said. "They are very beautiful."

She took her finger from his shirt. She turned back to the yard, and began twisting a strand of hair around her finger. Constantine stared at her finger with a wistful desire that lodged in his gullet like a stone.

"But they're wasting themselves over Newark," she said. "Look at them, shining away for all they're worth. It's sad, don't you think?"

Constantine was in love with Newark. He loved the proud thrust of smokestacks, the simple domestic serenity of square brick houses. Still, he knew Mary needed him to disdain all the ordinary beauties her presence had helped teach him to adore.

"Sad," he said. "Yes, it's very sad."

"Oh, Con, I'm tired of, I don't know. Everything."

"You are tired of everything?" he said.

She laughed, and her laughter had a mocking edge. Sometimes he said things that were humorous to her in ways he couldn't follow. Direct statements or questions of his often seemed to confirm some bitter joke known only to her.

"Well, I'm tired of school. I don't see the use of all this history and geometry. I want to get a job, like you."

"You want to work a construction crew?" he said.

"No, silly. I could work in an office, though. Or a dress shop."

"You should finish school."

"I can't think what for. I'm no good at it."

"You are good," he said. "You are good at everything you do."

She wrapped the hair tightly around her finger. She was angry again. How was it possible to know? Sometimes flattery was wanted. Sometimes flattery was hurled back like a handful of gravel.

"I know you think I'm perfect," she said in a low voice. "Well, I'm not. You and my father both need to realize that."

"I know you are not perfect," he said, and his voice sounded wrong. It was hollow and young, with an apologetic squeak. In a deeper voice he added, "You are the girl I love." Was a statement like that part of the immense, unguessable joke?

She didn't laugh. "We both say that." She continued looking deep into the yard. "Love love love. Con, how do you know you love me?"

"I know love," he said. "I think about you. Everything I do is for you."

"How would it make you feel if I told you I sometimes forget about you for whole hours?"

He didn't speak. A small animal, a cat or an opossum, browsed quietly among the garbage cans.

"It's not that I don't care about you," she said. "I do, I care about you awfully. Maybe I'm just shallow. But I keep wondering if love isn't supposed to change everything. I mean, I'm still myself. I still wake up in the mornings and, well, there I am, about to live another day."

Constantine's ears had filled with an echoing, oceanic sound. Was this the moment? Was she going to tell him it would be better if they didn't see each other for a while? To stop time, to fill the air, he said, "I can take you anyplace. I am assistant foreman, soon I'll know enough to get other jobs."

She looked at him. Her face was clear.

"I want to have a better life," she said. "I'm not so awfully greedy, really I'm not, I just—"

Her attention drifted from his face to the porch on which they stood. Constantine saw the porch through Mary's eyes. A rusty swing, a carton of milk bottles, a wan geranium growing in a small ceramic pot. He was aware of her parents and her brothers moving around inside the house, each nursing a private bouquet of complaints. Her father was poisoned by factory dust. Her mother lived among the ruins of a beauty she must once have thought would carry her into the next life. Her lazy brother Joey sought the bottom of everything with blind instincts, the way a catfish sought the bottom of a river.

Constantine took Mary's small hand, squeezed it in his. "You will," he said. "Yes. Everything you want can happen."

"Do you honestly think so?"

"Yes. Yes, I know it."

She closed her eyes. They were safe, at that moment, from the joke, and he knew that it was possible to kiss her.

1 9 5 8 / Mary was assembling a rabbit-shaped Easter cake according to the instructions in a magazine, cutting ears and a tail from a layer of yellow cake round and placidly innocent as a nursery moon. She worked in a transport of concentration. Her eyes were dark with their focus, and the tip of her tongue protruded from between her lips. She sliced out one perfect ear and was starting on the next when Zoe, her youngest, bumped against her ankle. Mary gasped, and cut a nick big as a man's thumbnail into the second ear.

"Darn," she whispered. Before Zoe bumped into her, Mary had been wholly usurped by the need to cut a flawless, symmetrical ear out of a freshly baked cake. She had been no one and nothing else.

She looked at Zoe, who was crouched at her feet, whimpering and slapping the speckled linoleum with the palms of her hands. Mary knew what was coming. Soon Zoe would topple over into a fit of dissatisfaction from which no comfort would rouse her. Zoe was the strangest of the children, a locked box Mary couldn't penetrate with kindness or impatience or little gifts of food. Susan and Billy were more comprehensible; they cried when they were hungry or tired. They'd look beseechingly at Mary, even in their worst tantrums, as if to say, Give me anything, any little reason to feel whole again. A toy could console them, or a cookie. But Zoe seemed to welcome misery. She could fuss for an hour or longer for no discernible reason—she was preparing to do so now. Mary could feel it coming, the way her own mother had claimed to feel the approach of rain on a fair day. She felt it in her joints. Spread before her on the countertop were cake layers, coconut icing, gumdrops, and licorice whips. She looked at her work and she looked down at the furious child who was about to fall into despair with a kind of voluptuous and hopeless pleasure, the way a grown woman might fall into bed after still another frustrating day.

"Con?" Mary called.

"Yeah?" he answered from the back yard.

"Con, the baby's all over the place in here. Would you take her out there with you for a few minutes till I finish this?"

She waited through the three-beat silence, during which he would be drawing a deep, moist breath, considering refusal. She waited until he said, "Okay. I'll be right there."

She straightened her knife on the Formica. "It's okay, sweetheart," she said to Zoe. "Daddy's going to take you outside for a while, to play with Susie and Billy. You've been cooped up in this old house way too long, haven't you?"

Constantine banged in through the screen door. "She's really bothering you?"

Mary took a breath, and turned to him. She put a lilt into her voice.

"Hi, honey," she said. "I'm working on my masterpiece here, and I need just a little tiny bit of peace and quiet to get it done. So would you be an angel?"

She touched her hair and offered a soft, embarrassed laugh. She was as lost in the demonstration of her own qualities as she had been in the slicing of the cake.

Constantine kissed her cheek, laid a hand on her shoulder. "This is a big deal you're putting together, huh?" he said.

"The biggest," she answered brightly. Zoe pounded the linoleum with the flats of her hands.

Constantine said to her, "Hey, you wanna go play with your brother and sister a little? Huh? You wanna go raise a little hell in the back yard, give your momma a break?"

He bent over to lift the baby. Mary caught a hint of his smell as he raised the child in his arms: his dank odor mixed with deodorant and the new cologne he'd taken up, a combination of sweetness and brine.

"You're a saint," she said.

Constantine bounced the baby in his arms. "How's it coming?"

"Fine," she said. "Just fine." She leaned over the cake to block his view. She was surprised to find that she didn't want him to see the damaged ear, though she knew he would neither notice nor care.

"It's a surprise?"

"Mm-hm. You kids just go out and play now, okay?"

"Yes. Come on, Zo. Let's see what your sister and brother are getting into out there. Let's go knock some sense into them."

He left with the baby, whose imminent fit of misery had been at least temporarily checked by motion. Mary waited for the sound of the screen door sighing shut. Then, with a relief that was palpable, like tiny valves opening inside her chest and belly, she returned to the cake. Although she was not artistic, she believed she understood an artist's temperament. She understood the absorption and the urgent, almost bodily hunger for time, simple uninterrupted time in which to work. She stayed up past midnight sewing and baking, carving pumpkins, twisting leftover pine branches into wreaths. Still, there were never enough hours and there was never enough money. Almost every day when the children cried, fought, or clung to her she lost her breath, as if the sheer disorganized passage of time was sucking the wind out of her. She grew dizzy and yawned enormously, struggling to fill her lungs as she tied shoelaces or read a favorite story one more time. Now, with Constantine watching all three children in the back yard, she breathed quietly while she finished cutting out the rabbit's second ear. She lifted both ears and placed them at jaunty angles atop the rabbit's spherical head. Yes, it would match the picture in the magazine. The gouge could be filled with icing.

It was nearly dusk. On the rear façades of the row houses lay a deep-colored light so tranquil that even this modest block in Elizabeth looked inspired and utterly empty, like a holy city of the dead. Sun slanted into orderly back yards, pulling shadows out of swingsets and aluminum lawn chairs. Someone flicked on a porch lamp, which shone pale yellow against the molten blue sky, and someone else three houses down turned on a lawn sprinkler, sending beads of water arcing up into the cooling air.

Constantine had gotten this far. He'd joined another crew, made a little more each week, and somehow there was enough money for this place, three bedrooms upstairs and a scrap of back yard. The neighborhood was lousy, mostly coloreds and Spanish, but at moments like this even a bad neighborhood could feel like part of a larger plan, an expanding and deepening future.

The final sliver of sun disappeared behind the paper mill, with only Constantine to see it. Susan sat on the ground playing an elaborate game with Billy, something she'd invented, involving dice and several stuffed animals and the tiny plastic hotels from the Monopoly set. Billy's attention kept wandering and Susan kept summoning it back, briskly indignant as a nurse. Constantine knew that soon she would slap her brother in righteous impatience, for he was an airy child, subject to endless distractions. He sometimes lost track of the real and stared with dumb fascination at an insect or a fallen leaf or simply at the empty space in front of his own eyes. Constantine walked in circles with Zoe, whispering nonsense to her, the only way he knew of calming her when she grew discontented. In a short-lived fit of nostalgia he had insisted on naming her Zoe, after his grandmother. Now he regretted it. Mary had favored American names like Joan or Patricia. Now, as Zoe proved to be a dark spirit, racked by indecipherable miseries, he wondered if he'd made a foreigner's life for her with something as simple as a name.

When the sun had fully set he took the children inside, before their fight gathered its final momentum. Zoe was fretful but not yet lost. If he could get them all reestablished in the house, they would once again be in Mary's realm, and subject to her more certain powers of comfort and control. He said to Susan and Billy, "Come on, kids, it's getting dark out here." He refused their pleas for five more minutes. He helped them pick up the tiny hotels, agreeing that they could finish the game in the living room. When he hustled them through the back door into the kitchen Mary looked up from the counter in surprise and annoyance. She was frosting a cake.

"Back already?" she said.

"Sun's gone down," he said. "It's getting too cold for them out there."

She nodded, yawned, and returned to her work. Constantine followed Susan and Billy into the living room, put Zoe down on the floor, at which she immediately started howling. He helped Susan and Billy put the red plastic hotels back into their proper order on the green pile carpet, where they kept toppling over.

"We can't *play* it in here," Susan said.

"I hate this game," Billy added.

"Play," Constantine said. "And no fights. Dinner will be in a few minutes."

He picked Zoe up again. He told her everything was all right, she was his little girl, an angel sent down from heaven, but her cries continued. He carried her back into the kitchen.

"How's dinner coming?" he asked.

"Dinner," Mary said. "It's after six, isn't it?"

"It's six forty-five. The kids are getting cranky."

She yawned again, gripping the edge of the counter as if the linoleum was unsteady under her feet. Before her lay a cake shaped like a rabbit, covered with white coconut icing that simulated fur.

"That's nice," he said, bouncing his wailing daughter in his arms. "Look, Zoe. Look, sweetheart. A bunny."

Mary smoothed the icing with a spatula and slipped a frigid glance at Constantine. He had, once again, erred in some obscure unpredictable way.

"The kids are starving."

"I've got fish sticks and Tater Tots in the freezer," she said. "Maybe you could help out a little. Maybe you could turn on the oven and take things out of the freezer for me." She smoothed the smooth icing and added, "Tomorrow is Easter, Constantine. I've got my whole family coming. There's a lot to do."

Constantine's face burned. He would not fight. He would concentrate on love and possibility, the small perfection of this cake. He jostled Zoe, whispering nonsense words into her howls. Without speaking he turned on the oven, took brightly colored frozen packets from the freezer and set them tenderly on the countertop, as if they might break. Later, after the children had eaten and been put to bed, he helped Mary fill Easter baskets at the dining-room table. The baskets were woven of lavender and pink raffia. He stuffed them with handfuls of green plastic straw while Mary assembled the candies and little toys.

"I've still got the baby's Easter dress to finish," she said. "And we've got to hide eggs for the egg hunt tomorrow."

"Yeah," he said. "Okay."

"Everything's so expensive." She sighed. "I just can't believe what everything costs."

Constantine swallowed, and put straw into a basket. Why did Mary refuse to understand about money? She went into the kitchen and came out with the rabbit-shaped cake, which she set in the middle of the dining-room table. She appraised it critically, her head cocked to one side. It had two red gumdrops for eyes, a black jelly bean for a nose, and whiskers made of licorice. Constantine's eyes teared at the sight of the cake. It was a marvel. It could have come from one of the downtown bakeries, the great white ones done in gleaming tile, their lavish confections tumbled out on silver trays, their hidden chimneys exhaling scents as deep and sweet as hope itself.

"I should have made Joey and Eleanor bring something," she said. "They're not that much worse off than we are. Con, put some newspaper in the bottoms of those baskets first, so the straw doesn't look so skimpy."

"Okay."

Mary sighed, a long dry exhalation with a faint rattle, a surprisingly elderly sound in a woman twenty-six years old. "It's Easter," she said.

He nodded. It was American Easter. Greek Easter would not fall for another three weeks, although he knew Mary wouldn't like his mentioning it. Whenever the occasion demanded it she'd say, "We're Americans, Con. *Amer*-icans." Her own mother, who'd gotten herself from Palermo to New Jersey so her children could be born U.S. citizens, flew an American flag next to the grieving plaster Madonna in her front yard.

"I feel so tired," Mary said. "It's the holidays, it seems like we should be having fun, but all I feel is exhausted."

"You work too hard," he said. "You should let up a little."

"Well, it all has to get done," she said. "Doesn't it?"

The baskets were nearly finished when Billy appeared, blink-

ing, wearing his cowboy pajamas. Mary had insisted on the pajamas, from Macy's, never mind what they cost. Billy stood barefoot
in the doorway, and when Mary looked up and saw him her face
filled with a mute, smiling panic. The baskets could not possibly
be hidden. Constantine heard the ragged intake of her breath.

"Honey, what's the matter?" she said.

"What are you guys doing?" Billy asked.

"Nothing, honey," Mary said. She went and knelt before him,
blocking his view. "Just sitting here. What's the matter? Did you
have a bad dream?"

Billy strained to look around his mother. Constantine felt a
hard little pellet of anger forming in his throat. "Go back to bed,"
he said.

"What is all that stuff?" Billy asked. "Are those our Easter
baskets?"

Constantine fought to contain himself. This is my little boy,
he told himself. My boy is just a curious kid. But another voice, a
voice not quite his own, railed against the boy for unnatural smallness, for a growing tendency to whine. For ruining Mary's surprise.
These new traditions were important and precarious, these visita-
tions by bearded saints and fairies and rabbits. They had to be
carefully guarded.

"No, honey," Mary said brightly, thinly. "Well, the Easter
Bunny was here, but he forgot a few things. He's very busy tonight.
He left the baskets with us, and he told us that we absolutely,
positively must not show them to anybody until he comes back."

"I want to *see*," Billy said, and the pellet of anger in Constantine's throat grew harder. This was his only son. At five, he had a
scrawny neck and a squeaky, pleading voice.

"Back to bed," Constantine said. Billy looked at him with an
expression at once craven and defiant.

"*I want to see,*" he said again, as if his parents didn't compre-
hend the simplicity and logic of his demand.

Constantine rose. The look of fear that crossed Billy's face further tightened the constriction in his throat. Mary took Billy's scrawny shoulders in her hand, saying, "Come on, sweetie. This is just a dream you're having, you won't even remember it in the morning."

"No," Billy screeched, and then Constantine was on him. He lifted him up, amazed at how little he weighed. Billy was like a sack of sticks.

"Bed," Constantine told him. He might have conquered his own anger if Billy had remained defiant. But Billy began to cry, and without quite having decided to, Constantine was shaking him, saying, "Shut up. Shut up and go back to bed."

"Con, stop," Mary said. "Stop it. Give him to me."

Her voice was distant. Constantine had lost himself in his own fury, and with ferocious clarity he shook Billy until Billy's face grew twisted and blurred.

"Oh, God," Mary said. "Con, stop. Please."

"Bed," Constantine shouted. He set Billy roughly onto the floor, where he collapsed as if his bones had dissolved. Mary reached for him but Constantine blocked her. He pulled Billy to his feet, held him upright, and aimed him toward the stairs. "Go," he shouted, and he slapped his son's bottom hard enough to send him stumbling halfway into the living room before he fell again, howling, gasping for breath. Constantine's hip bumped against the table and one of Mary's colored eggs, a limpid blue one, rolled unsteadily across the polished wood. Mary paused. He saw the shadow on her face. Then she ran to Billy and covered his body with her own. The egg hesitated at the table's edge. It fell.

"Stop," Mary screamed. "Oh, please. Just leave him alone."

Constantine was in a passion now, a crackling white glory. Delirious, he knocked the baskets off the table. Jelly beans sprayed like stones against the walls. Chocolate lambs broke on the floor, plastic eggs cracked open and spilled out the trinkets Mary had hidden inside. He started to ram his fist into the cake. He raised his arm over it—the insipid features made of candy, the jaunty ears. Then he stopped, his arm still raised. He might have brought his fist down into the fluffy round whiteness. He might have torn out handfuls and stuffed them into his mouth. He might have eaten the cake, gobbets of icing smeared over his face and shirtfront, and wept, begging with a full mouth to be forgiven. What he did was lower his arm, slowly, and stand beside the cake. He went to his wife and son and knelt beside them. "Don't touch me," Mary sobbed. "Oh, just leave us alone."

He picked up the baskets and placed them, gently, on the tabletop. He retrieved the straw, the foil-wrapped eggs.

"What happens to you?" Mary asked in a clotted voice.

"I don't know," he said. "I don't know."

"One minute you're fine and the next you're—"

He nestled a chocolate egg on the straw, then went and knelt beside his wife and son. Billy was huddled against Mary. Constantine put his hand, timidly, on his son's neck. The hall clock ticked.

"Please," he said. He wasn't sure what he was asking for. "I'll learn," he added. "Everything can change." He put his other hand on her shoulders. She neither welcomed nor recoiled from his touch. "I'd do anything for you," he said. When she did not respond he rose again, unsteadily, to pick up the rest of the candy. He returned the chicks to their straw, and put the little prizes back inside the eggs.

"Delicious," Mary's brother, Joey, said, patting his stomach. His stomach made a solid, beefy sound under the palm of his hand. Mary thought of his flesh, its hairy density and sour, bristling humors. She glanced at Joey's wife, Eleanor.

"Good," Mary said. "We aim to please."

She added Joey's plate to the stack she held, and looked quickly over the wreckage of the dinner. The food had been good enough, though she regretted the woody asparagus. She regretted the yellow napkins, which had looked bright and colorful in the store but somehow, on her table, had taken on a pallid, hospital quality. Her lungs tightened and she yawned, gulping air.

"Tired?" her mother asked. "You been working awful hard on this dinner, ain't you?"

"No," Mary said irritably. Her face burned, as if she'd been caught in some selfish indiscretion. "No, I'm not the least bit tired. I'm just, well, it's the holidays. You know."

"I know," her mother said. Mary's father sat beside her mother in his profound, submerged silence. Eddie's wife, Sophia, rose to help Mary clear the table. She took Constantine's plate, and he smiled with the frozen cordiality of a foreign prince. Throughout the dinner he'd been cautious and jovial, laughing sometimes before the jokes were finished. He wore his navy blazer and the striped tie Mary had given him for his birthday.

"Everything was perfect, honey," he said. "The best."

She smiled, and struggled for a full breath. "Thanks, sweetheart," she said.

In the living room, Billy and Susan were playing with Joey and Eleanor's sons. "—so give it here," she heard one of them say. Chuck, the older one. Thinking of the dinner's little failures, she listened for Billy.

"Don't," she heard Susan say. "Don't give it to him, he'll eat it."

"Kids?" Mary called. "Everything okay in there?"

A silence fell. She called, "Billy? Can you hear me?"

He appeared immediately in the doorway, his face red. "Chucky wants my Easter chick," he said.

Mary glanced at Eleanor. Eleanor called out, "Chuck, what are you doing in there?"

"Nothing," Chuck answered peevishly. "Playing."

Billy looked at the floor as if something enigmatic was stitched into the carpet. "He put my lamb in his mouth," he said.

"You can share with your cousin, can't you?" she said.

"Chuck," Eleanor said. "Are you behaving yourself?"

"Yeah, Ma," he answered.

Billy raised his eyes from the carpet and looked at Mary with an expression of mingled hope and terror. He wore the little yellow jacket she'd saved for, the paisley bow tie. "Come here, honey," she said. Her voice was louder than she'd meant it to be. "I want you to help me with the dessert."

He trotted to her side. "He was going to eat it," he said.

"Well, you have to share your things," Mary told him. "Come on, I need you to help me get out the ice cream." She touched his hair. It put out a faint electrical crackle, the tiny hum of his being.

"Mary, you spoil that kid," Joey said.

She shrugged. She remembered to smile.

Her little brother, Eddie, said, "Bill, why don't you go back out there and tell Chuck what you'll do to him if he eats your candy?"

Billy's eyes filled. Constantine smiled, and Mary kept her hand on top of Billy's head. She suffered an urge to take his hair in her fingers and yank on it.

"I need his help," she told Eddie sharply. "Come on, honey. We've got troops to feed."

She herded him into the kitchen, where Sophia was running dishwater. "Oh, leave everything," Mary told her. Sophia and Eddie had been trying for years to have children. Sophia was a hefty, sweet-natured woman who walked through her life in an attitude of hearty, optimistic defeat. The babies would grow to a certain point, then dissolve in her womb.

"I just thought I'd get things started," Sophia said.

"You know what you could do?" Mary said. "You could take out the dessert forks and plates. They're right over there, see?"

"Yes. Sure. I'd be happy to."

Mary went into the pantry for the cake. Billy followed her, his miniature black shoes making their clean rubber sounds on the floor. Her heart ached.

"Here it is," she said. "My masterpiece."

"Momma, I'm tired," Billy said.

"I know, honey." She lifted the cake platter. Her chest felt as if it was tied with iron bands.

"I hate Chucky," Billy said.

"They'll all be gone soon," Mary said. Billy looked at her with an expression of mute fear that was like a fist in her belly. She stood in the middle of the kitchen, holding the cake. Its icing was flawless as new snow. She felt the windy chaos of the world, its endless dangers, and she wanted to tell her son, 'I'm tired, too. I hate Chucky, too.' She wanted to give the cake only to Billy and, at the same time, she wanted to hold it out of his reach.

"When is he going?" Billy asked.

"Soon, honey," she said. "After we've had our cake. Come on now."

She took the cake into the dining room. Billy followed her. "Ta-daaa," she said, flourishing the plate. Constantine said, "Wait till you see this. She coulda been a baker, my wife."

Mary set the cake in the middle of the table, and modestly received her praise. The cake did in fact look perfect. The gouge she'd cut in the ear was undetectable. Susan and Chuck and Al, the baby, had reseated themselves at the table.

"Here goes," Mary said, taking up the cake knife. The rabbit cake was jaunty and whimsical, with just the right expression of benign surprise. She had done wonders with gumdrops and licorice. The air around her was dense, spangled with odd moments of light. Billy huddled beside her.

"So cut it," Joey said. "We're waiting. You got our mouths watering."

"Mary?" Constantine said. "Mary?"

"Hmm? Oh, sorry." She raised the knife and, with a firm smile, cut into the cake.

1 9 6 0 / Billy and Kate were playing when the voices started. Kate rolled the die, lost a turn because her boyfriend was late picking her up. She was fat and not nervous and she didn't mind. She only wanted to win. Billy rolled the die and got sent to his father's car to pin up his hem. It was his regular bedroom and it seemed like they were safe.

Then his father's voice, shivering with fresh rage, leaked in under the door. "Where do you think money comes from? Mary? You think I know a secret place where it grows? I don't. I do not know a place like that."

Kate leaned over the game board and said, "He's gonna murder her."

"No, he isn't."

Billy's mother said with furious patience, "Constantine, the money's gone. It's spent. So just get out of my way, all right? I'm trying to work." Billy could hear his mother in the kitchen, cleaning. The mop handle banged against the kitchen cabinets insistently, like a horse kicking its stall.

Kate said, "If you come home from school one day and she's

not around, call the police and tell them to look in the freezer. Don't look yourself. You'll go crazy if you see your mother in there."

"Shut up," Billy said. Kate maintained a system of complicated, ever-changing rules. She was Billy's best friend, a year older. She had five brothers in trouble, and she didn't mind about noise.

"That's the way it works, isn't it?" Billy's father shouted. "That's how it works. You spend the money, you don't talk to me about it, and then after you say, 'The money is spent.' That's the system here. Right?"

"What do you want, Con? Requisition forms? You want me to check with you every time one of the kids needs some new underwear?"

"You can buy 'em all the underwear you want. We're talking here about a goddamn stuffed monkey that cost nine dollars and fifty cents. Am I right? Did I miss something?"

"Of course you're right. You're always right."

The monkey sat pertly on Billy's bed, staring straight ahead with bright black eyes and a bemused, elderly expression. Its coat was a thick tangle of lush chocolate-colored curls. In the store with his mother Billy had looked at the monkey and she'd bought it without question, as if she herself felt the tidal pull of her son's desires. He wasn't even sure if he'd really wanted it. He wanted a Barbie like Susan's but his mother wanted him to want the stuffed monkey and so he did. He owned it now.

Kate said, "Seeing their mother dead is the one thing people never get over. If you see your mother dead, that's it, you go crazy, and nobody can help you."

She rolled the die, got a date with Bob, her favorite. Billy preferred Ken and Poindexter, though Poindexter was supposed to be the date nobody wanted. Billy liked the way Poindexter's harmless face looked on the card, his orange hair and his little harmless eyes.

"Yay, Bob," Kate shouted.

"Shh," Billy said. When his father was home he was supposed to play other games.

"I *love you*, Bob," Kate said. She kissed the card with Bob's face on it.

"Be quiet," Billy said.

"Mm-mm, *Bob*," Kate hollered. She stuck out her sharp pink tongue and licked the card. Billy threw the die at her. She threw it back, hard enough to hurt, and without quite having meant to, he told her she was so fat she'd need Bob and his whole family to take her to the prom. She left, weeping furiously, and Billy sat in his room for the rest of the afternoon, after the fight downstairs had worn itself out and after Kate had called from her house to tell him she'd grow out of being fat but he'd be stupid forever.

Billy was lying on his bed looking at his comic strip when his mother called him to dinner. It was an old strip, one his mother had given him, about a cat in love with a mouse who despised her. With every brick the mouse threw at her head the cat fell more deeply in love, until her head was lost in a whirlwind of hearts and exclamation points, the mingled signs of her devotion and her wounds. Billy had so adored the comic strip he'd begged his mother to let him keep it, and he looked at it almost every day, the big-nosed cat stupefied by love for the furious, spindle-armed mouse. His mother had read the words to him until he knew them by heart. "Ignatz my dollink. I loves ya a million times. Wham." The sequence of panels excited him, stirred around in his chest. He never tired of watching the cat and the mouse go through their unchanging sequence of injury and pure, bottomless affection.

He went downstairs to dinner and sat at his usual place, watching everything. His father didn't speak. His father ate with a finicky reluctance that was not his ordinary way, cutting each bite precisely, like a tailor. Occasionally as he cut his meat he emitted a low moan, as if the stroke of the knife had touched his own flesh. Billy glanced at his father's hands, red and veined, big enough to palm his head. He reminded himself that he must not stare. He concentrated instead on the other, less dangerous members of the dinner. Zoe sat playing with a spoon that sparked and dimmed and sparked again in the lamplight. Susan sat across from Billy, blank and perfectly behaved, although Billy knew that her whole attention was focused on making sure no food on her plate touched any other food.

Billy's mother ate with cool precision. Eating, for her, was a task to be done methodically and thoroughly. As she ate she kept up a vivid stream of talk. Everything was a subject. It was her job to buy and cook the food and it was her job to take in the world and offer it back to her family as conversation. "I stopped by Widerman's today," she said, "just to pick up a few things, and what do you think? They had a shelf full of transistor radios with a big sign that said, 'Special, Three Ninety-nine.' I couldn't believe it. I thought there had to be something wrong with them, so I asked Jewel, the one with the son who died at Pearl Harbor. Anyway, I said, 'Jewel, what's the matter with those radios?' And she said, 'Mary, I know what you mean, but there's not a thing wrong with them. They're Japanese.' The Japanese, it seems, will work for practically nothing, so these radios hardly cost more than the parts and the shipping. Can you beat that? These are the people who killed Jewel's only son, and now she's standing there selling their radios at prices no American company could possibly match. Jewel didn't seem to think anything about it, they're just cheap radios as far as she's concerned, but I told her I'd rather buy an American radio even if it cost four times as much. And you know what she did? She looked at me like I was crazy. This poor woman who's ruined her legs working at Widerman's for twenty years, and lost her only son to the Japanese, and she doesn't see anything wrong with people buying these radios. It made me wonder if she really understood about things. I wondered if, you know, she'd lost her mind a little. I think people can go crazy and just keep on about their business, I mean not every crazy person ends up in a strait-jacket. Like the other morning, when I was at the market—"

Billy marveled at his mother. Her inspiration never flagged. Each subject found its way to another. Billy's family lived in his mother's ongoing conversation the way they might have lived with a portable radio that played from early morning until after midnight, pouring out news and music and dramas both high and low. She was divine in the inexhaustible breadth of her interests. She worried over the extinction of nations and over a sparrow's tiny hiccup of death against the picture window.

Billy's father set his knife down on his plate and said, "So what's wrong with a cheap radio?"

His mother had moved on to something else, and was taken by surprise. "What?" she said.

"A cheap radio. A radio that costs three ninety-nine. What's the matter with that? Who cares where it comes from?"

"Con. The Japanese—"

"I know about the Japanese. You think I don't know about the Japanese?" He pointed at her with his fork. "The war is over, right? All over. You could get on an airplane today and fly to Japan. You could take your vacation there. But *you*"—he shook his fork at her—"you'd rather spend four times as much on a radio because it was made by some stranger in Philadelphia."

"I'm not buying any radio, Con," she said. "No one's buying any radio."

"No. Just toys that knock the hell out of a ten-dollar bill."

"Con—"

"This is the thinking that gets us into trouble." He looked at Billy and Susan. "This is the thinking that keeps us broke. We pay triple for things because we don't like the guy who's making them cheap. We're *Amer*-icans. We don't want a Japanese radio. We want a more expensive American radio. But toys. Hey. We want German stuffed animals. We want Italian shoes that cost five times as much as American. Never mind about Hitler and Mussolini. I want to tell you something." He shook his fork at Billy now. "Your enemy isn't the Japanese. Your enemy is whoever charges you too much. That's it. That's what you need to know about friends and enemies."

"Right," his mother said, so softly she could barely be heard. "That's a fine thing to teach them. Oh, very nice."

She had switched to her tiny voice. When she spoke in that voice she seemed to be addressing someone who lived inside her, an invisible friend who shared her belief that the world was great and wide but finally too exhausting for anyone to live in it.

After dinner, Billy lingered near his father. He didn't let himself get too close. His father sat in his chair, watching television. Billy played with his farm animals along the rug's opposite edge. He slipped away into the nowhere that hummed around the edges of everything. He arranged his pigs inside the plastic corral. He placed the pigs nose to nose and brought in the rust-colored horse that refused to stand straight on its plastic hooves.

In the kitchen, his mother rang the plates and glasses on the drainboard. With a rag she made squeakings that were the sound of cleanliness itself. She moved cleanly through the world; his father scattered spoor. Wherever he went he left hairs behind, threads of tobacco, limp pungent socks. In hot weather he stripped, massively hairy, to his undershorts and left his sweaty silhouette on the upholstery. Although Billy's mother mopped and vacuumed and nearly rubbed the skin off the furniture with her dustcloth, she couldn't expunge his father's intense, all-pervasive ownership.

The plastic horse fell again and again. It refused to stand, though Billy could not stop trying to force it. If he tried just a little harder, if he refused to give up, the little horse would finally straighten from the sheer size of his will. He bent and bent the legs until suddenly, with a crisply final sound, one snapped off at the knee. He held the severed leg, disbelievingly, in one hand and the crippled horse in the other. The leg was thin and articulate, its hoof edged in a ragged seam.

He set the leg down, carefully, as if it could feel pain. Still holding the three-legged horse, he walked to his father's chair and stood nervously until his father looked over at him.

"Uh-huh?" he said.

Billy couldn't speak. His father's knees showed a hint of their knobbed complexity through his thin gray slacks. His thighs, big as the hulls of boats, reflected light along their upper surfaces and, on their undersides, carried ragged shadows into the green depths of the chair. Billy stood inside his father's circle, breathing the sour particles of sweat and tobacco, the sweet underlayer of after-shave. "What is it?" his father asked.

Billy shrugged, and his father frowned in annoyance. "Speak up."

"I need a new horse," Billy said finally.

"Huh?"

"This horse is broken." Billy was surprised by the sound of tears in his voice. "Its leg broke off."

"You need something *else*?" his father said.

"It broke," Billy said.

His father nodded, gathering his calm and his kindness. "The horse is still good," he said. "This guy has just got hurt in a fight. He's basically okay. Three legs is plenty for a horse."

"No it *isn't*," Billy said. He realized he would cry soon. He was mortified, but helpless to prevent it.

His father sucked in a breath. "What if I got you a football instead?" he said. "What if you and me went down to Ike's tomorrow and got a football? How would that be?"

Billy hesitated. He wanted to go to Ike's with his father in the morning, to try out different footballs and select the best one. But he also wanted what he'd asked for—a small, muscular horse that had no defect, that would stand as it was meant to.

"I don't want a football," he said, though in fact he did want one. He wanted everything.

His father shook his head. "Forget it, then," he said. He looked back at the television, where a happy blond woman sang a song about something that was like cheese, but better.

Billy would have traded anything to be able to keep from crying, but his sorrow and outrage were too much for him and the crying won, as it usually did. Crying pulled him down. He turned away from his father, uncertain about where to go. He wanted to go someplace where his crying wasn't. He wanted to step outside of it and sit watching television with his father, both of them disgruntled and annoyed as the crying swarmed around them.

His mother came into the room. "'What's going on?" She carried a limp dish towel, and her black hair crackled. Billy looked at her, helplessly, from the middle of his own noise.

"Your son wants a new horse," Billy's father said. "He don't want a football. I told him I'd buy him a football, he don't want it. He wants a new toy horse."

Billy could feel himself as a spoiled, greedy, ungrateful little boy. The louder he cried, the more firmly he became that, but the feeling of becoming it only made him cry harder. If he could have managed it he'd have slipped underground like a gopher and burrowed his way to Germany or Japan, someplace where he hadn't yet affected the air with his little desires.

His mother came and crouched before Billy. She brought her colors and her stiff rustlings. "Is something the matter with your horse, honey?" she asked.

He didn't move or speak. The crying continued without his permission. His mother took the horse out of his hand, looked tenderly at its wound.

"It isn't much to want," she whispered. Then, louder, she said, "I guess he didn't *ask* for a football, did he? I guess he asked for a plastic horse that costs ten cents and is made right here in the U.S. of A."

"He's got a million of them little animals," Billy's father said. "He needs a million and one?"

"For heaven's sake, listen to yourself."

"He wants an American toy, I'll get him a football."

"You and I can talk about this later," Billy's mother said. "C'mon, Billy. Come in the kitchen with me, I could use a little help with the dishes."

He followed her, because he was unable to do anything of his own. He felt his father's silence pressing on the back of his head. In the kitchen his mother wiped his nose with a handkerchief that smelled like her. "We'll go out tomorrow and get a new horse," she said. "Okay? Accidents happen, it's no big deal. We'll just get you a new one. Okay?"

He nodded avidly. She smiled, deeply pleased, and told him he was a good little boy, a prize. She told him he deserved all sorts of good things, and if anyone tried to tell him differently, that person didn't know what he was talking about. Billy stared at her gratefully. She offered a practiced smile, one he'd seen thousands of times: a quick jerking upward of the corners of her mouth, a squeezing shut of the eyes, as if the act of smiling caused her a sharp and exquisite pain. Something bucked inside him, a feeling so unruly he thought he might be sick. She was his friend. She was the one who allowed. How could he dislike her? He heard, again, the sound the horse's leg had made, snapping off.

1 9 6 3 / It happened quickly. It happened because Constantine was Greek and because he stopped into a tavern for a beer. It upset everything he thought he'd learned about cause and effect. One damp yellow day just after the summer solstice he met a man named Kazanzakis, a thin man with gold buttons on his blazer. During his lunch hour Constantine had sought out the shade of a neighborhood tavern crowded with men watching the Mets game. The television, a big black-and-white, flickered on a shelf over rows of illuminated bottles. Beside it, a picture of an ice-blue mountain lake advertised beer. Constantine took the only empty stool, next to Kazanzakis, who watched the game and ate peanuts with unhungry avidity, as if his true objective was not to eat the peanuts but to reveal the bottom of the dish. Between batters Constantine and Kazanzakis started talking. They talked baseball, then they talked construction. Constantine was foreman on a job just winding up. Kazanzakis was a developer who'd started building sprawls of cheap houses—he called them planned communities— to the north and west of town. They introduced themselves and, upon hearing one another's names, declared their places of origin.

Kazanzakis's grandparents, as it turned out, had lived in a village less than thirty miles from the place where Constantine was born. The two men spoke Greek to each other. They laughed, ordered more beers. By the end of the third inning, Constantine had a new job. He was hired to oversee construction of Kazanzakis's newest planned community, which would soon be laid out on a flat brown stretch of reclaimed marshland twenty miles to the north. The men shook hands, ordered another round. Kazanzakis put his thin arm around Constantine's shoulders and announced to the bar, "Hey, sports fans, I want you to meet my new partner. A Greek, a man I can trust."

It was all chance, a throw of the dice. The unrelenting work of the past fifteen years had meant almost nothing, aside from what it taught Constantine about joists and sashes. What had made his fortune was the decision to go into a tavern on a Tuesday afternoon.

What had made his fortune was being Greek. After all those years of Mary's insistence, "We're Americans, Con. *Amer*-icans." Once it started, his Greek good fortune refused to quit. Kazanzakis proved to have a sharp eye for human wishes, a sure knowledge of what people wanted to buy. His houses were inexpensive, but he dressed them up with picket fences and false dormers. He advertised their several opulent features: top-of-the-line appliances, rumpus rooms, two-car garages. Constantine, for his part, knew the corners that could be invisibly cut. He knew about using green wood and plastic pipes; he knew how much time could be saved if you told your men to forget about drilling through the studs for wiring and just smack dents in them with hammers. The houses sold nearly as fast as he and Kazanzakis could get them built. Constantine, who was raised on a thrift hard as bone, kept overhead so low Kazanzakis was often moved to embrace him and call him a magician. He'd never imagined a tract might be so profitable.

Mary could hardly believe how the money grew. Now, finally, she could give beautiful things to the children, although her daughters consistently preferred the cheap and garish. Susan wanted more Barbie clothes and a toy oven in which a lightbulb scorched pans of batter into little round scabs of cake. Zoe wanted Lincoln Logs and a toy rifle and a ratty "coonskin" cap made of dyed rabbit fur that smelled faintly of urine. Mary bought those things and bought others as well, hoping her daughters would learn to see the shimmer that true quality produced in the air of a room. She bought gold bracelets and mohair sweaters and jewelry boxes that opened to reveal a tiny ballerina twirling to the tune of "Für Elise." Those gifts were briefly embraced and then discarded. The ruffled dresses were thrown indifferently onto the floor. The imported dolls were left outside, their delicate, hand-wrought faces smiling graciously up into the rain.

Of Mary's children, only Billy wanted the things she wanted to give. He was a dreamy boy who brought books home from the library, who sought hiding places where she could always find him. When she bought him an alpaca coat he wore it to church on Sundays in a spirit of miniature masculine sobriety that rinsed her heart with affection. Although she loved all three children, Billy was the one she could read. For him she bought soft V-necked sweaters from Scotland. She bought a burgundy leather briefcase when he started fifth grade, and a deep-green hunter's cap. For the girls she furnished a dollhouse, which sat first in Susan's room and then in Zoe's. Dust gathered on the intricate wooden furniture, the lamps that really worked. Mary cleaned the dollhouse periodically and, with a pang of guilty pleasure, rearranged the furniture.

1 9 6 4 / Susan led them onto the golf course. Before, there had been only fenced yards and the playground. There had been buildings and the alley with its rotting smell and the empty factory where weeds curled from the concrete. Now there was this bright field of green. Dead leaves sent up their smoke and a bird sang "Cree-cree-clara?" again and again.

Susan knew her father had gotten all this for her. She felt flattered and afraid.

"Come on, Billy," she called sternly. Billy was dreaming along, twenty feet behind, stirring up leaves with his sneakers.

"I'm coming," he answered. Zoe had run ahead. Susan turned to see Billy shuffling his feet as leaf shadows made bright and dark shapes on him. His ravaged beauty got under her breastbone and squeezed her lungs, a sharp inner contraction. She sometimes imagined dragging her brother from a burning building, knocking the incipient fire out of his clothes and hair.

She would rescue him. They would escape into the woods together and live there, away from the big immaculate house her father had bought for her. There must be woods, somewhere.

"Come *on*," she said. Her shadow stood before her, serrated on the leafy ground.

"What's your hurry?" Billy said. "We're going for a walk, right? We're not late for anything."

"I don't want Zoe to get lost," she said. "She keeps running all over the place, I can't stop her."

"She isn't lost," he said. "She's right up there, climbing that tree."

Susan turned and saw Zoe clinging to the lower branches of an enormous pine, working her way up. The colors of Zoe's clothes, her pale yellow shirt and indigo jeans, were cut into shapes by the pine needles.

Susan shouted, "Zoe. Stop that."

"She doesn't have to stop," Billy said. "She can climb a tree if she wants to."

Susan stood between Billy and Zoe, and her sense of her own promising future drained away. She would always be young, always unheeded, always insistent on rules of behavior no one else seemed willing to bother about. The world should have been so simple. All everyone had to do was speak softly but clearly, avoid fights, walk neither too fast nor too slow.

"She'll fall," Susan said, though she believed that Zoe was rising toward an accident, more endangered by the sky than the earth. "Zoe," she called again. "Come down."

She imagined herself catching Zoe in her arms.

"I can see the house," Billy said. "Look. That patch of white over there. You see it?"

Susan started for the tree. "Zoe, I mean it," she said.

"This is our home now," Billy said, although Susan had gone too far to hear him. "We're rich. Well, we're semi-rich."

Susan marched to the bottom of the tree and stood with her hands fisted on her hips. Standing on the level grass, squinting up into the canopy of pine needles with her shadow slanting behind her, she might have been a young handmaiden to a goddess of domestic exasperation. She wore a white windbreaker, pink pedal pushers, and anklets with little yarn balls sewn on at the heels to keep them from slipping down into her tennis shoes.

"Zoe," she shouted. "Come down here this instant."

Zoe was struggling to boost herself onto a forked branch nearly thirty feet above the ground. She didn't answer, which was as Susan expected. Susan sighed, and liked the sound she made. It was an adult sigh, with depths of intention. She'd lived in this neighborhood less than a month, and already knew of three boys whose eyes—brown, darker brown, and blue-green—sought the particulars of her life.

She imagined the boys stealing her from this new house, bringing her out here to the golf course. She would rule them, comfort them, make them behave.

"I mean it," she called. She thought, briefly, of her voice winding out among the tree trunks, following its own thread. Maybe there was a boy out here right now, walking heartsick and lost among the trees and the sand traps.

Billy came and stood beside her. He had a smell, not strong but unmistakable, a combination of bleach and stale bread. Susan wondered if he kept himself clean.

"She's not gonna come down till she's ready," he said. "You know that."

"She's going to break her *neck*," Susan said. "I promised I'd look out for her."

"I'm gonna climb it, too," Billy said. "I bet you can see the whole town from up there."

"Billy, no. You stay right here."

But he hoisted himself up onto the lowest branch, and then wriggled into the crotch of the tree. Susan watched his skinny butt twitch inside his dungarees and wondered, again, what sort of girls would someday want to ease his pain.

"Bill—ee," she cried. "Darn you."

He went quickly, and was soon pulling himself onto a branch just below Zoe's. She sat with one knee drawn up under her chin and a dirty hand rummaging through her hair. "Hey, Zo," he said, a little breathlessly. He had scraped his hands on the rough bark, and the small abrasions tingled in the moving air. She didn't answer. He watched her until he was sure she was firmly balanced on her branch, then turned and looked out through the scrim of needles down into Garden City.

"If you two don't get down here in exactly one minute, I'm coming up there after you," Susan called.

"Pretty," Billy said. From this height he could see the streets of his new neighborhood, neatly gridded, lined with trees in red and yellow leaf. He saw a sparrow hovering over a bird feeder, its wings making a little brown disturbance on the air. Farther away were steeples, the brick hulls of stores and banks, a gathering pale blue distance.

"The animals can see us," Zoe said. "They can climb this tree and look right down into our house."

"Are you afraid of that?" Billy asked.

"No. I like it."

Zoe pulled at her hair, scratched her knee. Although she had never told him, Billy knew Zoe thought of herself as an animal. She snatched food off her plate and ate it in small, eager bites. She slept curled up in a nest she made out of blankets and sheets.

"This is where we live now," Billy said, half to Zoe and half to himself. "Now we're semi-rich, and we live here."

Zoe nodded. "This is the tree kingdom," she said. "That's the cottage where the people live."

"It creeps me out a little," he said. "I mean, a new school and everything. You're lucky to only be in second grade."

Zoe watched time pass through the town. Billy found he could speak into Zoe's animal self and say things he'd never say to anyone else. She cupped a lost little glen of watchful quiet he could breathe with her.

"That's it," Susan called. "I'm coming up."

"Our babysitter," Billy said. Zoe smiled. She was a wiry little girl with black hair and heavy brows. She wore rubber beach thongs in October.

"Do you think we'll change, from being rich?" Billy said. "Do you think it'll make a difference?"

"We still get two more wishes," Zoe said.

"It could make a difference," Billy said. He settled back on his branch, feeling the small tremors Susan sent through the tree as she worked her way up.

"Darn you," she said finally, from several feet below. "*Darn* you, both of you. I think I tore my pants."

"Look," Billy said. "You can see the high school from here."

"We have to go back," Susan said. "It's getting late."

"Not yet," Billy answered. "I don't think it's safe yet. We should give it, like, another half hour."

"Everything's fine," Susan said. "Honestly, I don't know why you have to make such a big deal out of everything."

"You go home," he said. "We're gonna stay here awhile. Maybe we'll build a tree house up here."

"You're not building any tree house. This is private property."

"We're going to move here, Zoe and me."

"We have to go," Susan pleaded. "Come on, dinner's probably ready."

"You go," Billy said. "Zo and I are gonna stay here awhile."

"Don't you worry. I'm going." But she stayed where she was. A squirrel hopped through the leaves at the base of the tree, raised itself up on its hind legs, and disappeared as suddenly as if it had been snatched down into the earth. Susan looked away from the tree, down to the house her father had built for her. She knew herself as a thin and erect fourteen-year-old girl sitting astride a branch among the smells of leaves. She wanted to claim the house that was hers and she wanted to live up here, silent and fierce as a young mother of the wild. Cloud shadows shifted over the flat land. A tree lost its light and the copper roof of a steeple flashed suddenly, like something huge and precious risen from the bottom of the ocean. Briefly, with the changing of the shadows, Susan saw that she was powerful. She saw how much could be built for her, and how much brought down. A flush of excitement passed through her. She thought of a dam bursting. She thought of a silver wall of water tumbling down over the churches and the stores, the orderly streets. She could see it. She could see the water engulfing everything, shattering windows, lifting roofs up off their eaves, roiling on as ordinary objects—a cup, a wig, a bar of soap—bobbed to the surface and were caught in the suck. She saw the water churn its way over the rise and stop, finally, halfway up this tree, just below the branch on which she sat. Only she, Zoe, and Billy would escape. Afterward, there would be a brilliant brown silence. There would be a steeple, the top half of a stopped clock, the upper twigs of a few oaks and elms. There would be flocks of ducks and geese, settling down. And gradually, as the water began to subside, there would be rings and necklaces caught among the branches. She would lead Zoe and Billy back down to the wet, empty world and she would bedeck herself as they climbed down, orphans now, serene and grieving, facing a future in which anything could happen. She would arrive at the bottom covered in jewels.

1 9 6 5 / When Constantine took his night rides he imagined Mary sitting beside him. Not the Mary he lived with now but the Mary who'd been seventeen, a brisk mysterious girl latching a gate behind her. That Mary had managed to combine good sense with a scrubbed, feminine hopefulness. She hadn't yet begun to number his lacks. He was still in love with that Mary and he loved whatever traces of her remained—the self-possession, the devotion to order, the high-shouldered walk. When he went for his drives his companion was the young Mary, who sometimes blended in his mind with Susan. A smart girl who sat safely strapped in the passenger seat, watching the landscape with skepticism and stern admiration.

He showed her the development, row upon row of houses; a whole village done in soft colors and simple, comforting shapes. Sometimes he parked on one of his streets and allowed himself to sit, taking it in, cushioned by the Buick's burgundy plush. He and Kazanzakis had built this entire town. These were their roofs defining the horizon, their windows sending light out into the dusk. On nights like those, he felt truly accomplished.

It was a perfect village, new and orderly. Constantine's houses repeated themselves in series of three. One had a gabled roof; one a small front porch; and the third, his favorite, had a pair of bay windows trim and symmetrical as a young girl's breasts. The houses met the sky with their thrifty rhythms, and he was always surprised to see that they had in fact been called into existence. His days were made of details and arguments. *Jerry, I'm telling you, we don't need felt between the roof and the sub-roof. Who told you to order any goddamn stone, we can backfill the sewer lines with dirt.* Only at night, on his drives, did he fully apprehend the houses that now stood because he had ordered Sheetrock by the boxcar, five thousand rolls of insulation, a whole forest's worth of pine. Sometimes at night he chose a house and watched it, always from a reasonable distance. He lit one cigarette after another and watched the windows light up or darken, watched dogs bark to be let in. Some nights a car stopped and let out a teenager; some nights a man or woman came outside to water the lawn. Once a hardy-looking man in green plaid slacks walked out and stood on his front lawn as the last light was leached from the sky and the stars began. Constantine had watched him until the man went back into his house, a gabled model that had cost, what, maybe one-fifth what Constantine had paid for his own house. Briefly, he'd loved and pitied that guy. That guy could have been his kid brother, or his oldest son. Constantine wasn't sure what he was doing, what he wanted here. He couldn't have said why, once or twice a month, he took himself on these spying excursions after he closed up the office. He always imagined young Mary beside him, or someone like Mary, and he imagined the lives being lived inside the walls. When he started his car again and drove home, he always did so in a chaos of yearning. He didn't permit himself to make these trips often. Once or twice a month, tops. He told himself he liked to check up on things, to keep abreast. He saw a girl sit waiting on the curb for someone who never arrived. He saw an orange-striped cat catch a thrush, saw how the nervous life went out of the bird quick as a burst balloon. He heard conversations and music and once he believed he heard the cries of two people making love. He drove home in a state of arching, rarefied hope that was almost painful in its intensity. For his family he had built a substantial new house on a full acre. He had given them two working fireplaces and thirty-eight windows and a front door flanked by carved wooden columns white and fluted as wedding cakes. As he punched the remote-control button to open his garage door he was aware of the constellations—the Hunter, the Ram, the Sisters—and of the interstate highway system along which nails and produce and shoes and tractors were even now being conveyed to their rightful homes. He was aware of the network of underground pipes that conducted water through a world of burrowing animals and the roots of trees. As the garage door opened on its pulleys and oiled chains he took leave of his ordinary, restless thoughts and entered a realm of joy. He couldn't explain the feeling. It was a sense of imminence, of titanic plates shifting in the night sky, rearranging themselves according to a plan too simple for human comprehension. Full of happiness, he steered his car into the garage. There were his tools hanging in perfect order on their white pegboard. There was his mower, his vise, his screws and brads in labeled jars. He allowed himself to sit for an extra minute in the cool silence of his car. Then he went through the side door into the kitchen, where Mary had kept his dinner waiting for him. On the refrigerator, old drawings of Billy's and Zoe's were held with magnets shaped like fruits. A plastic apple, an orange, a banana.

"Hi," Mary called. She was making a list. She wore red slacks and a gray sweatshirt.

"Hi," he said. And just that quickly, with the utterance of a single mild syllable, the joy evaporated. Something was wrong here. Something diminished him, even as he earned good money and honored his marriage vows and fed and clothed his children.

"How'd the day go?" Mary asked. She continued with her list. When she wedded herself to a job, she was lost. She wore her dark hair pulled back tight.

"Fine," he said. "Smells good in here."

"Pork chops," she said. "And mashed potatoes. Are you hungry?"

"Yeah. I'm starved. What's that you're doing there?"

"Oh, just a list of all I've got to get for Zoe's birthday party. I can't believe I've invited eight little girls to spend the night here."

He nodded, and almost recaptured the clear, vaulting happiness of the garage. A pretty wife, oak cabinets, pork and potatoes waiting warm in the oven. He wanted to be happy in a solid, sustained way, hour to hour, not in turbulent little fits that gripped him at odd moments, usually when he was alone. He'd worked so hard. Sometimes he suspected that if he acted happy, if he said what a happy man would say, he could catch it again. He could grab it by its invisible wings and hold it, tightly, to his chest.

"Where are the kids?" he asked cheerfully.

"Susan's at ballet. Billy and Zoe are upstairs, supposedly doing their homework. You're real late tonight."

"Yeah. There's a hell of a lot to do."

"I know. There's a lot to do here, too."

He coughed, and wiped his lips with the back of his hand. "I don't hear you complain about the money," he said.

"You're in a pretty mood," she said. She kept on with her list. She held the pencil with a furious primness, and Constantine was afraid of her. She was angry and righteous. She was writing a list to be carved into the granite of his headstone.

"I'm just a working stiff," he said. "I just hope for a little appreciation every now and then, that's all."

She added something to the list. Her pencil scratched across the paper. "I work, too," she said. "As a matter of fact, I'm working right now."

The kitchen seemed to grow. He felt himself shrinking inside it, a small man standing hungrily on yellow linoleum. He turned on the oven light, looked through the tinted window at the casserole dishes within.

"So, how about dinner?" he asked. His voice was cheerful again. The voice of a happy man.

"Con, it's right there. I can get it for you in a minute. Or, if you want it right this second, well, you know how to open the oven door, don't you?"

"Right," he said. He took a hot pad and removed his dinner from the oven. He set the dishes on the countertop, lifted their beaded glass lids.

"Looks good," he said.

"Mm. Soft drinks, potato chips, marshmallows. Favors. Maybe little bottles of perfume. Or, I don't know. They may still be too young for that."

Constantine took a plate from the cupboard. He was spooning out potatoes when Billy came into the kitchen.

"Hello," Billy said. At twelve he was still as skinny as he'd been at five. The knobs and sticks of his frame poked against his milky skin. His face, a sharper version of Constantine's, was taking on a sly expression.

"Hi," Constantine said.

Billy went to the refrigerator and took out a Coke. Constantine felt a constriction in his throat, a spasm of ownership. That Coke is mine, I paid for it.

"What's going on?" he asked.

"Nothing," Billy said. "I'm doing my geography."

"Geography." Constantine squeezed the handle of the spoon. How could he fail to adore his son? What was lacking in him? *Talk*, Constantine silently commanded. *Tell me about geography.*

"What about geography?" Constantine said. He set the spoon on the counter, stabbed a chop with his fork.

Show me where you are on the map of the world. A boy who broods, who lives in books. Who refuses to know the names of tools and shows no interest in outdoor games.

Billy shrugged. He opened the Coke, which made a fizzing sound. "Latin America," he said. "Major imports and exports."

"Right," Constantine said. "Imports and exports. They ship a lot of diamonds out of Latin America, don't they?"

Billy sent him a blank-eyed, satisfied expression. Constantine knew the look. It was the victor's mask, the deep calm of superior accomplishment.

"No, Dad," Billy said with elaborate patience. "No diamonds. They export, well, bananas and coffee. And other things."

Constantine felt his anger rising. Maybe he was mistaken. Maybe it was some other country that mined diamonds. Maybe it was Africa, or Brazil.

"You're a smart kid, ain't you?" he said. "You're a real smart kid."

Maybe his voice carried a sharper edge than he'd meant it to. Sometimes the things he heard himself say didn't match what was in his heart.

"I don't know," Billy said.

"You don't know. Well, what *do* you know? I keep hearing from your mother all about how smart you are."

He watched his son's face. Billy stood before him in his frail armature of bone and pallid skin. His eyes, unnaturally large in his skull, ticked with unknowable thoughts.

"Where's Costa Rica, Dad?" he asked.

"Huh?"

"Costa Rica. The country. Do you know where it is?"

"What are you talking about, Costa Rica?"

Billy said, "I forget. Is it north or south of Panama?"

Constantine waved him away. "Go on," he said. "Go finish your homework."

"Okay," Billy said. He glanced at Mary and she looked back with such direct complicity Constantine's breath caught in his chest. He suspected that they plotted together, shared stories about his failings. Billy slurped his Coke and started out of the kitchen. He had a precise, girlish walk. He might have been balancing coins on his toes.

"Listen, mister," Constantine said to his back. "I don't like your attitude."

"Con, just let it go," Mary said. "Billy, get on upstairs."

Billy turned. His thin face was swarming with an emotion Constantine couldn't name. It might have been rage. It might have been terror.

"What's the capital of North Dakota, Dad?" Billy said.

"What're you saying to me here? What are you saying?"

"Con," Mary said. The anticipation in her voice only made him angrier.

"What's seven times nine?" Billy asked. "How do you spell 'rhythm'?"

"Mister, I'm warning you. Who in the hell do you think you are?"

"I'm a smart kid," Billy said. "That's what you called me."

"Well, you get the hell out of here. By the time I count three, I want you out of my sight. One."

Billy left the room. Constantine saw the relief on Mary's face. She held her list.

"Two, three," he said. He turned back to the counter to finish filling his plate. He was spearing a pork chop when Billy called from the stairwell, "The capital of North Dakota is Bismarck."

Constantine ran from the kitchen and mounted the stairs by twos. He caught Billy on the top stair. Mary was close behind, hollering, but her cries only fueled Constantine's passion. He grabbed Billy's skinny arms, lifted him off the carpet.

"What did you say to me?" Constantine said, and he heard the clenched power of his own voice. Billy looked into his face with an opaque, stubborn expression.

He said, "Seven times nine is sixty-three."

When Constantine hit him he felt he was obliterating a weakness in the house. He was cauterizing a wound. The back of his hand struck Billy's jaw hard, scraped across his teeth with a cleansing burn. He heard Mary's scream from a distance. Billy's head snapped back and Constantine hit him again, this time with the heel of his hand, a smack solid and sure as a hammer driving a nail deep into pine. When he let go of Billy's arms Billy crumpled and rolled down a few stairs, where Mary held him to her breast. She shouted and wept. Constantine couldn't hear what she was saying. He looked up and saw Zoe standing in the hallway, shyly, with her hands clutching her belly. "Go back to your room," he said. He watched until she had run into her room and shut the door. Then he stepped around Mary and his son and got himself downstairs.

"You monster," Mary screamed. "You stupid bastard."

Constantine didn't answer. He didn't look back. He made himself walk slowly, with buzzing calm, out the door and into the garage. He got into his car. Breathing steadily, he opened the garage door and backed down the drive, gunned the motor, and drove away. The needle of the speedometer touched fifty before he'd gone two blocks. He looked in the rearview mirror and saw his porch light receding, joining the welter of anonymous neighborhood lights. The sound of his heart drummed in his ears. His face burned with rage and shame. As he drove he promised to work harder. He promised to be better, kinder. He found himself driving back to his development, to watch the nocturnal life of the houses and to listen, like a penitent in church, to the murmur of the voices inside.

1 9 6 8 / The golf course was vast as an ocean, cut by a pale sliver of rising moon. Constellations glittered, and a northern wind, the first of autumn, tossed pine branches among the stars. Susan lay on the faint yellow square of the blanket, holding Todd's cock in her hand with cautious solicitude. She watched his face for changes.

"Oh," Todd murmured. Steam rose white from his mouth and nose. "Oh. Ohhhh. *Oh.*"

"Shh," she said, although he had not been loud. During the ordinary hours of his life he lived inside his own large flesh with astonishing ease. He seemed to find it unremarkable that his fingertips could grip a soup bowl around its edges and that his feet filled shoes massive and potentially lethal as cinder blocks. He obeyed rules, shook other boys' hands and told them, with profound conviction, that he was glad of their friendship. But at night, on the golf course or in his brother's car, something too big threatened to escape from him.

"*Ahh,*" he said, and she whispered again, "Shhh."

He groped his way along her thigh. She hoped her thigh was

beautiful, alabaster under the tossing branches. She hoped she was something to adore, in skirt and panties, wearing his rough cardigan over her bare breasts and the cold circle of his class ring on a chain around her neck. He slipped his fingers under the elastic of her panties. She shifted nervously. His fingers raised a queasiness in her belly, an unsettled feeling. They probed, rubbing her dark pubic hair (why was it so thick?), and then one dipped inside, quickly, almost furtively. The finger thrust, withdrew, thrust again. She fought a rising panic. He was so insistent. His finger burrowed through her in search of something else, a mysterious perfection she was afraid she lacked. Did he joke about her with his friends? She worked his cock faster, knowing that if she made him come he'd subside and return to himself, gentle gregarious Todd. To take her mind off her own fears she focused on his cock, its veined shaft and purple, strangely innocent head. Todd's was the only cock she knew, and when she fantasized, guiltily, about other boys, she imagined their chests and legs and asses but never their crotches. She put a white, illuminated patch where their cocks would have been; she made them powerful and inspired and neuter, like horses. Only Todd's cock appeared on her geography of the body. She wondered if he understood her loyalty's depth and breadth. She wondered if this diligence, this scrupulous and clinical interest of hers, was what people meant when they spoke about love.

"Aww," he said, a moist, guttural sound, and she knew he was getting close. His finger pounded inside her. She might have cried out for him to stop but instead she worked the loose skin up and down his shaft, up and down, aiming the whole of her will at it until, with a strangled moan, he shot a faintly luminous thread that fell, in little round spatters, on the smooth plane of his belly. "Mmm," she said, and "Shhh." Here was the smell of bleach. Here was the bucking surrender, frightening and sad. She held tight through his spasms, until his cock softened in her hands and his finger calmed and withdrew and she could lie beside him, comforting him, feeling the heat of his body.

They didn't speak. If the night had not been cold, they might have slept. Susan lay with her head on Todd's chest, rising and falling with the smooth animal effort of his breathing. She loved this time, when she could lie with him, just lie peacefully in shared ownership of his immensity. She liked the idea that her own body would fit completely inside his. She could wear him like a suit of armor. A wet, frigid smell rose from the grass and she contemplated his belly, where little pools of semen lay, opalescent in the shifting dark. At first his discharge had repelled her but gradually her revulsion had turned to interest. This viscous juice came from Todd's inward, secret self. Todd, the senior class president, whose mother ironed his undershirts. The spilling of semen was so unlike him that Susan couldn't help but be moved. His ejaculations implied some aspect of loss, and she loved to console him afterward. She watched the small puddles, knowing that in another second they'd turn translucent and lose their density, flowing off along his ribs. But now they lay in thick white circles under the October sky. She put out a finger and touched a drop that quivered, perfectly spherical, on his abdomen, just above the tangle of his pubic hair. She told herself she was touching starlight and Todd's sorrow, the secret hungers he revealed only to her. She held her moistened fingertip up in the cold air, watching its dull sparkle, and then she put it to her tongue.

"What are you doing?" he asked.

"Tasting you," she said. The taste resembled the smell, mushrooms and spray starch, although it had another thread, something raw and deeply human.

She felt the pause in his breathing. "Jesus, Sooz," he said.

"Strictly for scientific purposes," she said. "Youth wants to know." But she heard the thinness in her own voice. She had miscalculated. What she'd done was not the province of people in love. She was sluttish, grotesque.

He asked, "So, um, what do you think?"

"Well, it'll never replace ice cream."

"I guess not," he said.

They both laughed, but an awkwardness had settled between them. Susan pulled his cardigan more closely around her breasts. "I'm freezing," she said.

"I know. I am, too."

"We should probably go."

"Yeah. We probably should."

They sat up and began putting their clothes on. Todd took a handkerchief out of his back pocket and wiped his stomach with swift unsentimental motions, as if he was cleaning the windshield of a car.

"It's getting too cold for this," he said. "I guess we won't be coming out here any more this year."

"No. This is goodbye to the golf course."

They looked around as if they were both suddenly surprised to find themselves there at all. Sand traps glowed in the black fields of grass.

"We used to slide around out here on blocks of ice," Todd said. "Did I ever tell you about that? At night, when I was ten or eleven. Dan and Ronnie and I used to come out here and slide down the hills on these big blocks of ice."

Her pulse quickened. As a little girl, she hadn't known what a golf course was. Every day, the shadow of a smokestack had ticked across the façade of her family's row house. Now she was a citizen of another country, a lush green one, where a crescent moon answered the defiant snap of the golfers' flags. She looked, quickly but deeply, into Todd's placid face. He had an innocent intensity wide as a mountain's. All Todd's features—his heavily symmetrical face, his stubby hands, the flat muscular planes of his stomach and ass—put her in mind of continents.

"I'll bet you were a charmer as a little boy," she said. "I'll bet you were just about unbearably cute." In fact, she could imagine him: stocky and sweet-tempered, almost ostentatiously cheerful, the kind of child who never gives anyone any trouble.

He shrugged, pleased. He liked the myth of his own history. He liked its gentle curve.

"And you," he said, "were a princess. Right?"

She smoothed his hair with her fingertips, kissed his lips. It was hard sometimes to know what story they were inventing together. Was she a bored princess from an exotic land come to shed her magical strangeness on the golf course and the Dairy Queen? Or was she the impoverished girl from the fairy tales, with just one chance in a billion?

"Come on," she said. "I have a feeling my father's waiting up tonight."

"Right," he said. If he'd held her there another minute—if he'd said he didn't care about her father's life of rules and outrage—she might have started the long process of falling in love with him. But Todd's strength lay in doing perfectly all that was expected of him. He was known for his expansive, cheerful cooperation. He sometimes quoted Will Rogers: "I never met a man I didn't like."

They folded up the blanket and walked in silence across the sloped expanse of the fourteenth hole. Todd encircled Susan's shoulders with his arm. She could hear the strong skim of his breathing, could almost feel the thick, potent reliability of his heart. When they reached his brother's car he leaned against the curve of the fender and drew her to his chest. He put out his own warm atmosphere, sweetened with Old Spice and Vitalis. Standing close to him put Susan in mind of a barnyard: new hay and the furred, well-fed haunches of animals.

"Susan?" he whispered, and she felt his breath on her ear.

"Mmm?"

"Aw, Sooz, I, well. I think you're great."

She laughed, then sucked the laughter back in and tenderly kissed his ear. He was struggling with something.

"I think you're great, too, sweetheart," she whispered. A voice inside her seemed to say, This is romance. The asphalt road, pewter in the darkness, rolled away into trees and scattered porches. Todd's brother's Chevrolet gleamed with everything a car had to say about freedom and better luck. So why was some part of her unmoved? How was she able to retain her objective, cataloguing facility, the part that registered cars and porch lights and called them romance? She wanted to be swept away.

"This is our last year," Todd said. "After this, everything changes."

"I know. It'll be fun. I mean, college and everything."

He ran his finger along her spine. "Sure," he said. "It'll be great. I just . . . Aw, never mind."

"What? What is it, honey?"

"I've been here all my life. You know? I've never been any-where else."

"I know," she said. "I know that."

He breathed in, so deeply that she was crushed between his arms and the expansion of his chest. The ring pressed hard between her breasts.

"This is goodbye to the golf course," he said.

"Just for now. We can come back out here in the spring. Todd, honey, everything's going to be all right. Everything's going to be wonderful."

"Right," he said. "I know. Don't you think I know how won-derful everything's going to be?"

The note of peevishness in his voice surprised her. Todd was never irritable or morose. He was a table set with oranges and a pitcher of milk.

"It *is*, sweetie," she said with brisk determination. "Think about college. *Think* about it, there's so much that's going to happen. It's going to be a whole new world."

He nodded. "I like this world," he said. He looked past her to the golf course, where pines announced their ragged shapes against the sky.

"I like it, too," she said.

He turned from her, looked with a fierce scientific intensity at the row of darkened houses on the far side of the road. "Do you like two-story houses?" he asked. "I always want to have a house with an upstairs, these one-story jobs don't seem like real houses to me."

Susan believed she knew the truth about herself and Todd. She was still greedy for everything she didn't have, and he couldn't imagine wanting more than this. She was the stronger of the two, though he had all the advantages. The fact seemed to explode inside her head: We don't belong together. Then she tumbled into remorse. He needed her. She had to help keep him inside himself. Otherwise, the boy who lived within might fly out and run, howling and terrified, along this empty road.

"I like two-story houses," she said. "Sure, I do. Now come here."

She kissed him and lost herself again in the massive Chevrolet and the warm equine sweetness of his flesh. He was so large, so obedient. Someday she would leave him, she'd find out how much could happen to a smart and pretty girl. But for now, he was hers. She had unlimited rights to this flesh, this life of work and rewards. Soon they were inside the car, where, for the first time, she permitted him to touch her between the legs with the sweet, faintly impersonal head of his cock.

There had been a fight. She could feel its weight as she let herself in through the side door. "Hi," she called cheerfully into the empty kitchen. All was in order: dishes sparkling on the drainboard, counters wiped, the row of copper molds (a fish, a star, a rabbit) gleaming above the potted fern. Still, a hushed, exhausted quality lay in the air.

She passed through the kitchen, paused before her reflection in the hallway mirror. Her hair was fine, her clothes still looked clean and straight. Although she ordinarily tried to refrain from fantasies, she let herself imagine the football field as her name was read out and a crown, a wilder brilliance in the brilliant air, was lifted to her head. She looked herself up and down. Was she a queen or a princess? Had she let Todd go too far? She plucked a leaf of grass from her hair and, because she had no pockets, slipped it inside her blouse.

Whatever had happened, it was over now. Everyone must have gone to bed. The only evidence of discord, apart from the charge that lingered invisibly, was the lamps that still blazed in the empty rooms. Probably her father had gone off somewhere and her mother, having fled to the bedroom, had stayed there and fallen asleep. Susan moved from room to room, switching off lights, trying not to think of herself crowned, weeping, selected. It was bad luck to want it too much. She darkened the dining room and the den. Since moving to this town, she'd learned something no one else in her family knew. She'd learned that their house was an imitation. The sofas and chairs upholstered in roses, the chestnut gloss of tabletops and the gleaming brass of the lamps—all were simulated furnishings, held together with staples and glue. They were shrill in their newness; they smelled subtly of chemicals. Only she, Susan, had been to the real houses. Her mother—her poor mother—thought a blue leather jewelry box trimmed in gold was the pinnacle of elegance and good taste. Her father believed he was as well favored as anyone whose windows reflected the lawns and elm trees of these broad avenues. But she had been asked inside. She knew that other people's houses were full of books. Other people's houses chimed with the stately confidence of old clocks.

When she turned off the kitchen light she saw a figure standing in the back yard. At first she thought of her father, and a chill ran through her—why would he stand outside like that? What was he going to do? Then the figure raised the orange glow of a cigarette to its mouth and, in the small flare, she saw that it was Billy. She went out through the sliding glass door and stood on the concrete stoop.

"You shouldn't smoke," she said.

He was standing, just standing and smoking, on the grass. "You missed it," he said. "It was a whopper."

"Is everybody all right?"

"I guess. Mom and Zoe are in bed."

She folded her arms over her breasts and looked up at the stars. Todd would be getting into bed now, wearing only the bottoms of his pajamas. A row of trophies, little gold men with basketballs, would be shining on the shelf above his head like lavish, frozen dreams.

"Don't be so dramatic," she said. "Billy, why are you always so dramatic?"

"Well, things get pretty dramatic. You probably wouldn't be asking that question if you'd been here an hour ago."

Slowly, with deep weariness, she walked out onto the grass where Billy stood. "It's a pretty night," she said.

"I guess it is," he answered. "Yeah, I suppose you'd have to call this a pretty one."

He was fifteen now, a sophomore, and instead of growing up he seemed to be hardening into some sort of sulky, continuing childhood. He had no interests. He dressed ridiculously, in patched bell-bottoms and flowered, billowing shirts. His only friends were a handful of hippies and hoods who skulked around school like stray cats. Todd was nice enough to Billy, but she knew he didn't really like him. No, that wasn't true. Todd liked everybody. He didn't respect Billy. He thought of him as an oddity, a character. He said, 'He's a real nut, that brother of yours.'

"What was it all about?" she asked.

"Does it matter? What does that have to do with anything?" Billy sucked fiercely on the cigarette. His face was all sharp points and blank, empty spaces. Bony thrust of nose and chin, no cheekbones, a mouth that refused to assume any particular shape. His skin was blurred with acne. Susan worried that his unfinished quality might become permanent.

"Daddy's going through a hard time," she said. "He has a lot of responsibilities now. I think we have to be patient."

"Right," he said. "You should go in. It's cold out here."

"I'm all right. Where did you get that cigarette, anyway?"

"I do all kinds of things you don't know about. I have a whole other life."

She nodded. "Maybe I will go in," she said. "I'm beat."

"Okay."

"It's just that he loses control sometimes," she said. "I think he's getting better. He's trying. We have to be patient."

"Have you ever noticed how he never breaks *stuff*?" Billy said. "I used to think that, too. That he just, you know, lost control. But tonight after the fracas I was looking at that little glass chicken on the windowsill. You know? We've had it as long as I can remember, it's been sitting right out there in plain sight, and he's never touched it. So, you know, lately I've been thinking, it's us he wants to hurt. He knows what he's doing. If he was really out of control, he'd have smashed that chicken a long time ago."

"Did he do something to you?"

"*Daddy*? Nah. He never laid a hand on me."

"Billy. Come over here, in the light."

"I'm all right."

"Tell me what happened."

"Just a couple of slaps. Open-handed. They were like kisses."

"I want you to come over in the light. I want to look at you."

"Forget it," he said. "I'm really okay. I just want to tell you one thing."

"What?"

"I'm going to kill him one day, and when I do, I don't want people going around saying I lost control. Okay? When I kill him I'm not going to hurt anybody else, I'm not going to break anything. But still. I want it to be clear. I want you to say you stood out here with me one night and I told you I was going to kill him. Only him. Nobody else. Will you do that? Will you do that for me?"

She hugged her arms more tightly over her breasts. "You are so stupid," she said. "I wonder sometimes if you know how stupid you are."

Susan lay on her bed with the light off. Pink daisies swirled darkly on her wallpaper. When she heard the sound of her father's car she got up, put her robe on, and went downstairs. On her way into the kitchen she looked through the dining-room window, but couldn't see Billy in the back yard. Maybe he'd gone to bed; maybe he was walking around the neighborhood. She took milk from the refrigerator, and was setting a saucepan on the burner when her father came in.

"Hi, Daddy," she said.

He stood in the doorway, looking at her as if he'd known her once, long ago, but couldn't quite recall her name or the circumstances of their acquaintance. Had he been drinking?

"I couldn't sleep," she said. "You want to have a glass of milk with me?"

"Susan," he said.

"Sit down," she said. She pulled a chair out for him at the kitchen table.

"How are you, Susan?" he asked. "How is school?"

She knew this tone of voice: the careful articulation, the suave, earnest formality. When he drank, his accent returned.

"School's fine, Daddy. Well, school's school. Sit. I'm just going to heat this up, it'll only take a minute."

He leaned carefully against the refrigerator. His face was ardent and innocent as a boy's. He still wore his work clothes, his white shirt and somberly striped tie. He could beat Billy up, stomp out of the house to get drunk, and return hours later with his tie perfectly knotted.

"You are gonna be queen of the prom," he said. "Sweetheart, I am so proud of you."

"Homecoming, Daddy. The prom's in the spring. And as of

tonight I'm just a princess. Rosemary will probably be queen. She grew up here. She's got about a trillion friends at school."

"You will be queen," he said. "Yes. Oh, yes, you will be chosen."

The milk started bubbling around the edges, and she swirled it in the pan. "It's not like Elizabeth, Daddy," she said. "There are a lot of really pretty girls here. You can't imagine how they dress."

She sucked in a breath as if she hoped to pull her last sentence back into her mouth and swallow it. *Don't complain to him about money, not when he's like this.* But his face didn't change. He continued looking at her with moist, unfocused eyes.

"Princess," he said. "They are gonna make you queen. I promise."

He was big and dangerous and full of love. What would happen if she wasn't chosen?

"It's a big honor just being one of the princesses," she said. "Now sit *down*, Daddy. The milk is ready."

She wondered where Billy had gone. He wouldn't kill their father, she knew that, but if he came into the kitchen now and acted a certain way there was no telling what their father might do.

"You're somethin' else," he said as he lowered himself onto a chair. "How's everything? You happy? How's Todd?"

"Todd is Todd," she said, pouring the steaming milk into two mugs.

"School is school and Todd is Todd," he said. "This does not sound so good. This does not sound like happiness."

She set a mug on the table in front of him. "Don't listen to me," she said. "Everything's great. I guess I have a touch of senioritis, or something."

"Huh?"

"Oh, senioritis. A desperate urge to be done with school just about the time you've reached the top of the heap. It has medical science baffled."

He nodded. He looked into his milk. "Your brother and me, we had a little disagreement tonight," he said.

He wanted so much. He could do such damage.

"I heard," she said. "I wish you two wouldn't fight like that."

"Don't tell me. Tell him. You want to know what he called me?"

"What?"

"He called me a pig. A *pig*."

"Oh, Daddy."

"Like what he calls the police. He called me a fucking pig, excuse the language. That's how your brother talks these days."

"You have to ignore him sometimes."

"Your mother, she told me to get out of the house—"

His voice was filling with emotion, a clotted sound. His face was darkening.

"She gets upset," Susan said. "She's high-strung, you know that, these fights are too much for her."

"I guess so. I guess that's true. You know a lot, don't you? Only eighteen, and you know so much."

"Not all that much. Listen, Daddy, it's late. I should get to bed."

"I wish your mother knew half the things you know. God. I wish she wasn't so mad all the time."

"I have to get up in about five hours—"

He put his hand on top of hers. She recognized what was in his face, the love and the hunger and the bottomless grief.

"Susie," he said. His face was imploring as a baby's, full of a baby's inchoate, violent need.

"I'm here," she said. "I'm right here."

She didn't move. She was frightened and vaguely excited. It wasn't desire; not exactly desire. She saw the power she could have. She heard her name being called out on the football field, saw a crown lifted in the floodlit air. Slowly, with tenderness, she took his big suffering head in her slender hands and guided his face to her own. His breath was full of beer, strong but not unpleasant. Human. She thought he would pull away. He didn't. She was frightened. She let the kiss go on.

1 9 6 8 / Words caught in Zoe's throat. She watched instead. A leaf fluttered down from the ivy plant that was inching its way out of its Chinese pot. Dust brightened and dimmed in the square of light. A ghost slipped across the carpet, crying silently for all it couldn't find.

"Zoe?" Momma called. "Zoe, are you in there?"

She nodded. Momma tapped with her heels on the floorboards. She entered in a fury of perfume and sly glistenings. Her nylons hissed against her skirt.

"Right," she said. "Not dressed. Hair's a rat's nest. Zoe, he's going to be here in twenty minutes. Do you get it? Do you understand?"

"Uh-huh," Zoe said.

"Then will you *move*?"

"I hate my dress."

Momma's mouth made a noise, a dry sucking. Momma's mouth refused the cravings, made itself into a line.

"Last week was the time to tell me you hated your dress," she said. "Last week, there was time to do something about it. Right now I want you *in* the dress, hair brushed and face washed, in exactly ten minutes. Got it?"

Zoe nodded. She poked her fingers between her toes. From upstairs, Poppa whistled a song known only to him. Momma hated his whistling, though she'd never say so. His songs were like needles on her skin and she'd learned to enjoy the pain.

"*Zoe.*" Momma wrapped a pink-nailed hand around Zoe's arm, yanked her out of the chair. "You're driving me to distraction. Do you know that? Now come on. I'm going to dress you myself."

Zoe let Momma pull her out of the room, up the stairs past the pictures. She passed herself as a baby, terrified in pajamas covered with dancing bears. She passed her parents' wedding, and Susan in her baptismal dress. She passed Momma as a girl, with a pearl necklace and a hard, hopeful smile.

Zoe knew she'd never marry. A bride had to have a plan; she had to live in a house. Zoe would live in the outside, eat soup made from bark and rainwater. She was wrong for houses.

"—not so much to ask," Momma was saying. "A twelve-year-old girl can be trusted to get herself ready, to not have to be watched and babied every single second. Honestly, I don't know what to do with you sometimes."

Momma took her into the main bedroom, where time was slower. There, a white bedspread spoke silently about the patience of whiteness. Two silver dancers, a man and a woman, were stopped in mid-leap on the wall. Momma sat her down at the dressing table, which was cluttered with jars and tubes and little glass bottles, a miniature city of cosmetics. It had a jumbled, intricate life of its own. It was the center of something.

Zoe would live elsewhere, let her hair go free. She'd smell like moss and fur.

"Just sit still," Momma said, taking up her brush. "If this smarts a little, I can't help it. Zoe, how do you get so many tangles in your hair? What do you *do* to it?"

Zoe saw herself and Momma in the round mirror. She saw that she was the end of beauty. She had unruly brows and a hooked nose. Something that had started in Momma and advanced into Susan had crashed against her small black eyes, her jutting chin.

She was somebody else. She couldn't carry the family manners.

"Mmm," Momma moaned, forcing the brush through. From down the hall, from the bathroom, Poppa whistled. When he whistled, Momma pulled the bristles harder through the thick black snarls. Zoe bit down on the pain.

"It'll be over in a second," Momma said. "If you'd done this an hour ago, when you were supposed to, we wouldn't have to rush."

Susan's voice came in from the hall. "Momma, have you seen my sharmbreslet?"

"Your what?"

Susan stood in the door. Her face came into the mirror.

"My *charm bracelet*," she said. Her face moved next to Momma's face. They were all three in the mirror together. Zoe's eyes cupped their silence.

"It's in your jewelry box, isn't it?"

"I guess I would have checked there, wouldn't I?"

"How about the pocket of your coat? Remember, the last time you thought you'd lost it—"

"I looked there, too. I've looked everywhere."

"Do you have to wear it?"

"I want to wear it."

Momma made the exhausted noise, the little growl that lived at the back of her throat. "All right," she said. "You finish Zoe's hair, I'll go find the charm bracelet."

She gave the brush to Susan. She left the mirror and made impatient high-heel sounds in the hallway.

"Yikes, Zo, look at this *hair*," Susan said. She brought her skimming, soaped smell. She brought the optimism and the swift, confident clicking of herself.

"I don't want to have my picture taken," Zoe told her.

"Well, there's no escape. The Christmas picture is going to get you whether you like it or not. Now brace yourself, this might hurt a little."

"Ow," Zoe cried, although Susan's strokes hurt less than Momma's had.

"Just be brave."

"I hate having my picture taken," Zoe said. "I hate the dress she got me."

"I know, I know. Things are terrible. Criminy, look at this *knot*."

Poppa came into the mirror. He brought his size. He brought his eager, turbulent face.

"Hello, ladies," he said. "How goes it?"

"I'm just wrestling with Zoe's hair," Susan said. "It's the most amazing thing. It looks like hair, but then you try to get a brush through it and you see it's really something else. Wire, or something."

Poppa laid a hand on Susan's shoulder. "We got to hurry," he said softly. "The photo guy's gonna be here any minute now. Your mother's going out of her head."

"I guess there'll still be Christmas if he has to wait five minutes," Susan said.

Poppa nodded, and smiled. That had been the right answer.

"Found it," Momma called. "It was in the clothes hamper, for heaven's sake. I might have put it through the washing machine."

She came into the room but didn't enter the mirror. Poppa took his hand off Susan's shoulder.

"Zoe's almost ready," Susan said.

Momma came into the mirror. The air took on noisy possibilities, an electric impatience.

"Let me finish," Momma said. She took the brush from Susan and forced it through Zoe's hair so hard that buried thoughts were pulled to the surface of her brain. Zoe let her eyes water, let the thoughts boil. She didn't make a sound.

Later, they all sat in the afternoon dusk of the living room while Mr. Fleming made his adjustments. Mr. Fleming was a small, busy man with heavy glasses and an astonished aspect. Something invisible, known only to him, seemed always to be happening a foot in front of his thin, serious face. His camera stood on three stork legs, aiming its blind eye at the room.

"Just relax, everybody," he said, lowering a lamp. "This'll only take a few minutes. Right? A few minutes."

Zoe sat on the sofa with Billy. He wore his blue blazer, with a red handkerchief peeking out of the breast pocket like a proud secret. Billy sat to make himself bigger, with his legs wide and his skinny arms splayed on the cushions. He believed things were important but not necessarily serious.

"Great dress," he said to Zoe from the side of his mouth. She hunched up. Her forehead burned. Sometimes Billy meant what he said and sometimes he meant the opposite. The dress was green, tied at the middle with a red bow the size of a cabbage. When Momma brought it home, Zoe had shrugged in haphazard assent. She had somehow not fully understood that she was meant to wear it, and soon.

"Let's have the kids on the sofa," Momma said. "And Con, you and I can stand back here." She had about her an air of avid, defiant sorrow. She was already preparing to be dissatisfied with all the proofs Mr. Fleming would send.

"Ma," Billy said. "That's what we do every year."

"Well, professor," Momma said, "do you have a better idea?"

"I want to stand this year," Susan said. "I look fat when I'm sitting down."

Susan wore the dress she'd fought for, white ruffles with an emerald sash. Momma had insisted it wasn't Christmasy enough.

But Susan wanted what she wanted with a glacial singularity. Momma's desires were too far-flung. She wanted Susan in a more Christmasy dress but at the same time she wanted new cordovan loafers for Billy and a different hairstyle for herself (would it look too young?) and six boxes of white Christmas lights instead of the colored ones she'd bought. Susan could always win that way, by knowing with a jeweler's precision.

Momma said, "It'll look funny if three of us are standing behind the sofa and just Zoe and Billy are sitting on it."

"Why don't you sit between Zoe and Bill," Poppa said to Momma, "and Susie and I can stand back here."

Momma's mouth made its line. It said its no, silently, while Momma turned inside herself. She wore a red dress with a sprig of holly and three gold glass balls trembling at the breast.

"What if you and I sat on the sofa," she said. "And all three kids stood in back?"

"Zoe's too short," Billy said. "All you'll see is the top of her head."

Momma nodded. "All right," she said. "Fine. Whatever. I'll sit. Susan, you stand in back with your father."

She was lost in multiplicity. She wanted to stand behind the sofa with Poppa but she also wanted new records of Christmas carols and a set of dishes hand-painted with candy canes and a real pearl necklace to give to Susan for high school graduation.

"Get ready," Mr. Fleming said. "Get in your positions. Right?"

Momma put herself on the sofa between Billy and Zoe. She blued the air with her nervous shining and her pride, the tiny music of her earrings. In three weeks the cards would be back from the printer: Season's Greetings from the Stassos Family.

"Mr. Fleming?" she said. "How does this look to you? As a composition."

Mr. Fleming rotated a lamp a fraction of an inch. He looked at the Stassos family with awestruck myopia.

"Right," he said. "Perfect. Just about perfect. Susan, move a little to the left of your father. Right. There. That's perfect."

Zoe shifted on the sofa cushion. She repositioned her arms in an effort to conceal the red bow at her waist.

"Zoe, don't fidget," Momma said. She leaned toward Billy, adjusted the handkerchief in his pocket. She whispered to him, and he put out a helpless spasm of laughter. Zoe glanced back at Poppa and Susan standing behind the sofa. Briefly, she thought Susan was wearing a wedding dress, all sheen and lace. Susan stood next to Poppa. She was calm and beautiful.

"Fine," Mr. Fleming said. "You look aces, all of you. Now you're all going to smile for me. Right?"

Zoe saw that she was not in the picture. She shifted her weight, moved closer toward the center. She still wasn't in the picture.

"Hey, Zoe," Mr. Fleming said. "Are you going to smile? For me?"

She nodded. She started to smile. The room exploded with light.

1 9 6 8 / It was too late not to have done it. The kisses had become something Susan did and now there was no language to say no in. Now it was only possible to let it happen. Not saying anything gave it no shape, no beginning or end; it was only possible to not say anything.

If she hadn't started it, if she was innocent, she might have been somebody who could say no. An innocent girl could have done that.

As herself, with no one else to be, she let it happen. She wanted it. She didn't *not* want it. And it was only kisses and hugs. It only happened when he drank. She was like a little girl and she was like a nurse. He kissed her with romance, playfully. He was careful about his hands.

He wasn't to blame, not really. She had started it and now it existed, a secret they shared. Saying no would have given it a name.

It was two minutes to halftime. The band waited in formation under the bleachers, quick glimmers of gold glancing off their trumpets and trombones. As Susan and Rosemary led the victory cheer, they smiled at one another. Two minutes. All four cheerleaders turned cartwheels, and Dottie Wiggins, popular in spite of her looks, mugged for the crowd, wiping her brow as if it had been a strenuous effort. Laughter rose up into the chill air. Someone threw a streamer, a liquid ribbon of dark red against the black sky.

"Victory victory is our cry, V-I-C-T-O-R-Y."

When play started up again, Susan and Rosemary stood close together, watching the field. "Are you nervous?" Rosemary whispered.

"No. A little. Are you?"

"No. You're going to win."

"No, you are."

The ball was snapped. Maroon jerseys collided with orange. Susan heard the grunts and cries, the musical click of one helmet striking another. The ball sailed, spiraling, in a graceful arc, and Rosemary whispered, "Have you seen Marcia? She looks like she's ready for Halloween."

Susan nodded, grimacing. Marcia Rosselini was a tough, beautiful girl who did everything. When the nominations were announced, Rosemary had said to Susan, "Marcia just got all the boys she's slept with to vote for her." Although Susan didn't despise her the way Rosemary did, she understood about Marcia's unsuitability. No one could question her lavish, cocoa-colored hair and hazel eyes, the buoyant languor of her body. She was the most beautiful girl in school. But she drifted from boy to boy, went all the way. She squandered her beauty like an heiress spending her whole fortune in a few crazy, glittering years. Boys gathered around her like hungry dogs, growling and snapping, and for all her good fortune Marcia was, finally, a pathetic case. Because she fed herself to the dogs. Because she laughed too knowingly and wore tight skirts and would end in an apartment in Elmont or Uniondale, married to the fiercest, sexiest boy, who'd carve the years straight into her skin with his tempers and habits. You could see the Marcia Rosselinis of ten and twenty years ago, working as waitresses or cashiers or shouting from front porches at their own wild children. They'd lived a life of desire and desire had burned to ash in their perfect, practiced hands.

Being queen didn't mean anything so simple and doomed as desirability. The homecoming queen was destined. She had grace. She was someone particular. She was vivid enough to live without shame, and any mistakes she'd made were burned clean by the radiance of what she'd become.

"Marcia can't win," Susan said. "She can't. You're going to win."

"No, I think you are," Rosemary said. "I have a feeling, I just do."

Impulsively, Susan squeezed Rosemary's hand. All right, she'd admit it, at least to herself. She desperately wanted to win. She needed to win, more than Rosemary did. She permitted herself a prayer. *Please, God, let me be chosen. Let me be the one.*

At halftime, as the band marched onto the field, Susan waited with Rosemary and Marcia at the fifty-yard line. Susan and Rosemary wore their cheerleading outfits. Marcia wore a low-cut powder-blue dress and a sapphire on a thin gold chain. She had a prominent collarbone and a small, well-shaped head. She'd outlined her eyes with heavy black pencil, and brushed sparkling blue shadow from her lids to her brows. She looked at Susan and Rosemary with the sleepy, irritated expression that had become her trademark.

"This is it, girls," she said.

Rosemary smiled, and picked a speck of lint from her sweater. She hated Marcia the way a housewife hates disorder. Susan harbored a certain admiration for Marcia's harsh self-confidence, but so feared the fate Marcia would make for herself that she felt a twinge of nausea in her presence.

"Right," Susan said wanly. "The big one."

Todd walked up to them, grinning, his shoulders thrown back and his left hand thrust casually into his pocket. He moved as if this occasion, the next second and the next, contained a series of openings exactly his size. He held the sealed envelope. It was his duty as class president to read out the name of the winner. He wore his gray slacks and navy-blue blazer, which Susan knew as intimately as she knew her own clothes. She felt related to prominence, magnified, because she had lain with her head on that blazer, barebreasted under the stars. Then she felt shamed by what she'd done, accused. It was impossible to know what to feel.

"Hi, everybody." Todd smiled. "You ready?"

Because he believed in duty, Todd didn't look directly at Susan. He didn't wink at her, or sneak her a special smile. In his official capacity he conducted himself as if he were on cordial but distant terms with all three contestants, and Susan briefly and bitterly hated him. She glanced at Marcia, who probably considered Todd a joke. A team player, too dull and honorable.

"Let's get it over with," Marcia said. Susan wondered if she was so certain, so lost to her own future, that she genuinely did not care about being chosen. If she won—for being foolish and beautiful and doomed—would she end the evening drunk, laughing, makeup smeared, setting the rhinestone crown over Eddie Gagliostra's erection? Susan felt an envy more potent than anything she'd known with Rosemary or the other celebrated, well-behaved girls. By being mean and sluttish, Marcia had taken herself to a realm where losing meant nothing because winning meant nothing.

Rosemary pinched Susan's arm, gently, through her sweater, and Susan returned to herself. Rosemary was her best friend, her true sister. Rosemary was what she wanted to be. Todd led all three girls to the middle of the field, where the band members had arranged themselves in a half circle around the pale green Cadillac convertible that would drive the queen and her court around the track. Underclass boys stood ready with flash cameras. Peggy Chandler, last year's queen, waited to crown the new winner. Peggy, a handsome, forceful girl wearing an expensive dress covered with red poppies, had taken the train down from Albany, where she would soon marry a state attorney's aide. "Good luck," Rosemary whispered, and Susan said "Good luck" back. She felt dizzy, short of breath. The world shrank before her. *Please*, she said silently. *Please, God.* Neither Rosemary nor Marcia needed the crown the way she did. They were already on their way to the places they were going.

The girls stood in a line before the Cadillac, facing the bleachers. Peggy Chandler stood on one side, waiting, staunch and satisfied within her dress. Susan knew where her family was sitting, though from where she stood they were merely part of the shifting, admiring crowd. The world was so large. There was so much to win or lose. Todd stepped up to the microphone stand. He adjusted the mike, grimaced over its squawk, then smiled expansively at the crowd.

"Welcome, everybody." His voice boomed, hollowed and deepened, through the loudspeakers. "Welcome fellow students and alumni. Hope you're enjoying the game. No. I stand corrected. Hope you're enjoying the way we're clobbering those Panthers."

The night filled with cheers and hoots. Maroon streamers flew. Clouds of confetti cascaded through the electric light.

"We Trojans are known around these parts for our team spirit, our honor, our ferociousness on the playing field. Well, some of us are. Others are just as well known for beauty and charm. Now the time has come to crown the girl who best represents those qualities. Ladies and gentlemen, it's my privilege to announce the queen of the 1968 homecoming game."

Again, the crowd cheered, but not as loudly. Todd leaned closer to the microphone. His face in profile was grave and competent. He had a low forehead and a short nose, a jaw so heavy Susan sometimes thought, without meaning to, of the shape of his skull.

"Let me begin by saying that all three of these lovely ladies deserve to be queen. All three, each in her own way, represent the Trojan ideal. But tradition dictates that only one can be chosen. So, without further ado . . . ."

He held up the envelope, sparkling white. He tore it open, pulled out a sheet of white paper. Nothing changed on his broad, mild face.

He said, "Permit me to present the first princess of the 1968 homecoming game. Marcia Rosselini."

Cheers and whoops, scattered boos, rose from the crowd. Marcia smiled and lifted her chin higher, as if defying Peggy Chandler to place the single red princess's rose in her hand. Rosemary and Susan turned to each other at the same instant. Each knew not to permit any sign of relief or triumph to show on her face. Rosemary mouthed the words, "It's you," and Susan shook her head slightly, mouthing back, "No, it's you." For a moment Susan wanted Rosemary to win so that no disappointment would ever stain her. For a moment she wanted Rosemary's perfection to expand and expand until she embodied everything, every feminine virtue, and she, Susan, could become her acolyte. Her kind and deserving daughter.

"This is it," Todd said into the microphone. A silence cut through the air, marked only by the loudspeaker's soft crackle and the remote shrill of a baby crying.

"May I present princess Susan Stassos, and the queen of the 1968 homecoming, Rosemary Potter."

Rosemary and Susan fell into each other's arms. Susan felt relief and a flood of devotion. Yes, of course. Rosemary was always going to win; it was what she was born for. Susan felt the touch of Rosemary's hair, and thought, 'I'm the first to hold the queen.' The crowd cheered. When Rosemary and Susan drew back, Rosemary was weeping and Susan realized that she herself was not. "Congratulations," she said. She had not expected the tone of formality she heard in her own voice. Rosemary nodded, helpless with tears, and Susan saw, with a shock, how much she, too, had wanted to win. How much she had wanted to finish school in complete, untarnished victory. Susan felt herself stiffen inside Rosemary's embrace. Rosemary had said, 'It's you,' knowing—she'd surely known—that Susan could not win. Susan had a Greek name. She wasn't blond.

They parted. They smiled out into the cheering crowd. Peggy Chandler hugged Rosemary, and carefully placed the rhinestone circlet on her head. She gave Susan her single rose, put a dry kiss on her cheek, and then placed a dozen roses, wrapped in tissue, in Rosemary's arms. Susan glanced at Todd. He was looking straight at her, smiling, and she smiled back, thinking, 'I can survive this, I'm being changed by it but I'll survive.'

The band played "Stardust," and all three girls took their places in the back seat of the convertible. Rosemary held Susan's hand. They didn't speak. They waved to the crowd. As the car was driven slowly around the track, before the noise and waves of the spectators, Susan fingered the stem of her single rose and wondered what she had expected. Maybe she was surprised because her expectations had been so entirely met. Maybe she'd believed that Rosemary's obvious destiny, the ease with which she'd always won, somehow disqualified her. As the car rounded the far end of the track Susan saw that the world's capacity for surprise was limited. Facts prevailed over romantic unlikelihoods. A poor girl—a dark, foreign girl—could be a princess. The horizon extended no farther than that.

When the car finished its circuit, the girls were told to remain in the back seat, still waving up into the bleachers, while the band finished its number. Then Todd opened the rear door. Marcia got out first, followed by Rosemary, whose emergence inspired scattered applause. Susan got out and Todd took her in his arms with such force she gasped. "I'm so proud of you," he whispered. When he released her she scanned his face for signs of sympathy or disappointment. She saw none, but he was impossible to trust. He claimed he'd never met a man he didn't like.

Several girls, those who'd expected to be nominated but had been passed over, congratulated Susan and she began to know, for the first time, the particular kindness the world extends to those who do not win. Rosemary stood several feet away, beside her boyfriend, Randy, her face still shining with tears. Tonight it was safely behind her—a girlhood of unqualified success. Flashbulbs snapped, igniting Rosemary's crown, and when Susan blinked she saw the crown's phosphorescent red image.

"The yearbook people told me I've got to keep you three together for pictures," Todd said softly. It was uncharacteristic phrasing. Ordinarily Todd would have said, 'You have to stay together for your pictures.' Ordinarily he acknowledged no gap between what was expected and what was necessary. He squeezed the back of Susan's neck, and she grazed his cuff with her fingernails.

Two more girls offered congratulations, and then Susan's family emerged from the crowd. Her mother reached her first, clasped her quickly to her breasts, and said, "You looked so beautiful out there." Her father chucked her under the chin with his thumb, laughed, and said, "Robbery. There should be a recount. Don't you think so, Todd?"

Todd said, "Sir, there's no doubt in my mind who the winner is."

Her father nodded, and shrugged. "Blondes," he said. "The whole world goes crazy over blond hair. I've never understood it, myself."

Susan shifted her weight toward Todd. Her father blamed her, though he wouldn't admit it. She'd never missed the honor roll, never lost a club election. She'd danced the lead in her ballet recital. Now she stood uncrowned, with one rose, while cameras clicked and flashed around a girl who had somehow worked harder, exerted subtler charms, been more. Susan Stassos was a handmaiden. Of three sisters, she was one of the two the prince disdained to marry.

Now she belonged to her father.

Zoe hung back, embarrassed, but Billy punched Susan's arm and said, "You should get the goddamn purple heart for this. I mean, the whole rest of your life is going to seem safe and tame compared to this."

She didn't want to be this rancorous girl, standing with a single rose under crepe-paper bunting in the cafeteria as the band played "Cherish." If she couldn't win she wanted at least to be blasé like Marcia, who stood at the edge of the dance floor proud as a captive Amazon, surrounded by her friends—tough girls in makeup and short skirts—and by Eddie Gagliostra, an ill-tempered, handsome boy who was, in Marcia's own words, only good for one thing. One of her girlfriends said loudly, "Let's duck into the ladies' for a smoke, *Princess,*" and Marcia laughed. Maybe she'd prove mean enough to escape her fate, the two-story brick apartment building, the wild husband who couldn't keep a job. Before she left for her cigarette Eddie whispered something to her and she smiled knowingly. Eddie had thick lips and a broken nose, a curl of oily hair that trembled on his forehead. Susan pretended to be listening to Dottie Wiggins but in fact she imagined what it would be like to be Marcia, later that evening, drunk and naked in a car or a borrowed bedroom. She imagined Eddie—those fat, obscene lips. Dottie Wiggins was saying something about college and Susan thought of Eddie, of the sneering self-satisfied pleasure he would take in making a girl lose control. He broke into houses, bullied the younger boys. He had twice menaced Billy in the locker room. Susan imagined the sinews of his arms and thighs, his insolent tongue, the spare hard muscles of his chest and stomach. She returned, flushed, to Dottie Wiggins, who was saying, "—Tufts is a better school but the University of Colorado would be a lot more fun and I think there's a lot to be said for having fun, don't you?"

"I don't think anybody around here has any fun, really," Susan said. "I think we've all just learned to make a lot of noise together and call it fun."

Dottie looked at her suspiciously. "Well," she said, "if you want to get all *tragic* and everything."

Susan twirled the rose in her hands. "No, honey," she said. She had never called another girl 'honey' before. 'Honey' was what Marcia called people she considered drips. "No, I don't want to get tragic. I want to have fun, real fun. I honestly do."

She knew what she was doing. She was starting the story: Susan Stassos got nasty about failing to win. Dottie would tell everyone. She was a good mimic and she would do Susan, standing tense at the edge of the dance floor, twirling her rose and saying, in a voice Dottie would borrow from Marlene Dietrich, 'Honey, no vun hass any fon, not reeely.'

"Well," Dottie said. "There's no real trick to it. Fun's the easiest thing in the world, especially for someone like you."

"Someone like me," she said.

She thought about going home that night. Would her father be awake? Would he have been drinking? Now that she was less than she'd been, how could she ever say no? How could she ever say yes?

Todd returned from whatever duty he'd been attending to. "Hey, Sooz," he said. "Hi, Dottie."

"Hi, Todd," Dottie said brightly, mockingly. She was racked by envy, electrified by it, and her efforts to be brisk and fun and carefree had eaten her flesh nearly to the bone.

"Sooz, you want to go outside for a minute?" Todd asked. "It's a nice night, I wouldn't mind a little breath of air."

"All right," Susan said. "See you later, Dottie."

"See you," Dottie said, and as Susan left with Todd she knew Dottie was already looking for someone to tell the story to. *No vun hass any fon, not reeely.*

Susan went with Todd to the asphalt square immediately outside the cafeteria, where students were officially permitted to go if they left the dance. Beyond the square, which was mercilessly lit, stood the mullioned bulk of the gym and, beyond that, the empty football field. Several other couples whispered in the blaring circle of light. They registered Todd's and Susan's presence, shifted slightly. One, an ambitious boy from the junior class, abandoned his date to shake Todd's hand and discuss his own upcoming campaign for next year's presidency. "Congratulations, Susan," the boy added. Susan thanked him. Rays of deep red from her cheerleading sweater skimmed through the blinding air as Todd disengaged himself from the boy and led her to the far edge of the light. Out in the soft black, cigarettes flared. Scraps of cloud sped past the moon.

"What a night," Todd said.

"Mm-hm. To tell you the truth, I'm glad it's almost over."

He paused. He had something to say. Susan thought, 'If he's been practicing a consolation speech for me, I'll break up with him.' She hoped he would. She was ready to scream.

"Sooz?" he said. "Susan?"

"Yes?"

She twirled the rose, insolently. He was going to advise her to think of this as a learning experience, to thank God for giving her a chance to strengthen her character. She thought of Marcia, called 'princess' as a joke. Marcia moving out into the world, powerful and free.

"Well, you see," Todd said, "I've been thinking."

"Mm."

"About next year. You know. We didn't apply to any of the same schools. And now it's too late."

"I know."

"And we haven't really talked about that."

"That's right. We haven't."

"So I've been thinking. Suzy. Wherever I go, I want you to come with me. If it's Yale, you know. Or Princeton."

His face reddened, and his eyes took on a rheumy, unhealthy cast. She had never seen him flustered like this, except when they had sex. Suddenly she wanted to help him reestablish himself, to find his way back.

"What are you saying?" she asked softly.

"I guess. It seems like I'm saying I want us to get married. You and me. I want to marry you."

The blood rushed to her head. All she could think of was, 'This is happening now, right now.' Someone wanted to marry her. He was asking her now, outside the cafeteria, on the night of her defeat. She thought, 'I'm not ready for this. This shouldn't be happening here.'

"Oh, Todd," she said. "I don't know."

"You don't know if you want to get married? Or you don't know if you want to marry me?"

"Well, both. No, forget I said that. This is just—well, *could* we?"

She didn't know what she meant by that. She wanted to be told whether getting married was something a person like her could do. She wanted to know if Todd was the kind of boy you married.

"Well, yeah," he said, and he managed a smile. "We could, if you wanted to."

"My father," she said.

"I know he's old-fashioned," Todd said. "I'd talk to him. I'd be very—"

Then Susan knew the answer. She knew what to do.

She was going somewhere. If she and Todd went home that night and announced their engagement, she'd have a new language to say no in. She'd be protected.

"We could," she said. "Yes. This is really something we could do, isn't it?"

"Sure," Todd said, and laughed affectionately. "We can absolutely, positively do it."

His poise was back. His forthright, practiced Toddness.

"We could do it," Susan said. "Oh, sure. Let's get married."

"Really? You really want to?"

"Yes. Oh, yes. Right away."

"Right away?"

"Well, as soon as we graduate. I can wear the veil under my mortarboard, we can go straight to the church after we get our diplomas."

"You're funny," he said. "You know that? You're a funny girl."

1 9 6 9 / Mary wrote on the envelope the phone bill came in: I will not steal. She put the pledge in writing. But she went on stealing. She didn't know why she did it. She remembered the first day, in Englehart's. She'd gone to look at stationery for Susan's wedding invitations, just to see if Englehart's stocked anything decent or if she and Susan would have to drive to New York. The salesgirl, young, tentatively pretty under too much base, had shown her the samples. Ordinary cream, a yellowish ivory, a blue milky and shallow as a bus ticket. Borders trimmed with lilies, with doves and spectral white bells. Englehart's wouldn't do. She'd have to take Susan to the city after all. Mary thanked the salesgirl, told her she'd think about it. As she rose from her seat at the counter she knew herself to be an attractive woman in her late thirties, carrying a good navy clutch and graciously rejecting the wares of a store that hired salesgirls like this one, a girl whose common prettiness was wearing away with her youth. In her own youth Mary had seen women like herself, prosperous wives who kindly and firmly rejected the merchandise in neighborhood stores. As she stood, as the sheer satin of her slip fell with liquid ease over her nylons, she saw herself with such clarity she might have been standing outside her own body. She might have been the salesgirl, watching as a woman of stature and property, a woman who wrapped all her gifts perfectly, withdrew from the local stationery store, where the quality was not of the best. Mary's heart rose and she knew a calm, shimmering satisfaction that hovered inside her and then turned to uncertainty, quick as a shattered plate. Her older daughter, an acknowledged beauty, was about to marry a handsome boy on his way to Yale. It was a triumph to have a daughter like that and yet, even as it delighted Mary, Susan's good fortune seemed also to diminish her in some way. She worried that when they appeared in public together she looked fraudulent beside her daughter. She suspected Susan found her sad and slightly humorous. She reminded herself, with a pang of guilt and pleasure, that Susan had not been elected queen. As Mary walked toward the door she heard the salesgirl close the sample book; she heard the heavy muffled thump of the cover. On her way out she stopped to look at address books, because it had occurred to her that Billy was getting to an age when he might need one. The address books Englehart's stocked were second-rate. Their covers were simulated leather, their bindings indifferently glued. Mary stood frowning over one of the books, bound in oxblood plastic, emblazoned with the golden word *Addresses*, the final *s* of which had already begun to chip. It was such a flimsy thing, so beneath her, that she felt foolish even looking at it. She glanced around, saw that no one was watching, and almost before she knew she would do it she slipped the address book into her bag. Her forehead burned. Calmly, walking as herself, in heels and pearl earrings, she left the store with the tacky little address book hidden in her bag, its price tag still attached. The tag, when she looked at it, said that the book had cost ninety-nine cents.

She didn't know why she'd done it. She didn't want the awful address book. It had not been covetousness she'd felt; the impulse had had more to do with cleaning up. Afterward she'd felt a nervous sensation of relief, as if some promise of bad luck—some debt— had been forestalled but not fully answered. Now she had the ad- dress book, this insubstantial thing, and she wasn't sure what to do with it. She couldn't give it to Billy, but she found that she couldn't quite bring herself to throw it away, either. She'd risked so much for it. She removed the price tag and tucked the little book into her top drawer, thinking maybe she'd give it to someone some- day. Eventually, she'd be able to put it to some kind of use.

Since then, she'd stolen any number of little things, and always felt the same queasy satisfaction, as if she'd risked herself to create a little more cleanliness and order. The stealing was a minor aspect of her life. It occupied roughly the same interior space a dull hobby would, or the occasional perusal of *National Geographic*, with its simultaneous suggestions that the regions of the earth were un- utterably strange and yet, in the final analysis, all more or less alike. Mary lost herself in the plans for Susan's wedding, which demanded endless decisions right down to the rosebuds on the cake. The wedding was so much, it weighed so heavily on her lungs, that she finally asked her doctor if something might be wrong with her and was given a prescription for pale yellow pills. She took a pill on the day of the wedding itself, and was surprised that for an instant, as Susan stood at the altar with Todd, she felt a stab of anger sharp enough to penetrate the pill's sweet flotation. The anger was sourceless—just nerves, she'd tell herself later—and seemed to have to do with Susan's white dress, with the placid handsomeness of Todd's square face as he bent to kiss her. Nerves, Mary thought, and the inevitable fears on a mother's part about her daughter's happiness, given all she herself had learned about what can go wrong.

The wedding was flawless, except for the guests. It had of course been necessary to invite the people who worked for Constantine, and they were for the most part boisterous men in cheap, outdated suits, escorting wives who were variously cowed or shrill but were, in every instance, badly dressed. With the help of Todd's father, Mary had rented the ballroom at the country club, and had had it impeccably decorated with urns of white lilacs and center-pieces of cream-colored roses. She'd enlisted a caterer to provide Rock Cornish game hens, wild rice, and French-cut string beans with slivered almonds for over two hundred. She had made no mistakes, and now into her white-and-cream reception marched a brigade of foremen who'd been hired specifically because they could bully other men into building houses as quickly and cheaply as possible. They were married to just the kind of women you'd expect: brassy, in loud dresses and too much jewelry, their hair teased and tortured into great stiff piles on top of their heads. Todd's mother and his two aunts wore simple page boys and dressed in pure colors, and Mary suffered over her own French twist. Her dress was frosted pink—she silently thanked God she had decided against a ruffle at the bodice. As she danced with Billy, who was straight-backed and self-conscious in his blue gabardine suit, she watched Susan laughing with two of her bridesmaids, and it seemed that Susan had gone to another country, where all the girls were effortlessly thin and beautiful and all the boys had futures sturdy as suspension bridges. Even through the graceful hush of the pill she felt, again, a little storm of emotion that might have been anger and might have been fear. She didn't want either feeling, not on a day like this. She concentrated on her daughter's beauty, her remarkable ease and charm. This one, at least, was safe. Mary hummed along with the band, a few bars of "Begin the Beguine." She said to Billy, "Seems like the wedding's a success."

He said, "I guess any wedding's a success, huh? I mean, as long as they really get married, it's worked."

"If that was all that mattered, they could've gone to a justice of the peace and saved your father about five thousand dollars."

"C'mon. Did this shindig really cost five grand?"

"You'd be surprised how things add up. You kids have no idea."
He whistled. "Five grand," he said. "For one party."

"When you get married," she said, "your father'll be off the
hook. Your wife's family will have to pay."

"When I get married," he said, "we'll go to a justice of the
peace. If somebody wants to fork over five thousand bucks, we'll
take the cash and spend, like, a year in Europe."

"The girl you marry may feel differently."

"I wouldn't marry somebody who felt that differently."

The number ended, and Billy walked Mary back to her table.
As she walked with her hand on her son's elbow, Mary's pink shoes
shed their cool minty light against the indigo carpet of the country-
club ballroom. This was her son, on his way to Harvard. She was
conscious of his new height, the size of his hands. She loved him
so. He was still hers, the most intelligent of her children, full of
promise and afflicted with a ravaged complexion that only increased
the terrible weight of her love. He was at once ethereal and painfully
human. He, alone among her children, suffered hurts and prides
she could read.

That night she lay in bed in her nightgown, watching Constantine undress. His body, gone slack and hairy, now inspired in
her a tenderness that had almost as much to do with motherhood
as it did with passion. Her husband might have been her oldest
child, a difficult and obstreperous boy who lived outside the realm
of her control. She could love him, more or less, when she thought
of him as a wayward boy, one who occasionally did harm to others,
who was subject to violent fits of temper, but whose decent heart
would outlive his youthful fury. In his middle age Constantine had
turned boyish, and she lived with him that way, as a boy with a
pudgy body and a petulant streak. Wearing only his Jockey shorts,
he sat on the edge of the bed and said, "Well, there she goes. She's
married."

"Mm-hm." Mary still inhabited the outer edge of the yellow

pill, its soft declining side. The world retained its feathery aspect.

"Married," Constantine said.

"I think the wedding went fine, don't you?" Mary said. "I had a few doubts about the band, but really, on the whole I think it was a real success."

Constantine rose without speaking, put his pajamas on over his shorts. He had had a few during the reception, he was moving with elaborate caution, but Mary didn't think about that. She thought about the wedding she'd produced, a sit-down dinner for over two hundred. She tried not to worry about its coarse aspects: the off-color toast made by Constantine's partner, the foreman who'd argued with a wife in a dress crawling with fuchsia flowers. She tried not to imagine the future weddings of Susan's bridesmaids, girls whose families Mary scarcely knew because she was an Italian woman married to a Greek construction man. None of Todd's people had gotten drunk.

"I could have done without Nick Kazanzakis's toast," she said. The hard edges were returning. "What's the matter with him? A toast like that, at a wedding."

"Nick's all right," Constantine said. "He likes a little joke. Nobody minded."

"Betty Emory minded. I was sitting right beside her. I saw her go stiff."

"Fuck Betty Emory. She's got a stick up her ass, just look at her."

"Oh, lovely. That's a very nice thing to say about a lady. I'll tell you one thing, she *is* a lady. Which was not true of about half the women there today."

Constantine got into bed. The smell of liquor was mixed with his old personal smells.

"Let's not fight," he said. "Not tonight."

"Fine. I'd be delighted to not fight."

He pulled the covers up to his chest. She saw how haggard his face looked, how worn. He was getting older.

"This was our daughter's wedding day," he said.

"Yes."

"Now her name is Mrs. Emory. Susan Emory."

"I know."

She turned off the light. The room went black, and pieces of objects slowly materialized: half of Mary's vanity with its oval mirror, the nearer legs of the chaise on which no one ever sat. Mary lay looking at the room, her mind so tangled with thoughts that she might have been thinking of nothing at all. The bedside clock put out its buzz. There was something else, a strange sound she thought at first was coming from outside but which she realized was the sound of Constantine weeping beside her. He was turned away, and she laid her hand on his back, which was covered with the broad stripes of his pajamas.

"Con?" she said. He didn't answer.

"Con? Are you all right?"

"I'm okay," he said thickly.

"Con, what is it?"

"Nothing."

"It can't be nothing."

A minute passed, filled only with the sound of his weeping. She thought, My life is going on outside me. I don't know anything about it.

He said, "I can't believe she's really gone."

His own words seemed to inspire in him a fresh wave of sobs, and his crying had a tone that was not quite fleshly, a sound like wet paper tearing. She hadn't heard him cry in years. Mary was sympathetic and irritated, to almost equal degrees.

"She isn't gone," she said. "She just has a life of her own now. New Haven isn't so very far away."

"She's gone," Constantine said. "She isn't ours anymore."

"Well, she hasn't really been ours for a long time, has she?"

"She's been mine," Constantine said.

Mary understood. She pushed the thought away.

"You're just tired," she said. "And you've had too much to drink. Everything will be okay in the morning."

He turned and faced her. In the dimness, distorted by weeping, his face looked haunted, ancient. Mary saw, with awful clarity, what he would look like when he was helpless, and needed her care to survive.

"Please," he said. He held out his arms and, when she did not move into his embrace, he took her and pressed his hot wet face onto her neck. "Please," he said.

"You're just tired," she said. "And drunk."

"I'm more than that," he said. "Oh, God." He kissed her neck, took her chin in his hand and put his lips on hers. They hadn't made love in—what?—six months? Longer? Tonight would not be the night, not as far as she was concerned. Long ago, she'd started winning the battle with her own feelings. For years now she'd felt desire closing down in her, the lights going out like the lights of a household preparing itself for sleep. At moments, lying right here in this bed, she'd fallen into a panic. This was her fate being made; this was the future stitching itself onto her skin. There would be no other life than this. The feelings, the fear itself, had come to seem familiar to her—they were part of what she meant when she used the words 'my life.' Now, tonight, she was in no mood to change her life. Not with Constantine maudlin and drunk, not after a day as wearing as this had been.

She disengaged her mouth and said, "Honey, go to sleep. You'll feel better in the morning."

"I can't sleep," he said.

"Yes you can." She spoke to him just the way she'd spoken to the children when they awoke from nightmares. Now, as then, she marveled at the maternal certainty she heard in her own voice. *They believe I'm their mother. They believe I know what I'm doing.*

"Just close your eyes," she said. "It'll happen before you know it."

And, to her surprise, he obeyed her. He returned quietly to his own side of the bed like a randy boy who wanted discipline even when he said he wanted every noise and thrill in the world. She lay quietly beside him, listening to his abating sobs with motherly concern. It was only after he'd fallen asleep that she was stricken with a horror so powerful and nameless she got out of bed and took three of the pills, to give herself the simple unremarkable gift of sleep.

She took a hairbrush, a cheap bracelet, a bar of amber-colored soap. She knew she had to stop. She consoled herself with a short list of virtues. Everything she stole was cheap, and she never used what she took. As long as she didn't use the objects, she did not feel indicted by them. Susan sent postcards from her honeymoon in Hawaii, short and undetailed assertions of happiness written in a hand more scrolled, more adult, than Mary remembered her handwriting to be. Mary attached the postcards to the refrigerator with fruit-shaped magnets. She kept the objects she stole in her drawer, hidden away, until her holdings began to look like the trousseau of an impoverished bride.

1 9 7 0 / He called it car ballet. It had that strength and grace, that musical stillness. Out on the back roads, trees hung blackly, fence posts were dark and important as tombstones. Behind the trees and the fence posts, farmers slept under roofs blue with moon. Billy liked to imagine the silence. When he pictured the silence he loved all the more what their headlights did to it. What their music and engines brought. Tree limbs jumped, sizzling with gold and silver light. Dust boiled up, yellow at their approach and red in their wake. Bits of his favorite songs found their way into farmers' dreams.

"Car ballet!" he'd call from the back seat. He'd put his feet, big in boots, out the window. At moments, at night, he felt a huge new world of freedom and love cracking open.

Sometimes it was Larry's father's car, sometimes it was Bix's. Sometimes, on lucky nights, they got both. Larry's father had the green Chevy Impala, Bix's had the Ford Galaxie. The Chevy was slightly racier, but the Ford had a rubberized, floating ride that gave you nervous stomach and a hard-on when things got rockety. Billy always hoped for the Ford.

"Faster," he said. "Floor it." He was the voice of speed. He was the smallest, the smartest, the one most intricately loved and hated. The radio played "Eight Miles High."

"You're crazy," Dina said. She rode in the back seat with Billy, pressing her big knee against his skinny one. She smeared sugary pink lipstick over her heavy lips, blackened her brows with a grease pencil. Her boots were higher than Billy's. She called herself a pirate queen.

"Yeah," he said. "Oh, yes. I'm crazy."

She rubbed his knee with hers. The old nervousness came to him, the breathless trapped sensation. In front, Bix and Larry passed the vodka through the blare of the music. Sometimes it was vodka, sometimes beer. Whatever they could get. Once Dina stole a bottle of crème de menthe from her father, and Billy and Larry vomited green along three miles of road.

"Hey, boys, can a lady get a drink around here?" Dina said. Larry handed her the bottle. Bix sat straight-armed at the wheel, silent and murderously blissful. He was the one with the meanness in him. Night flashed by, with its insects and its threads of deeper and lesser black.

When Dina had had her swig of vodka and passed the bottle to Billy, she left the taste of her lipstick. Billy watched the shaggy brown curve of Bix's head. He filled his mouth with vodka and felt the burn, the little explosion. He kept himself from screaming with the pure rush and happiness of it. The future kept coming and coming.

"Car ballet," he said. "Time for stunts."

"What kind of stunts?" Larry said. He had the worst skin, the least complicated sweetness. He gave you things you never asked for. His hair model was Keith Richards.

"Figure eights," Billy said. He sat up, put his head between Bix's and Larry's. He put his head deeper into the music. On the dashboard, dials and numbers made their hushed glow. Tree trunks hurdled past.

"Figure eights," Billy said again, handing the bottle to Larry.

Bix swerved to the far side of the road and back again. The tires made their protest, a clean swiping sound.

"Figure S," Bix said. "Just warming up."

Bix had a military brain. He aimed himself at the world like a torpedo.

"Don't you boys hog that bottle up there," Dina said.

"Let's go crazy," Billy said into Bix's ear. The motion had given him a hard-on. He loved Bix and feared him. A low branch brushed the car like a gigantic wing.

"Wow," Larry said.

"Girl could die of thirst," Dina said. Her perfume was everywhere.

"How crazy?" Bix asked. He gave the bottle back to Billy.

"We been on this road too long," Billy answered. "Let's fly."

"Fly? You want to fly?"

"Yeah. Oh, yes."

"Right. Here goes."

Bix hit the brakes and turned sharply. The car bottomed into a ditch, then bounced up again. Drops of vodka flew glistening into Billy's face. A stick cracked under the axle, loud as a broken bone.

"Whoa," Larry said.

The car bounced a second time, then settled itself. They were in a field. The headlights showed the field going on until it met a stand of thin, shocked-looking trees.

Billy whooped. Dina screamed, "What's happening?"

"Figure eights," Billy hollered. "Come on." He put the bottle to Bix's lips, tilted it. Vodka poured into Bix's mouth and down his shirt. Bix revved the engine and the car shot forward, headlights shining into knee-high grass.

"Whoa, far out," Larry said with an appreciative smile. Dina put her hand on Billy's shoulder. She wore six rings. Some were silver, some plastic.

"Where are we?" she said. Her voice was thick with the vodka.

"We're in space," Billy told her. "We're flying."

The DJ, sitting somewhere in music and electric light, played "Ruby Tuesday."

"This is dangerous," Dina said.

"I know."

Bix steered the Ford in a wide arc. Darkness and a rank green smell blew in through the windows. The axles bumped in the ruts so hard they couldn't get the bottle to their mouths. Grass and trees and wedges of night sky tilted in the headlights. Billy laughed, and Dina laughed, too.

"Figure eight," Bix said with the suave cruelty of a bomber pilot. Billy's heart swelled. He told himself he was in love with crazy motion.

"Yeah," he said. Because he couldn't get the bottle to Bix's lips he poured a splash of vodka over his head. Billy felt the edge of the world, the harsh blossoming happiness that moved too fast for ordinary life. Only when you raced, only when you took the risks, could you enter this other dimension that shot through time and space at triple speed.

Larry hummed the "Blue Danube Waltz." "Da da da da da, taa taa, taa taa."

"Go," Billy screamed. "Go go go go go."

The cow came from nowhere. They swerved into the final loop of their figure eight and there it was, black and white, big as an oncoming car. Billy saw its shining black eye. He saw its nicked white ear. He screamed. Larry screamed. Bix cranked the wheel and the car jackknifed with a shrill mechanical screech. Dirt sprayed up through the windows. Billy's eyes and mouth were filled with dirt. The car skidded, lurched, and stopped so suddenly Billy was thrown into the front seat. He couldn't see. He felt his forehead crack against something that wasn't hard and wasn't soft. A splinter of a dream flashed inside his head: a desert sandstorm with a dark, cloaked figure running through it. Mick Jagger sang, "Who could hang a name on you?"

A silence came up under the music, a steaming windy silence.

Billy blinked, rubbed the dirt from his eyes, blinked again. He saw that he was lying on his stomach, looking down at a boot. A brown work boot. Bix's. He turned around and looked up at Bix.

Bix still sat behind the wheel, smiling and bleeding.

"Shit." Bix grinned. "Sweet shitting mother of Christ."

Billy saw that he was lying on the front seat with his head under the dashboard. Bix and Larry were still in their seats. Dina sat blinking in the back with a confused but polite expression, as if the conversation had turned to a topic she didn't fully understand.

"A wreck," Billy said. "We had a wreck."

"Wow."

"Shit. Sweet Jesus." Bix chuckled. Lines of blood ran freely down his forehead. A garnet-colored drop trembled on his nose.

"Bix, you got hurt," Billy said.

"I did?"

"Man, you're bleeding."

"I am?"

"The car could blow up," Billy said. "Don't crashed cars blow up?"

"I don't know."

"We better get out of here. Come on."

Everyone remained utterly still, as if they had all suddenly realized that the car was balanced on the edge of a cliff and any movement could send it toppling into the abyss. Bix remained with his hands on the wheel, smiling and bleeding majestically. Larry looked forward with his habitual expression of good-natured awe, and Dina continued to sit, polite and confused as a great-grandmother, in the back seat.

Billy said, "Move. It's going to blow up." They all scrambled out into the altered night, the settling whirlwind of dirt. Billy ran a half dozen paces, then turned. Dina was behind him. Bix and Larry had run the other way. The car stood at an angle, its nose in a ditch and its rear wheels a foot off the ground. It was, at once, both titanic and pathetic.

"God," Dina breathed. "Are you all right?"

He nodded. "I just bumped my head a little. Bix is the one who's hurt. Hey, Bix."

Billy ran to the far side of the wreck, where Bix and Larry stood in attitudes of calm appraisal, hands fisted on their hips. "Unbelievable," Larry said.

"Bix," Billy said. "Hey. Let me see your head."

Bix put his hand to his forehead with a certain reverence, as if his wound was something precious. "It's okay," he said. "I just knocked against the wheel a little." When he brought his hand down the fingers were slick with blood. He smiled.

"We flew," he said.

"Yeah," Billy said. He stood close to Bix. He could smell the blood, mixed with grass and the faintly fried odor of Bix himself. "You sure you're all right?"

"Never better. You?"

"I'm okay. A little bump."

Bix looked at his bloodied fingers. He put his hand to Billy's forehead and made a slow, deliberate circle.

"War paint," he said.

Billy's forehead tingled. He was wearing Bix's blood. Dina, the pirate queen, came up whitely from across the field.

"God," she said. "Are we all right? What was that that happened?"

"We lived," Billy said, and he felt the thrill rising in his voice. "We all lived."

"We wrecked Bix's father's car," Dina said.

"It isn't wrecked," Bix said. "I bet we can push it out of that ditch."

"Wait a second," Larry said. He ran back to the car.

"Don't," Billy called. "It's going to blow."

Bix started to laugh. Then Billy started, then Dina did. Larry went into the car and came out again with the vodka bottle. "There's still some in here," he called.

"It's a miracle." Billy laughed.

"Look." Dina pointed. Her rings put out a dull flash. Fifty yards away the cow stood placidly, staring at them. Billy yelped with laughter. Bix pounded his back. Billy fell in the grass and Bix tumbled onto him. Billy smelled the blood and the crisp personal essence of Bix. Billy was laughing so hard he could barely breathe. He had a hard-on. Larry took a sip of the vodka, passed the bottle around. When it was empty Bix stood up and threw it at the cow. The bottle fell thirty yards short, and broke against a stone. The cow didn't move.

"Argh," Bix hollered. He smeared both his hands with blood from his forehead and went running at the cow, screaming and waving his hands. As he watched Bix run toward the cow Billy was overcome with a feeling of recognition. There was the car at its crazy angle, still playing music, its headlights illuminating the ground. There was the spotted cow and there was Bix, running bloody and ecstatic in his army jacket. It was not déjà vu. Billy didn't feel as if he'd seen all this before. He felt instead that it had been waiting for him, this strange perfection, and now that he was seeing it he was becoming someone new, someone particular, after the long confusion of his childhood. A surge rose in him and, with a whoop, he jumped up and ran after Bix. The earth was soft and uneven under his boots and he felt himself entering a moment so real he could only run toward it, shouting. He caught up with Bix just as the cow turned, with a disgruntled moan, and trotted away. He and Bix chased it until it broke into an ungainly swaying lope that had no true element of haste. The cow was just placid appetite moving, temporarily, at a faster rate. Billy and Bix kept chasing it, screaming, until at the same instant, with a singular accord, they stopped and stood screaming at one another. Bix's face was wild and shining, streaked with blood. They screamed, and something invisible happened. An enormous love arced and crackled between them. Billy stopped screaming. He stood, mute and suddenly frightened. Bix looked at him with no expression, with a face gone blank and stupid as a statue's. Then he turned and ran back to the car. Billy stood alone in the grass, with passion and fear turning hugely inside him. Bix took the moment away and Billy ran after him, greedy for more of whatever could happen. When he and Bix reached the others they all fell briefly into a spasmodic, gleeful dance. The radio played "Light My Fire." The moment filled everything. It seemed, somehow, that they'd won some kind of victory.

When the song ended they all sat down in the grass. Crickets buzzed, and the DJ played "Incense and Peppermints." Billy touched the place on his forehead where Bix's blood had dried.

"We got to push the car out," Bix said.

"Think we can?" Billy asked.

"Yeah."

No one spoke for a while. Dina sat close to Billy, pulling up handfuls of grass, and he watched Bix. Bix was silent and fierce. He had a soldierly self-containment. Billy's heart swelled. He'd do anything, suffer any loss.

"We flew," he said. His voice sounded smaller than he'd expected it to. He was aware of the sky—pale stars and the flashing red lights of a plane. The now started to shrink. A whistling, windy nowhere wanted to return.

"We fucking flew," he said.

Bix stood up. He had square shoulders and a graceful, weighted way of standing. He stood as if his pockets were full of stones.

"Come on," he said. "We got to get that goddamn car out."

By pushing on the front fenders, they were able to inch the car out of the ditch, as Bix had predicted. He slid into the driver's seat and, after several tries, got the engine to turn over. There was no damage. A quiet caught and held. Something had ended, at least for the night. There was no damage. Larry got into the front seat, Billy and Dina into the back. Bix steered the Ford back onto the road.

"Some night," Billy said.

"Far out," Larry said. Bix and Dina didn't speak. Billy wasn't ready for the nowhere yet.

"I think I need a little more war paint," he said. He reached over and touched the blood on Bix's cheek. Bix cuffed him with the back of his hand. He caught Billy on the chin, snapped his head back. The car veered to the far side of the road

"Bix," Dina said. "What's the matter with you?"

"Don't touch me," Bix said. "I don't want you touching me."

"You all right, Billy?" she asked. Her knee pressed against his. He shoved her knee away.

"I'm fine," he said. "Leave me alone."

The quiet sealed itself, but as long as the pain throbbed in him he was somewhere. The radio played on. Billy held his jaw in his hand and put his boots out the window. His heart was pounding with a love so awful it made him giddy and a little faint. The car sped along and Billy watched the tree limbs flash by. He felt Dina's perfume working itself into his skin. Bix drove in silence and Billy ran his fingertips tenderly along his jawbone, fondling the injury as if it belonged to someone else, someone he adored. The car hurled itself into the growing somewhere. He believed he could drive all night.

When he got home a pale, tentative light was seeping down the stairwell. He walked as lightly as he could in his boots but they were made for noise. That was the point of them.

"Billy?" His mother's voice drifted down with the light. He paused on the landing, sucking air between his teeth.

"Yeah, Ma." *Let me get to my room. All I want, all I need, is quiet and darkness.* He got to the top of the stairs and halfway down the hall but his mother came out of her room and caught him with her anxious smile. She was puffy and radiant in a rose-colored bathrobe.

"It's late," she said.

"I know. I know it's late."

He stood in his boots and his leather jacket, not looking at her. He knew he smelled of vodka and cow manure. He knew he had blood on his face.

"Look at you," she said. "What have you been doing?"

"Nothing," he said. He wanted a mother like Bix's, who carried a cocktail from room to room. Who didn't need anything but Kents and Scotch and her own bitter, wised-up personality.

"What happened to your forehead?" she asked. "Did you hurt yourself?"

"No. I'm totally fine. I'm going to bed."

She tried to touch his forehead but he took a heavy-heeled step away from her. She managed to catch his sleeve. His lungs tightened and he pulled in air through his clenched teeth, striving for a full breath. Lately he'd been suffering these attacks of breathlessness, though he hadn't told anyone about them. He suspected he had lung cancer.

"This is no way for a Harvard man to act," his mother said with whispered cheerfulness.

"I'm not a Harvard man, Ma."

"You will be in September, Billy. Do you know how special you are? Do you know how much is going to happen to you?"

"Maybe I don't want to go to Harvard after all," he said.

"Don't be ridiculous. After all that work."

"I haven't even told anybody about it. I mean, Bix and Larry and everybody. They don't even know."

She put her face closer to his. She smelled of powder and sleep and something else, a vague but insinuating sweetness that frightened him. "Bix and Larry," she said. "I want you to watch yourself with them. Do you hear me? Bix and Larry are basically nothing but juvenile delinquents."

"Yeah. Well, that's what I like about 'em."

"Honey," his mother said, and her voice took on deeper, more harshly whispered urgency. "What's wrong with you? What's going on?"

"Nothing's wrong," he said evenly. "I'm tired. I need to go to sleep."

"You're not the same," she said. "You're not the same boy. I don't know who you are these days."

He wanted to put his hands in her hair, to grab hold and tell her—what? A new world was coming, and she would have to stay home. He stood briefly in a transport of love and fury, surrounded by dim unbreathable air, wanting to touch her for what felt like the last time.

"Right," he said. "I'm somebody else. I'm already gone."

1 9 7 0 / Constantine had been specific—no interruptions, not for any reason. Not when he was with Bob Nupp. Nupp, obese in a red-striped shirt, was the trickiest of the county inspectors. You had to tickle Nupp; you had to make talk. You had to woo him like a girl, flatter him, and then slip him the money the way a schoolboy might drop his hand onto a girl's breast, with suave and showy indifference. It was a performance, and if you lost momentum at a crucial point you could lose Nupp completely. Constantine had seen it happen. Nupp lived in a sluggish agony of mixed feelings, and if the meeting got interrupted he was capable of heaving his burdened frame up out of his chair, going off empty-handed, and showing up the next morning, sharp-eyed and wheezing, to look over the work and start issuing citations.

So when Sandy opened the office door and put her nervous head into the room Constantine thought to himself, That's it, she's finished. He couldn't fire her now, not in front of Nupp. For now he frowned and said sharply, "Sandy, I told you. No interruptions. Did I tell you that?"

"Mr. Stassos, I'm sorry. I know. I just, well. It's the police. They said it was important."

Constantine sucked in a breath that tasted of pine-scented air freshener and Nupp's sweat. The police. Was it Susan, who now lived outside the sphere of his protection? Was it Billy, racing with those friends of his? The world was all danger. Having children gave you a lifelong acquaintance with fear.

"Thanks, Sandy," he said. He hesitated over the phone on his desk, glancing at Nupp. If it was bad news, he didn't want to hear it in front of this fat imbecile. Nupp had lips thick and mottled as sausages. He wore his big-collared shirts with the top three buttons open, showing the hirsute sag of his breasts as if they were rare and beautiful.

"I've got to be going, anyway," he said. "I'll show myself out."

Constantine nodded. "See you tomorrow morning, Bob," he said, and with a clarity for which he would later despise himself he regretted the fact that this telephone call was going to cost him a fortune in cited violations. He would definitely fire Sandy.

He waited until Nupp had negotiated his way out of the chair and through the door. He punched the button on his phone.

"Constantine Stassos," he said. "What can I do for you?"

"Mr. Stassos?" The voice, male, was flat and measured. It might have been the voice of the telephone itself.

"Yeah. Stassos. What's up?"

"Mr. Stassos, this is officer Dan Fitzgerald. We need you to come to the Nassau County sheriff's office. As soon as possible. It's located on Old Country Road in Mineola, are you familiar with that location?"

"What is it, officer? Is one of my kids—?" He stopped. He couldn't bear to give this voice so much power over his future. Before the voice had a chance to speak again he added, "I want to talk to the man in charge there. Get me the sergeant."

"Mr. Stassos, if you'll come down to the sheriff's office—"

"Just tell me, you son of a bitch. Tell me. Is my daughter all right?"

There was a pause, filled with the soft crackle of the phone lines. Constantine could hear the ghost of another conversation. He heard the words "whole days," faintly, in a woman's voice.

"I don't believe she's your daughter, sir," the voice said hesitantly. Constantine thought that for some reason they were calling him about another man's daughter, an unknown girl. Susan, he thought, in a silent prayer.

"Sir," the voice continued, "the woman we're holding is your wife."

He and Mary drove back from the sheriff's office in a silence that would not break. Constantine took her to the downtown street where her car was parked, and she got out of his car and into her own without a word, without a gesture of recognition. She was blank, uninhabited. Her makeup had blurred, giving her a slightly melted aspect, baleful and furious.

Constantine followed her home, keeping close behind the sloped rear end of her Dodge Dart. Not the first time, the police had said. They wouldn't arrest a respectable woman, a member of the community, if she'd just once slipped a few inexpensive items into her purse. No, Mary had been watched over a period of months. Security didn't like to make trouble. They let the first two go, then they gave her a warning. *Ma'am, I think you've made a mistake here. I'm sure you didn't mean to put that hairbrush in your bag.* When she did it again, they had her arrested.

The cops were polite, even embarrassed. This was America. If you were accomplished, if you'd made money, even the police wanted to believe in your innocence. Their embarrassment was more dreadful to Constantine than their hatred would have been. They suggested that Mary see a psychologist. He'd nodded, signed the papers, shaken the hand of the man who brought his wife to jail. What else could he have done?

Mary pulled into the driveway and he followed her. Inside the house, she stood in the kitchen holding her pocketbook in two hands and looked around with a dazzled expression, as if this familiar room had been suddenly rearranged.

"Mary," Constantine said, behind her. She was nicely dressed, in a short dark skirt and green jacket. Constantine was surprised to find himself noticing her shape, the swell of her hips and the strong symmetry of her stockinged legs.

"Don't," Mary said.

"Don't what?"

"I don't know. I don't want to talk. I don't have any right to ask that, do I?"

He heard the ragged intake of her breath. He came and stood in front of her. She was crying, though she stood straight and held her pocketbook in both hands. He could hear the effort of her breathing.

He knew he should be angry. He knew in fact that he was angry, but his anger burned somewhere outside of him. It dipped and glistened, just out of reach. All he could seem to feel was confusion and shame, as if he himself had committed a crime.

"Mary," he said again.

"Oh, please, Constantine," she said, and her voice was strong through her tears. "There's no conversation for us to have."

"Cologne," he said. "A key ring. A bar of soap."

She nodded. "They were for Billy," she said.

"Huh?"

"I was thinking about him when I took them. Oh, Con, I'm going to bed. I think I just need to go to bed for a while."

"Why?" he said. "We have enough money. We could have bought that stuff. What did it cost? Ten, fifteen dollars?"

"About that, I suppose."

"Then why?"

"I don't know."

Constantine looked at her, and saw the girl she had been. He saw her breezy self-assurance, her hard shining indignation and the heartbreaking ease with which she had danced, conversed, sipped from a glass. He saw that now, in this kitchen, she was and was not that girl. Something had wilted and dampened, touched the hard underlayer of bone. Something erect and determined remained.

"I don't understand," he said.

"That makes two of us," she said. "Maybe you should scream at me and break the dishes. Maybe you should knock me down. I wonder if that might make us both feel better."

"Mary, I—I'm sorry."

She laughed, a sudden breathy little sound, as if she was blowing out a candle. "All these years," she said. "And you finally feel regret—"

She stopped, and stared at him with a black emptiness he had never seen on her face before.

"I'm going to bed," she said. "I'll talk about this in the morning, I'll do whatever I have to do, but right now all I can think about is going to bed."

She left the room without touching him. He heard her footsteps, soft and unwavering, as she ascended the stairs.

Constantine poured himself a drink and stood in the kitchen sipping it. The ice cracked; the new teapot-shaped clock swept its face with the thin red line of its second hand. He watched the house go through its own silent life until Billy came in through the front door. Constantine heard his footsteps in the hall, the particular clatter those boots of his made on the tiles, a reckless sound, like a pony.

Billy came into the kitchen, expecting Mary. When he saw Constantine his face changed.

"Hey, Dad," he said.

He wore a flowered shirt, purple and orange, with sleeves so full and fluttering Constantine wondered if the shirt had been made for a woman. His hair tumbled wispily down over his eyebrows, shrinking his face, and that along with his erupted skin gave him a dim-witted, oafish look.

He's a scholar, Constantine reminded himself. He's got a scholarship to Harvard.

"How ya doin', Bill?" he asked.

"Groovy." He opened the refrigerator, peered inside, closed it again. He took an Oreo from the cookie jar, nibbled delicately along its outer edge.

"You're home early," Billy said.

"Yeah," Constantine answered. "I am."

"Where's Mom? Out?"

"She went to bed. She's not feeling so good."

"Oh."

Constantine could not imagine what a father would say next to his son. He sipped his drink. Almost before he'd decided to, he heard himself saying, "If that damn hair gets any longer you won't be able to see."

"I can see," Billy told him. "I've got eyes all over my head."

Constantine nodded. Every answer had to be smart, every movement had to mock and defy him. He knew that he loved his son—what sort of man doesn't?—but he wanted him to be different. He wanted, right now, to stand in this kitchen with his boy and talk to him about the world's elusive glory and its baffling, persistent disappointments. He wanted to wrestle with his son, to throw a football at him with all his strength.

"You borrow that shirt from your sister?" he said.

"I have to go, Dad."

"We're talking. Are we talking here?"

"I have to go over to Dina's. Tell Mom I'm having dinner there, okay?"

"I asked you a question."

"I know you did. It's my shirt, Dad. It's my hair and my shirt and my life."

"Nobody said it wasn't your life. But I'm the one the principal's gonna call about the hair. And I paid for the fag shirt."

Billy stood in the middle of the room. He stood, it seemed, in exactly the same place Mary had stood, weeping and holding her purse with both hands.

"As a matter of fact, you didn't pay for it," he said. "I bought it with my own money. That's why I work at Kroeger's, so I don't need to accept any more from you than I absolutely have to."

"Calm down," Constantine said. "No need to get all hot and bothered here."

"You didn't pay for this shirt," Billy said, "but listen. I'm going to give it to you anyway. This'll cancel out one shirt you bought for me when I was still too young to make my own money. How's that sound to you?"

He began unbuttoning the shirt, revealing with each button a wider V of skinny, blue-white flesh.

"Bill. For Christ's sake."

He stripped off the shirt and held it out to Constantine. His bare chest was skeletal, luminous, dotted here and there with livid red pustules. How could a young boy, on the verge of manhood, look so sick and elderly?

"Take it," he said.

"Stop," Constantine told him. "Stop this."

Billy dropped the shirt to the floor. "How about the boots?" he said. "These were expensive. These ought to cancel out two or three pairs you bought me in the fifth grade."

He raised one thin leg and struggled out of an ankle-high brown boot. As he was pulling it off he nearly lost his balance, and Constantine couldn't help laughing. For the first time in memory he pitied and admired his son. His son had rage and a shrill potency.

"Bill," he said affectionately. "Billy." As his son worked the boot free Constantine reached out to tousle his overgrown hair. Maybe they'd have a drink together. Billy was seventeen, old enough for a little bourbon at home.

At the touch of Constantine's hand, Billy jumped back as if he'd been stung with an electric wire. "Don't," he said, flinching.

Constantine realized Billy had thought he was about to be hit. "Bill," he smiled. "C'mon, calm down." He held out his hand, palm up—a gesture of penury, of harmless intentions.

But Billy, ashamed of having flinched, took another two steps back. He still wore one boot, which clopped loudly on the floor.

"I'm going to pay you back," he said. "For everything. For every single thing you ever gave me."

"You're acting crazy," Constantine said.

Billy turned and strode, single-booted, off-balance, back to the front door.

"Don't talk to me that way," Constantine said sharply, but he made no move to follow. He hadn't the heart right now. He heard the door opening and closing. Then he heard the sound of his son's single boot heel striking the door, hard. Now Constantine was ready to fight. He ran to the door but when he got there and opened it all he found was the other empty boot, lying on its side on the stoop.

The house was quiet. Pipes and ducts made their soft, efficient sounds. Kitchen appliances droned. Mary was upstairs sleeping, dreaming her dreams. A thief, a repeat offender; a woman who'd sat silently in the fluorescence of the sheriff's office with her makeup bleeding onto her pale, mortified skin. Billy was gone to his friends, half naked. As Constantine poured himself another drink he thought of Susan, brave and clever and forgiving, moving with smooth-limbed certainty into a future that held only better and better news. What had happened didn't matter. It was only a couple of times, drunk; a small thing. It was only kisses and hugs. It was love, that's all. He thought of calling Susan but knew his pride would not recover from the memory of a half-drunken conversation with his own daughter in which he begged for forgiveness. He'd be old one day. He had to be careful about the past he made for himself.

Billy's shirt lay in a bright heap on the floor. Constantine bent over, hearing the faint crackings of his stiff knees, and picked it up. It was light as smoke, made of some gauzy fabric. Thumbnail-sized orange poppies and trumpet-shaped purple flowers bloomed on a field of black. Constantine lifted the shirt to his face, inhaled its odor. It smelled like his son—his sweet cologne and deodorant, a hint of the wintergreen candies he chewed for his breath. Billy was obsessed with the idea that he smelled bad, and Constantine understood his boyish terror. He himself had chewed anise, doused himself in scent, scrubbed his teeth three times a day. What thoughts of Billy's so terrified him that he drenched himself in perfume, scalded his flesh with showers that steamed windows all over the house? What thoughts? Constantine dropped the shirt back on the floor. Then, because he was a family man, because he had love for his son shot through with hatred, he picked it up again and draped it carefully across the back of a kitchen chair.

How many people had seen his wife being arrested? How many were talking about it now, over dinner? *I told you this would happen sooner or later, what can you expect from people like that?* His eyes burned. So much work, so much daily caution. All so precariously balanced.

He went to the sliding glass door, looked out into the back yard. Susan, up north in a tidy little apartment, setting out dinner. That's what he wanted to think about. But the idea of Susan, like his happiness and his outrage, flew defiantly around the room and refused to settle where his rightful feelings were housed. What pulsed in him were bitter prayers for Billy and Mary and himself. Deliver us from our nameless defeats, the rats inside the walls.

He walked out into the yard and stood for a while, looking up.

It would be dark soon. The sky was flattening, losing its blue depths, settling in around the earth. A jet pulled a vapor trail, pink-gold in the dying light. Constantine's house looked big and dense as a battleship. Its windows reflected the sky and the black branches of neighbors' trees.

This yard would be perfect for a garden if the Wilkinsons' maple didn't throw too much shade. Over there, at the south end, that would be the spot. Holding his empty glass, he walked over and paced off the modest square that seemed the most promising place. Yes, a garden. Bean rows, lettuce, the gawky beauty of sunflowers. Right here. Strawberries winking like jewels. Tomatoes big and fleshy as men's hearts. He looked down at the grass beneath his feet. His feet looked trim and prosperous, sheathed in expensive white loafers. Their gold buckles gleamed. He took a sip from his empty glass and continued looking down at the ground he owned.

Zoe had heard what happened in the kitchen. She'd been watching everything. Now she saw him through her bedroom window, standing alone in a new smallness. She sat smoking a joint and watching him on the lawn with night coming around him. She felt the whole house shrinking.

She put out the joint and walked down the hall, past the living silence that came from Momma's room. She walked through the colors and the quiet order into the back yard, where the evening insects made their circles.

"Hi, Poppa," she said.

He turned, surprised. He took her in. She saw from his face that she was pale and wild, the strangest of the children. She was loved but she was not known.

She was going somewhere else. Every day she said goodbye.

"Zoe," he said. She saw that he had forgotten about her.

"Uh-huh," she said.

"Aw, Zoe. Look. It's you."

"I know. I know it's me. I saw you from the window."

"I—" Poppa raised his arms and lowered them again. "Are you okay?" he asked.

"Sure."

A silence passed. Then Poppa said, "I was thinking about maybe starting a garden here. In the yard."

"Mm?"

"They're a lot of work," he told her. "You watch over a garden all the time. Bugs get in. Weeds. Too much sun, too little."

She shrugged. "I'd like it," she said. "I'd like to have a garden."

"We could grow a lot of things here," he said. "We could grow squash, beans, tomatoes."

"I hate tomatoes."

"Okay. No tomatoes."

She shivered at the thought of a tomato. He crouched and dug into the grass with his fingertips. He scooped out a small handful of earth.

"It isn't bad soil," he said, straightening up. "Look here. See how dark?"

She nodded. "I'd want to have flowers, too," she said. "Could we grow flowers here?"

A garden would be something to come back to. A garden would remember her.

"Sure," he said. "This soil is made for flowers."

Carefully, as if it were fragile, he gave her the little ball of dirt. She held it close to her face and inhaled its rich black smell.

"It's good dirt," he said. She pretended not to notice the one tear that crept down his face. She didn't know what to say about it.

"I'd water the garden," she said. "I'd take care of it."

"You would," he said. "I know you would."

He touched her hair. His hand was big and unsure. She held the dirt in her hand and watched her father's white shirt catch and hold the last of the light.

"I know you would," he said again.

II

CRIMINAL

WISDOM

1 9 7 1 / The sky over Cambridge was an Arctic blue, a blue burned clean of sentiment or the suggestion of simple kindness. Although it was just past noon on a warm October day it did not seem impossible to Billy that the sky would begin producing frigid little stars. He lay on the grass of the Yard, looking up. Inez, sitting on her Hegel and Kierkegaard to protect her skirt, put out her birdlike grandeur, all her powers of frank, sharp-eyed disapproval.

"Billy is too nice," she said. "Whoever named you Billy wanted you to spend your whole life behaving yourself."

Inez had a thin golden body and a riot of wiry black hair. Her face was round and incisive and blankly mysterious as an owl's. Sun and the movements of other people flashed on her little round glasses.

"My parents named me Billy," Billy told her. "Who did you think?"

"William is better," she answered. "Or Willy."

"Not *William*," said Charlotte. "William. Uck."

Charlotte was a Midwestern girl, pale as milk, with powerful hands that would not settle. She touched her hair, touched the buttons of her thrift-store tweed jacket, touched Inez's bare golden knee.

"Right," Inez said. "Willy. Or Will. For formal occasions."

"I could maybe do Will," he said. "Willy is too, I don't know. Presumptuous. Cutesy. I could probably live with Will."

Inez and Charlotte consulted one another silently. "Done," Charlotte said. "We name you Will. The child Billy is dead. You're a new man, sugar. Rise up and go forth into the world."

"You can't just change my name," he said.

"We can. We have."

"Okay. Let's see. Inez, I hereby rename you Sister Agatha of Modesto. Charlotte, from henceforward you will be known as Zsa Zsa."

Again, the women consulted each other. They shook their heads.

"We already have the right names," Inez said. Charlotte picked up a fallen leaf and tore it in half, as if that was the ceremony that would make a fact of the hour and the conversation. Even her nervous gestures had an ordained aspect.

"Sugar, we're doing this for your own good," she said. "We're not being capricious. Billy is just something you've outgrown."

"Fine," he said. "That's fine. You call me Will. I'll call you Sister Agatha and Zsa Zsa."

"They won't stick to us," Charlotte told him. "Wait and see."

"I've been Billy for eighteen years," he said. "It's too late to change." But, privately, he was starving for a new name. He barely believed it was possible.

"Wait and see," Inez said. The Yard fluttered around her, leaves sparking and skimming on the air. Everyone hurried; everyone carried books through a weighted autumn light that broke around them like fog. Billy believed that if there was a heaven it would be the first in an endless series of heavens, each one shocking and strange and perfect in ways you could not possibly have imagined. In every heaven you'd be someone new.

"It's pretentious," he said. "It would be such a pathetic display of ego."

"Mellow out," Charlotte advised him, and he agreed to try.

They lived together, the three of them, on the top floor of a faded brown house on Massachusetts Avenue. Paisley bedspreads blew from its rattling windows; silver chimes glittered fretfully on its prim front porch. Billy adored the house. He loved Charlotte for being wry and mannered and faintly masculine. He loved Inez for her willful and methodical rejection of common sense. Because of her, there was speed and blotter acid. Because of her, a procession of strangers, usually thin contemplative men, appeared in the shower or fingered guitars on the porch or sat shy and unshaven at breakfast. Billy called Inez and Charlotte the Holy Sisters of Permission. He told them all his secrets, and then began inventing new ones.

The name Will stuck to him, as he'd scarcely dared hope it would. His other friends took it up readily, because it seemed that almost everything in the world was old and out of plumb and needed renaming. The name Will became first his sly privilege, then his right, and finally an outward fact. Among his friends he was no longer someone called Billy. Billy belonged to the old past, the dying era of cars and sorrow and colonial greed, the prosperous desolation of houses. Will had a new beauty: clear skin, a sharp delicate face framed by hair that fell past his shoulders. Will was sinewy and even-tempered, symmetrical of body, with long legs and a soft, ragged triangle of hair at his breastbone. He moved gracefully, a little tentatively, inside his army jacket and shapeless khaki pants. Sometimes, in certain lights, he was able to believe he had turned into a man named Will. Then it passed and he returned to himself, a boy named Billy, someone small and foolish. Others called him

Will but in his dreams and his thoughts he was Billy, just that, a boy smart enough to fake his way through, a boy well acquainted with the limits of the possible.

On a warm evening in April, when the air smelled like rain and people walked on Brattle Street carrying tulips in paper cones, a man leaned over Billy and said, "You know, you're a rare soul. Do you mind me telling you that?"

Billy, who had been reading Faulkner and drinking coffee at a white marble table, looked up in a bright panic, as if a disembodied voice had publicly announced his most embarrassing secret wish. The man leaned over the table. He was well past thirty, with complex, vaguely geological facial bones and liquid eyes. He had a lunatic enormity, although he wasn't large. His hair was windblown on a windless day.

"No," Billy told him. He was full of fear but his voice came out steady and slightly bored, as if he was used to attentions of exactly this kind. He couldn't tell whether the man was crazy or inspired. The man's face had a doglike ardor. He wore white bell-bottoms and a brown leather vest and a yin-yang symbol on a thong around his neck.

"A rare and ancient soul," the man said in a speculative tone. "I had to stop and tell you that. You shouldn't drink coffee, it excites the body but kills the spirit. That coffee has got orange light crackling all over you."

Billy nodded. He knew the man was ridiculous, and possibly even dangerous, but he didn't want him to leave quite yet. The man was watching him with such naked reverence.

"I like orange," Billy said, sipping his coffee.

"Right, youth," the man said. "Burn it up, it'll last forever. I don't blame you, I was like that, too. My name's Cody."

"Do you always just start talking to strangers like this?"

"Not all of them. I see something I recognize in you, just like I can see the light you're putting out. Orange, but with an outer layer of the most beautiful pure blue. Think of the color of the flame on a gas stove."

"I'm Will," Billy said defiantly, and he felt, immediately, that he was giving a false name. When he caught up with the name a flood of possibility opened in his blood.

"Lovely," Cody said. "Charmed, I'm sure."

Cody shook his hand in the new way, palm first, so that his hand and Billy's joined like a boxer's gesture of triumph. Cody's hand was large and dry and uncallused.

"Do you—are you from around here?" Billy asked.

"I'm from Mars, child," Cody said. His eyes were shot through with green. He had an angular woody handsomeness that flicked fitfully across a ravaged, homely face. He might have been as old as forty. "You're a student? Hah-vahd?"

Billy nodded. He'd learned to feel pride and embarrassment over his privileges. In any conversation he sought to make it known that he did not come from a grand or protected place, but whenever he said that he felt as if he had lied. Hadn't he known money and love? Weren't his troubles, in fact, the complaints of the privileged?

"Hah-vahd," Cody said again, pleased and disdainful. "The new crop of saviors. What are you reading there?"

Billy held up his copy of *Absalom, Absalom!* Cody nodded.

"The grand old man himself," he said. "Tell me, Will, what do you love in this world?"

"What?"

"What do you love?"

Billy smiled nervously, and felt that he himself was at once desirable and slightly absurd. He wanted this man's continued attentions, not because he enjoyed them but because, if they were withdrawn—if Cody suddenly dismissed him as a dull Harvard boy—his own uncertain promise might start to wither inside him. Dullness might become a fact about him.

"Well, I love Faulkner," he said, and his ears burned at the well-behaved insufficiency of the answer. The more he needed to fascinate this Cody, the more he found himself hating him.

"Not a book," Cody said. "Not somebody dead. What do you love in the world, I mean the living, breathing organism?"

"I love coffee," Billy said thoughtlessly. "I love a good sale at Kmart. Now I'm afraid I've got to go."

Cody put his hand on Billy's forearm. His fingernails were a turgid, living pink, cut short.

"Don't go yet," he said. "Just walk with me for a minute first. I've got a feeling about you. I need to find out if I'm right."

Billy spoke to Cody's hand. "You really are pushing it," he said.

"Just walk with me a few blocks. Things are happening, Will. Things are clicking and turning and opening and closing all around us. Do you know what I mean?"

"No."

"Yes you do. Come on."

He hesitated. Then he decided he could do this as Will, a brave, reckless figure who did not quite exist. With mingled sensations of abandon and dread, Billy paid for his coffee and walked away with Cody. The streetlights had switched themselves on, pale lemon against the pale evening sky.

"You don't really love sales at Kmart," Cody said. "You were just being clever."

"Well, it was a pretentious question."

"Clever clever clever. You've got to be careful or that fancy school you go to will get you so clever and wised up and cynical that you'll think you can see through everything. You don't want to be that old."

Cody, as he walked, put out a faint scent of wood shavings. He was a compact man who moved through his own nimbus of odors and small metallic sounds: keys in his pockets, bracelets on his wrists. Billy was nervous and faintly humiliated. He felt a swelling at his crotch. He had always known what he wanted but he couldn't imagine turning his desires into flesh and so he'd lived like an aesthete, a young disciple. He'd been a friend and a scholar and a demure object of questioning glances, thin and talkative, elusively romantic, no one's. All his congress had been with himself, a hurried business. He'd been careful about his dreams.

"I do want to be old," he said. "And I don't see what's wrong with being clever."

"Poison," Cody said. "Wit and cleverness, worse for you than thirty cups of coffee. Talk about surrounding yourself with static electricity. But listen here, Will. Do you think you could love me?"

"What?"

"I think I could love you. For an hour. Maybe longer. There's no point in speaking in code. I see a purity in you I'd love to touch."

"What?" Billy laughed. His laugh had a swaying, arid squeak.

"Don't act shocked. No is no, no is your business, but don't act like I'm asking a question you never thought of."

"Well." The laugh again, though he hadn't meant to laugh. "I just—"

He stopped walking. He and Cody stood in the middle of the block, with people passing around them. Ahead and to the right was a doughnut shop, part of a chain that had an outlet in Billy's hometown. He looked at the shop's bright sign, the rows of ordinary, lurid confections displayed on metal trays. He thought of his room, the books on his shelf.

"I'm staying right down the street," Cody said. "Why don't you come up and smoke a joint with me?"

He looked at Cody's burnished, harmed face, and realized the question could answer itself. He didn't have to work at this; he didn't have to seek or decide. All he had to do was not say no.

"Where are you staying?" he said.

"This way," Cody said. "Follow me."

He went with Cody down Brattle, past the usual stores. Cody talked and Will answered but the conversation didn't settle in him.

He thought about danger and permission, the swelling in his crotch. He thought about changing his mind. Charlotte would praise his good sense, Inez would tease him for cowardice. The world shimmered around him, its streetlights and the colors of traffic. Inez preached a life of risks. Charlotte advocated wisdom, the careful weighing of losses and rewards. He couldn't tell what he, Billy, believed. A dog barked. He didn't know what he would do in a situation like this, so he let Cody lead him down Story Street and up the brick walk of an oatmeal-colored apartment building.

Billy knew the building—he knew all the buildings in Harvard Square—and as Cody opened the lobby door with a key Billy felt a spasm of irritation. Cody was casting his strangeness onto the limitlessness of his streets. Now, forever, this building would emanate.

"A friend's place," Cody said. "She's off on a mission, I'm here to keep the demons out."

Billy laughed again, the high-pitched panicked sound. It wasn't the way he wanted to laugh. He wanted to be cool. He wanted to be brave and desired, free.

"Don't think there aren't demons," Cody said. "Demons and angels, wrestling over our souls. The world is a more important place than the corporations want you to believe. Let people get too serious, let them start thinking too much about good and evil, and they lose their urge to be customers. Pow. The whole idea of shopping goes right out the window."

"Well," Billy said. He followed Cody up two flights of stairs, down a hallway featureless as a dream, and through a heavy brown door.

The apartment was covered in tapestries, aswarm with flowers and paisleys and the stolid, walleyed profiles of elephants. The tapestries hung taut on the walls and in fat billows from the ceilings. Wan evening light seeped in through the windows and was absorbed by the layers of fabric, so that the room appeared murky and deep, a grotto. It smelled faintly of frankincense. Cody lit a candle, and another, and a third.

"A lot of bedspreads," Billy said. "This is someone who believes in bedspreads."

"Sit down," Cody said. "I'm going to make some tea."

He went into what would have been the kitchen, and Billy sat on a pillow. Then he stood up again and walked to the window. Headlights shone in the street now. The neon was lit. In an apartment across the street Billy could see the blue-gray flicker of television, and he knew a sharp, sudden envy. Someone was living the most ordinary and unsurprising of lives. Someone was sitting on his own sofa, popping a beer and watching the seven o'clock news. Billy resolved that he would drink a little tea, tell Cody it had been fine to meet him, and leave. He'd return to the order of his days, the simplicity of his skin.

Cody brought out two mugs of tea and stood with them in the light of the candles. He let Billy come to him. "Long life," Cody said, raising his mug. The tea smelled bitter. Billy let the steam wash over his face but did not drink.

"Burdock root," Cody said.

"What?"

"It's burdock-root tea. At first you hate it because you've lived on sugar all your life. Drink it, it's good for calming all needless anxieties."

Carefully, Billy tipped the mug to his lips. The tea did in fact have a foul taste, like water that had pooled on a forest floor. Cody laughed.

"You have to give it a chance," he said. He opened a box that sat on a wooden table, took out a plastic bag full of dull green-brown dope, and rolled a joint quickly, with the skill and focus of a baker. The box was elaborately carved, inlaid with mother-of-pearl. When Cody lit the joint, his face took the light of the match like a painting revealed on the wall of a cave. Cody's face was pocked, extravagantly lined. In repose, all his handsomeness fell away from him.

He gave the joint to Billy. Billy sucked the smoke deep into his lungs, felt with gratitude the familiar sweet burning. When he passed the joint back to Cody, Cody put his hand, gently, on Billy's chest.

"I can feel your heart," he said. "Child, what are you so afraid of?"

"I'm not afraid," Billy said. He let Cody take his hit, got the joint back, filled his lungs again.

"Well, if you *were* afraid, you'd have no reason to be," Cody said. "This is just love, Mr. Will. This is just what you nose around for every day of your life. It only means good things about you."

"I think—" Billy said. "Listen, I should go." He gave the joint back to Cody.

"So soon?"

"Yeah. Well, I could say something really ridiculous like I just remembered I was supposed to meet someone, but really—" He hoped to be loved for his honesty. He was a good and kindly boy who still knew the limits of what should be allowed. Cody, a sweet fatherly man, would love him for everything he decided not to do. The air was full of shade and unsteady light.

"Listen, really—" Billy said, and his voice sounded remote, as if it were coming from another boy who stood in another room. He watched Cody put the joint in the ashtray and move closer to him. He felt Cody's hand settle, gently, on his shoulders. There was the woody smell. There were the faint clickings. Billy wanted and didn't want.

"All's well, child," Cody said. "Don't you worry. This is goodness here, every bit of it."

Cody's hands moved down Billy's spine and then Billy was on the other side of something. Then something was happening and even if Billy pulled away and ran from the apartment it would still have happened. He was on the other side and with a terrible sense of relief he let Cody unbutton his shirt. He felt, briefly, as calm and entitled as a child being undressed for bed.

"Lovely," Cody whispered. "You're a lovely boy and that's a fine thing, to be thin and pretty like you are."

Billy let the word roll around in him. Pretty. He put his fingers on the top button of Cody's shirt and with a rush of exhilaration he opened it. There was a new patch of Cody's skin, brown, speckled with black hair. Billy could not believe he had permission to do this. Blood hammered in his skull and a part of him floated up and watched, exultant, terrified, as his hands moved down the buttons of Cody's shirt. Cody's shirt hung open. Billy could see the soft muscles of his chest, the furred mound of his stomach. Billy careened between squeamish desire and a hot, howling embarrassment.

"Come here," Cody said. "Come over here." He led Billy to a mattress covered with pillows, and there he took Billy's shirt off with steady, almost clinical certainty, as if he, Cody, was a doctor and the shirt was doing Billy some slow undetectable harm. "Now lie down," Cody said.

"I—"

"Shh." Cody put a thick brown finger to his lips. Billy obeyed. All he had to do was not say no. Candlelight moved across the tapestries like a breeze. He felt Cody unlacing his shoes. Suddenly, Billy needed to speak. Suddenly he believed that if he didn't hear his own voice in the room he'd lose himself. He'd disappear into the nowhere that hovered around the edges of the world.

"Listen, Cody," he said, and his voice was small in the dusky air. "I don't think I want to do this, I mean, I think I'd better go."

"You don't want to go," Cody said. "That's just your voice talking."

Billy was filled with rage. He could have kicked Cody—Cody's intent, lined face was bent over the toe of his shoe—and jumped up screaming, 'Don't tell me what I want.'

He didn't move. His own rage rose hotly to the surface of his skin and then turned into something else, something unfamiliar.

Anger and desire and fear were so intertwined in him he couldn't tell one from the other. He lay quietly under the combined weight of them as Cody, with a soft grunt of effort, took his boots off and set them on the floor. As Billy watched his boots being set aside like that he thought, quickly and not fearfully, of his own death.

"I—" he said, and he said no more than that. As urgently as he had needed to speak he now needed to be quiet, to slip in among the pillows and tapestries and the jar of peacock feathers that winked in the semi-dark. He joined the room and anything could happen to him. Everything was all right.

Tenderly, but with the same clinical sureness, Cody opened the buttons of Billy's pants and pulled them off. Billy lay in his socks and boxer shorts, breathing. He had a hard-on and he was still embarrassed but now in an abstract way—he was embarrassed and pleased and he watched a line of pale green elephants bisect the fabric overhead. He had joined the room. Anything could happen. He saw his pants and his shirt puddled on the floor and they were the clothes of someone else, someone he'd invented.

Cody took Billy's shorts off. Cody whispered, "Lovely." Billy was breathing. He was naked except for his socks. He was someone to whom the word *lovely* applied. Cody removed his own clothes. Billy raised his head and watched with a queasy, prickling interest as Cody shrugged away his shirt, kicked off his shoes, stepped out of his bell-bottoms. He wore no underwear. He stood furrily naked, erect. His arms were thin; he had a belly. Cody knelt on the mattress and rubbed Billy's chest with the palms of his hands. Billy didn't look at him. He looked back up at the ceiling, where the elephants marched trunk to tail, and he felt Cody's lips on his belly. Briefly, he panicked. His heart fluttered. This can't happen. This can't. But he held still and it was allowed. It did happen. Cody's lips, ticklish with their stubble, moved down and then they had taken Billy inside. Billy's stomach heaved. He worried about teeth. He didn't look anywhere but up. Cody's mouth moved. Billy said to himself,

This is happening. He felt powerful and ridiculous. He remembered the forearm of the waiter who'd given him his coffee an hour ago. The waiter had been handsome in a pallid, dissatisfied way. His forearms had been pale and hairless, ropy with little muscles that jumped. Billy looked at Cody's bare shoulders, the top of Cody's windblown head. Cody's head moved and there was the sensation, strong but remote, edged with vertigo, nothing like the familiar thrills Billy summoned in himself, quickly, with his own hand. Cody's hair was black, disordered, innocent. The waiter had seemed hurt by his own beauty. He'd been sullen. The muscles in his arms had jumped as he poured the coffee. Billy saw that he could think of the waiter's arm and say to himself the word *beautiful*. There was permission and he said the word, silently. The arm became beautiful and then the man did, an unhappy stranger with a shadow of mustache. A man who was naked sometimes, who would have slim hips and a sullen way of standing, with his arms folded over his bare chest. Billy thought of the waiter's sculpted unhappiness. He watched the top of Cody's head. Yes. Bix had put his blood on Billy's face. The waiter's buttocks would be small and precise. Yes. He thought of Bix—the quiet rage of him, the crazy light in his eyes—and he thought of the waiter's small innocent buttocks and he thought of himself lifted by strong arms and then with a single exclamation of surprise, he came.

That was it. It was over.

Immediately, it turned to nothing. It had been so much and now it was nothing, just dull shame and the desire to be elsewhere. Cody wiped his mouth, smiled. He patted Billy's stomach and reached with his other hand into the ashtray for the joint.

"Mmm," he said, relighting the joint. "Delicious."

Billy didn't speak. He saw that he was alone in a room with a lustful, crazy old man.

"It's all right," Cody said, offering him the joint. "You're all right, everything's fine."

"I have to go," Billy said. He did not accept the joint.

"I know."

Billy got himself off the mattress, put his clothes back on. Cody watched. Billy could feel him watching. He didn't want to look back at Cody but when he was dressed he had to and what he saw was a thin homely man sitting cross-legged, smoking the last of a joint, with a round belly and the purple stub of a penis protruding from a splotch of dark hair. Billy couldn't believe it. This ugliness, this sad flesh.

"Bye," he said.

"Goodbye. Don't worry."

"I'm not."

"I'll be here another two days," Cody said.

"I probably won't be seeing you. I mean, I have a lot of studying—"

"I know. Have a good trip. Please torture yourself as little as possible."

"Yeah. Well."

"Go. Go in peace, child."

Billy nodded. He knew he could go now, and be forgiven. All his desire had evaporated. This episode didn't have to mean anything beyond simple curiosity, the open-mindedness all adventurers brought with them into a new world. Then he walked up to Cody —three steps—and put a kiss on Cody's lips. Neither of them spoke. Billy turned to leave. He felt a drop of moisture on his lower lip, Cody's saliva or his own cum. He could hear his boots clopping on the floorboards. He closed the door behind him, strode down the bare hallway, took the stairs two at a time. He crossed the malignant little lobby, with its varnished yellow wood and its rows of smudged chrome mailboxes, opened the glass door and walked out into the altered Cambridge night. It was April, the air had a living smell, though there would still be fitful little furies of snow in the weeks to come. Will took a breath, and another. He was out of the room but he wasn't out of it. He carried it. He had kissed another man, and he knew, abruptly, who he would be. As he turned onto Brattle he touched his own lips, curiously. A wild roil of happiness and terror caught up with him and took him so suddenly, so unexpectedly, that he stopped and stood, just stood, before his reflection in the window of a bookstore. He was exultant and full of dread. He had kissed another man. He let himself be inhabited by this new thing, this possibility. A leaf of newspaper scraped across his feet and in the electric lights of Cambridge he said his new name, quietly, to himself, in a tone of tenderness and surprise, as if he were speaking to a strange brother who'd been away for years and had suddenly returned, unannounced, to stand before him radiant and fierce and crazy as an angel, full of an angel's wised-up, immaculate sorrow.

1 9 7 1 / It refused to happen. Susan thought it should have by now but nothing took hold. No tiny hooks caught on other hooks and began the long process of tangling themselves into hands, feet, the first stirrings of a silent red slumber. She charted her days carefully; she always knew. There were times when she thought, That's it. That was the little puncture. Now it's going to start. But nothing started. She was alone inside herself.

She didn't want to wait much longer. She wanted a family of her own. When she and Todd had a child they would be separate, complete; they would be respected. They would no longer visit their families on holidays.

Aside from the baby—a temporary problem—her life was good. Good enough. She didn't mind her job, typing and filing in the admissions office. She didn't mind Yale, though it did not open to her. Privately, she called it the fortress. She and Todd and everyone they knew lived within the fieldstone and lawns of the campus itself. Next to the campus a cluster of stores and inexpensive restaurants had grown up around a green and an ancient church. That was what offered itself; that was where you could go. Beyond the stores and cafés it was broken glass, black men and women, the dim dirty glow of the Greyhound terminal. Susan kept her circles small. She never complained. She made friends with the other girls in her department, young Yale wives like herself. She loved her boss, Mr. Morst, a reedy jovial man who smelled somehow like an overheated vacuum cleaner and had no aspect of sexuality, none. Mr. Morst made only modest demands. Please refile these folders, please type up these forms. He knew Susan and the other girls wouldn't be around for long, just as he knew that if this job began to displease them they could get other, equally meaningless jobs tomorrow. After the riot of confused, contradictory desires Susan had known in school this island life, this life of simple undemanding tasks, felt sometimes like a guilty pleasure. She did exactly what was needed, neither more nor less. The hours passed like boxcars, steadily, with a mechanical rhythm and order that possessed something of a cross-country train's measured, stately grandeur. Todd worked hard at his classes, and did as well as he'd expected to. There were no surprises. Law school became an increasing certainty, either at Yale or at Harvard. The days kept arriving. But nothing grew inside Susan, and she wanted it to. Until that happened, until the baby began to manifest itself, her days would be made of waiting. She typed student records onto forms, and always typed exactly on the line. She shopped, and cooked, and cleaned the apartment, and drank coffee with Ellie and Beth and Linda, the other girls at work. The others were trying to avoid pregnancy until their husbands graduated, until they knew whether their adult lives would be lived in New York or California or somewhere on the plains.

"I'm going to be raising a family for the next twenty years," Beth said over coffee during the midmorning break. "I don't mind if my life's a little breezy for another year or two."

Ellie added, "My mom made me promise to wait till I'm twenty-three. She says a girl any younger than that can't raise a child because she's still a child herself."

"I guess," Susan said. "But you know, I have this feeling that somebody's waiting for me. I mean, my baby is."

"How's that?"

She sighed, and her breath rippled across the surface of her coffee. "Oh, don't pay me any attention," she said. "I don't know what I'm saying half the time. It's just that I have this, I don't know, feeling. It's like my baby already exists, and he's just waiting for me to catch up with him so he can get started on his life."

"Or her," Linda said.

"But I feel like the first one will be a he. I feel sure about it. That's what I mean. I keep thinking this is already a person, right now, and I'm just holding things up. Like if I wait too long this person will just disappear."

"It's better to have a baby after you're settled," Beth said. "You don't know where you and Todd'll be this time next year. If you got pregnant now, I mean right now, tonight, you could be moving to some remote place with a three-month-old."

"Todd isn't applying to law schools in any remote places," Susan said, and she felt a furtive glow of satisfaction. Of the four girls, she had married the boy whose future seemed least subject to question. Beth's husband, Arnie, had switched his major suddenly, from engineering to journalism. Linda's Bob had failed two of his classes. These girls needed to protect themselves, to measure their lives as best they could, because they might be blown anywhere.

Linda said, "I bet when you've got a three-month-old, the supermarket feels like a remote place."

"Oh, everybody makes too much of a fuss," Susan said. "My mother had my brother and me before she was twenty-one, and no money, and she did just fine."

Again, Beth and Ellie glanced at each other. "Well, I'm not my mother," Ellie said. Susan knew she was the outsider, the one banded against. After she left the job she wouldn't know these girls anymore.

"I'd better get back to work." She sighed. "Terrible calamities will happen if I don't get my folders filed by noon today."

"Right," Beth said with exaggerated patience. As they left the employees' lounge Linda's skirt caught on her nylons and showed the rippled white heft of her thighs. Susan saw, with a brief and terrible clarity, how Linda's future would fall. Linda's husband wouldn't make enough money. Linda would get fat—it was already starting—and stay at home with her children as her husband's orbits grew wider and wider around a house like the ones Susan's father built, a house made of wire brads and false wood.

Her father's houses were waiting for people who didn't do well enough.

Susan knew Linda had been cheerful and unremarkable in high school, a friend of the more popular girls because she carried no hint of danger. She knew Ellie had offered willingness as apology for her flat bust and her lack of chin. Susan saw these things automatically, the way a jeweler can't help seeing the relative value of a stone. She tried not to pass judgments but she saw what she saw and could not seem to see in any other way. To punish herself she remembered Rosemary, crowned and weeping on the football field. She reminded herself, Don't start feeling too superior. You were only a princess, you didn't win. But the more she thought about that, the more obdurately her mind seemed to insist on Linda's plainness, Beth's lack of spark, Ellie's habit of wearing too much rouge and eyeliner.

When she got home, she found Todd at his desk. He was turning into someone. She watched it happen. He'd bought himself new glasses, with licorice-colored rims. A certain boyishness had evaporated—his old, transparent need to be loved—and in its place was a newer need to work. Susan thought of his studies as devourings. He worked through his books with an implacable hunger. Somewhere, buried, was repose and satisfaction, the golden moment, but to get there he had to eat his way through miles of printed pages. He had to write his way to it, to answer every question fully and correctly, to so thoroughly understand the concepts that the concepts themselves were remade in his stern, laboring image.

"Hi," she said from the doorway.

"Hi." He looked up, smiled, pushed his glasses higher on his nose. His forearms were heavy and powerful, lush with bright blond hair.

She went to him, rubbed his shoulders. "How's it going?" she asked.

"Okay," he said. "International finance is a monster."

"I'm sure." Now that he was an upperclassman, the subjects he studied were vast and remote as the rumors of mountain ranges in Asia. During the first two years, Susan had kept track. She could imagine twentieth-century literature; she could imagine cellular biology. But now he studied invisible laws of commerce, the history of ideas. She watched him grow denser, older, with what he knew. She thought about babies, who would need her to teach them goodness. Who would require goodness of her, every hour.

"How was your day?" he asked.

"Fine. Same as always. I'm going to put dinner together."

"Okay."

She gave his shoulders a final squeeze, and went into the kitchen. The apartment was snug and unremarkable. It was their first home together but Susan couldn't seem to make it mean anything. It was so obviously temporary, like her job. She kept it clean, bought flowers occasionally. Every morning, she knew what she would fix for dinner that night. Each day spawned the next and at odd hopeful moments she felt something struggling to come through her, a gentle but insistent pushing on the fabric of her skin.

The telephone rang while she was rinsing lettuce.

"Hello?"

"Hi, honey."

"Hi, Mom."

"Am I calling at a bad time?"

"No. I'm just starting dinner. How are you?"

"Oh, we're okay."

Susan heard it, and knew. She knew from the buzz that lingered on the wire.

"What's happened?" she asked. "What's wrong?"

"Nothing. Nothing big. Billy just called from school and told me he's not coming home for Christmas, it's no big deal."

"Where's he going?"

"Some friend of his. Someone with a cabin somewhere. Vermont. A cabin in Vermont."

"Well, that sounds like fun," Susan said. "Mom, Billy's got his own life now. He's not necessarily going to be coming home every holiday."

"Oh, I know that. Don't you think I know that? He's got to do his own thing. I want him to."

"But?" Susan said.

"I beg your pardon?"

"But what? I know you're not happy about this."

"Well, honey, of course I'm not *happy* about it. What mother doesn't want her children to come home for Christmas?"

Susan held the headpiece to her ear with her shoulder and started tearing up lettuce for the salad. "It's something else," she said. "What is it?"

"Oh, honey, you know."

"Tell me."

"You and I know perfectly well that Billy doesn't want to come home for Christmas because of your father. I knew this would happen. I've been expecting it. Do you remember last Christmas?"

"I'll never forget it."

Susan heard her mother take a breath. She heard the thickness in her mother's throat.

"Your father's driving Billy away," her mother said. "It makes me so darn mad."

"No one's driving Billy away, Mom. He's in college, his life is changing. He'll be back."

"Sometimes I could murder your father. I mean, why is he so stubborn? Do you have any idea? I watch him pick these fights and I beg him to stop but he won't. He won't stop. He can't stop, he's like a bull."

"Well, Mom."

"I beg your pardon?"

"I mean, well, you married him, didn't you?"

"What kind of thing is that to say? I married a boy, twenty-two years ago. People change. You don't know that yet. Not that I think Todd will change. Todd is different."

"I don't believe anybody changes that much," Susan said. "If Dad can be a bully now, he must have been a bully then."

"He's not a bully. Honey, I never said he was a bully. I said he was like a *bull*."

"Oh, come off it. He can be terrible. He's—"

"Honey, I love your father. Your father is my whole life."

"I didn't say you didn't love him."

"I'd do anything for your father."

"Mom, listen—"

"So, tell me. How's Todd?"

"Todd's fine. Working hard, as always."

"That's great," her mother said. "He's a real workhorse, that Todd. And what about you, honey? That job of yours isn't getting you down, is it?"

"No, the job's fine. Listen, it'll be okay, about Billy. He'll grow up and he and Dad will work things out."

"Oh, I know. I know that. These are just growing pains, every boy goes through it. I'm going to let you get back to your dinner, Todd must be starving."

"Okay. Mom?"

"Mm-hm?"

"Nothing. Daddy's not home now, is he?"

"Your father? Oh no, he's still working. You know him. He and Todd are two of a kind, a pair of workhorses. When you come home for Christmas, don't let him bring any books with him."

"I'll see what I can do."

"I can't wait to see you, honey. Christmas can't come soon enough. Give Todd my love."

"Okay. Bye, Mom."

"Bye. Nice talking to you, sweetheart."

Susan hung up and stood for a while. She waited for time to pass. She would not cry, not tonight. She finished tearing up the lettuce, got a tomato from the refrigerator. She waited, and returned to her life, its regular motions, the unhaunted brightness of her temporary kitchen. This is my life, she thought, and I'm standing right here in the middle of it. She sliced the tomato. She didn't think of anything.

That night, she and Todd made love. She knew he was exhausted. He'd happily have given her one brief dry kiss and slipped away. But it was one of her nights. She ran her palms down his broad back, kissed him lingeringly, and he understood. He cupped her breasts, worked his mouth along the nape of her neck. He moved up under her nightgown, touched her gently between the legs. She moaned over his simple probing. Marriage had diminished and deepened the mystery. She'd seen him on the toilet. She'd known him rank and sour. She'd caught him looking so empty and stupid and self-satisfied that she'd thought, This is the end of my interest. He can't return from this. But at the same time his flesh expanded with familiarity. His particulars—the cross-stitch of fine hairs on his abdomen, the single thick vein that slumbered along his biceps—had become hers as well, so that the sight of them inspired a wash of mournful tenderness she'd neither known nor imagined, a careening sensation of possibility and loss. She believed, now, that no one was ever sure about love. Love arrived obliquely, at angles, but even when it lay dormant a boundary had been crossed, a sanctity relinquished. All her certainty, the sameness of her days, was infiltrated now with the fear that something might happen to Todd. If he was hurt or grew ill, if he died, some part of her would be set free but another part, a part that weighed more, that had more of Susan about it, would be silenced forever.

"Oh," she whispered. There it was, the tip, pushing against her, pushing itself in. Todd was tired. This would be especially short. She ran her hands up and down the muscles of his back. The strength of him still impressed her. The flesh that lay under his skin was so knotted, so continually tense. She imagined Todd living in a state of ongoing physical pain that only released its hold when he slept and when he made love. She believed a body so large and muscled must hurt, and as she touched him she thought of smoothing him out, untangling him.

"Oh," she said again, louder. She usually made more noise than he did, which embarrassed her. She worried that she took too much pleasure in this, that she was too lascivious and greedy. She told herself, It's for the baby. As Todd worked his way into her she thought of the baby, waiting. Maybe this would be the night. She knew so much. She knew he'd be dark, like her. She knew he'd be serious, and kind, and never tempted by weakness. Todd pumped in her and she felt the hard painful muscles of his back with her hands. Poor thing, she thought. His breath tickled her ear. Poor thing. He pumped with steadfast concentration, silent except for his breathing, and the sensation grew. She kept opening and opening. With every thrust she opened wider, until she heard herself gasping and moaning and felt the sweat pop out along Todd's spine. Here it comes. She thought about the baby, waiting, and this might be the time, this, now. There was the high tingling, the bright inner nowhere. She thought of the baby and she thought of Todd, and as he emptied himself with a single surprised exhalation the two were momentarily mixed up in her mind, Todd and the baby, the inside and the outside, all the flesh that was waiting for her to become herself so it could be released from its sorrow and its pain.

1 9 7 2 / Trancas's mother had left everything: a husband, petunia beds, a blue-shuttered house on Zoe's street. She'd taken Trancas to live with her in drunken renunciation until she found the hard kernel of nothing from which she could start again. She was drinking her way to it, smoking Chesterfields two at a time. She was watching television, waiting for the day she'd wasted so many hours that the hours themselves would be ground down, the days indistinguishable from the nights, and she'd be able to look for a different self amid the wreckage. She wanted to drop acid with her daughter, but Trancas claimed she didn't know where to get any.

"So long, girls," Trancas's mother called cheerfully from the colored twilight. Television light changed and changed in her glass of Scotch. She'd decided to think of herself and Trancas as sisters, two young criminal girls with everything ahead of them.

Zoe understood about Trancas's mother. She'd left the curtains and the shelf paper, gone to live in the wild. She wanted to look at her human life through an animal's eyes, to see where the mistakes were buried.

"Fuck off," Trancas muttered.

Zoe pinched Trancas's arm, which was hard and fat as a sausage. Zoe loved Trancas's mother. She respected her exhausted and ironic hope for rebirth.

"Have fun," Trancas's mother said. She looked at the television screen through her Scotch. It would have looked like a kaleidoscope, Zoe thought. Trancas's mother was skinny and precise as an ancient ballerina, grandly slovenly as an insane queen. She wore an Indian blouse embroidered with flowers and furtive glintings of mirror. She put out a wan, unsteady light that matched the light of the television. She could have been a figure from the television, projected into the room.

"Good night, Mrs. Harris," Zoe said. Trancas pushed her out the door, closed it as if she were shutting in deadly radiation. Trancas pitied and feared her mother with an ardor more potent than romance.

"Fuck off," Trancas said again, louder, to the scarred, thickly painted wood of the door.

"Don't be so hard on her," Zoe said.

"You're not her daughter," Trancas answered. "You go back to Garden City tomorrow."

"You hate Garden City."

"She burned up a chair last night," Trancas said. "With one of her cigarettes. I came out of my bedroom and there she was, fast asleep, with smoke all over the place and this little lick of fire right next to her ass."

"She should be more careful," Zoe said, but she understood even the desire to burn. Trancas's mother had probably dreamed about sitting on a chair of fire, going up with the smoke and looking down at the old business of the world.

"Damn right," Trancas said. "If she wants to kill herself, okay. Just don't take me and half the building along with her."

"She's depressed."

"She's a fucking lunatic, is what she is. Come on, let's get out of here."

Trancas and Zoe walked down Jane Street together, under the night shimmer of the trees. Trancas had been Zoe's best friend since they were both nine years old, and now Trancas had left the old world of rules and girlish hungers. Zoe visited on weekends. She kept other clothes in Trancas's closet: a black miniskirt, a translucent blouse the color of strong coffee. In New York, some men treated her as if she were beautiful.

"Tomorrow," Trancas said, "I want to go look at a motorcycle."

"What kind of motorcycle?"

Trancas pulled a scrap of newspaper from her back pocket. "Somebody on West Tenth is selling an old Harley for three hundred dollars," she said.

"You don't have three hundred dollars. You don't have any money at all."

"If I like this bike well enough, I'll get the three hundred."

Trancas was trying out a new heedlessness, a big mean-spirited freedom that never worried. She was planning her own escape. Lately she'd been packing on weight, pushing her jaw out to make her face look squarer and less kind. She talked about buying a motorcycle, a leather jacket, a pearl-handled knife. Zoe was still her best friend and, in some obscure new way, the bride of her new ideas. They walked the streets like lovers.

"Where could you get three hundred dollars?" Zoe asked.

"You can do it," Trancas said. "There are ways."

She was cultivating secrets. When she and Zoe met, Trancas had been tall and intelligent, clumsy, undesired. She'd lived in bulky, slow-moving confusion among her own chaos of mistakes and hopes. Now she was taking on size. She was talking about California.

"Maybe your mother would buy it for you," Zoe said.

"Right," Trancas answered.

"You could ask her."

"She doesn't have any money."

"Your father must send her some."

"She won't cash his checks. She wiped her ass with the last one and sent it back to him."

Trancas had fallen in love with her mother's bad behavior. Some of the stories were true.

"Why don't you ask your father, then?" Zoe said.

"For money for a motorcycle? He wants to buy me ballet shoes. He keeps telling me it's not too late to start."

Zoe took her friend's hand as they crossed Hudson Street. The night sky was filled with tight little fists of cloud, bright gray against the red-black.

They went to one of the bars Trancas liked, over in the East Village. The bar burned a damp blue light inside its own stale darkness. Men danced in leather cowboy clothes, and no one ever seemed to notice or care that Zoe and Trancas were sixteen. It was the kind of bar you could walk into with a snake draped over your shoulders. On the jukebox, James Brown sang "Super Bad."

Trancas and Zoe sat on the broken sofa at the back, near the pool table and the reek of the bathrooms. Trancas lit up a joint, passed it to Zoe.

"Crowded in here tonight," Trancas said.

"Mm-hm."

"Look at that guy with the tattoos."

"Where?"

"Right there. Playing pool."

A sinewy, feline-faced man leaned into the puddle of brighter light that fell onto the pool table, took aim at the seven ball. His arms swarmed with hearts and daggers and grinning skulls, the snaky bodies and alert, hungry faces of dragons.

"Cool," Trancas said.

"Mm-hm."

"I'm getting a tattoo."

"What kind?"

"Maybe a rose," Trancas said. "On my ass."

"You'd have it forever," Zoe told her.

"I'd like to know I was going to have something forever. Wouldn't you?"

"Well. Yes, I guess I would."

They smoked the joint, listened to the music. Time didn't pass in the bar, there was just music and different kinds of dark. Zoe was afraid and she liked it. She liked night in the city in bars like this, all the little dangers and promises. It was like going to live in the woods. Back in Garden City, the food stood on the shelves in alphabetical order.

"Maybe a lightning bolt," Trancas said.

"What?" Zoe was getting stoned. She could feel the music moving in her. She could see that the worn brown plush of the sofa arm was a world unto itself.

"A lightning bolt instead of a rose," Trancas said. "I think maybe a rose'd be too, you know. A *rose*."

"I like roses," Zoe said.

"Then you should get one."

"Maybe I will."

"You can get a rose, and I'll get a lightning bolt. Or a dragon. I like the one dragon that guy's got on his arm."

"You can get a lightning bolt *and* a dragon," Zoe said.

"I will. I just have to decide which I want first."

Trancas took out another joint and then a man was sitting on the arm of the sofa. Zoe hadn't seen him sit down. She wondered if he'd been there all along. No, a few minutes ago she'd been staring at the bare brown plush.

"Hey," the man said. He smiled. He was haloed with hair. He had a brittle storm of black hair on his head and he had prickly black sideburns and an electric little V of beard. He was dark and blurred, like a tattoo.

"Hi," Zoe said. She got a buzz from him right away, this compact smiling man ablaze with hair. Dope made her languid and prone to sex.

"What's up?"

"Nothing. Sitting here."

She offered him the joint and he took a hit. His face pulled in cartoonishly around the joint, eyes squeezed shut and lips puckered. Zoe laughed.

"What's so funny?" he asked, handing back the joint.

She shook her head, took another hit. There was something sexy about this sweet little cartoon man. There was something alert and lost, canine. He wore black motorcycle boots, a black velvet shirt. He could have been a figure who popped out of a black cuckoo clock to announce the hour.

"You're very pretty," he said. "Do you mind me telling you that?"

"I'm not really pretty," she said. "I wish I was."

"You are."

"No. Maybe I look pretty in this light because I want to, I mean you're probably not seeing *me*, you're just seeing how much I'd like to be a pretty girl sitting on a sofa in a bar."

She laughed again. It was good dope.

"What was that?" he said.

"I don't know. I don't have any idea what I just said."

"You're a weird girl, huh?"

"Yes. I'm a weird girl."

"That's good. I like weird. You're a girl, ain't you?"

"What?"

"You're not a boy."

"No. I'm not a boy."

"Good," he said. "Hey, I like boys, but I like to know what's what. You understand what I'm saying?"

"I guess so. No. Not really."

"A lot of the girls who come in this place ain't really girls."

"I know that," she said. Did she know? She was losing track.

"I can tell you are, though. You've got this thing they can't fake, it's like a glow. You know what I'm saying?"

"You're saying I glow."

"Uh-huh. My name is Ted."

"Hi, Ted. I'm Zoe. This is my friend Trancas."

"Pleased to meet you. Listen, you two want to do a few lines?" he asked.

"Okay. Sure."

"I got a gram or two up at my place. I live right across the street there, how'd you two like to run over there with me and do a few quick lines?"

Zoe looked at Trancas, who shrugged. Trancas refused to say no. She wasn't turning into the kind of person who'd use that word.

"Okay," Zoe said.

"Come on."

The man stood up and Zoe and Trancas were standing up, too, when a voice said, "Girls, don't go with that one."

Zoe saw his shoes first, red sling-back pumps with a five-inch heel. She thought, My mother has a pair like that, but not so high. The rest of him was army fatigues, a ruffled off-the-shoulder blouse, a platinum wig that fell with a bright chemical crackle to his shoulders. He stood with his hands on his hips, emitting a faint, powdery light. His face was sharp and narrow, full of brash indignant complications.

"Fuck off, Cassandra," Ted said.

"That one is bad news, ladies," the man in the wig said. "Don't mess with him unless you like it rough and I mean *rough*."

"Fuck you."

"He had a girl in the hospital last month, and I told him if he started working this bar again I would hound his ass. You think I was bluffing, Nick, honey?"

"Actually, his name is Ted," Zoe said.

The man said to Zoe and Trancas, "This bar pulls scum in off the street like shit pulls in flies. Come on."

"Up to you, ladies," the man in the wig said. "As long as you know what you're getting yourselves into."

Zoe paused, half standing. She knew Trancas wouldn't change her mind. She couldn't; any show of fear or common sense would push her backward toward the tall unloved nervous girl she'd resolved to stop being. Zoe looked at the cartoon man, scowling now, and she looked at the man in the wig, who stood like a crazy goddess of propriety and delusion, his sharp face jutting out from between the silver curtains of his wig and piles of colored bracelets winking on his arms. Zoe thought of Alice on the far side of the looking glass, an innocent and sensible girl. What Alice brought to Wonderland was her calm good sense, her Englishness. She saved herself by being correct, by listening seriously to talking animals and crazy people.

Zoe decided. She said to Ted or Nick, "Maybe we'll just stay here." To Trancas she added, "Unless you want to go."

Trancas, relieved, shook her head. "I'll stay with you," she said. "Hey, girl, I can't leave you alone in a place like this."

The man said, "You're going to let yourselves get scared off by this sleazeball? You're joking. You're playing a joke on me, right?"

"No," Zoe said. "We're going to stay. Thanks, anyway."

His face puckered in on itself. He might have been trying to make his head smaller. "Right," he said. "Listen to bag ladies, listen to bums, they know what they're talking about. Listen to drag queens that were locked up in Bellevue a week ago."

"Not true," the wigged man said to Zoe. His voice was full of a dowager's conviction, a drawling and leisurely grandness. "I've never been to Bellevue or any other institution for the criminally insane. I don't deny that I've done a little time for shoplifting, but, honey, it didn't in any way compromise my ability to know a pervert when I see one."

"A pervert," the man said. "Right. You're calling me a pervert."

"A pervert," said the man in the wig, "is somebody who does things to other people they don't want done to them. Period."

"Come on," the man said to Zoe. "I don't want to look at this fucker's ugly face anymore."

"We're not going," Zoe told him. "Really."

He shook his head. "Stupid bitch," he said.

The man in the wig raised his hands and waggled his fingers. "Be gone," he said. "You have no power here."

And Nick or Ted was gone, whispering insults, scattering them like little poison roses.

"You made the right choice, girls," the man in the wig said. "Believe me."

Zoe was filled with gratitude and fear, a slippery respect. She'd seen drag queens in the bar before but it had never occurred to her that she was visible to them.

"My name is Trancas," Trancas said eagerly, "and this is my friend Zoe. What's your name?" Trancas wanted to live a bar life, to know all the drag queens by their names.

"Cassandra," the man said. "Charmed, I'm sure." Now that Nick or Ted had gone, Cassandra appeared to have lost interest. He glanced around, preparing to leave. He glittered in the heavy air like a school of fish.

"I like your earrings," Zoe said. One of Cassandra's earrings was a silver rocket ship, the other a copper moon with an irritable, unsettled face.

Trancas said, "Yeah, they're great."

Cassandra touched his earrings. "Oh, the rocket and the moon," he said. "Fabulous, aren't they? You want 'em?"

"Oh, no," Zoe said.

"I insist." Cassandra pulled the moon out of his ear. Its tiny copper face darkened in the bar light.

"No, really, please," Zoe said. "I couldn't."

"Is it a question of sanitation?" Cassandra asked.

"*No.* I just—"

"Let's split them," he said. "You take the moon, I'll keep the rocket." He dangled the moon, the size of a penny, before her face.

"Really?" Zoe said. "I mean, you don't know me."

"Honey," Cassandra told her, "I am a Christmas tree. I drop a little tinsel here, a little there. There is always, always more stuff. Trust me. It's a great big world and it is just *made* of stuff. Besides, I stole this trash, I can always steal more."

Zoe reached for the earring. Trancas helped her run the post through her earlobe. "This is a great little thing," Trancas said. "This is a treasure, here."

"Now we're earring sisters," Cassandra said. "Bound together for life."

"Thank you," Zoe said.

"You're welcome," Cassandra said. "Now excuse me, will you, girls?" He walked away, expert in his heels. His platinum wig sizzled with artificial light.

"Wow," Trancas said. "Now *that's* a character."

"I wonder if he saved our lives," Zoe said.

"Probably. He's our fairy fucking godmother, is what he is."

Trancas and Zoe went back to smoking dope on the sofa, but now only less could happen. They finished the joint and left the bar. They went to a few other places, smoked another joint, danced together and watched the men. When they got back to Trancas's apartment they found her mother snoring in front of the television. Zoe checked for the first stirrings of fire. Trancas put her finger to her mother's sleeping head. She said, "Bang." Her mother smiled over a dream, and did not awaken.

Momma said, "I wish you'd stay home this weekend. What's so endlessly fascinating about New York?"

"Trancas is lonely up there," Zoe said. "She needs me to come."

Momma wore red tennis shoes. She put her shadow over the tiny beans and lettuces, the darker, more confident unfurling of the squash. Momma stood in a swarm of little hungers. When the beans were ready she'd pull them off the vines, toss them in boiling water.

"Trancas," she said, "can probably manage on her own for a weekend or two."

"I miss her," Zoe said. "I'm lonely here, too."

She wore Cassandra's copper moon in her ear. She wore the clothes of her household life, patched jeans and a tie-dyed T-shirt. She squatted among the labeled rows, pulling weeds. The dirt threw up its own shade, something cool and slumbering it pulled from deep inside.

"Let her go, Mary," Poppa said. He carried a flat of marigolds so bright it seemed they must put out heat. Poppa himself had a hot brightness, a sorrow keen as fire.

"I just think it's getting to be a bit much," Momma said. "Every single weekend."

Poppa came and stood beside Zoe. He touched her hair. When they were in the garden together, he defended her right to do everything she wanted. Outside the garden, he lost track of her. His love still held but he couldn't hold on to the idea of her without a language of roots and topsoil; the shared, legible ambition to encourage growth.

"This is her best friend," he said. "And hey, it ain't like there's much happening here on Long Island on a Saturday night. Am I right, Zo?"

Zoe shrugged. There was a lot happening everywhere. But she had some kind of business in New York. She wasn't after fame and the victory of self-destruction like Trancas was. She wanted something else, something more like what Alice must have had after she'd gone to Wonderland and then returned to the world of gardens and schoolbooks and laundry on the line. She wanted to feel larger inside herself.

"Fine," Momma said, and her voice took on a gratified bitterness. She loved defeat with a sour, grudging appetite, the way she loved food. "Do whatever you like."

She went back into the house, stepping on the grass in red canvas shoes. Poppa stood over Zoe, still touching her hair with one hand and holding the flat of marigolds in the other. The smell of the flowers cascaded down, rank and sweet. Marigolds collapsed helplessly inside their own odor. They were just smell and color, no rude vegetable integrity.

"Let's get these planted," Poppa said tenderly. "And I'll take you to the twelve-thirty train."

"Thanks," she said. "I'm sorry I go away so much."

"It's okay," he told her, and she knew he was telling the truth. Susan's absence punched a hole in the house, and Billy's did, too. Susan took a piece of the future with her when she went; Billy took the mistakes of the past and made them permanent. Her own departure had a different kind of logic. It was part of her job to leave.

Sometimes Cassandra was in the bar. Sometimes he wasn't. Zoe found that she waited all week for the nights she went out to the bar with Trancas, and when Cassandra wasn't there Zoe felt dejected and diminished, as if a promise had not been kept. When Cassandra was there Zoe said hello to him with a swell of anxious hope, the way she'd speak to a boy she loved. Cassandra always said, 'Hello, honey,' and moved on. Zoe wasn't in love with Cassandra but she wanted something from him. She couldn't tell what it was.

Trancas started turning tricks to earn the money for a motorcycle. She told the first story as an accomplishment.

"I hung around in front of this theater on Forty-second," she said to Zoe in a coffee shop on Waverly. "I was so scared, I was like, what if nobody wants me? What if nobody even knows what I'm doing?"

Trancas's face was bright and homely, red with an exaltation that resembled rage. She dumped five spoonfuls of sugar into her coffee. She wore her gray denim jacket and a Grateful Dead T-shirt, a skeleton crowned with roses.

She said, "I told myself I'd stand there, like, fifteen minutes, and if nothing happened, I'd go home. So, like, about fourteen and a half minutes go by and suddenly this guy comes up to me, just a regular guy about fifty. He didn't look rich but he didn't look like a creep either, he was just all polyester, one of those *guys*, you know, just a guy, probably worked in an office and did something all day and then went home again. Anyway, he comes up to me and at first I thought, he's a friend of my father's. Then I thought, no, he's gonna tell me something like the bus stop is down at the corner or give me some kind of Jesus pamphlet or something. But no. He walks right up to me and says, 'Hi.' I say hello back, and he says, 'Can we make a deal?' And my heart is pounding and I'm so scared but my voice comes out like I've done this a thousand times before, like I'm an old hand at it. I look at him a minute and then I say, 'Maybe.' And it was *weird*, Zo. It was like I knew exactly what to do and what to say and how to be. He asks, 'What do you charge?' and I say, 'Depends on what you want.' I was so *cool*, I don't know where it came from."

"What did *he* say?" Zoe asked. She leaned forward over the scarred, speckled surface of the table. In the kitchen of the coffee shop, a man with an accent sang, "Hang down, Sloopy, Sloopy, hang down."

Trancas said, "He said, 'I want to get blown, and I want a little affection.' And you know what I said?"

"What?"

"I said, 'A blow job costs thirty dollars, and I don't do affection.' "

"I don't believe you."

"It's true. I was cool, Zo. I was playing a part and I was perfect at it."

"Then what happened?"

"He said, 'How's about twenty-five?' And I just *looked* at him, like, stop wasting my time, jerk. And he sort of laughed, this big old haw-haw-haw with his big teeth showing, and he said okay, thirty it is. Then I thought, shit, what happens now? Am I supposed to know a hotel for us to go to? But he said to come with him, and we went, like, a few blocks over to this hotel he was staying in, the Edison or something. Yeah, the Edison. And we went up to his room and I said, 'Before we go any farther, how about my thirty bucks?' He did that haw-haw-haw thing again, and he gave me the money. Man. His teeth were as big as dice. He didn't ask me any questions. He didn't even ask how old I was. He just took his clothes off and he wasn't a pretty sight but he wasn't the worst thing I've ever seen either and I took my clothes off and blew the motherfucker right there on the bed and then I put my clothes back on and got the hell out."

"That's it?" Zoe asked.

"That's it. Thirty bucks."

"You really did it?"

"Only way to get the money."

"Weren't you scared?"

"Zoe, I *told* you I was scared."

"I mean, of him."

"No. He was nothing to be scared of, you'd know that if you'd seen him."

Zoe sipped her coffee, looked out the steamed window at Waverly Place. An obese man walked a gleeful-looking yellow dog he had dressed in a white blouse and a plaid skirt. There was a new world with no rules and there was the old world with too many. She didn't know how to live in either place. Her mother was the guardian spirit of the old world. Her mother was proud and offended and she warned Zoe: Never let a boy talk you into losing control, boys want to ruin everything you prize.

Cassandra was the guardian spirit of the new world. He believed in sex but he believed in safety, too. He cautioned girls against going off with men who secretly worshipped harm.

Zoe said to Trancas, "I don't know if you should be doing this." Trancas's face held its rapt, furious light. She was already gone. "Thirty dollars, Zo," she said. "For, like, twenty minutes' work. Nine more guys, and I can get myself that Harley."

"It's prostitution, though."

"Man. So is being a waitress or secretary. This just pays better."

Zoe looked at Trancas and tried to know. Was she setting herself free, or was she beginning the long work of killing herself? How could you be sure of the difference between emancipation and suicide?

"If you're going to keep doing it, be careful," Zoe said.

"Right," Trancas answered, and Zoe could see her dead. She could see her blue-white skin and the faint smile she'd wear, having beaten her mother, having gotten first to the wildest, most remote place of all. Having won.

Cassandra stood at the bar that night in an old prom dress, a chaos of emerald satin and lime-green chiffon. Zoe waited until Trancas had gone to the bathroom and went quickly up to Cassandra. Cassandra held a drink in his hand, talked to a tall black man in a velvet cloak and a canary-colored pillbox hat.

Zoe said, "Hello, Cassandra."

Cassandra's face was clever and squashed-looking under his pancake makeup, his lipstick and eyelashes. Cosmetics and the intricate cross-purposes of being a man and being a woman seemed to impel him forward, and he could look, at times, as if he were pressing his face against a pane of glass, speaking distinctly and a little too loud to someone on the other side.

"Why, hello, baby," he said. "How are you?"

"I'm all right. Actually, I wondered if I could talk to you for a minute."

"Honey, you can talk all you want. Start at the beginning and just work your way straight through to the end."

"Maybe, alone? It will just take a minute."

"There's nothing in this world that could possibly shock Miss Cinnamon here," Cassandra said.

"You got that right," Miss Cinnamon said. A scrap of yellow veil quivered like insect wings over his shining brow.

Zoe paused nervously. "Well," she said. "You know Trancas, my friend?"

"Sure I do."

Zoe paused. She wanted to bury her face in Cassandra's gaudy dress, the slick, livid sheen of it. She wanted to sit on Cassandra's skinny lap, to whisper secrets in his ear and be told that a wicked and fabulous safety waited beyond the dangers of the ordinary world.

"Speak up, honey," Cassandra said. His voice was hard and sure as rain in a gutter.

Zoe said, "She's started turning tricks."

"Well, I'm sure that's very profitable."

Miss Cinnamon put a huge hand on Zoe's arm. "Does she have herself a can of Mace, honey?"

"I'm worried about her," Zoe said.

"She should carry Mace and a knife," Miss Cinnamon said. "She can get herself a cute little knife, it doesn't have to be any big old thing. She can slip it right down inside her boot."

"Why are you worried?" Cassandra asked.

"I'm afraid she'll get hurt."

"That's why you need Mace and a knife, honey. Listen to what I'm telling you."

"People do get hurt," Cassandra said. "Terrible things happen."

"I know," Zoe said.

"You girls are so *young*. Don't you have parents, or something? Who takes care of you?"

"Trancas and her mother live here in the city. I come up on weekends, I live with my family out on Long Island."

"Another planet," Cassandra said.

"Terrible things happen there, too," Zoe told her.

"Honey, I can imagine. Oh, look, here comes your friend."

Trancas was back from the bathroom. She saw Zoe talking to Cassandra and came over, full of her own greedy happiness, her love of trials and ruin. Zoe thought of her folding money into her pocket before sucking off a man with teeth the size of dice.

"Hey, Cassandra," Trancas said in her big-voiced, ranch-hand style. To Miss Cinnamon she added, "Great hat."

"Thank you, baby," Miss Cinnamon said demurely. Zoe saw that Miss Cinnamon had once been a little boy going to church with his mother. He had sat before an altar, under the suffering wooden eyes of Christ, as a chorus of velvets and brocades and crinolines sighed around him.

Cassandra said, "We were just discussing the ins and outs of the business."

Trancas glanced at Zoe. Trancas's face was clouded with embarrassment and a defiant anger that resembled pride but was not pride.

"Right," she said. "The business."

"My only advice to you, dear," Cassandra said, "is don't undersell. Not at your age. You could get twenty dollars for taking off your *shirt*, don't suck cock for less than fifty. If somebody tries to tell you he can get a blow job for half that much up the block, he's talking about getting it from some tired old thing who can barely walk unassisted and who needs her glasses to find a hard-on. Tell him to go right ahead and get himself a bargain, if that's what he's after. Now, if you're willing to fuck 'em, charge a hundred, at least. Don't flinch when you name your price. Don't bargain. And if you *do* fuck, make them all wear condoms. You don't know *where* some of those cocks have been."

"Okay," Trancas said.

"And, baby," Miss Cinnamon said, "I was telling your friend here, carry protection. You get yourself some Mace, and a pretty little knife you can slip down in your boot."

"Right," Trancas said.

"We're the voices of experience, dear," Cassandra said. "Listen to your aunts."

"Okay," Trancas said, and her face briefly shed its habitual expression of ardent mistrust.

They stood for a moment in silence, the four of them. Zoe was filled with a queasy mixture of love and fear unlike any emotion she could remember. She felt herself leaving her old life, the dinners and furniture, the calm green emptiness of the back yard. As a little girl she'd imagined living in the woods, but she knew she couldn't do that, not really. She couldn't build a nest in a tree, eat mushrooms and berries. Even if she'd had the courage to try it, someone would have come for her. She'd have been sent to one of the places that received girls who believed they could escape a life of rooms, and kept there until she'd renounced her wishes.

These were woods no one could stop her from living in. This was a destiny a girl was allowed to make for herself, this immense promiscuous city that harbored the strangest children.

She said to Cassandra, "Could I take you to tea sometime?"

Cassandra blinked, started to smile. "Excuse me? Tea?"

"Or, you know. A cup of coffee. I'd just like to talk to you. You're my aunt, right?"

Cassandra paused, considering. She smiled at Miss Cinnamon. Zoe felt as if she were talking to two wealthy, celebrated women. They had that private entitlement. They had that lofty, sneering grace.

"Tea," he said to Miss Cinnamon, and he pronounced the word as if it was both funny and frightening. Then he got a pen from the bartender and wrote his number on a napkin.

"You should know," he said as he handed the napkin to Zoe, "that your Aunt Cassandra will kill you if you ever, under any circumstances, call this number before three in the afternoon. Do you understand me?"

"Yes," Zoe said. "I understand."

Miss Cinnamon said, "There is nothing more evil than a drag queen getting woken up before she's ready. Believe me, baby, you don't want to mess with *that*."

1 9 7 2 / Will and Inez and Charlotte dropped acid together one last time, declared their devotion, and all went back to their parents' houses for the summer. When Will's parents picked him up at the train station in Garden City and took him home, he was surprised to see that the town looked both ridiculous and deeply familiar, familiar in an almost otherworldly sense. He might have been a hypnotist's subject on the verge of remembering a past life. He might have been traveling in another country where he knew supernaturally that the driver would take the next left turn, and that a gabled yellow house would appear from behind the scrubby blackness of a mulberry tree. He'd been prepared for his feeling of bored irritation at the sight of the unaltered lawns and the prim, prosperous houses. He'd imagined exactly his own sense of weightlessness as his father drove with both hands on the wheel and his mother talked about the new swimming trunks she'd bought for him on sale. What he hadn't expected was the sense of comfort, of almost surreal location. He'd never expected to feel, as his father's Buick turned the familiar corner, that he had in any sense come home. When he got out of the car he stood on the lawn staring at the house his father's money had built, grand in its suburban way, a big rambling folly with mansard roofs and bay windows, clean as bone in the summer light. There were no books inside, except the paperback bestsellers his mother read on summer vacations. There was no object, no dish or furnishing, older than Will. But there was familiar food. There was sanctuary. His father commanded the house from a position of profound and eternal ownership, and Will remained his father's servant in some way that was all the more powerful for being nameless.

"Penny for your thoughts," his mother said.

"Huh? Oh, sorry."

"I made chicken salad. Are you hungry?"

"I guess so. Sure."

"Come on in, then. It's so good to have you home."

He stayed less than two days. His flight was decided the first night. His father asked over dinner, "So, what do you think about a major?"

"I think I want to teach," Will said.

It was a lie. He was surprised to hear himself telling it. He didn't want to teach. Teaching was monotonous, thankless, underpaid. He wanted to study architecture. He wanted to build.

His mother, thinner and more prone to smiling silences than he remembered, ran her fingernail along the rim of her plate. Iridescent flecks, hard little rainbows of electric light, flashed and faded in the prismed chandelier.

"Teach," his father said. He pronounced the word with disdainful neutrality. He made a little brick of sound. Will's father had grown larger. His flesh had the puffed, padded quality of fat loaded onto a man born to be thin. Will suspected his father had gained precisely the amount of weight his mother had lost.

"Yeah. Teach."

Zoe sat across from Will in her carnival colors, her patchy hobogirl clothes and her tinkling gypsy jewelry. She smiled helplessly at him.

"Teach what?" his father asked.

"Kids," Will said. Everything he said surprised him. He'd declared English literature originally, then switched to linguistics, and had now more or less settled on taking the courses he would need to apply to architecture schools after he graduated. He'd signed up to study Palladio and Frank Lloyd Wright in the fall. He'd be learning about the conduction of electricity through a room. But he needed a different life to show his father. He needed a self that didn't touch him.

He said, "I think I'd like to teach the kids everybody's written off. Like, maybe work with Head Start."

"I think you'd be very good with children," his mother said. "You'd be a wonderful teacher."

"You need to go to Harvard for that?" his father said. "You could teach pickaninnies with two years of junior college."

"Don't use a word like that when I'm here," Will told him.

"Sorry. Nee-groes. Colored children. I don't get it. Where does the fancy education come in?"

"No, you answer one for me, Dad. Where does all this hate come from? What's the point? What does it get you?"

"Now, don't start, you two," his mother said. Her fingernail made its faint scratching, a clean dry sound, on the china.

"What hate?" his father said. "I don't hate anybody, unless they give me a reason to. What I want to know is, why are you going to Harvard, to goddamn *Harvard*, if all you want to do is teach Neee-gro children?"

"That's it," Will said. He took his napkin from his lap and threw it onto his plate. "Mom, dinner was delicious."

"Honey, you've hardly eaten anything."

"I've lost my appetite."

"Come on," his father said. "Don't be a prima donna. If you can't take a little straight talk, I don't know how you think you're gonna do in a classroom full of jungle bunnies."

Will stood. He looked down at his father, who sat surrounded by his wealth, chewing. His father wore green plaid pants. On the wallpaper, blue pagodas rose over country bridges and wading cranes. Will wanted only one thing—to be strange to his family. To disappear. For a moment he thought of looking calmly into his father's satisfied feeding and saying, 'I sleep with men.' He thought of kissing his father goodbye. He was filled with fury and shame and an uncertain desire that sizzled in his blood like a swarm of bees.

"Billy," his mother said. "Honey, sit down and finish your dinner."

Billy. At the sound of his old name, spoken in his mother's voice, Will left the room. He hadn't told them about his new name. He felt dizzy with his emotions. He heard his father say, "If you can't take a little frank talk, I wish you luck with the world." Will's stomach lurched. He wasn't ready to disappear, not yet. He still didn't know what was true about him, and if he said too much he could never come back.

Later that night, Zoe came to his room. She knocked so softly that he knew without having to ask. "Come in, Zo," he said. His father would have pounded. His mother would have rapped, courteous but firm and measured, the sound of a body of intentions steady as hail. Only Zoe conveyed the impression that she could be ignored.

She wore a torn orange T-shirt that advertised the Carlsbad Caverns, where she'd never been, and a gauzy skirt covered with red arabesques. A bell the size and shape of a woman's thumbnail hung from a black velvet ribbon she'd tied around her neck.

"Hi," she said.

"Come *in*, Zoe," he said. The room still held artifacts. A Dylan poster, foil stars pasted to the ceiling. "Come on, sit here on the bed with me."

He thought, briefly, of Cody, who claimed to see the light of human emanations. Sometimes Will believed he could see a faint light that hovered around Zoe, though it didn't resemble the electrified fields Cody described. It was barely visible, a phosphorescence, as if some ghost of Zoe occasionally rose a quarter inch off the surface of her skin. Will wasn't mystical. He never thought with any seriousness about tricks of vision. But right now he admitted to himself that sometimes, when he looked at Zoe quickly, he seemed to surprise a pale flickering light that skittered over her when no one watched.

She entered, smelling of patchouli, and sat on the edge of his bed. How had such a noisy, covetous family produced her?

"What's up?" he said. He touched the black tangle of her hair. Only for Zoe did he feel this painful affection. He loved others but Zoe was the one he worried over, the one who inspired his fear. She was precarious; she came and went.

"I'm glad you're home," she said. "I've been missing you."

"Zo, I won't make it through a whole summer here," Will said. "I think I'd better go back to Cambridge."

"Already?" she said.

"God, Zoe, what do you do to your hair? You don't have spiders or anything in here, do you?"

"It's so soon," she said. "You haven't seen Bix or Larry or anybody."

"Things'll get worse. Dad and I will be slugging it out in another few days. Remember last summer?"

"What would you do in Cambridge?" she said.

"I can find a job, I don't care what it is. You can always get a job if you don't care what you do."

"Couldn't you stay for a while? A week?"

"I think I'd better just go," he said. "I'm not even going to unpack."

"Please?"

"Come on."

She nodded. "I'm mostly being selfish," she said. "I'm afraid one day we'll just be, you know. Relatives."

"I'll always recognize you, Zo. I'll know you by your hair."

"I wish I could go, too," she said.

He took her hand. He wanted to say to her, I can't stay because I don't belong to the family anymore, but I can't find a way to leave it either. He wanted to tell her everything. But Zoe was still part of the house, and he needed this secret. He needed flight.

"You'll be gone soon enough," he said. "And you can come up and stay with me in Cambridge anytime, okay? I can always afford a train ticket for you. Okay?"

"Okay," she said.

"You want to smoke a joint?" he asked.

"Mm-hm."

He took a joint from his jacket pocket, lit it, and handed it to her. She inhaled, gave it back to him, brushed the hair out of her face, and something in the combined gestures showed him that she was grown. It had happened. She had a life of her own, a plan and a body of secrets. He watched her with a certain mute wonder. This, he realized, was where adults came from. They developed, suddenly, out of strange unhappy children like Zoe and himself. They would live into the next century.

"Zo?" he said.

"Mm-hm?"

"Nothing."

What had he wanted to tell her? That he loved her and feared for her, that he wanted to save her from pain. That he was turning into someone else and she was, too. They sat quietly together, passing the joint. The foil stars, glued to the ceiling when he was twelve years old, shed their tiny light.

1 9 7 3 / Constantine worked seed into the soil and the soil answered him with red-leaf lettuce, with the curl of string beans and the sexual heaviness of bell peppers. He and Zoe worked the garden together, and there were times. He might find a perfect crookneck squash, just the length of his ring finger, shimmering under a leaf, or Zoe might stand up in the afternoon light with her arms full of basil. There were times when he believed he had gotten where he'd wanted to go. But they passed. They always passed.

There used to be a tumble. There used to be a queasy brightness.

Now Mary wore gloves to bed at night; she arranged flowers on a little circle of pins. Susan had gone. She'd hardly glanced at him from under her veil as he'd led her down the aisle. She called sometimes, but she wasn't company anymore.

And what had happened to his son? At twenty, he was a boy with little round eyeglasses, the kind worn by bitter old maids. A boy whose hair touched his thin shoulders with a nervous dryness, like an old woman's curtains. Sitting up at Harvard, getting pious about the meek of the earth who in the whole of their lives never worked as hard as Constantine did in a single week. He could tell a few stories about disadvantages. Try coming to this country with no money, knowing no English beyond 'hello' and 'please.' From 'hello' and 'please,' how many men could build what he'd built? So you're black. I'm sorry. Now tell me your real story.

What had happened? Someone like Billy, a young man so well provided for, should be devouring the world. He should be striding through his life, able as a horse, smart as a wolf, squeezing the rich meek blood out of women's hearts. When Mary'd given birth to a son, Constantine had imagined himself taking handfuls of the future and stuffing them in his mouth. Daughters, even the best of them, disappeared into the lives of men. But a son carried you. His pleasures included you; you lived in your skin and you lived in his as well.

Maybe, Constantine thought, I made mistakes. He knew he suffered from fits of passion, a violent largeness that refused to live in the small. He had always numbered his passions among his virtues. He'd had every reason to believe a boy needs discipline the way a tree needs pruning. Constantine's own father had cracked Constantine's head open on the stove, had pulled his arm so hard it slipped from the socket as easily as a bean popping out of its skin. The punishments had cauterized Constantine's will, made him into someone. The punishments had invented him, a strong ambitious man who'd survived enough damage to live fearlessly. But he did not love his father. He'd taken his first chance, and crossed the ocean to make a self so big his father couldn't touch him. Could it be, was it possible, that Billy was doing the same thing? Could the hair and the beads be his idea of accomplishments strange enough to protect him from his father? *Life* magazine said it was the Age of Aquarius. *Life* showed pictures of men with hair to their shoulders, standing cheerfully beside women who didn't worry about the vows. These guys had sex whenever they wanted to, swam naked, claimed to have no plans beyond the trees and the water, the women and children in their beds. There was a new permission. There was a lewd world being born right here inside the old one, another country with its own customs and language. Now it seemed that Billy was going there, just as Constantine had left Greece and come to America. He couldn't tell whether he wanted to call his son back or be taken along. Constantine was a husband and father, a steady if less than ardent lover, a hardworking man. He didn't see himself anywhere in the pages of *Life*.

Her name was Magda, like one of the Gabor sisters. Constantine lost himself in her the way a coin gets lost through a storm drain. With Magda he felt himself falling and then shining up from the darkness, a prize, hidden and hard to reach. Magda was Hungarian, like the Gabor sisters, although her accent had been tamed and flattened by two decades in New Jersey. When he gave himself to her, when he inhabited her big white body, Constantine made the wild exultant sounds he'd always swallowed for Mary's benefit. At forty-one, Mary was an aging girl; Magda had been a woman most of her life. Constantine pushed hard into her big wet opening—she didn't want delicacy—and as he nailed her, as he thrust and thrust, her cries drowned his just as her body absorbed his own. She must have weighed a hundred and fifty pounds; he was only about one sixty-five himself. He hammered into her. He bit her breasts, pulled at her hair. She cried out, sometimes so loud she'd set his ears ringing, and afterward, when they lay sweating on the sheets, with the sound of a next-door radio leaking through the plaster, she'd put a pink-nailed hand on his chest and whisper, "Fantastic, baby. Fan fucking tastic."

The obviousness was part of what he loved. He was banging his partner's secretary in a motel room on his lunch hour. It was a tryst right out of the funny papers, and he felt as if he'd joined a club, a national fraternity with its own rites and history. He enjoyed not only the sex itself but the whole business of parking his Buick around the back, of picking up the key from a smirking old desk clerk with crusty eyes and a half-dozen long hairs cemented to his bald head. He loved the daytime crackle of the neon sign (red *Vacancy*, three pink arrows); he loved the two pictures of blue daisies, identical, screwed to the wall over each double bed. He loved the fact that, at the age of forty-six, he got a hard-on every time he heard Tom Jones or Engelbert Humperdinck on the radio. They were like his brothers, singing their songs of desire and loss out into a world big enough to contain every surprise.

Age of Aquarius. Goddamn right.

"You're too much, baby," Magda said, and the motel room seemed to agree with her. He was too much for this room, with its water-stained gypsum-board ceiling and matted shag carpet. He was too much for this woman, an overweight bleached blonde who shared a duplex with her mother and four cats. He patted her huge rippled flank, told her, "You're not bad yourself." His desire for her astonished him. His dreams had always been of beauty, and now he got hard sitting at his desk in the mornings with the radio on, thinking of a great spill of belly, an ass like two white pumpkins. *"It's not unusual to make love with anyone,"* Tom Jones sang. Sometimes, at work, Constantine ducked into the bathroom and whacked off, thinking of Magda, a boat of flesh. At forty-seven, he was horny as a fifteen-year-old. He could have been his own son, the son he'd wanted. He smiled at himself in the bathroom mirror, pumping his cock over the sink, due for a proper workout at the Mayflower Motel in another two hours. The surprises weren't over yet. Age was a sad fiction, a story for the weak.

His life with Mary receded, and he found that he could live more freely. Something softened. Something that had lived with him inside his skin, a prickly current of anger and disappointment, began to relax and in its place were only the hours, one and then another, work and a good hard fuck and more work and dinner and sleep. Mary lived her life alongside his. She tried new recipes (cheese fondue, quiche Lorraine), bought what she needed. As their battles and their love subsided, Constantine began to see a simplicity that had always been there, flowing under the daily strife. He began to see that it was enough to fuck and earn money, to talk on the phone to your beautiful daughter whenever she happened to call and to weed the garden with your youngest girl, to exclaim with her over the first radish. Try not to think too much about the boy. Constantine's lunch-hour sessions with Magda, who expected nothing of him beyond what he wanted to give her, seemed to have rescued him in some deep way he could not possibly have anticipated. He felt as if he were living a new and easier life, and all that remained of his old life, the single stubborn convention, was his habit of driving out to his houses at night to watch the inhabitants go about their ordinary business. He did it less often now, just once every couple of months. But still he went. Still he parked his car and listened, with a terrible yearning, as these mysterious men and women went about their nocturnal feedings and arguments, their lovemaking, their endless worrying about the fate they had made for their children. Still he sat in the silence of his Buick, smoking one cigarette after another, listening to the little neighborhood noises with the furious attention of a priest in the confessional, straining to hear the machinery of real good and evil humming under his parishoners' clumsy anecdotes about the failings of their flesh.

1 9 7 4 / Mary dressed in cream for the ceremony. She wore a cream-colored straw hat and a simple cream dress under a beige linen jacket. As she walked through the campus with her gloved hand on Constantine's elbow, as leaf shadows shifted on the grass around them, she knew she'd arrived at a moment that would hold for her, whatever else happened. Whatever mistakes she'd made, whatever humiliations suffered, she would always have this: herself walking beside her husband at Harvard as strange music drifted out of dormitory windows and children on their way to promising futures mugged for the cameras in cap and gown. She knew how her gold earrings gave back the light. From one of the windows, a pure tenor voice sang something about a wild world. Or a *wide* world.

"Quite a place," Constantine said.

"Mm-hm," she said, with a tick of annoyance. She didn't want to be appreciative. She wanted only to be with and of this place, to be exactly who she was right now, an attractive woman in a smart outfit come to see her son graduate from Harvard. Come to sit between her husband in a navy-blue suit and her daughter, the wife of a promising young Yale law student.

"I made the reservations for lunch," Constantine said. "At that place the Florios are so crazy about."

"Fine," she said. She didn't want a conversation. She didn't want to dwell on her fear that Paul and Liz Florio's idea of a good restaurant would be expensive but wrong, a flashy place with elaborate, bad food; a place other families told jokes about as they drove past on their way to restaurants Mary and Constantine couldn't know about. She'd asked Billy where they should go for lunch after the ceremony but Billy was acting strange these days. All he'd been willing to say was, "Please, let's not make a big deal out of this. Let's just get a hamburger someplace. I don't want a Hallmark card scenario, not with everything that's going down in the world." She hadn't known what to tell him, beyond the obvious: "You know, you're the first one in my family or your father's family to graduate from college. Ever."

"I know, Ma. I know."

Billy would be the only one. Susan was married and Zoe was Zoe. Constantine's people were still farmers in Greece, as far as anybody knew, and Mary's brothers' children would all be lucky to see thirty without doing time. She wanted to make Billy see that this ceremony was as important as a wedding or a funeral. Billy had lived his life under her protection. He couldn't imagine what he was escaping: all the long hopeless years, men crouched over rusty machines and women muttering into the soup. He didn't know how time hung in rooms. He believed life urged all its children toward good ends.

"One o'clock," Constantine said. "That's what you wanted, right?"

"Hmm?"

They turned into the Yard, where the commencement ceremony would be held. Rows of folding wooden chairs stood in mute, perfect order, and up ahead, on a platform, a suited man white-haired and hale as success itself discussed particulars of the microphone with a younger man in blue jeans.

"For lunch," Constantine said. "I made the reservation for one o'clock. That ought to give us plenty of time to find the place."

"Fine."

He sighed, and she could hear the phlegmy workings of his lungs. His body was prone to mucus; hers tended to parch. She believed that when they grew old, he'd be thick and viscous and hairy while she'd be thin and dry as a hickory stick. They'd grow deeper into their differences. She worried sometimes about growing old with Constantine but now, right now, she felt she was about to tear through her old caul of doubt into a solid, imperishable future that glittered among the leaves, that sparked and sang along the white drainpipes of these old brick buildings, where great men had once been young.

Constantine said, "We should get over to Billy's place."

"In a minute," she answered. "There's still time. I want to walk around the campus a little longer."

"Pretty, ain't it?" he said.

Mary's forehead burned and a thin film of perspiration popped out along her upper lip. She loved Constantine for everything he felt about Harvard, his pride in its shaded walks and broad stairs, but he was a man who said 'ain't.' He'd earned the money, and he'd stood beside her, and he loved her, in his way. But he would take them this afternoon to the Florios' restaurant, Chez Something-or-other.

"Let's go get Billy," she said abruptly.

"I thought you wanted to keep walking."

"We can't. I don't know what I was thinking about, we're late as it is."

As she would later tell her friends at home, the less said about Billy's apartment, the better. At first, she and Constantine believed they'd gotten the wrong address. The building looked as if it were about to emit one last dusty exhalation and tumble down into the weeds of its yard, leaving only a skeleton of rusty pipes and a crumbling chimney. Mary squinted at the slip of paper on which she'd written the address. "No, this is it," she said.

"Jesus Christ," Constantine said. "Wouldn't you know it."

"Please don't start," she said. "This is a happy day. There's no need to rain on anyone's parade."

He nodded grimly. "I hope it's safe in there," he said. He kept his hand on her elbow as they crossed over the rough boards of the porch and mounted a set of stairs that were not much more than kindling, each painted a different garish color. "Christ," Constantine muttered. The air was heavy with sweet, feral odors Mary couldn't name. Cats, certainly, and incense—she knew that smell from church. The building had the air of a deconsecrated chapel, a once-sanctified place given over to stray cats and the steady appetites of vermin. "Wouldn't you know," Constantine said, and Mary told him to hush.

When they knocked at the battered door Billy called, "It's open." They walked in and found him wearing patched jeans and a ragged flannel shirt, sitting with Zoe on a sofa that must have come straight from the junkyard. The apartment was, well, indescribable—it might have been the home of a lunatic, someone so lost to the fundamental principles of order and cleanliness that he'd drag any filthy piece of trash up from the street and display it proudly. As Mary and Constantine stepped inside she involuntarily touched one of her earrings with her fingertips.

"Hey, folks," Billy said. "Welcome to the House of Usher."

"Christ, will you look at this dump," Constantine said. He managed a growlish laugh and Mary thought, Fine, they can get through it with banter. They can make this into a rough masculine joke.

"I call it home," Billy said.

"It's sure colorful." Mary smiled. To Constantine she added, "I like it. It's fun."

Again, her emotions rose in such confusion that she felt the moisture break out along her upper lip. She wanted to defend Billy from his father. She wanted to stand next to Constantine and demand to know who Billy had turned himself into. How had he gotten so lost? Her lungs clenched up and she struggled for a breath.

"Goddamn rat's nest," Constantine said. The grudging humor still hadn't left his voice. Please, Mary said silently. "What're you now," he asked, "some kind of beatnik?"

"That's it, Dad," Billy said. "Once again, you've hit the nail right on the head. I am, in fact, a beatnik. You've gone straight to the heart of the matter."

"Now listen here, friend—"

"Come on, guys," Mary said, though she could barely speak for lack of wind. The invisible metal bands pressed on her lungs and seemed to tighten another notch with every breath she accomplished. "It's a happy day, we don't want to fight."

Billy and Zoe sat together on the sofa, which looked as if it might be infested with something that would get into their hair. Mary shuddered, and pulled in a breath. She saw, suddenly, that Billy's and Zoe's hobo clothes—the costumes she'd considered foolish but harmless—were part of a larger perversity. There they sat, her son and daughter, heir and heiress to centuries of daily struggle, the recitation of prayers for luck and better weather, the husbanding of funds. There they sat in rags, hair unkempt, slumped like the poorest of white trash on a piece of furniture that had been dowdy and threadbare even when new. Mary's drunken father had had more pride. Her Sicilian grandmother, too poor to buy drinking glasses, had kept her jelly jars in immaculate rows. For the first time in her life, Mary knew her son as a stranger. As someone who might do anything, whose head was full of thoughts and desires she couldn't imagine.

"Right," Constantine said. He raised his arm and looked at his watch. The dark blue wool blend of his jacket, the crisp white line of his shirtsleeve, drew back to reveal his Rolex in all its placid certainty. At the sight of her husband's watch Mary briefly imagined him and her son as officers in two hostile factions: one strong and wealthy, armed with tanks; the other nimble and wily, anarchic, armed with little darts tipped in unknown poisons.

"Better get your cap and gown," Constantine said. "We've got to swing by the hotel and pick Susan up on our way."

Billy said, "I'm not wearing a cap and gown."

"Huh?"

"I'm not wearing a cap and gown. I'm willing to go through commencement and everything, the works. But I'm not wearing the monkey suit."

"Don't be stupid," Constantine said. "C'mon, go get it, we're gonna be late."

"There's nothing for me to get," Billy said. "I didn't order a cap and gown."

"Oh, Billy," Mary said.

Constantine swallowed. Mary could hear the juice of him, the thick angry inner workings. She wanted only to lie down somewhere clean and safe until she could catch her breath.

Constantine said, "So. You want to go to commencement in your beatnik suit? You want to just stroll in there looking like a deadbeat?"

"I want to go in my own clothes," Billy said. "Why should it be a big deal?"

"You've gotta be different, don't you?" Constantine said. "You've got to stand out."

"Hey, guys," Mary said, but she knew her voice was barely audible.

"Look," Billy said, "I've got friends who are laughing at me for even *doing* this. Sitting there listening to speeches about this grand old institution, brought to us by the folks who helped invent napalm.

You know what napalm does? It's like fire that sticks to you. It eats right down to the bone."

"I don't know what you're talking about," Constantine said. "What does that have to do with anything?"

"Harvard has big research contracts with the government," Billy said. "Did you notice how nice the campus is, how well maintained? Where do you think all that money comes from? Tuition? Sweatshirt sales?"

"Mister, I could tell *you* a few things about where money comes from—"

"Guys," Mary said. "Come on. Susan's waiting for us."

"Dad, I'm happy you and Mom are here," Billy said. "I'm very pleased we can share all this. But there are limits. Get my drift?"

"I don't know what you're talking—"

"It's my show. It's my life. And I won't wear the goddamned suit."

"Right," Constantine said. "It's got to be your way, huh? You don't care that your mother and Zoe and Susan and I drove all the way up here."

"No. I do care. I honestly thank you for driving all the way here to my graduation. Which I'm attending for your benefit. In my own clothes."

"Forget it, then," Constantine said. "Don't do anything for our benefit. Don't strain yourself."

Billy shook his head. Mary felt herself beginning to cry. She watched through a hot film of tears as Billy stood and said, "There are two ways to do things, aren't there, Dad? Your way and the wrong way. We've got to take advantage of all the photo opportunities in Harvard Yard, and then after the ceremony we've got to get into the car and drive to some horrible fancy French restaurant. You're not here to see me graduate. You're here to see the son you *want* graduate. I've got news for you. They're two different people."

"Nice speech," Constantine said. "Very nice. Where's your goddamned *heart*, mister? You know what you're doing to your mother here?"

"Mom and I can talk about whatever it is I'm doing to Mom. This is about you and me. Right? You want to come up to Harvard like a big cheese and pose for pictures with a guy in a cap and gown. Listen, I can set you up with half a dozen guys. Big strapping guys, short hair, on their way to law school or business school. I've got connections, bring your camera and we can go straight to the Yard—"

"Shut up," Constantine shouted. "You shut up, mister." His face was dark, his arms rigid at his sides. Mary knew that in another second, with another quarter ounce of provocation, he'd lunge.

"Oh, Con, Billy, please," she whispered.

"Mom doesn't care what I graduate in. Do you, Mom?"

"I don't know," she said. "I just—please. Don't fight."

"Don't do this to her," Constantine said. "Don't you dare."

Billy nodded. "This was a mistake," he said softly. "Mom, Dad, I'm sorry you came all the way up here for nothing." He stepped carefully around his father and walked to the door.

"Where do you think you're going?" Constantine demanded.

"For a walk. Maybe I'll go to the movies later. What do you say, Zo? Want to come? *Midnight Cowboy* is playing at the Orson Welles."

Zoe blinked, as if she herself had forgotten she was present. Mary thought, Everything has failed. All the effort, all the love, the careful stitching of the days, has added up to nothing.

Zoe said, "I can't. I'm sorry. I've got to stay with Mary and Constantine."

She had begun to insist on calling them by their Christian names. No discipline or persuasion would stop her.

"Okay," Billy said. "See you."

He left. The door clicked shut behind him. Mary thought Constantine would run after him but he didn't move. No one moved.

"Unbelievable," Constantine said. "*Un*believable."

Tears were running down Mary's face now, hot heavy ones that ran to her jawline. She took a handkerchief from her pocketbook. "What do we do now?" she said in a small voice.

"We're going to the goddamn commencement ceremony, is what," Constantine told her. "Come on. We got to get Susan from the hotel, she's waiting for us."

No one moved. Zoe remained on the sofa, looking down at her shoes, and Mary had all she could do to keep from striding over to Zoe and screaming, What's wrong with you? What's going on?

"Come *on*," Constantine said.

"Con."

"Nothing. Not another word. Susie's waiting for us. We're on our way."

"I've got to use the ladies' room," Mary said.

"You okay?"

"I'm fine. Just wait for me a minute, all right?"

She crossed the living room and walked down the hallway. She passed an untidy yellow-tiled kitchen, a closed door, another closed door. She didn't need to use the bathroom; she needed to be alone, if only for a minute or two. She needed to concentrate on filling her lungs with air. When she found the bathroom she locked the door and took a pill from her purse. She swallowed the pill and stood for a while at the sink, breathing. In the sink lay a long dark hair, curled like a question mark. There was a spotted mirror; there was a ceramic cup that contained three toothbrushes, Billy's and those of his two roommates, whom she'd never met. Mary didn't know which toothbrush was Billy's. The yellow, squashed-looking one? The newer one, stubbier, bright green, with bristles stiff as a hairbrush? The clear one with a little half-moon of toothpaste stuck to its lip? None of them spoke obviously of her son, and none was unquestionably alien. She saw, suddenly, how entirely she'd lost track. Her own life, the rhythms of the house, its maintenance and upkeep, had seemed so real, so quintessential, that lives lived else-where, even the lives of her children, had taken place along the margins, in a realm singular and immutable as a photograph. Al-though she thought of Billy constantly she thought of him in faintly abstract terms, the way she'd think of a character in a television show when the show wasn't on. But here was this bathroom, with its sour mildewed smell floating under a scrim of chlorine. Here were these toothbrushes. Looking at them, she was stricken by a wave of anxiety so powerful she had to sit on the edge of the bathtub and lean forward until her forehead nearly brushed her knees. Breathe, she told herself. Relax. Let the air in. It seemed no time at all had passed before she heard Constantine knocking at the door, demanding to know if she was all right. "Fine," she called cheerfully. She reached over and flushed the toilet. As she stood she was taken by an impulse to slip the toothbrushes, all three of them, into her handbag, so that she could examine them later and try to sort out which one belonged to her son. But that would be crazy. Everyone would know who'd done it. Constantine knocked again.

"Mary? I'm coming in."

"*Don't*," she said, too sharply. She added, in a softer voice, "I'm fine. Really."

She took one last breath. Then, before opening the door, she took a faded pink washcloth from the towel rack and put it quickly, almost thoughtlessly, into her bag.

When Susan heard they were going to the ceremony without Billy she said, "Well, really, what's the point?" She wore a green A-line dress covered with white flowers. It was shorter than Mary would have liked, but, otherwise, Susan was impeccable. Her lips were glossily pink, her hair fell only to her shoulders. She looked straight at Constantine when she spoke. The hotel room, like Susan herself, gleamed with cleanliness and rectitude.

"We're going," Constantine told her. "Come on."

"That's silly," Susan said. "If Billy's being a brat, let him be a brat. There's no reason for us to sit through commencement with a bunch of strangers."

Mary couldn't help marveling at her elder daughter's fearless shoulders, her staunch certainty, the crispness of her dress. She knew to call Billy a brat. She knew the word that would render his bad behavior small and transitory. Mary couldn't imagine why she so often felt irritated with Susan for no reason, and why Billy, the least respectful of her children, the most destructive, inspired in her only a dull ache that seemed to arise, somehow, from her own embarrassment.

"*I'm* going," Constantine said. "The rest of you can do whatever you want."

Susan looked at Mary, who offered a wan smile. Susan shrugged dismissively. Mary knew the gesture: Forget about Momma, she'll do whatever's easiest. Mary's face burned but she knew that if she spoke, if she said one word, she'd start crying again and this time she might not be able to stop. She hated her family, every one of them. No one had any idea what it felt like inside her skin, this tightrope sensation, the terrible hunger for air.

"All right, fine," Susan said. "Let's go to Billy's commencement without Billy. Todd went to see an old friend of his, he's going to meet us there."

They went to the commencement ceremony. They took seats toward the rear of the field of wooden chairs. Now that she was here, among the mothers in pastel dresses and the fathers in dark suits, Mary felt a sense of foolishness that turned quickly to rage. Billy had made them look like idiots. He'd humiliated them in front of all these people; these men with hearty, successful faces and these cool, talkative women with lacquered fingernails. Mary's irritation at Susan vanished and was replaced by a skittish gratitude. She felt grateful to Susan, who sat on her left, and to Todd, sitting beside Susan, handsome and grave in a suit the same inky blue as Constantine's. Mary touched her earring, shifted her weight toward Constantine, who sat in a cold fury to her right. She tried not to let her irritation turn itself on Zoe, sitting beside Constantine in her baggy muslin dress, her disordered hair, and the old-fashioned lace-up shoes she'd insisted on. Zoe had taken to dressing like a figure in a daguerreotype, one of the frizzy-haired women who stared out of old brown-and-white pictures with harsh-eyed solemnity, who looked stolid and afraid and insanely formal and who were, by now, all dead.

"I think Billy's going to show up," Mary whispered to Susan. "I think he's bluffing."

"Don't hold your breath," Susan answered. "He's got all of you-know-who's stubbornness."

Mary nodded knowingly, although she seldom thought of her husband and son as resembling each other in any respect. They inhabited different spheres of air, subscribed to different systems of logic.

"I still think he'll show up," she said. "Why on earth would he want to miss his own graduation, after all that work?"

"Well, don't hold your breath."

Mary wondered, briefly, with a flush of fear, whether Susan had guessed about her breathing trouble. No, it was only a figure of speech. She laid her hand, gently, on the taut stockinged curve of her daughter's knee.

The ceremony began. It was all speeches, delivered in voices rendered deep and hollow by loudspeakers mounted in the trees. Mary didn't listen. To distract herself, she picked out a boy sitting toward the front, in the students' section. He looked a little like Billy—he had the thin, broad shoulders that made Mary think of wings, and he had the wide jaw that seemed slightly too large and heavy for his thin, graceful neck. This boy's hair, though, was neatly trimmed, and he was, well, present. She wondered who his parents might be. Directly in front of her sat a man who looked too old to have a son graduating from college but who was clearly married to a much younger woman, one of those round-faced, tiny-featured women who were touted as beauties though they were not in fact particularly beautiful. They were simply the daughters of wealthy families powerful enough to demand that the concept of beauty be expanded to include them. A knot of envy and admiration formed in Mary's stomach, like wet fabric bunching up. Their son was probably the product of the old man's second marriage, and Mary thought she could imagine the embattled, aging woman (was she barren? was she poor?) who had been set aside for this gunmetal blonde with her pert chin and her fertility, her miniature nose and her trust fund. Mary looked from the couple in front of her to the boy who resembled Billy. She watched him whisper to the boy who sat beside him as a deep male voice crackled from the loudspeakers, saying something about the long but rewarding work that lay ahead.

When Mary and her family filed out with the others after the ceremony, she tried to locate the boy who resembled Billy.

"I can't believe we did that," Susan said. "I can't believe I've just spent two hours of my life this way."

Todd held her hand and managed to arrange his face in a way that was at once optimistic and sympathetic. Zoe moved inside her shapeless dress, thinking whatever it was she thought.

"Billy's a rebel," Todd said. "It takes all kinds."

"Okay, everybody," Constantine said. "We've got about a half hour to kill. I made our lunch reservations for one."

"We're going to go all the way with this, aren't we?" Susan said.

"You want us to not eat because your brother's got a wild hair up his ass? Should we skip lunch because of that?"

"Oh, no," Susan said. "Absolutely not."

As they left the Yard, Mary touched Susan's arm and said, "Thanks for being a good sport."

"Don't thank me," she said. Mary was surprised by the tone of reproach in her voice. Her daughter's hatred still surprised her, after all these years. She wanted, as always, to put her hands on Susan's shoulders and say, 'How can you dislike me, when I'm the one who suffers?'

"I don't know what I'm going to do with these two," she said, and she liked the lightness she was able to put into her voice, the chipper quality. Better days would come.

"What can you do?" Susan said. "What could you possibly do?"

"Well, nothing, I suppose. Billy will come around. Hey, is everything okay with you?"

"Everything's fine, Momma. Everything's perfectly fine."

Susan walked away, said something inaudible to Todd. Mary and her family made their way toward the Square amid the knots of graduates and their parents. All around them, young men and women whooped and embraced one another as their robes flashed darkly in the simple, shadowless light of early summer. Someone opened a bottle of champagne. A half moon had risen over the library roof. When they passed through the gateway and reached the street Mary saw the boy again, getting into a car with his parents (ordinary-looking people) and a pretty blond girl in a white dress. The girl squeezed the boy's hand, and his father, one arm draped easily over the shoulders of his pink-skinned wife, said something that made the rest of them laugh. Mary watched them drive away. She couldn't help wondering where they were going, what they'd eat that night, how they'd talk to one another, where they'd go after that. Casually, as if reaching for a tissue or a mint, she slipped her hand into her bag and touched the washcloth she'd taken from Billy's apartment.

1 9 7 5 / Susan awoke one night and knew, suddenly and completely, that she and Todd would not have a baby
together. It had simply refused to happen. Waiting to have the baby
had been her occupation; it had explained her. Now she would
need to do something else. Todd slept beside her, one strong arm
thrown over his face. She got up out of bed and went into the
bathroom for a glass of water. Her flannel nightgown touched her
as she moved. She was aware of herself in these dark rooms, a faint
blue shape among the squat blacknesses of bed, lamp, bureau.

She went into the bathroom, filled a glass from the tap, and
took it back into the bedroom. The air was full of Todd's breathing,
the sound of his easy, rhythmic little snores. Asleep, Todd reminded
her of a submarine. He churned steadily through the hours of his
slumber, and the sounds he made—the nasal rasp, the sporadic
murmurs—implied a certain blind progress, guided by sonar waves
that bounced invisibly off coral reefs and submerged mountain
ranges. Even in sleep, he was going somewhere. He was moving
steadily toward morning, when he would wake and rise eagerly to
the resumption of his work.

Susan sipped her water and walked to the window, parted the curtains. Behind the curtains was a layer of cold air, trapped between the glass and the fabric, and when the cold touched her face she thought, briefly, that something alive was flying out at her. The New Haven street was quiet under the thin orange haze of the streetlights. There was the world of sleep and purpose, the unlit windows of people like Todd and herself, who were having their portion of rest before the new day arrived with its endless accomplishments. She thought sometimes, with a sense of wonder, that right here on this street lived people who would help reshape the world. They'd be the scientists and politicians; they'd find the cures and draft the laws. She touched the rim of the glass to her chin. Outside, a cat slunk along the sidewalk, racing over its own shadow. She followed the cat with her eyes and when it darted under the lilac bush she thought she saw a figure standing behind the bush. He was looking up at the window, at her. He had her father's heavy shoulders, her father's wounded, pugilistic stance, and she was overcome with dread, with a conviction that everything, everything she wanted would now be taken from her. Then she blinked, and saw that it was only a trick of the bare branches, a confluence of shadows. Nothing really happened, she reminded herself. Kisses, it never went any farther than that. She closed the curtains firmly, as she would close a drawer. She waited until she felt calm again.

1 9 7 6 / Cassandra called her her daughter. Cassandra had business of her own but she kept track the way a mother does. Zoe had other friends, an apartment, a job that more or less covered the rent. She had lovers. Her life was full of facts and they all commanded her daily attention with more weight and urgency than Cassandra exerted from her cynical private religion based on clothes and men and on the love of surprise and the conviction that surprise was impossible. Cassandra lived in the mirror. She lived in bars (Zoe had learned to think of Cassandra as "she"). Still, she claimed she had adopted Zoe. She performed a mother's rituals of praise and complaint. At the bar, she picked out men for Zoe. "That one there, honey," she'd whisper, pointing a long finger. "He says he's gay but he's been known to do a girl or two and I have it on the best authority that he's got the dick of death between those scrawny legs."

Cassandra instructed Zoe on the particulars of giving blow jobs. She sewed clothes for her, urged her to tame her hair.

"Wild is one thing," she said. "Medusa is something else. You're scaring men off with that jungle do. Why don't you let me give it a cream rinse and a little trim, just to see if we can get it to move in a windstorm?"

But Zoe didn't want her hair to change. Something resided there, something heavy and tangled she wanted to keep.

She had rented an apartment with Trancas when they grad-uated from high school but now Trancas was gone and Zoe lived with her friends Ford and Sharon in a fourth-floor walk-up on East Third Street, across from the Hell's Angels' headquarters. Trancas was in Oregon, in love with three women at once. Zoe worked in a secondhand clothing store on MacDougal Street. She smoked joints in the cramped little office at the back of the store, helped strangers decide whether or not to buy old party dresses, silk shawls, Hawaiian shirts. The musk of the used clothes seeped into her skin and she took hot baths at night, dabbed herself with grass oil in an effort to feel new again. At home she smoked more joints and drank wine with Sharon, who worked as a waitress, and Ford, who played guitar on the streets. She hung bad portraits of strangers on the walls of her bedroom, covered the lamp with colored scarves. She lived in New York like Alice, thinking someday she'd go back to the other world. Gardens, schoolbooks, wash on a line. For now there were her sweet-tempered friends and her undemanding job, cash paid off the books. There was sex with men who could turn out to be anybody. There was acid in Central Park; there were syringes full of crystal meth that made her slip through the hours like thread slipping through the eye of a needle. She'd learn what she could. As a young girl she'd lived in her parents' house and watched the daughters and sons of the old era dancing on television, dressed in discarded clothes and pieces of the flag, with flowers twisted into their hair. By the time she was grown a kind of promise had already faded, a lost, light-headed belief that humans could live innocently among the animals. Zoe mourned and did not mourn the passing of the old future. She had too much desire in her, too many electrical circuits snapping, to want a life growing dope and feeding chickens and goats. She wanted the true dangers of the forest; pastures and barnyards were too much like houses.

Cassandra called when she thought about it. Sometimes she came over. She didn't do drag in daylight. She came in her ordinary skinniness, her thin red hair. She wore loose khaki pants, big shirts, sometimes a bracelet or two.

"So, what's the dish, honey?" she said, sipping coffee at the kitchen table. In men's clothes she looked more feminine. In dresses and wigs she looked like a man in a dress and a wig.

"I met somebody new," Zoe said. She tried always to have a story or two.

"Do tell." Cassandra sat with her sharp elbows on the tabletop, looking over the rim of her coffee cup like somebody's shrewd wife.

"Well, I met him in Tompkins Square Park," Zoe said. "I was smoking a little hash by the band shell, and he was throwing a Frisbee to a dog."

"Men with dogs," Cassandra said, "are generally trustworthy, but no great shakes in bed."

"The dog came up to me, she was a nice dog, just a mutt, and I petted her and this guy and I started talking."

"And what was he like?"

"Sweet. Sort of untouched. He said 'Wow.' "

"Only that?"

"No. He said things like, 'Wow, are you smoking hash right out here in the open?' and 'Wow, that's a cool necklace you're wearing.' He was like a ten-year-old boy who'd turned twenty-five, you know what I mean?"

"Oh, I recognize the type from a distance. They don't come within fifty yards of nasty old drag queens."

"We smoked what was in the pipe, and then we both started throwing the Frisbee for the dog."

"Better go straight to the sex, this is getting boring."

"We got all sweaty, he took off his shirt."

"And revealed what?" Cassandra said.

"A nice body. Skinny. Sort of a boy's body, with tiny little nipples. But I liked it. I don't need muscles."

"You straight girls are a marvel. No wonder you all get married. It's only *men* who disappear up their own assholes searching for perfection, isn't it?"

"I don't know," Zoe said. "I wouldn't marry this guy."

"Never mind about that. Did you bring him home?"

"Mm-hm. I told him I lived right around the corner, he could take a shower at my place if he wanted to."

"Good girl," Cassandra said. "Like a lion bringing down a gazelle."

"I'm a slut," Zoe said. "What can I say?"

"So you got him home."

"Mm-hm. And he took a shower, and you know. There we were."

"What did he do with the *dog*, for god's sake?"

"I gave her a bowl of water, and she just lay down in the living room. She was a good dog."

"And how was the sex?" Cassandra said. "Tell Momma."

"Nice. Well, he was fast. He was too fast for me. But sweet. He fell right to sleep after, he rolled off of me and I think he was asleep before he hit the mattress."

"Just as I told you," Cassandra said. "Men with dogs."

Cassandra worked as a seamstress, and she performed in plays put on in basement clubs. She wasn't the star. She played hand-maidens and slave girls, or the heroine's best friend. Zoe always went to see her. In *Bluebeard* Cassandra played the doomed wife, standing outside a painted cardboard door and saying, "Oh, my master hath warned me never to trespass upon the sanctity and privation of this, his most inner chamber, but I've just *got* to know what's in there." In *Anna Karenina, or, Night Train* she was part of a chorus that sang "Can't Stop Loving That Man of Mine." In *Secrets of the Chun King Empire* she entered in a kimono and said, "The emperor has chosen Wing Li to be his concubine and the mother of his heir, to ascend with him to the realm of tranquillity that lies beyond the Blue Mountains, so all the rest of you girls can just get your butts on out of here."

Zoe always applauded with pride and a lurking, stinging embarrassment. She loved Cassandra. She was vaguely burdened by her. She felt herself to be increased and diminished because Cassandra carried around the idea of her, Zoe, a girl who had set herself free. A girl who wasn't nice or ordinary. Sometimes she could be that girl. Sometimes she wanted only to sleep in a small white bedroom while Cassandra and the other Zoe walked through the streets glittering with all they wanted.

After her performances Cassandra would come out and have a drink with Zoe. The clubs were black as ice, full of ancient smells, a rot Zoe recognized from the bins of unwashed clothes kept at the back of the store. Cassandra introduced Zoe around. "This is my girl here, yes, ladies, the one hundred percent real thing. She's my protégée, isn't she gorgeous?"

People agreed that she was gorgeous. Who knew what they thought? Zoe sat on a barstool in her dark clothes, the black distance of the kohl she'd started wearing on her eyes. She sipped a beer and listened to them talk. The men in dresses didn't need conversation. They were a performance, they only needed her to watch.

"You know what I envy? Those little feet. Imagine being able to walk into a store and just buy any pair of shoes that caught your fancy."

"Frankly, darling, I can think of nothing more depressing. It's so easy, any fool can walk into a store. What I love is the challenge. Finding a pair of pretty pumps in a size thirteen, now that's an accomplishment a girl can take pride in."

"Uh-huh. Didn't I see that pair you got on hanging from a pole over the shoe-repair shop last week?"

"Look who's talking. Honey, the police are *still* trying to figure out who took that pair of canoes out of the lake in Central Park, but my lips are *sealed*."

Cassandra and her friends didn't need Zoe for long. She said good night, left them talking and laughing together at the bar. Cassandra usually walked her to the door.

"Thanks for coming, angel."

"It was a good show, Cassandra."

"Well, there's a reason they call it the big time, and there's a reason most people aren't in it. Call me."

"All right."

"Not too early."

"Never."

When Cassandra came in the afternoons, in pants and a T-shirt, she sat at Zoe's kitchen table picking up crumbs with her fingertip. She said, "You kids should clean up a little more, you'll have this place crawling with roaches."

Sometimes Zoe thought she should have a plan. She should have an ambition, so that if somebody asked her, 'What are you doing?' she could have given a better answer than 'I'm doing opium suppositories,' or 'I'm doing the bass player on the fifth floor.' Her most conspicuous talent was for being, and sometimes she thought that was enough. Sometimes she thought, I'm a witness. I'm here to watch things happen.

When she turned twenty-one she quit the used-clothing store and got a better-paying job as a cocktail waitress. She fell in love with one of the bartenders, a beautiful, edgy man whose hair had been gray since childhood. She moved out of the apartment on East Third to live with him in his loft in SoHo, then moved back again after he slugged her in a transport of jealousy. She got a job in another bar, worked until until four in the morning, slept until twelve or one the following afternoon. She watched soap operas with Ford and Sharon, took up smoking and stopped again. She fell into and out of love with a firm-tempered, quiet woman named Brenda, who read tarot cards and earned her living as a lighting technician on Broadway.

Sometimes Zoe didn't hear from Cassandra for months. Sometimes Cassandra called five times a week. Sometimes—not often—she came to the apartment and stayed all afternoon.

She said, "I like knowing someone as young as you. I like it that you're not fabulous."

"I'm fabulous enough for my own purposes," Zoe said.

"I mean *fab*ulous, honey, the kind of fabulous that can quote from every movie Ida Lupino ever made. I can dish the dirt with the rest of the girls but frankly, dear, it's a little like speaking in French. It's not my native tongue no matter how fluent I may have become. It's nice to just come over here sometimes and sit around playing Scrabble."

Cassandra and Zoe had taken to playing Scrabble every time they were together. Cassandra always won.

"I like it, too," Zoe said.

"My little girl, oh, the daughter I never had. Now tell me, angel, are you fucking anybody new?"

1 9 7 7 /   Mary knew. She knew by the smells he brought home with him, by the tunes he hummed. Constantine wore the woman on his face. The fact itself didn't surprise her. Men strayed, they were driven by appetites. She'd been educated as a little girl, and she'd never let sentiment pass for thought. What surprised her was not the fact but her own sense of distance and even, on certain exhausted nights, of relief. Constantine was unfaithful to her, and it made sense. She was far from a perfect wife, though she'd set out to be one. She'd suffered over the birthday cakes, cleaned everything, sewn flawless hems. But years went by and she never picked up the habit of desire. She was cool and reluctant in bed. She stole, and could not seem to stop. She failed to befriend the prominent women, to become their intimate, though she served on endless committees. If Constantine had something going, if he'd found a way to crush his yearnings the way other men stepped outside for a cigarette, it was all right with her. She knew, with rock-hard certainty, that he wasn't in love. The smug, self-satisfied limits of his affection clung to him like the woman's perfume. It was Constantine's nature to build, to acquire, and he might add a woman or two to his life but he would never voluntarily relinquish any of his holdings. He wouldn't sacrifice the prickly friendship he and Mary had found, the comforts of the home they'd built. So she went along. She disliked pretending ignorance. She could feel so stupid, so underestimated. Still, it seemed a small enough price. She couldn't live inside an arrangement. She couldn't water her ivy or try new recipes as a woman who openly consented to her husband's infidelity. But she could keep a secret.

She kept the secret for nearly a year, and might have kept it much longer, but one day in the middle of a heat wave unprecedented since the turn of the century she stopped by Constantine's office on her way to the grocery store to drop off a contract he'd forgotten at home. She rarely went to his office. She had no business there. It was not the kind of place wives were meant to visit. It had no amenities, no magazines or comfortable chairs, and the bathroom, a communal one down the hall to which one carried the key on an oversized brass ring, was unspeakable. If Constantine and his partner were ruthless in the economies they applied to the houses they built, they were, at least, similarly severe about their own professional comforts. Their offices, on the third floor of a vaguely Tudor-style commercial building, were sheathed in Masonite paneling and furnished, haphazardly, with imitation-wood desks and green Leatherette chairs. Mary disliked entering the office at all. Its cheapness made her uneasy, and on the rare occasions when she was forced to go there she felt for some time afterward edgy and insecure, as if she'd caught a glimpse of termites browsing the foundations of her house.

Still, the contract was needed, and so she went to the office just before ten on a scorching morning, dressed in a beige linen skirt and an eggshell-colored silk blouse. She found Constantine at his desk, looking so hectic and overworked, so much like the living embodiment of those conditions, she suspected that upon hearing the outer door opening he had picked up the phone, lit all three hold buttons, and begun scribbling nonsense words on a yellow legal tablet. She thought it might be a public-relations gesture, a protocol designed to seduce creditors and investors alike, and as soon as he saw her he'd relax, hang up the telephone, sit back in the big wheeled chair that produced a harsh, serrated sound whenever it moved over the clear plastic panel Constantine kept on the floor behind his desk to protect the carpet.

But he kept talking. "—I said a low estimate, if that's your idea of a fucking low estimate, Jimmy, I don't know what to tell you—" He waved at her, a chopping gesture at once welcoming and dismissive. He pointed to the right-hand corner of his desk, where she laid the contract. He mouthed the words Thank you, and continued talking into the receiver.

"—I want you to get a good price, is what I want, you want me to tell you what a good price is, I'll tell you, a *good price* is—"

Mary turned to go, anxious to return to the relative hush and clean, cushioned surfaces of her own life. She came flat up against Nick Kazanzakis's secretary, what was her name, the fat girl she'd met at the Christmas party two years ago.

"Oh," Mary said, and smiled. "Hello. How are you?"

What *was* her name? Martha, Margaret. No, something foreign.

The girl stood staring at Mary with an expression so empty, so dumbly astonished, that Mary suspected she must be feebleminded. She had something of that look, fat and small-headed, with blondish no-color hair pulled tightly into a little blond fist at the top of her head. Mary's first impulse was to speak slowly and distinctly, as she would to a child. She might have said something like, I'm Mrs. Stassos, what a pretty dress you're wearing.

"Hello," the girl said, in a voice harsh and accented but not in any way simple. Mary saw her face fill with expression just as a colored glass fills with clear liquid. Under her makeup the girl's face became petulant and triumphant, as if she alone knew of some past transgression of Mary's, an ancient sin Mary had thought was safely buried away.

"We've met, I think," Mary said. "I'm Mary Stassos."

"Magda Bolchik," the girl said. She continued looking at Mary with a victorious hatred so naked it seemed to emanate from her in waves, like heat rising from asphalt.

"The Christmas party, I believe," Mary said. "I'm on my way out, I just dropped off some papers."

"Yeah, the Christmas party," Magda said.

"Yes. Well, it was nice seeing you again." Mary stepped around the girl, went to the door, and she might have left with no more than a puzzled feeling, a sour sense of unrest, but she turned and saw it. She saw that the girl had stepped quickly around Constantine's desk and that she stood there with her hand on his shoulder. She saw Constantine brush the girl's hand away and she saw him look up at her, at Mary, with panic in his eyes, even as he continued talking about the proper price to pay for lathwork.

This was the girl.

Mary lost herself; she lost her own inner convictions of cause and effect. She'd known Constantine was having an affair but the girl she'd imagined was so different, so superior to this one, that the very laws of physics seemed to have been violated. If this plain, overweight girl could be sleeping with her husband—could be her rival—then the papers on Constantine's desk could shriek, rise up like birds, and fly around the room. The coffeepot could explode, the walls could crack. Mary stood through the moment as Magda stared at her with the furious satisfaction of a gorging bear and Constantine looked up pleadingly, guiltily, while he argued into the telephone.

Mary did the only thing she knew how to do. She said, in a pleasant voice, "See you later." She touched her earring. And she left.

———

She found that she couldn't be in her house, even after she'd taken a pill. The rooms felt infected, filled with a silence so dreadful it seemed weighted, as if a lethal, invisible gas were seeping in through the walls. It occurred to Mary that her breathing trouble might come from something in the house, some vapor floating up through the earth that was poisoning only her because she spent more time there than anyone else. Of course, that was ridiculous. She'd had these fits of breathlessness most of her adult life. Still, she couldn't be in the house right now. She couldn't breathe there. She couldn't stay at home. She couldn't go shopping. She couldn't visit a friend because all her friendships were formal ones, related either to Constantine's business or to her own charities. The women she liked best, the calm well-bred women who chaired the committees and gave the luncheons, had never offered her more than the outer edge of their affectionate attention. While she'd subsisted on that for years she could not have it now; she couldn't possibly pay an unannounced call on someone who would cordially tolerate her presence. Assuming she was received, accepted into a living room and given a glass of iced tea, she was too afraid she'd break down. And if she broke down in front of any of those cool assured women she'd be little more than an immigrant, full of an immigrant's hysterical, bottomless trouble—gesticulating, babbling, keening at the white ship as it sailed away. She knew they'd treat her kindly but she knew as well that they'd think her pathetic, and she knew she could not survive that.

She drove, instead, to New York and took a room at the Plaza.

The Plaza calmed her a little. In the ornate golden hush of its lobby she felt, once again, like a woman who could handle herself, a woman of power and means who could do whatever must be done. She let herself be shown to her room, murmured something to the bellhop about her bags arriving later, and when she was alone she turned the air-conditioning on as high as it would go and lay down on the double bed. Her room faced south, which was not as she'd wanted it, but there'd been none available overlooking the park, at least none available to a woman arriving alone, without luggage or a reservation. Outside the window, New York lay bleached and roiling in the heat. It didn't stop, not even on a day like this. Taxis still bellowed down Fifth Avenue, and across the street, in Bergdorf's, saleswomen still moved with swift, icy assurance among the racks. Heat didn't stall this striving, this wide-ranging quest for perfection, the slipper or the jewel or the glass of wine; the golden egg you could hold in your hand and say, Yes, here it is, this, right now. New York was the opposite of Garden City. There time altered itself to match your mood and there, if you let yourself fall into torpor or futility, the world seemed to share your lapse of faith, which it demonstrated by showing you empty rooms full of furniture, the bird feeder standing unused as old Mrs. Ramble across the street came out in her coat and scarf to remove a scrap of paper that had blown onto her lawn. New York carried on, it didn't mind about you, and for nearly ten minutes Mary was able to lie on the bed in a state of relative peace, breathing, sur-rounded by muffled street noise and the immaculate gelid luxury of her room, the roses on the wallpaper, the basket of expensive toiletries she knew would be waiting beside the sink.

Then she thought of the girl again, with her sated expression and the row of pearlized plastic buttons shining on her synthetic, apricot-colored blouse. Touching her husband's shoulder. The girl Constantine had chosen.

Mary sat up and dialed the telephone. She wanted, suddenly, to talk to her children. Not, certainly, to tell them what their father was doing, but simply to hear their voices, to receive whatever affection they had to offer her, to be reminded that their lives had been set in motion and would continue. Billy was the one she most wanted to talk to but Billy was off somewhere, traveling, following a mysterious itinerary, having refused all courtesies beyond the promise to drop a postcard in the mail every few weeks. In a year she'd gotten three cards, one from San Francisco, one from Gallup, New Mexico, and one from British Columbia. She tried Susan in Connecticut but she got no answer, and as the phone rang she could see the empty rooms of her daughter's house, the prim Early American antiques and the sedate, formal wallpaper. She felt a loneliness more piercing than any she could remember. Finally she dialed Zoe's number. Zoe lived less than a mile from where Mary lay on her rented bed, but she seemed, somehow, the most remote of the children; the one she was calling from across the greatest distance.

The phone rang three times before someone picked it up and said, "Hello?" It was a woman's voice, husky and dark.

"Oh, sorry," Mary said. "I've got the wrong number."

"No, no, this is Zoe Stassos's number, she just stepped out for a minute. I'm the maid."

"I beg your pardon."

"Little joke. I'm a friend of Zoe's, she'll be back in about two shakes. Can I give her a message?"

"Well. This is her mother."

"*Oh*. Mrs. Stassos. I've heard so much about you."

"Really?"

"Mm-hm. I'm a friend of Zoe's, I've actually been dying to meet you. My name's Cassandra."

"Oh, yes," Mary said. "Zoe's mentioned your name."

Zoe had not, in fact, as far as Mary could recall, said anything about anyone named Cassandra. Still, one offered these little gestures. The woman sounded older than Zoe, which seemed strange, but she had a warm, refined voice. Better than that homely, gallumphing child Trancas, and the other oddities Zoe had brought home over the years.

"Shall I have her telephone when she gets in?" Cassandra asked.

"No, that's all right. Just tell her I called to say hello."

"Certainly."

"I hope she's managing in the heat," Mary said. "I hope you both are."

She knew it was time to get off the phone but she wasn't eager to return to the silence of the hotel room, the uncertainty of this hour and the next. She'd talk for a minute or two, just ordinary idle things with a pleasant stranger.

"Oh, I don't mind the heat," Cassandra said. "I learned the secret years ago. You have to give yourself over to it. When it gets like this I put on not one lick of makeup, and I don't care *who* I scare on the street."

Finally, Mary thought, here was someone who spoke in a language she could understand. Here was someone who didn't scoff at nylons or makeup, who didn't insist on going around bare-legged, wild-haired, dressed in scraps strangers had thrown away.

"I only wear silk and linen in the summer," Mary said.

"Perfect," the woman answered.

"And can I tell you a little secret of mine?"

"Please do."

"I put my bra and panties in the freezer overnight."

"Oh, I'm going to try that."

"It's wonderful," Mary said. "And if you get enough sun on your legs you can sneak by without nylons."

"I love the sun. But you know, I freckle terribly."

"You want to watch that if you're fair."

"I'm the exact color of an egg." Cassandra sighed. "Scandinavian stock, all my forebears just huddled around the banks of the fjords and kept marrying the palest girl in the village."

"Oh, but very white skin can be lovely. What kind of lipstick do you use, do you tend toward frosted pinks?"

"You know, if I get too frosty and pink I can look like somebody who just washed up on the beach after a couple of weeks. I know this may shock you, but I've started dabbling in red. I mean *red* red. Scarlet."

"Really?" Mary said.

"You couldn't wear it just anywhere. But you know, here in New York I sometimes find it's best to shock them before they can shock you."

"I suppose. Hey, I shouldn't be taking up your time like this."

"Not at all. I've enjoyed this little talk immensely."

"Me too. I'm sure I'll be speaking to you again."

"I hope so. I'll tell Zoe you called. Bye bye."

"Bye."

Mary hung up the phone and lay down on the bed again. As she expected, the silence and uncertainty were waiting for her. But she felt, in some small measure, comforted. There was someone in the world she could talk to about simple unimportant things, a charming woman who spoke without grandeur or condescension. Mary looked up at the snowy plaster of the ceiling, listened to the jostle of traffic. The next time she talked to Zoe she'd chide her, gently, for keeping this lovely new friend of hers a secret.

1 9 7 9 / The songs said love was everywhere. Under Will's window a man in a hunter's cap and crusty plaid pants spent half the night crying out, "Hey, do you love me, do you love me, hey, motherfucker, I'm talking to you." You could call the police but he just came back again—this was his territory. Will played records to drown him out, rock singers and jazz trombonists who were all asking, with music, the same insistent question. *Do you love me, do you love me, hey, fucker, do you love me?* Will couldn't seem to fall in love with anything so complex and elusive as another person. He didn't worry. He didn't worry much. He shared a big cold apartment with a woman friend and her five-year-old daughter. He had a tight little orbit of friends. Romance happened elsewhere, to other people. It could come to him in its own time. He was twenty-six, and didn't dislike himself too much. Only a little, only at moments. Sometimes, when no one could hear, after a day of classes he sat at his desk and let himself emit a series of sharp little moans over all the meetings, the shifty victories with students, the potential for humiliation that seemed to grow endlessly from the seam connecting his job as the students' master to his more complex, and perhaps truer, role as their servant. Will thought sometimes of the night years ago when he'd looked into his father's angry face, his steady feeding, and said, 'I'm going to be a teacher.' He'd said it merely for effect, to confound his father's expectations. But afterward he'd kept thinking of his father's outraged response: 'You got to go to Harvard to teach pickaninnies?' The speck of sauce on his father's chin, the soft dead blue of the dining-room wallpaper. As Will had traveled around the country, picking up jobs as a waiter or an errand boy—as he'd prepared himself to leave his childhood and begin a life of work—he'd found his old ideas about architecture slipping away and he'd begun to know, gradually, with a kind of heady, satisfying helplessness, that a teacher was what he would in fact become.

So he taught fifth grade on Beacon Hill, for sixteen thousand dollars a year. He had his friends, his carefully inexpensive dinners out, his French or Italian movies. He walked, read, bought clothes in discount stores. He looked for love.

He met the man on an ordinary night. He met him in a downtown bar where old men offered drinks and porcelain smiles, the muscular hunger of fathers, to young cowboys just off the bus. Will went there for the strangeness of it. He wasn't expecting anything. He'd drink a beer or two, talk to the old guys. He liked them; he thought of them as ghostly heroes gone to the shadow realm. They came from another era. They'd spent their best years crouched in public toilets, bravely searching the silences of city parks. Now they were like refugees arrived in a land of plenty. If their smiles were ravenous, if they bird-dogged some kid just in from Worcester or Fall River, Will could forgive them. They were his uncles, they'd been misused. They had stories you wouldn't believe.

The man stood near the door, drinking a beer. He stood in the jukebox light as if it were an ordinary thing to be so large and fair and handsome, to have a firm heavy jaw and shoulders broad as the wings of a plow. He was too much for this place. Even the uncles were afraid of him. The uncles could manage a nervous boy from a dying textile town. They could speak with wry insistence into the face of some skinny kid's jerry-rigged self-assurance, because they knew what was in his heart. They knew fear better than anybody. They'd lived fear, they'd survived it. They'd married without love, they'd been beaten by criminals and by the police, spit their own teeth out on the pavement. Now they sat boldly on barstools, neat and perfumed, prosperous, talking in gentle voices to the more privileged manifestations of themselves from twenty or thirty years ago. They had the serene disregard of child emperors grown old. But this man was too perfect. No one went near him.

Will leaned on the bar, talking to a man named Rockwell. Rockwell was a ringer for Everett Dirksen. He wore a hothouse tulip in his lapel. "Must be some mistake," he said, sipping at his daiquiri and nodding toward the man. "His feathers must've caught fire and he plopped down on Washington Street. It happens sometimes, you know. They fly too close to the sun."

Will said, "I don't think he's real. I think he's a hallucination we're all having. It's mass hysteria, you get enough gay men together in one place and sometimes their dreams sort of, like, coalesce."

"Oh, he's no dream, Willy. He's real, he's on the prowl. Trust me, he's out tonight looking for something."

"Love," Will said. "Love love love love love. What's anybody looking for?"

"Lots of things," Rockwell said. He sang, *"Most gentlemen don't like love, they just like to kick it around.* Cole Porter, the sage of our century."

"I don't know," Will said. "We're afraid of love, don't you think? We say we want what we can get. If we can get laid, we say that's all we want. But really, don't you think everybody just wants to fall in love?"

"A very pretty view of human nature. Frankly, I half wish he'd go away. He's making me nervous. What does he *want* here? Just veneration, if you ask me. There are men like that. Admiration queens. I'll bet you the price of a drink he's going to go to a half-dozen bars tonight, speak to no one, and then go home and get off in front of a mirror."

"Who knows?" Will said. "Do you think it's fair to judge some-body like that just because he's handsome?"

"Old crones have been passing harsh judgments on pretty young things since time immemorial. Those of us who were once pretty young things ourselves are usually correct."

"He could just be here hoping to meet somebody. Why not?"

Rockwell said, "The Duchess of Windsor could be browsing Woolworth's hoping to find something she'd like, but the odds are she'd have an ulterior motive. How old are you, Willy? Aren't you about ready to shed your youthful idealism? Past a certain age, it's no longer becoming."

"What will you give me if I go talk to him?"

"My undying respect."

"If he turns out to be just a regular, decent guy, you'll have to buy me my drinks for the rest of the month. How's that?"

"All right. Go. Report back."

Will took his beer and walked purposefully up to the man. It was the only way. He got courage from Rockwell, from the idea of being seen as someone heedless and courageous. He said, "Excuse me, but I have to ask. What are you doing here?"

"Huh?" The man's face was blunt, placid, deeply carved. He was Will's age, a little older.

"This bar is the exclusive province of sad old queens," Will said. "I'm afraid I'll have to ask you to leave."

"You're not an old queen," the man said. He tilted his beer bottle to his lips. An oval of reflected light slipped along the bottle's shaft.

"I have visiting rights here," Will said. "My name is Will."

"Matt," the man said. They shook hands. Matt wore a white dress shirt and pale blue corduroys, smelled too strongly of cologne. His hair, a lavish abundance of dark-blond curls, did not quite touch his collar.

"You really are getting everybody all upset," Will said softly, conspiratorially. "You're too handsome for this place. You're making everybody else feel like they look the way they really do look."

"Maybe I should leave," Matt said.

A shock of uncertainty ran through Will. Was he driving the man off? He knew that when he was nervous he could be too slick, too clever, though he knew, too, that in a sense he did want this Matt to go. He was too finely wrought, too fortunate. The ease of his beauty hung awkwardly in the unfresh air.

"No," Will said. "I didn't really mean it, I'm just trying, you know, to be clever."

"I'm getting tired, anyway," Matt said. "I have to get up in the morning."

"Oh. Well."

Matt yawned to illustrate his fatigue. A thread of clear saliva stretched from his upper to his lower teeth.

"I actually have to get up, too," Will said. "I have to teach in the morning. I just came out for a quick beer with my aunts and uncles."

"You're a teacher?" Matt asked.

"Yeah."

"I just finished school."

"Really?"

"I just got my master's in government. From Harvard."

"Well. Somebody's got to do it."

"Uh-huh," Matt said. "Hey, I've got to go."

"Okay."

There was a shuffling, a nameless transition. Will and Matt looked at each other, shrugged as if they shared a joke. Matt asked, "Do you feel like coming over to my place for one more beer?"

Will blinked. Matt must, in fact, be a hallucination. It did not seem possible that a man like this, a man heavy-jawed and muscular as all his dreams, would invite him home. He didn't live in that kind of world.

"Okay," Will said. "Sure."

"So. Let's go."

They got their coats. As he left the bar with Matt, Will glanced back at Rockwell. Rockwell lifted his daiquiri glass, and Will imagined him at a harbor, standing among the parents and the abandoned sweethearts, watching a ship depart. Rockwell had been handsome once, he'd lived in the network of possibilities, and Will felt, briefly, the plain loneliness that waited for everyone. The little bag of groceries, the long walk up the stairs. Then he stepped out of the bar behind Matt.

Outside, the air sparkled with a fine mist of ice. Matt hailed a cab, and their conversation ended. He gave the driver an address in Cambridge, six blocks or so from the house Will had lived in when he himself was at Harvard, settled into the back seat next to Will, and disappeared inside himself. Will asked a couple of questions, simple ones about school and place of origin, but Matt answered with single syllables and watched the city pass outside the window. To calm his nerves, Will checked Matt for human signs. His fingernails were not well trimmed. His cologne (Will knew the brand) was cheap and ordinary. He would have hopes and an inner grove of disappointments, even with his beauty and girth. He would once have been a child, crying with frustration.

Matt lived in a brown brick high-rise, one of the buildings Will used to pass and wonder, with a shiver, who would choose to live there. The silence held as Matt led Will into the lobby and into the elevator. Matt's beauty was untainted by the harsh elevator light but his face, in its rocky quietude, did not look so open or so calmly benevolent as it had in the bar and the taxi. Suddenly, Will could not imagine kissing him. He began to tell himself, This will pass. Whatever happens, I'll be back on the street soon, back in my life.

He thought about what he would eat when he got home. There were bananas, a little overripe. There was leftover Chinese food.

Matt's apartment held only piles of cartons and a beanbag chair. The bare walls glared white in the white light of the ceiling globe. There were no shadows. On one of the cartons the word *Records* had been written in a steady hand. "I'm moving," Matt said. "I'm leaving for Washington day after tomorrow."

"Oh. Well, have a good trip."

"You want a beer?" Matt asked.

"Sure."

Matt went to the kitchen and returned with two beers. The light was steady and colorless as tap water. Enter this, Will told himself. Do it, do whatever happens, and then go. But the air resisted him. This room was the opposite of sex. He felt as if flash-bulbs were exploding in his face. He and Matt stood together, drinking their beers. Will felt lost in his clothes. His shoes seemed enormous. It occurred to him that he and Matt had misunderstood each other. Matt had somehow failed to realize that he'd gone to a gay bar. He had simply invited Will up for a comradely beer before he slipped out of his old life and into the new. That idea appealed to Will—he wouldn't need to risk sex with someone so remote and well made.

"What kind of job have you got?" Will asked.

"I can't tell you my boss's name. But he's very high in government, and I'm going to be his personal assistant. It's a great job. I'm lucky."

"That's good. Congratulations."

"Thanks."

They finished their beers. Matt turned his bottle over in his hand and said, "I haven't done this much. This is really kind of new to me."

"Oh," Will said. "You're, like, just coming out?"

Matt raised his shoulders, hefted the bottle in his hand, and

Will believed he understood. Here was the sullen unnamed thing, the clumsiness. Everything opened; everything made sense. Matt was new. He'd turned up in the bar because he didn't know what bar to go to—he'd probably heard the name somewhere. An old fear lived inside that perfect body. Finally, after years of deception, before he left his old life and entered a new one, Matt was going to let his desires show. A spasm of tenderness rose in Will's throat.

"It's hard, isn't it?" he said. "I mean, I was nervous as hell my first few times."

Matt took a deep swig of his empty beer bottle. All right, Will thought. He stepped forward, put his arms around Matt's broad shoulders. This close, he could smell Matt's sweat mingled with the sweetness of his cologne. It occurred to him that a circle was completing itself. He had it in him now to be patient and generous, to help someone come around to himself. He said, "There's nothing to be afraid of. It's all goodness here. I mean, relax. I'll take care of everything."

"Good," Matt said, and his voice turned surprisingly harsh. He might have been granted something that was rightfully his, after a long and bitter fight.

"Do you still have a bed?" Will asked. "Or has it already gone to Washington?"

"It's in here," Matt said.

He led Will into the next room, flicked a switch that filled it with the same light. The room contained a double bed, unmade, and more cartons. "Great," Will said. "I mean, I'm glad to see the bed's still here."

"You want to take my clothes off?" Matt said.

"Do you want me to?"

"I'm asking you."

"Well, yeah. I do."

Matt stood in the middle of the room and let himself be undressed. Will peeled off Matt's shirt, told him to sit on the bed so he could remove his shoes and socks. Matt asked, "You like this? You like taking a guy's clothes off?"

"I do," Will said. Something was wrong. Matt didn't look nervous. He looked disdainful, bullyish. His voice had a sneering edge.

"I thought you did."

Will reminded himself to act kindly. Different men did different things with their fears. Kindness was the answer, the gentle competence of a parent. He took off Matt's shoes and socks, had him stand up again. Matt grinned.

"Yes, you like this," he said.

"Sure I do," Will said. "What's not to like?" He unbuckled Matt's belt, slid his pants and then his boxer shorts down around his ankles. Matt stepped out of his pants, smiling. He was half erect. A medallion of golden hair on his chest trickled down into a serrated line that led to his crotch. Will saw that Matt's cock was smaller than his own.

"What are you going to do now?" Matt asked.

"Well, I guess I'm going to take my clothes off, too," Will said. Matt nodded. Will undressed quickly, embarrassed by his scrawny flesh but proud of his cock. "There," he said when he, too, was naked. The two men faced each other.

"And what are you going to do now?" Matt asked.

"I'm going to lay you down on that bed," Will said. He hoped his voice had been commanding, not questioning. For all his determination to be kind and fatherly, he could not shake the feeling that this was a test he would either pass or fail.

"I'll lie down myself," Matt said calmly. He lay across the mattress in a posture of ease, his hands clasped behind his head. His armpits bristled with dark golden hair, and suddenly Will was angry. This man was too certain, too full of entitlement.

"Don't move," Will said. "Stay right where you are."

He knelt on the bed, straddling Matt's thighs with his own. He knew he was pale and skinny in the shadowless light. He didn't mind. He set to work. He tongued Matt's pale nipples, bit them gently, moved slowly down Matt's belly with his mouth. He traced the herringbone trail of hairs. There was the smell of Matt's cologne and of Matt himself, a faint but harsh smell, like iron on a freezing day. Will circled around Matt's cock with his mouth. Matt's cock was small and straight, the head dark pink, the shaft ringed with lighter pink. He kissed Matt's thighs, licked his scrotum, pulled lightly at his pubic hair with his lips. When Matt started to groan Will bit at his thighs, burrowed under his balls with his tongue. Will thought of his tongue as a flame, Matt's flesh as a kettle that wanted to boil. There. And again, there. The flame's going to touch you everywhere. You're going to be boiling soon. Matt's hips started to move and Will let himself touch the shaft of Matt's cock, lightly, with his lips. "Aw," Matt exclaimed, and Will took his mouth away. Suffer, he thought. Want it.

"Roll over," he said.

"I'm fine like this," Matt said. His voice was thinner now, with a throaty edge.

"Roll over. Do what I tell you."

To his surprise, Matt obeyed. There were the golden muscles of his back, the buttons of his spine. There was his ass, so lovely and guileless Will's mouth went dry at the sight of it. He adored men's asses. They were the benign, childlike part. When you saw a man's bare ass you saw that this big noisy aggressive creature, all muscle and swagger, had once been fearful and small.

Will licked the back of Matt's knee, worked slowly up his thigh. Matt groaned again. His hips rolled. At the top of his thigh Will licked the crease where the thigh joined the buttock. He couldn't believe he commanded all this flesh, this immensity. He licked his way up over the mound of Matt's right cheek, bit the flesh a little harder than he'd meant to, though Matt didn't seem to mind. Will bit Matt's ass and he felt more potent, larger, than he'd ever felt before. He was a cannibal who'd captured a mercenary. The big white man from the world of money and guns was just food here, just dinner. Will slid his tongue into the crack of Matt's ass. His ass had a sour, human smell, and it excited in Will a renewed surge of desire and rage. He didn't think of his own pleasure. He had to devour Matt. He had to dominate Matt's flesh so he'd never act superior again. He'd never be a bully. Will licked the crack of Matt's ass, put the tip of his tongue into his asshole. Yes, white man, yes, gun runner, there's nothing I won't eat. Your guns can't match the tongue and teeth of true hunger. I'm eating them, all your rules. Your bullying. I'm eating you. Now.

"Awww," Matt cried. "Aw God."

"Turn over again," Will commanded. Matt did as he was told. His cock was burstingly erect. Will licked the tip of it, the pink softness. Matt was panting now, short bursts of wind, like a sprinter. With every breath a moan leaked out of him, a low pleading sound. "Awww? Awww? Awww?" Will slid his mouth over Matt's cock. Now I'm eating the truest part of you. Now you're coming into me and you'll never have yourself back again. I'm eating you and part of you will be inside me forever. Will took the whole of Matt's cock. He moved his mouth up and down, not too quickly. He tickled Matt's balls with his fingers, dipped down and prodded, lightly, at his asshole.

Matt came with a little shriek, a high-pitched sound Will hadn't expected. Matt's thighs pressed Will's head and Will was lost in Matt's flesh, his ears blocked and his mouth filled with Matt's cum.

Then it was over. Matt's thighs fell away and Will released his cock. "Whew," Matt said.

Will smiled. Matt tugged at his own cock twice, put his fingers to his nose. Will waited to see what would happen next. Matt yawned.

"So, that's it," he said. "That's the show."

"It's just the first act," Will said. "Are you okay?"

"I'm fine, guy. I'm perfect. Hey, it's late. I've got to get to sleep."

Will wasn't sure what he meant. Did he expect them to spend the night together?

"Well, it is sort of late," he said. He was still dizzy from the sex, from his own erection. He wanted to comfort Matt, to be congratulated on his own skill, and to come all over Matt's thick muscular belly.

"I've got a big day tomorrow," Matt said. "You'd better go."

"Right," Will said. His face burned but he could not bring himself to demand reciprocation. He couldn't make himself that humble. He stood and began putting on his clothes. As he dressed, Matt said to him, "I don't think I told you. I'm getting married."

"Oh. Congratulations. You haven't seen my left shoe, have you?"

"You ever think about getting married?"

"No. I never have."

"You should. You're a good guy, you could get yourself a really nice girl."

"That's not what I want," Will said.

"What do you want? You want to make a career out of this?"

"Out of what?"

"This." He made a gesture that took in the whole bare room, their two bodies. "Fag stuff."

"I like fag stuff."

Matt shook his head. "You want to see a picture of the girl I'm going to marry?" he said.

"Not especially."

Matt got off the bed and walked naked into the next room. He returned with a picture in a silver frame. His flaccid cock trailed a filament of cum.

"This is her," he said. He showed Will a photograph of a pretty blond girl with an alert V-shaped face and a string of pearls around her neck.

"Nice, huh?" Matt said.

"Very nice. I've got to go."

Matt stood with the photograph in his hands. His face was flushed, his eyes bright. "I want to tell you something," he said.

"What?"

"I did this just to see if I'd like it. A guy's about to take on a lifetime commitment, he's naturally a little curious. And you know what? It made me sick. This fag stuff makes me want to puke."

"Sorry you feel that way," Will said. "Good night."

"So in a way I want to thank you. For helping me know who I am."

"Don't mention it." Will left the room. The front door wavered in front of him as he found the knob.

"Good night, faggot," Matt said behind him.

When Will got home he took a shower, as hot as he could stand it. He poured himself a shot of bourbon, got into bed. Later, when he told the story to friends, they all agreed that these things happened. Sometimes you picked a creep. His friend Dennis told him about a soft-voiced, neatly dressed man who'd kept him handcuffed to a bed for two days and who'd seemed convinced that all Dennis's protests were elaborate signals of his pleasure. Rockwell had a half-dozen tales of more ordinary humiliations in truck stops, in parks, in the men's room of the British Museum. Every gay man had stories. They'd been robbed, beaten up, dumped naked on a highway in New Jersey. These were usual things; they happened. They lived as anecdotes, war stories, and once you were on the far side of them they fattened your reputation. Matt the Nazi angel, as Rockwell called him, was just an episode in the passion play. He told Will, "Think of that poor fuck married to that nice dumb girl, sneaking around to bars and movies. Believe me, I've seen this plenty of times. They only get ugly when you've struck a nerve. Have a moment of silence for the pathetic schmuck, and get on with things."

Will believed what Rockwell said. Still, the memory of Matt

stuck to him. Something about Matt's calm disdain, the way he'd stood, naked, with hard white light falling on him and the girl's photograph in his hands. Will saw Matt striding, suited, firm-jawed, calmly determined, into the hush of a government building, and he was filled with a dread that stung like ice water.

1 9 7 9 / It wasn't an affair. *Affair* was the wrong word for what Susan was having. It was—what? A mistake she permitted. An ongoing temptation she found herself, temporarily, unable or unwilling to resist. When she thought of a woman having an affair she thought of hotel rooms, tearful afternoons, a whole galaxy of longings and regrets. This was sex and something else, a modest affection that resembled, to a surprising extent, the friendships she'd had as a girl. Affairs were premeditated; they were kept alive by a tortured system of meetings. She and Joel, on the other hand, simply had sex when they felt like it and when circumstances permitted. He was a tree surgeon. She knew there was a dirty joke to be made out of that though she didn't make it to herself—she wasn't quite sure how it would go. She and Todd had been in the Connecticut house less than three months when Joel came to work on the mature elm that had somehow survived Dutch elm disease, the only one in a neighborhood once known for its trees. When Todd and Susan bought the house they learned they were considered the custodians of something precious, a monument. They were advised—ordered, really—by their neighbors to continue the previous owners' custom of having Joel out every six months to monitor the tree's inexplicable good health. The tree spoke to Darien about deliverance, a future that could not be wholly obliterated even by the bottomless appetite of disease. Susan dutifully called Joel, a short, affable man of forty or so, who smoked a pipe and carried about him a faint air of apology mixed with his scents of tobacco and wood. He was like a forest creature, watchful and ready for flight. He had an animal's mix of caution and mysterious purpose. The first time he came, she watched him climb fearlessly up his chrome extension ladder to cut away a dead branch, and she was impressed by how thoroughly he appeared to have married his simple work. He sawed the branch with quick delicate strokes, and when it fell he descended the ladder and carried the branch to his truck with a certain tenderness, as if it were a pet that had died. His black hair was cropped close to his skull; he wore yellow work boots and a green plaid jacket. Susan felt the romance of him, a sturdy competent man who had only this one ambition and who, she suspected, could take you into the woods and tell you the names of everything you saw. He whistled; he drove a truck with his name painted on the door in bright blue letters.

It happened on his second visit. After checking the tree, he came to the house for his payment. She offered a cup of coffee, he accepted, and they stood in the kitchen talking about the miraculous deliverance of Susan's tree. There was only that one subject. "It's a strange thing," he said in his soft monotone. "There's no pattern, no pattern at all. A tornado can level a house, level it, and leave one wall standing with a shelf full of china cups. China cups. Not one of them even cracked."

"I guess that's where religion comes in," she said, and he shrugged, embarrassed by any reference to the otherworldly. He was probably a man who acknowledged only the real. As he was preparing to leave, Susan shook his hand and he looked questioningly at her with his soft, feral eyes. He was discreet. All she needed to do was drop her eyes and withdraw her hand. But she hesitated, and softly, with deliberation, he drew her close to him. He was scarcely an inch taller than she. He knew, somehow, not to kiss her lips. He kissed her cheek with a gentleness that was almost chaste. Then he kissed her forehead and hair. If he'd tried to court her, she'd have refused him. If he'd been aggressive, if he'd grabbed her or pinned her against the wall, she'd have ordered him out and called Todd at the office. His manner was what made it possible, his simple and slightly apologetic friendliness. Sex, he seemed to say, was the obvious and correct thing—it was what two people in this position would naturally do. She went along the way she'd have followed an unexpected turn in a conversation with someone older and better educated than she. They stood embracing in the foyer and he whispered, "Let's go upstairs, what do you think?" She hesitated. There was only one way to say it. "I don't use birth control, I don't have anything in the house." "That's okay, it's okay," he told her. "We won't need that." She paused again, conscious of the bentwood coatrack, the striped wallpaper. She nodded. As they climbed the stairs, it seemed to her that she did not lead and did not follow. His hand rode the small of her back but didn't press her forward. He seemed only to want to maintain contact, as if the loss of it might mean the loss of all their aims. She was excited and nervous but she walked with purpose down the hall and into the guest room. She did not take him to the bed she shared with Todd. As she stood with him on the rag rug amid the odd furnishings— the guest room was a catchall for leftovers—it occurred to her that she was only twenty-nine and was the owner, half owner, of this house, a three-bedroom colonial on a full acre, probably a more substantial house than the one Joel would own. She was the mistress and the willing victim of everything that happened. She let him unbutton her blouse. Her head was clear. She knew what was happening. If she'd ever thought of anything like this she'd imagined it as an extended swoon, a turmoil of drink and passion. But now she watched with almost clinical composure as he took off her clothes and then removed his own. She felt neither proud nor ashamed of her body. Her body was a fact, it had the inevitability of the elm outside, the same unquestioned privilege. His own flesh was solid, sparsely haired, not as muscular as she'd imagined. She looked with interest at his penis—aside from Todd's, she'd seen them only in pictures. Joel's was larger than Todd's, the head blunter and redder, and she knew size was supposed to be a virtue but it didn't strike her that way at all. She loved Todd's penis, its brown-pink shaft and delicate lavender tip. Joel's was raw, thickly veined, and at the sight of it she passed through her single moment of doubt. It struck her that his penis might be an aberration, something freakish and unwholesome. Maybe she should change her mind, send him away. She almost spoke but he took her in his arms again, peppered her hair and neck with kisses, and she decided to let it happen. She would remember, afterward, that there had been a decision.

He took her to the bed, an old double that had belonged to her parents, and drew back the covers. She was touched by his domesticity, his gentleness. She slid under the blankets and felt like a girl in a fairy tale, captured by a beast with immense paws and powerful haunches, a beast that devoured others but adored her. When she'd thought of something like this she'd thought of danger, hard predatory breaths and the tearing of fabric. She'd never imagined it kind or courtly.

Joel lay beside her, and she put her hand on his shoulder. He smiled, shyly. His face was neither ugly nor handsome. It was simply a face, with a round nose and ordinary eyes and shaggy black brows. He ran his fingers along her arm, touched her elbow consolingly, as a friend would. This is happening, she thought. This is what it's like. He brought his hand up to her breast and, as he grazed the nipple with his fingertips, his mouth formed an O, as if he, too, had felt the touch, found it surprising and pleasant.

He circled her nipple with the tip of his index finger, then ran the finger under her breast and weighed it, gently, in his palm. "Mm," he whispered. She was moved but not excited and she began to think that it would all be tender, remote, and small. It would happen outside her; she could see herself making the bed again after he'd gone. Her theory had probably been right: sex at best was a pleasant and minor experience, widely overpraised. Because it didn't matter, because this would end soon and nothing would change, she let her hand fall to his chest. She'd explore him like a nurse and then she'd know something other women knew, the heft and grain of men's bodies. It was a casual curiosity, it didn't smolder. She was satisfied with Todd. But sometimes she'd wondered how he conformed and how he differed. She'd wondered what, exactly, other women meant when they talked about their men in bed. Joel's chest was solid under a layer of fat, like Susan's own thighs. A fountain of curly dark hair sprouted in the middle, circled his nipples (longer than Todd's, more pointed and womanly) and straggled down along the curve of his belly. He must have been a dream at twenty, and as she thought of that she pictured him as a schoolboy. Quiet, she thought. Athletic but not heroic, neither celebrated nor shunned, one of the steady boys who faithfully dated the same girl (a decent girl, semi-pretty, who sang in the school choir), and married her soon after. By now he might have been married twenty years or more, and his habits of fidelity had finally worn thin. He bent toward her, smiling, and put his mouth on her nipple, which faintly resembled his own. She felt queasy and she almost pushed his face away, but his lips were velvety and he kissed her nipple without a hint of tooth. Then he touched it with his tongue and the first true sensation ran through her, a high ticklish feeling that made her draw her breath sharply in. She hadn't expected that. He tongued her nipple and then he tongued the other, and she caromed between pleasure and squeamishness, as she had when she was a little girl and her father had held her down and tickled her. She couldn't say whether she liked this or not. The squeamish sensation rose from her belly to her throat, and without removing his lips Joel let his fingers wander down her belly to her crotch. "Oh," she said, loudly enough to surprise herself. Joel's fingers teased her pubic hair, spider-walked among the tufts and she felt as if a wind was blowing between her legs. That settled into her, the idea of being touched by wind, and as he brushed her pubic hair she began to wish he'd touch her more deeply. What if he did nothing more than this? She pushed her pelvis out to meet his fingers, and when he withdrew them she was briefly angry. Who was he, this quiet unspectacular boy grown to middle age? Who did he think she was? She cleared her throat. He smiled up at her and began kissing his way down her belly. He was making a sound, a faint whistle and moan. She lay quietly, watching his ears and his thinning hair, unsure of what she wanted or didn't want. She watched him trace a line of kisses along her belly and then she realized what he intended to do. Todd had never done that; he'd never ventured there with his mouth. She didn't want it, she'd feel too exposed, but Joel kissed the insides of her thighs and she didn't ask him to stop. She waited. She was full of fear and a new kind of queasy excitement. She regretted having done this. She wanted to be alone in her kitchen, brewing a fresh pot of coffee, watering the plants. He worked his face between her legs. He touched her there with his tongue. The feeling was electric, slightly sickening, a hot moist sensation that shot through her. She moaned, though she hadn't meant to. He lapped at her with his tongue, spread the flesh with his thumbs and then he found it. He found the spot, and he knew. At first she thought he'd just grazed it, men didn't know about that, but he worked his tongue around it in circles and he knew, he knew, he'd found it and he knew to touch her there. She was moaning now, she didn't want to stop. She put her hands on his head, the coarse thinning bristles of his hair, and held on because she was afraid he'd quit. She was afraid he'd lose what he seemed to know. "Oh, god," she said. This was something else moving through her blood. She'd felt the opening, the high quivering expansion, but this was going someplace different. She was used to a rise and fall, a quickness. A warm red shadow that flicked past, left the memory of heat behind. This wasn't stopping. His tongue was relentless, it kept finding her, and she writhed, half hoping she'd elude the tongue but she didn't, it found her and found her and she was crying out, "Oh oh oh, oh god, oh." It kept opening inside her, the ragged immensity. She couldn't stand it, it couldn't open any wider, it was gushing all through her. He found her and found her and found her and she went up and over. It rushed up at her and filled her and she was tumbling, she didn't care, she was inside herself and the flood didn't stop, the hot wet pulses, they didn't stop, and then, finally, they did.

He lifted his face, smiled at her. She watched him with a certain incomprehension, a small embarrassment that was already starting to grow. She saw that she was covered in a thin film of sweat. Tenderly, he kissed the crook of her knee. He brushed a strand of hair from her forehead.

And then she began crying. She didn't expect it. The crying started softly, nothing more than a stinging wetness in her eyes, but as she looked at Joel's capable face the crying continued on its own, not loud but deep, punctuated by soft ragged intakes of breath. She let herself cry. She was filled with sorrow and relief, as if she'd escaped simple happiness and entered something larger, more complex and promising. Joel stroked her hair.

"There, there," he whispered, and she imagined he spoke that way to the trees as he sat among their branches, sawing away their afflicted parts.

When she was through crying they both put their clothes back on and walked down the hall together, past the closed door of the third bedroom, which was reserved as a nursery. Susan was slightly disoriented, as if she'd awoken at night in a new house that seemed strange at first and then revealed itself to be the place she in fact belonged. Here was the striped wallpaper she'd chosen, here was the antique mirror hanging at the bottom of the stairs. Joel paused at the front door. His work boots, stained with the sap of trees, were nearly the same color as the varnished pine floorboards. He took her hand.

"That was nice," he said.

"Was it?" she said. Then she laughed and brushed at her eyes. "Yes. It was nice."

He could have killed it so easily. He could have been lewd or self-satisfied. He could have indicated, by his face or his body, that he pitied her. He could have asked her when they'd do it again.

"Bye," he said.

"Goodbye." He opened the door and she stepped out onto the porch with him. It was still a warm clear day. It was still autumn. She still lived on a street of clapboard colonials in Darien, pumpkins grinning on the doorsteps. In another few days other people's children would dress in costumes and ring her doorbell, demanding candy.

"Oh," she said, "did you remember your check?"

He put his hand on the breast pocket of his jacket. They both laughed. "Got it," he said. He walked out to his truck and drove away. He waved to her from the road.

It surprised her that when she saw his truck a week later on her way to the supermarket, she parked her car and went boldly to speak to him. He was working on the grounds of an elementary school, pruning a haphazard arrangement of young trees that had been planted to soften the dour sprawl of blond brick buildings. He wore his boots and a navy-blue sweater, jeans that hung too low on his waist. Colored leaves cut from construction paper were taped to the windows of the single-story building that rose behind him.

"Hi," he said, apparently glad to see her. His eyes were brown, ordinary. His skin glowed in the cloudy light.

"Hi."

A silence passed. She said, "Is it all right that I stopped to talk to you?"

"Sure," he said. "Sure, why wouldn't it be?"

"Well. I don't know. Do you have a wife?"

"Oh, we live way off. In Wilton. She wouldn't come over here. She wouldn't. Are you okay?"

She nodded. "I've never done anything like that," she said. "I guess that's probably what they all say."

He shrugged. "It's not like there are so many."

"Oh, come on." She wasn't jealous. She wanted this to be a usual thing; she wanted to have joined a group.

He shrugged again, and laughed. "Okay. There are a few."

"I should be going," she said. "I saw you and, I don't know. It seemed like it would be strange to just drive by."

"It's nice to see you," he said.

"Maybe we'll see each other again. I mean, before it's time for the tree's checkup. Am I being too forward?"

"No. It'd be nice to see each other again, I'd like to."

"I guess you can't come by in that big truck," she said. "You know, the neighbors. God, that's such a housewife thing, isn't it strange to be saying this?"

"You could come by my office," he said. "You got the address, it's over in Norwalk. You could come by there."

"I could. What about Thursday, in the afternoon?"

"Four o'clock? Four o'clock would be good."

"That's a little late," she said. "Would three be okay?"

"I have a job in New Canaan. I could be back by three-thirty."

"All right, then. Three-thirty."

"Okay."

"See you then."

"Yeah. See you then."

She got back in her car and drove to the supermarket. She couldn't believe the strangeness of it. There was no tumult, no chaos of emotion. There was only the working out of schedules and this sad but unmistakable sense of relief.

It surprised her that she could sneak away to Norwalk for Joel and yet continue to love Todd. She'd imagined devotion to be finite. She'd believed that if you focused an affectionate energy on someone new you had to deduct corresponding affection from someone you loved already. But her love for Todd held steady; at times it seemed to have grown. She retained all her tenderness toward him. She still liked reassuring him when he returned from the rigor and gravity of his days in the city. She'd learned that the mantle of work Todd had begun shouldering in college would not end. She'd been wrong in her belief that he'd emerge from his studies complete, magnified, and free. His labors at Yale had not been a trial, they'd been the first in an ascending process of labors. By now it was clear that the work led only to other work. His value would always be questioned and he would need to prove himself again and again and again. If anything, the strife became more ferocious, the stakes higher, as the lesser men fell away. Todd's firm hired only the best, and expected to dismiss fully half of them. Todd had no intention of being dismissed, and further, he had no intention of ending merely as a successful attorney. He wanted to govern. He wanted to create new systems of order. In whatever time he could shave out of his schedule he advised the city planning commission in Darien and provided counsel to the school board. He was getting his name around. He had reason to believe he could one day become a representative, a senator; he might even be able to go beyond that. There was nothing stopping him. He was smart and handsome, he had a solemn undangerous charm. He was married to a smart and handsome woman who had worked to help support him through college and law school and who now took classes at the community college. The idea that Susan would do terrible damage if discovered seemed abstract to her, like tales of the punishment inflicted on women accused of witchcraft. She did what she needed to do, lived on the edge of a forest far from what Todd meant by the world. She worked on the house, attended her classes, comforted her husband after the long struggle of his days.

What happened with Joel kept increasing. She wanted nothing beyond the sensations and the simple friendship. She wasn't looking for love. She didn't bother with birth control. She'd come to believe she couldn't have babies, anyway. What she loved about Joel was not thinking about babies; not thinking about defeat and insufficiency. With Joel she unabashedly sought pleasure. She straddled him, pushed herself up and down on his big red cock. She thrust herself in his face, tugged screaming at his hair, told him he must not stop. She'd never expected this, the hot ragged climb and the implosion. She'd never imagined herself so washed in it. Afterward, driving home again, she felt cleansed, lightened, as if a layer of dust had been scrubbed off her. The cold air touched her differently. Her skirt lay differently on her thighs.

Her mother called early one morning the following September. "Hi, honey," she said in a cheerfully haggard voice, and Susan knew immediately that something had happened.

"Mom. What's up?"

"Well, I have something to tell you."

"What? Mom, what's happened?"

"Sweetheart, I've asked your father to leave. He's staying at the Garden City Hotel, for now."

"What? What do you mean?"

"We've separated. I don't know exactly what will happen. I'm sorry to be telling you over the telephone, but I thought I should let you know."

"What happened?"

"This has been brewing for a long time, honey," her mother said. "You must have known your father and I have always had, well, a little trouble."

"But why now?" Susan said. "Something must have happened."

Her mother paused. The line hummed faintly with static. "You know what it really is, honey?" her mother said. "It's that I'm finally coming into my own. I haven't turned into a women's libber or anything like that, believe me. I'm not going to start burning my bras. But. I'm not sure how to say this. I guess I've known for a long time that I need my own life. Your father and I raised you kids, we hung in there, and now that you're all on your own we need to be on our own, too. Does that make any sense?"

Susan had stiffened. All she could think of was that she had failed. She'd been discovered. She wasn't sure what she meant. She wasn't sure what she thought.

"I don't know," she said. "I don't know what to say."

"This is a shock," her mother said. "I understand."

"I have to go."

"Susan, it'll be all right. We're still your parents, nothing about that has changed."

"Mother, I really have to go. I can't talk to you right now."

"Whatever you think is best. I understand."

"You don't understand," Susan said. "You don't understand anything."

"I don't blame you for being angry."

"Thank you."

"Your father, well. His temper. I just—"

"I have to go. I'm sorry."

"Okay, honey. Whatever you want."

Susan was sitting at the dining-room table when Todd came home. She hadn't called him at the office. She hadn't called anyone. She'd kept the receiver in her hand and touched the dial, intending to call her husband, her brother and sister, anyone. Then she'd taken her hand away and walked into the dining room, where she'd sat at the mahogany table that had been a housewarming gift from her parents. She'd let the phone ring as somebody called, then somebody else, and a third person. She felt nauseous and disoriented, as if she was seasick. Through the French doors she could see the back yard, the brilliant living green of the grass. When she and Todd had decided on the house, they'd remarked to each other about the yard, which was well removed from traffic and offered plenty of room for a swing set, a sandbox, a wading pool. A tree house could have been built among the limbs of the celebrated elm. It all rushed in at her, how much she was risking, how selfish she'd been. She saw now—how could she ever have failed to see?—how fragile everything was. She'd made a terrible mistake, and she couldn't offer it as a lapse, a brief failure of flesh. She'd lied. She'd done it again and again. Though she wasn't religious she prayed now, sitting in her empty dining room. Please, let this go unpunished and I'll be good for the rest of my life. She stayed where she was, in a mahogany Queen Anne chair, for almost two hours. She didn't move and after a while she stopped thinking about anything. She couldn't imagine where to go, what to do with herself, and so she did nothing. When Todd came home he found her sitting in the dark. He rushed up to her and said, "Sweetheart, what are you doing?" He brought his smell, his concern, his vocabulary of gestures.

"Sitting," she said. "I'm just sitting here."

"Why? What is it? What happened?"

"My mother called today. She and Daddy are splitting up."

"What?"

"Splitting up, *separating*. He's gone off to a hotel."

"Jesus," Todd said. "What do you know?"

"I just, I can't."

"Darling. Oh, darling, it's a shock, I know."

"I. There's too much."

"Come on," he said. "Come in the kitchen with me, I'll make us something to eat, and then I'm putting you to bed. Okay?"

"Okay."

He made scrambled eggs and bacon for both of them, and after she'd eaten he took her upstairs and drew back the covers on their bed as tenderly as Joel had once done in the guest room. Her face burned with shame. "Get in bed with me," she said. "Okay? Don't stay up and work, don't read."

"Sure," he said. He undressed and got into bed beside her. His body was exactly that, his body, almost as familiar as her own. She tried not to stare at his penis, the marvelous commonplace of its shape and color.

"I thought they'd gotten through the worst of it," she said. "I really thought that if they went this far—"

"Give them time," Todd said. "I'll bet old Constantine'll be back home within the week."

"Maybe. I'm not so sure."

"Trust me. What'd they do without each other?"

She put her hand on the smooth soft plane of his chest. An emptiness was opening in her, a fear like nothing she could remember. Forgive me, she said silently. I'll never do it again. She kissed Todd, ran her fingers along his ribs. She whispered, close to his ear, "Oh, I love you, I love you so much."

"I love you, too, sweetie," he said.

She kissed him tenderly on the mouth. He was her only true friend and she'd betrayed him. The kiss held and he worked himself around, got on top of her. She parted her legs and he slid himself in for the first time in—what?—a year? Longer? Here he was, pumping, and here came the old familiar flush, the red shadow. She lay as she always did, clutching the hard muscles of his back, smoothing them out. She put grateful kisses on his cheek and ear. The old warmth filled her, the sweet flickering agitation. She was careful not to do anything unusual, not to practice any of what she'd learned from Joel. She might have asked Todd to thrust more slowly, to give her time to catch up with herself. She might have asked him to touch her, down there, with his tongue. But then he'd know, he'd figure it out. She felt translucent, her faithlessness ticking just under the surface of her skin. Her greed and lasciviousness; her capacity for destruction. She whispered, "Todd, oh, I love you." He grimaced, sighed, and fell away, his outer arm resting companionably across her breasts. He kissed her and she lay beside him, praying silently. In another three weeks, when she found out she was pregnant—possibly with Todd's baby, more likely with Joel's—she'd take a final vow. She'd be faithful forever. She'd quit her classes, stop thinking about a job. She'd be perfect, unfailing, a miracle of kindness and good works.

1 9 8 2 / The sight of him nude on the fire escape, singing "Didn't It Rain" as the darkness thinned around his sleek dark body and the hooker upstairs screamed at him to shut the fuck up—the sight of him that way was everything Zoe needed to know about love. She sat on the mattress humming "Dark Angel." Those two words, over and over, as music leaked into the brightening air and the furious hooker stomped a counter-rhythm on the plaster overhead. "I got a dark angel gonna visit me tonight." If Zoe had that kind of talent, she'd write the song. Black wings, smooth flanks, the cut and tumble of muscle stitched straight to the bone. No mortal fat. The last of the acid sifted through her blood and she hummed "Dark angel in my window." He'd said he wanted to sing a hymn for Annie, floating crazy-haired somewhere in the East River, a silent angel of the drowned drifting amid the glitter of fish and lost jewelry. There were other people between him and the water but this music wasn't for them.

"Hey," Zoe said, and she watched her voice cut through the fog of the room. She watched it dart to the place where Levon was standing. "Hey."

He didn't stop. She watched her voice swim into his ear and stay there. Another part of her was inside him now. He didn't always give back.

She would have said, "Come here, come back to bed," but she didn't want to let go of that. She didn't want him to keep it. She rose from the mattress and wrapped the spread around her. Paisleys sparked. The fabric was electric in the cool, damp air. A nimbus gathered, and followed her across the floorboards to the window.

"Hey," she said again, climbing out. From above, the hooker's voice rained down. "You fucking maniacs, shut up or I'm calling the police." She wouldn't call anybody. Zoe was sorry she didn't know this one's name. Floretta had been sweet, and Luz funny and harmed, but since then there'd been three different girls and all were black holes in the world, without generosity or even glee in their own meanness. You couldn't know their names.

"Levon," she whispered, one limpid word he could keep because it was his, anyway. He sang on. He was lost in his singing. On the far side of the cemetery, scattered lights burned in tenement windows. Zoe thought the people awake behind those windows might look out and see Levon, perfectly naked, singing a hymn into the first hesitant light. She thought they might feel comforted, or they might feel afraid. *Big naked black man singing a song over the cemetery. Judgment Day, just as you were starting the coffee and checking to see if your socks dried on the radiator overnight.*

"Levon, it's like an ocean out here." She wasn't sure what she'd meant, but she'd found that if she let her mouth go, it would say things her brain didn't know yet. "It's like standing at the edge of Atlantis," she heard herself say. And she began to understand herself. New York in its last foggy darkness was like a lost city, cupping underwater caverns of deep black as the sky thinned and lightened overhead. An aqueous silence floated through the old graveyard, and a pilot whale paddled languorously, its flukes studded with barnacles, among the tombstones and the electric lights. Fish swerved, quick and silvery as thoughts.

"Oh, Levon," she whispered. "Isn't it strange? Isn't it just so beautiful and, well, *strange*?"

She knew he could hear her. He heard everything. His whole life had taught him how to listen. But he never took risks. He was a fisherman who kept everything he caught.

She stroked the hard plates of his shoulders, walked her fingers slowly down his spine. Levon was wholly visible. Here were his muscles, shifting under the satiny, eggplant-colored skin. Here was the ladder of his spine. The inner workings of his body were implicit under his skin the way most men's nakedness was implicit under their clothes, and she imagined undressing him, peeling the skin away from the wet purple skeins of muscle and reaching in for the lungs and intestines. She imagined taking out his rampant, glistening heart, and holding it—its obstreperous thump—in her hands. Levon's body was blatant, unashamed, unmysterious. His only secret resided in his brain, where he kept a tight little knot of Levonness, strange griefs and needs that nothing, no comfort or sex, no ceremony, could touch.

"Levon," she said, and she was glad he didn't respond. What did she mean to tell him? That she loved him so much she wanted to dismantle him, organ by organ, and hold each part reverently as the sun rose over the tenements. That she wanted to fuck him right there, on the fire escape, to be blotted out and sung to and moved around until she was something else, another shape in the changing world.

He finished the song in his own time. While she waited, running her open hands over the ropy surface of his back, Zoe knew what it was like to be a sea captain's widow, out on the walk with her husband's ghost who was wailing her the news an hour before the messenger arrived. She knew the shock, the echo, and the windy, hollow satisfaction. Mourning was straightforward, a simple anguish. From now on, your life would be easier. No more wondering if he was safe. No more worrying that his love had started to ravel and fade.

"Levon," she said, one more time, just to see the shape his name cut out of the air.

"Mmm." His voice was always soft and guarded. Anyone could be listening, taking notes, plotting a future in which Levon counted less.

"Baby, it's daytime. Better come in, you could get arrested."

He nodded. The cords of his shoulders shifted, thin lazy snakes warming in the sun. He stood, considering, as if getting arrested might be a good idea. A purgative, something harsh but redeeming. Then he turned to face her. His erection bumped against her hip and she thought, 'He's been standing out here singing a hymn with a hard-on.' He held her. From upstairs, the hooker screamed for the police.

Zoe didn't remember going inside. It happened; they were outside and then they were in. They were back on the mattress, fucking, sending moans and small moist suction sounds into the room. This acid wouldn't quit. Zoe felt his cock inside her and she felt the colors it shot through her blood, the hot oranges and yellows, liquid and jangly, like spurts of electrified water. She felt herself with her legs slung over Levon's shoulders, whimpering, and she felt the room, the old furniture draped in sheets and bedspreads, the pictures in their chipped gilt frames. She saw that it was a storage room, made only of waiting. As she fucked she lost track of herself. She floated out. She began to see that she and Levon were fucking in a dead room in a building full of hookers and drug people and ancient, mortified women. Someone in another room boiled an egg. Someone searched in the gray light for a vein. Traffic rumbled up Second Avenue, and a bus driver sighed over the thin pleasures of the night before. The present stretched until it bled over into the past and the future. Shadows of immigrants and sailors and merchants threaded their way among the drowsy living, and there was Levon on the fire escape, with his song and a hard-on, putting out music for the shade of Crazy Annie, who'd decided that the violent ecstasy of the long drop and the shimmering, oil-black water was better than another day of wondering. Here was Levon, fucking with silent, sweaty absorption. Fucking was a tunneling process; he had to dig his way out of jail with a teaspoon. Oh, she loved him. She loved his patience and his disregard, his habit of disappearing before he'd left the room. She loved him and in some way she could not quite name she wished him dead. She saw the future, in which Levon would leave her without explanation, with mournful, deliberate reverence, the same way he sang his hymns.

Then the fuck was over, and the hot colors cooled to blue. Levon sighed, rolled away from her. She could never come on acid; she didn't think about it. Coming would have been too much. It would have blown her up like a firecracker inside a melon. It would have opened her too wide. Her body was cooling and she put her head on Levon's sweaty chest, inhaling his sharp citrus smell. She played with his limp, wet cock. He was different from other men, not just because he was dark. He kept all his hatred, cupped it inside himself as if it was something precious he refused to share with the world.

"Pretty," she whispered.

"Huh?"

"You're so pretty."

He grunted, in boredom or disdain. He kept her words, scraps of ribbon he'd hold forever inside his skull. She held on the way she'd taught herself to, with invisible hands that embraced her insides. You could flip if you let yourself count your losses and your human flaws.

"You're *beautiful*," she said. Just let it go. Just don't worry about what gets kept and what's returned. "You have the most fantastic cock I've ever seen on a man."

He chuckled, as a parent would over the rampaging enthusiasms of a child. "The Negra is famous for his physical endowment,"

Levon said. "Explorers to the dark continent sometimes brought them back as curiosities. It ain't personal. It's a African thing."

"I might love you," she said. "What would happen if that was true?"

He grunted again, ran the palm of his hand up her thigh. Outside, a dove called. Ants crawled busily over the trees that stood among the old graves, the battered brown hulks of the buildings.

"Listen," she said. "Maybe we should sleep a little."

"Mmm."

She reached into the crate beside the mattress, shook two reds out of a crystal bottle. "Let's just sleep a little," she said, handing him one.

"Yeah," he murmured, swallowing the pill. "Sleep and dream."

She swallowed her own pill and waited for the gray lull, the gloved feeling. Levon breathed beside her, eyes closed, though he couldn't be asleep that quickly. She touched him, lightly, with a fingertip, on his forehead, chest, and belly, as if looking for the button. The mechanism that would spring it all open. She wanted what he wouldn't give her. His childhood, his fears. His explanations. He was not unkind but he lived in his own country. She could only learn the rules by breaking them. In Levon's country, compliments were insults and stories were lies. Of all human sounds, only music carried no hidden taint of defeat or domination.

What worried Zoe: She may in fact have sought to murder him. He was her first gentle man, her first black man, and she loved him with a hunter's ferocity. Didn't she think about putting her hands inside him? Couldn't she get herself wet by imagining biting his perfect ass, not gently but ravenously, sinking her teeth into the roundness of his cheeks, their maddening, muscular innocence? She thought of herself inhabiting Levon, scooping him out. She ran her fingers through his pubic hair and had an acid thought about Cassandra at dinner, her jaw hinged so it opened as a snake's jaw does, so she could swallow bodies nearly as large as her own. Hold on, she thought. Don't get too loose. She thought of trees dripping with snakes. She watched Levon's profile.

Yes, he would leave soon. He had never been here, not really, and he was going somewhere she couldn't follow. He dreamed in a language different from hers.

She ran her finger slowly down over her breasts to the curve of her stomach. Nothing stirred there, not yet. She thought he would leave before the child started showing itself, and she thought that was probably right. She wouldn't tell him. She didn't have the words. And, anyway, this was her child, hers alone. Levon would want to give it a name she couldn't know. He'd want to cup the child's feathery soul in his hands and add it to his own fierce inventory. She looked at him for a long time. She watched the progress of sleep on his strange, beautiful face.

She had the nameless part of him. She would keep it safe; she'd talk to it in a language that was perfect and true.

"Goodbye, lover," she whispered. Without opening his eyes, he said, "Good night."

Then the drug kicked in, and she followed a dream out of the room.

1 9 8 2 /   The evening of the day the divorce papers were signed Constantine bought a six-pack and drove out to his houses. He didn't want to see Magda. He didn't want to do anything and he didn't want to do nothing. He parked on a street, smoking cigarettes and drinking beer. He waited for a sense of calm to arrive but as time passed he only found himself growing more and more irritated with the lighted windows, the little arrivals and departures, the formation of yellow ceramic ducklings lined up behind a white ceramic mother duck. Who did they think they were, these people? Suckers, rubes, busting their nuts to make the payments on these shitbox houses, walls you could break through with a kitchen spoon and aluminum window frames that would keep out the cold about as well as a raincoat would keep you dry if you fell in the ocean. He drove to another street—Amity Lane— and then to a third, Meadowview. On Meadowview, in the middle of a block, one of the units stood empty. Number 17, right. Everybody who built on spec knew that, for some reason, certain houses seemed to carry a curse. They were dogs, they were lemons, though they'd been built from the same material, the same pine and plaster, as all the others. Same two-car garage, same wall-to-wall, same kitchen fixtures. In Constantine's tracts, they were three or four doors down from their identical *twins*, for Christ's sake. But, for some reason, these houses wouldn't sell. They'd stay dark and empty as the rest of the tract filled up. Birds would start nesting in the eaves, skunks would whelp pups in the sub-basements. Kids would break in to smoke marijuana or to fuck in the empty rooms, to write smut on the walls. Finally you'd cut someone a deal, let him have the place for five grand or so below market value, and sometimes that was the end of it but sometimes, with a few of these houses, the trouble just refused to go. The new owners would default on their payments, and then after the bank foreclosed and Constantine bought the place back from the bank the next new owners—nice people, regular types—would die in a car accident or lose a child or just disappear one day, with the dishes still neatly stacked in the cupboards. No one in the business believed in curses or ghosts, sacred burial grounds, anything like that, but occasionally, for whatever reason, there were these houses like the one at 17 Meadowview, empty more often than not and prone, when occupied, to ill fortune. There were these houses that stood in a little vortex of bad luck, though their paint was fresh and their chimneys straight.

Constantine got out of his car and walked slowly around the silent house, taking in its simple details. White aluminum siding, aluminum eight-over-eights, green fiberboard shutters he'd bought by the gross. Too new and clean to be haunted, he thought. The house held its darkness inside it, the empty silence of its rooms, though he knew the interior as well as he knew the rooms of his own home. From the foyer (the wives loved little touches like calling the entrance a "foyer"), you went straight ahead to the living room with its dining el. To the left was a kitchen and a little linoleumed foxhole called a family room. To the right were three tiny bedrooms, two baths. Total square footage, eleven hundred fifty-five. Constantine strolled to the back yard, a patch of raw dirt that had been trucked in from Passaic to fill in the marshland that had once been here, just a big wet tangle of cattails and frogs and the occasional whooping crane. He stood on the bare earth, facing the house he'd built. There was the sliding glass door that would open into the living room, there the high rectangular window of the master bedroom. He stooped, picked up a stone and threw it, without rage, almost speculatively, at the bedroom window. The stone went through the glass the way it would disappear into black ice, with a small clean sound, leaving its jagged, white-edged shape behind. Constantine wasn't sure how he felt. Angry, maybe, but maybe it was more like empty, like he needed to break every window in this goddamned house just to get to zero again, just to start feeling something simple like rage. He threw another stone, and another. He broke all three panes of the master-bedroom window, then broke the sliding glass door, which would not shatter but only took the stones like a body taking bullets, one hole and then another. He hurled stone after stone and then, growing nervous about the police but still full of nothing at all, no particular feeling beyond a vague urge to be out of there, he got quickly back into his car and drove away.

It was a clear, warm night. The thruway had its own steady rhythm, its soft white glow. There was some kind of comfort in driving and he told himself, for almost fifty miles, that he was in fact just driving, working something out of his system. It wasn't until he'd passed Manhattan that he admitted, sheepishly, that he was probably going to drive all the way to Susan's place in Connecticut.

He got there after midnight. The sight of Susan's house, a substantial colonial standing among mature trees on a solid piece of property, brought tears to his eyes. She had made it. She was happy, safe; she had the life he'd wanted for his children and himself. He got out of his car and walked quietly across the lawn, listening. He could hear nothing except the crickets and the faint sigh and rustle of the night itself. No sound of the baby crying. But, hey, the lights were on upstairs. He stepped up onto the porch and stopped there. What would he tell Susan when she came to the door? The truth would have to do. Today he and her mother were officially divorced and he couldn't stand the thought of being with anyone but Susan. Still, he didn't knock on the door or ring the bell. Something moved in him, some furious remorse, and he didn't want Susan to see it. He didn't want the liquor and sympathy of her husband, a Milquetoast, a nice boy who'd made it because his parents were rich and because he wasn't torn by the passions that sometimes ruled other men. Constantine didn't want to be old in this house, or alone, or defeated in any way. And yet he didn't want to be anywhere else. He loved the house, the sturdy prosperous lines of it, the dormers and dovecote, the eight-over-eights. This was the real thing, here. These were the details he and Nick Kazanzakis reproduced, in particle board and aluminum, on the houses they built down in Jersey and Long Island. It had a few of the same details—Dutch-style door, bay window—as the little haunted number on Meadowview Drive. Constantine wasn't ready to drive away, but he couldn't ring the bell. He couldn't present himself as a sad case, a creature in need of shelter. He stood on the porch for a while until he heard the baby's soft fretful crying, drifting down from an upstairs window, and then, as if he'd been summoned, he went back to his car. He stayed there until all the lights were out. He watched the progress of darkness, the play of shadows over clapboard, as mother and husband and baby slept within. An hour passed, and another. He watched the stealthy, restless business of the night being conducted until the night itself forgot he was there, until his waking presence had been subsumed and he had joined the silence that rose up from the earth and met another silence, a deeper, icier one, that fell from the stars. He saw a raccoon waddle with unhurried propriety across his daughter's lawn. He saw an owl lift silently out of an elm tree like the spirit of the tree itself. He heard callings, little chirps of pleasure or alarm or simple assertions of being. He heard one long birdcall, a terrified sound that was unmistakably a question. Quickly, in shrill bursts: *Can it be? Can it be? Can it be?* He lit another cigarette, opened another beer. It had only been kisses and hugs. He'd never messed with her. He *loved* her, for Christ's sake. He *was* her, in a way, and she was him. If that made any sense. Kisses were harmless. Kisses were okay. He watched the night pass. At one moment he felt as if he were guarding the house from the living darkness that swarmed around it. At another he felt that he was homeless, destitute, come to confess his shortcomings and seek whatever protection he could find at the gate of a nocturnal city.

1 9 8 2 / Smallness was over for him. He'd lost all interest in being lithe and clever, a monkey boy. At twenty-nine, Will wanted size. He wanted to move with the ease and authority of geography. No more nervous little thin-boy dance. He was tired of making jokes. He was ready to look a little dangerous, to need no apology.

He started at a gym on the outskirts. He went faithfully, in a cold tumult of shame. He was ashamed of his aging boy's body and he was ashamed of his desire to improve it. It was easier to be cynically, defiantly skinny. It was easier to sit on a barstool and make cracks. Now he was admitting it—he owned this vanity. He wanted what fools want; he shared their belief in the flesh. Still, shivering with embarrassment, he went. He drove to the gym after school let out, put himself through his routines. The gym he'd chosen lay in a failing shopping center in Malden, far from the orbits of all his worlds. At this gym, middle-aged men sweated on exercise bikes. Bands of thickly muscled boys with outdated haircuts hoisted enormous weights and spoke to one another in loud, encouraging insults. The boys could have been the brothers of his old friend Biff, noisily confident, in love with their own beauty and ready to murder any man who admired it as they did. Will kept to himself. He detested and, grudgingly, admired them from across the carpeted field of barbells and machinery.

He was mortified and he was faithful. He grimaced under five-pound weights. Sometimes, when he was red-faced and exhausted after lifting an especially insignificant weight, he glanced around and smiled, helplessly eager to let any witnesses know he was in on the joke. When he saw that no one had been watching him and no one appeared to care, he picked up another weight and started again.

The five-pound barbells became easy for him and he promoted himself to tens, then to fifteens. After almost two months he began to notice a slight swelling in his chest. At first he refused to believe it was the result of his efforts. He had not imagined his body capable of responding to discipline or hard work. His body had always seemed to live on its own. It had looked the way it looked, stayed healthy without sufficient rest or abstention from liquor or any elaborate attention to questions of nourishment. Now Will examined his reflection and saw that two small mounds of muscle were beginning to rise under the flat white skin of his chest. He turned sideways, then faced front again. There they were, undeniably. Little humps of muscle he'd made.

He worked harder, and he grew. It felt like a miracle. The muscles of his chest revealed themselves and then, more slowly, the muscles of his shoulders and back. He felt as if a second body were emerging. He watched as it asserted its shape: the raised straps of his triceps, the solid pillows of biceps. He started buying books on nutrition and, still stinging with shame, buying exercise magazines in which glossy, tanned men demonstrated new exercises. He tried the new exercises. He bought vitamins, forced himself to eat five meals a day. He lived inside this new body, watching its changes with a hope he had not yet been able to manage for another man. He was embarrassed about that, too—what kind of person was he turning into?—but he let himself go. He let himself be admired, by his own eyes and the eyes of others. He was becoming a hunk. He, Billy, the skinny boy whose only powers were his wit and his talent for saying no. At the gym, as he grimaced under his increasing loads, he spurred himself on by thinking about bulk and power, the end of doubt. When the weather turned he bought tank tops; he bought his first pair of Speedos. He began living as two people, the self who had been a frightened child and the self whose landscape of musculature threw small flesh-colored shadows on his own skin. Occasionally he imagined showing his enlarged body to his father. He imagined his father's admiration and, more obliquely, his father's desire. Sometimes Will felt guilty for spending his time and his energies on a project so perishable. Sometimes he was filled with a soaring sense of possibility that took him back to the days, more than ten years ago, when he went driving at night with his friends, in those big borrowed cars that could take them anywhere.

1 9 8 2 / "Hello?"

"Mary Stassos, please."

"Speaking."

"Mary, this is Cassandra. Zoe's friend. Do you remember me?"

"Cassandra. Yes."

"Mary, listen. Zoe's okay, but she's in the hospital."

"What?"

"Don't get all plucked, she's *okay*."

"What is it? What happened?"

"Well, honey, she took a few too many pills."

"*What?*"

"She slipped up a little. Too many little red something-or-others, it could happen to anybody. Now listen, she's *fine*, they say they'll let her out tomorrow or the next day. She didn't want me to call you, and I almost didn't, but then I thought, what the hell, I've never obeyed anyone, why start now? And really, a mother ought to know about these things."

"Where is she? What hospital?"

"St. Vincent's. I'm here now."

"I'll be right there. And, Cassandra?"

"Mm-hm?"

"Will you stay with her until I get there?"

"I wouldn't abandon my daughter, now, would I?"

"I beg your pardon?"

"Figure of speech. Now, honey, get in that car of yours and *drive*."

"I can be there in an hour."

"Don't break your neck, love. She's fine, honestly, I'd tell you if she wasn't. A girl makes a mistake every now and then. And, Mary?"

"Yes?"

"The baby's fine. When you get here, you and I have got to do some serious talking to this girl about behaving like she has in her condition. We'll be an avalanche of nagging—"

"The baby?"

"Listen, just *get* here. Girl, you've got some catching up to do."

Zoe was asleep, lying thin and gray in a hospital bed. Mary stood watching for signs of her daughter. The girl in the bed had a blankness, an anyone quality. She was thin, not pretty, her hair lank and unclean on the pillow. Mary found herself staring at Zoe's hands. The face was waxen, slumbering, lost in its silent demonstration of how skin can lie upon a skull. Mary looked at Zoe's hands and saw her there, in the curl and twitch of the fingers. There was her daughter's inchoate being, the creaturely push and pull Mary remembered. There was the fretful one-year-old, asleep and dreaming in Mary's lap, cutting off the circulation in Mary's legs because she dared not shift her position for fear of waking Zoe and setting into motion another hour's worth of sourceless, inconsolable weeping.

She was still watching Zoe's hands when a voice behind her said, "Mary?"

It was a man in a dress.

He stood in the hospital light, a tall man with garish red lips and enormous, spidery black fans of false eyelashes. He wore a black beehive wig and a red square-dancing dress, bristling with net and chiffon and synthetic red lace.

"Yes?" Mary said.

"It's Cassandra."

Mary passed through an interval of dislocation, a loss of order like what she'd felt in Constantine's office the day she'd realized he was having an affair with fat, homely Magda. This was Cassandra. The words appeared in her head. Her daughter had taken an overdose and this was the woman Mary had liked so much on the telephone.

"Sorry about all this," Cassandra said. "I didn't have time to change, it's not what I ordinarily wear to emergency rooms."

Mary nodded. She said, "Cassandra."

"Oh, I know, I know. Life is full of surprises, isn't it? Have you talked to the doctor?"

"Yes."

"So you see? She's going to be fine."

"What happened?"

"She wasn't doing Marilyn, if that's what you mean. I'm sure of it. Like I told you over the phone, it was a simple mistake. But she's got to stop this. You know how the young are, they think nothing can possibly happen to them."

A part of Mary floated to the ceiling and hovered there, watching herself stand beside her sleeping daughter and talk to a tall man in a red dress. A part of Mary asked questions and wanted answers.

"Did you say something about a baby?" she said.

"I thought you knew. She *told* me she'd told you. I kept saying to her, 'What do you think you're going to do, *hide* the kid for the first eighteen years?' I said, 'You're not Lucy Ricardo, don't try to come up with some kind of zany scheme.' "

"How long has she been pregnant?"

"Four months."

"And the father?"

"I never had the pleasure."

"Well," Mary said.

She stood there, just like that. She didn't cry. She didn't move.

Cassandra put a hand on Mary's shoulder. His hand was soft and light and Mary found, to her surprise, that she was not repelled by his touch.

"I know, honey," he said. "It's a big dose, isn't it?"

III

INSIDE

THE MUSIC

1 9 8 3   /   Magda wasn't a beauty, not in the magazine way that some guys went for. Those stick women with no hips or tits, a big cloud of hair like the end of a Q-Tip. Mary was that kind of beauty. She had those magazine fingernails, those thighs that didn't touch. Constantine had been there, with that. He knew exactly what kind of hunger lay on the other side of it. He knew about the primness of bedside tables. He knew about the sourceless, infinite anger that had no cure because it had no cause, nothing you could get to beyond the plain facts of a hard-working man and a woman whose beauty led her to expect more than the world could provide. He'd been there—maybe that was the difference between him and other men. He'd already had what most guys spent their lives reaching for. Maybe he knew something most men didn't. Maybe he'd pushed his way through to a kind of genius, a bigger and more fabulous vision that lay beyond the rules of ordinary beauty.

All right, then. If Mary was going to divorce him over Magda, if she was going to take the house he'd built plus a big greedy bite out of his income every month, if she was going to poison the kids' minds toward him . . . All right. He had an answer, and it was simple and it was true. There was a genius in his love for Magda. It wasn't a usual love, some poor shlunk leaving his wife for a little leopard of a blonde who'd leave *him* as soon as she got herself a better offer. This was something else, this love of his, and if you didn't get it, if you were still so unsure of yourself that you needed to parade around with prom queens, well, too bad for you.

At home, in his rented apartment, Constantine played his old records and thought about Magda. He played Tom Jones, Engelbert Humperdinck. He played them in private because all the kids, even Susan, teased him about his taste in music, and these days he didn't like being teased. Okay, he'd never liked being teased, but these days he got furious over any joke made at his expense, any clever little remark that suggested he was a figure of fun. And getting mad in front of the kids just gave Mary more ammunition for the poison she was spreading against him. So he listened to his records alone, after work. Tom Jones sang, *It's not unusual to make love at any time.* He kept the records in a drawer, not hidden exactly, but out of sight, so that if one of the kids came over and looked through them they wouldn't start in on him. He'd had enough of that. These days, he just wanted to be loved.

He wanted to be loved. What was wrong with that?

He married Magda at St. Bartholomew's, the biggest Episcopal church in six counties. Fuck Catholicism with its curses and re-demptions, its insistence on cheerful misery as the only virtue. Fuck the Greek Orthodox church of his childhood, with its veils and secrets and roadside shrines. Episcopalians understood that Christ came to earth as an advertisement for the flesh, to tell us it's all right to be human. It's all right to want things. It's all right to own, as long as you keep yourself humble by remembering that you'll turn it all in again anyway, when your time comes. So Constantine insisted on an Episcopal wedding, and Magda's old Catholic mother, reduced by arthritis to a life of television and sly, joking complaints, didn't put up anything he couldn't handle. If he could beat county inspectors and a squadron of crooked day laborers, he could overrule a sick, good-humored old Hungarian woman in a housecoat the color of stale bread. Besides, she wasn't a fool. She knew a good deal when she saw one.

Constantine and Magda put on the grandest wedding St. Bartholomew's had ever seen. For the wedding a thousand white gladioli were cut. A cake almost five feet high was baked and covered with white sugar roses, swans, and bells, and topped by a little porcelain bride and groom—porcelain, not plastic—with blurred, rapturous faces and identical tiny red mouths. For Magda's dress, forty yards of white lace was tatted by whoever, Belgian or French nuns, whoever it was that made lace, along with slightly less than an acre of white silk and chiffon and white sequins and pearls no bigger than a sparrow's eyeball. Mary had told Constantine once about something called the forbidden stitch, some Chinese thing, a kind of embroidery so fine they had to ban women from doing it because they went blind over their needles. As Constantine stood at the altar he glanced at Billy. His best man, his only son and heir, built up now, bulkily petulant in a rented tux. Blood rose, hot, to Constantine's temples. He knew what Billy was but he couldn't say the word, not even inside his own head. Here he stood in front of everybody with his brawny, girlish son and there in the first pew sat Zoe with the little black bastard, and beside her was Susan— perfect Susan, who barely spoke to him—and her cheerful kiss-ass husband and their son, his grandson, clear-faced, in a miniature dark blue suit. His grandson. At three, the kid could already write his name; he could throw a softball hard enough to sting your hand. He had a precocious air of gravity, a personal importance. Here was the future Constantine had worked for, this sturdy, affectionate boy with a Greek jaw and wide-set American eyes. This one thread, at least, was coming out of the tangle straight and true and strong. At the altar Constantine knew a soaring happiness, the old kind, born of a piercing consciousness of the world's shifting and inscrutable order. He had suffered, maybe he'd even failed in certain ways, but here he was at the head of an immense church, big and proud as a lion in his tux, and he said to himself, All right. He said, Let it happen, all of it. As if in response to his silent command the wedding march started up and Magda walked toward him down the red-carpeted aisle in her shimmering lunar garden of a dress. He found that . . . Okay, maybe this was a little strange, but he found that he liked the idea of seamstresses going blind to create this, this huge moment of stained glass and music and the staunch white rods of all those gladioli, bright and clean as torches in the colored dusk of the church. It had something to do with resurrection, with liberation from the world of the small. It seemed regrettable but right that this plenty he'd created, this magnificence, should take something out of the world. Some people found love and an immense comfort. Some women went blind, sewing. That was the way of things. Matter can't be created or destroyed, only rearranged. A little more here means a little less over there.

1 9 8 4 / Mary went to the window and looked out at the ruins of Constantine's garden. It was her single concession to rage, to whatever she possessed of an urge to do harm. The house remained immaculate, the beds made and the floors swept, the top of the dining-room table rubbed to a rich, burnished life even though she ate her meals in the kitchen or on a tray in front of the TV. But she did nothing to Constantine's garden. She watched with a slightly irritated indifference as the tomatoes ripened and burst on the vines, as the beans withered and the basil turned brown. She watched the zucchini vines grow and strangle the rest of the garden, the zucchini themselves swollen grotesquely, big as waterlogged baseball bats, their flesh turned to wood, inedible. Then she watched the zucchini die, collapsing leadenly onto themselves, shriveling, until finally there was nothing left but dead leaves crisped by the first frosts and the inert carcasses of the squash themselves, long and flaccid and utterly dead. Mary covered the rosebushes, bedded the perennial flower bulbs with peat moss, pruned the deadwood off the pear tree. She took perfect care of every other living thing and did not touch, did not so much as step into, the little deceased shrine of Constantine's garden. Snow, when it came, dusted the blackened heads of lettuce, whatever had gone too foul for the rabbits to eat. Wind blew the bean poles down, and once, on a blustery day in early December, Mary looked out the window just in time to see a little snake of vine, with one perfect fan-shaped brown leaf, blowing away over the fence and into the restless, icy gray.

1 9 8 6 / Jamal was eating the sky. He opened his mouth so wide he felt a small crackle of hinges deep in his jaw as he sucked it in, the fat heavy whiteness that blew and twisted around him. It turned to nothing on his tongue. He ran in a circle, eating a patch of the dense white falling sky, and he saw himself filling up with it, the cold and distance, the big arcing empty space.

"Jamal." It was Cassandra, coming in blue glasses and a white jacket. Jamal sucked in a last mouthful. He looked mournfully at all the sky he wouldn't eat.

"Let's go, baby." Cassandra came, big in her boots. "Everybody's ready."

Jamal stood waiting. He'd eaten some of the white silence, but there was so much more.

"Pretty, huh?" Cassandra said. She put her big hand on his head. "If you like nature. Now, personally, I'm partial to a cocktail lounge or an apartment, someplace where you can control the light a little. Daytime's for the young. But come along, now, your grandma's about to bust out of her panty hose in there."

Jamal reached up for her hand. Her hand was almost hot,

knobby with rings. Flakes blew onto her white jacket, disappeared. As she led him back toward the house he opened his mouth, wide, and ate a little more.

"You turn to stone if you don't get out of Connecticut before nightfall," Cassandra said. "Now wait a minute, that's not true. I've promised your grandmother I'd quit exaggerating around you, she worries about your sense of reality. So listen, I retract the statement. You do not turn to stone if you stay in Connecticut after dark. You just go on with your life, but in Connecticut."

Jamal filled his mouth, made footprints. The house came, white, with white lines on its black shutters. Flakes fell past the yellow window squares.

"Here we are," Cassandra called into the back door. Inside, it was warm and full of rules. His grandmother came from the kitchen, crouched in front of him.

"Here you are," she said. She made her painful little smile. She was darker than Cassandra, more happy and worried. She and Cassandra had the same mouth.

"Look at you," his grandmother said. "You were out there without your mittens."

"Seized by an urge," Cassandra said.

"His hands are freezing." Grandma's face gathered in on itself. Worry was something she could taste.

"Come on into the kitchen, Jamal," Cassandra said. "Let's warm up those little mitts of yours."

"Honestly," his grandmother said. "You can't go running out half dressed like this, it's *freezing* out there."

"True, true," Cassandra said. "Thank the lord for central heat."

"Jamal, are you listening to me? You have to *think*, you can't just do whatever enters your mind."

"Oh, Mary," Cassandra said.

His grandmother's face stopped. She was angry, and she was deciding.

"Really," she said. "I'm his grandmother."

"And I'm his *god*mother. And I think every now and then a four-year-old boy runs out into the snow without his mittens on. It doesn't mean he's embarking on a life of crime."

"Cassandra—"

Grandma looked down, then up. "All right," she said. She was sucking a hard ball of anger and worry with a sweet-sour taste. "Let's get going, you two."

Jamal let his grandmother take his hand and lead him into the room where the party used to be. Balloons still bobbed and jostled on the ceiling. Half the cake stood whitely on the white table, circled by the melted stubs of candles. Ben sat in his chair at the head of the table, next to Aunt Susan. Their grandfather stood behind, looking hungrily at the room. He wanted to eat the house. Jamal wanted to eat everything outside the house. Ben ran his new orange truck over the cloth. He looked at Jamal with his hard eyes.

"You're still here," Ben said.

Jamal nodded. Ben and their grandfather both looked at him and saw that he was small and dark and prone to vanishing. He saw them see him that way.

"Sure you're still here," Grandpa said. "You wouldn't run away from your own birthday party, would you, buddy?"

"Everybody thought you were lost," Ben said.

Aunt Susan touched Ben's hair. Then she came over and waited a quarter second before touching Jamal's hair. He felt her hand, waiting, and then he felt her touch.

"We lost track of you, sweetheart," Aunt Susan said.

Jamal nodded. He'd been eating the frozen air. He'd been nowhere, and everywhere.

"We've got to hit the road," his grandmother said. "I don't want to be driving in this after dark."

She spoke to his grandfather, though she didn't look at him.

There were bad roads and darkness. There was something else, a patient appetite that waited.

"Mm-hm," Aunt Susan said. "Jamal, honey, it was nice having you."

Uncle Will came in from somewhere else. He was not in the room, and then he was.

"Hey," he said. "We thought you'd decided to walk home."

Jamal looked at the rug. It had people hidden in it. There was the fat Japanese woman with her arms out. There was the smiling devil. When he looked up again, Uncle Will was still there. He stood with Aunt Susan. Aunt Susan smiled in her dress that was like his grandmother's but brighter, with more buttons. Aunt Susan wore the gold bird at her breast, the bright silent bird with the sharp beak.

"Come on, gang," his grandmother said. Jamal looked around, fearfully, for Cassandra. She was gone and then she was there, behind him. She had her shine and her smell. He reached up and touched his own hair, then reached for her hand. The room shone and sparked.

"Ta, everybody," Cassandra said. There was the long work of coats and goodbyes. When the front door opened, snow blew in. Jamal watched it vanish into the boards. He thought of all he hadn't eaten. He held some of his presents: an orange truck like Ben's and a Star Trek spaceship. Uncle Will held the big stuffed bear that Jamal had wanted and that now embarrassed him, though he still wanted it and, in some uncertain way, despised it. The bear had blank black eyes, a pale orange tongue.

"Tell Zoe we hope she's feeling better," Aunt Susan said.

"Of course I will," Grandma said. She kissed Aunt Susan. Aunt Susan was like his grandmother but darker, more worried and smooth. The bird glittered on her breast. Jamal walked to the car between Cassandra and Uncle Will, his arms full of gifts. There were intricate waves of love and hatred, a low complicated buzz.

When he looked back he saw Ben and Grandpa in the doorway, outlined in yellow, watching him go. Uncle Will drove, and Grandma sat in front. Jamal sat in back, with Cassandra.

"Well, that's over," Uncle Will said.

"I thought it was fine," Grandma said.

"Sure," Uncle Will answered. "It was fine. It was a lovely little party."

Jamal watched the flakes tap against the car windows. He watched trees go by, and other cars, and houses. He saw himself taking everything, reaching out the window and gathering up every house and tree as they drove through the blowing white. He saw himself taking them home and showing them to his mother.

"Tell it again," he whispered to Cassandra.

"What?"

"You know."

"The same one?" she said.

"Yes."

"Honey, you are ob*sessed.*"

"Tell it."

"Okay. You were brand new, you were the tiniest little thing—"

"How tiny?"

"Hmm. You were just slightly smaller than one of those chickens in the window at Lee Chow's."

"No."

"We're not going to vary from this one inch, are we? Okay, you were as tiny as Mrs. García's puppy. The Mysteriously Unnamed."

"Yes."

"And we put you in the car and drove you all the way up to the Green River in Massachusetts."

"It took a long time," Jamal said.

"Yes, it did. Over two hours. There were rivers that were more conveniently located, but your mother had been to the Green River once and she'd seen that there was something magic about it, so when you were born nothing would do but that we baptize you up there."

"Yes."

"We drove more than two hours," Cassandra said. "It was a pretty day in July, there were tiger lilies and black-eyed Susans growing alongside the road. I was wearing, if I do say so myself, a very fetching little christening outfit, white leather pants and a white tuxedo jacket and a pair of hiking boots because, honey, it was a *hike* to that magic river, your mother didn't choose one that was close to the road, no, she didn't."

"We were riding in a blue car."

"Yes, we were. A borrowed Toyota, nothing grand, but reliable. It was you and your mother and Will and me."

"Uh-huh."

"And when we got there we parked the car and carried you all the way to the river."

"How long?" Jamal said.

"Oh, let's see, what's the correct response here? Longer than walking from Canal Street all the way to Central Park."

"That's right."

"And we finally got there, and your Aunt Cassandra's hairdo was a little bit disarranged but she was a *trouper*, a very distant relation of Daniel Boone. And really, the river was beautiful. It was a big wide river with trees on both sides of it, and lord knows there was hardly anybody else there, because not many people would choose to walk that far just to see something that flows right out of their taps at home—"

"There were fish."

"Mm-hm. Trout. You could see them. We all took our shoes off and waded in, that water was ice-cold, and Aunt Cassandra had a brief cranky moment from which she recovered admirably. The water was very clear and the bottom was covered with little round stones and it *was* really quite pretty, even if the temperature would've made an Eskimo nervous."

"Momma was carrying me."

"Yes, she was," Cassandra said. "We carried you out into the water and said a few words, and Will and I promised to look after you, and then in spite of your Aunt Cassandra's objections Will poured a little of that frigid water over your head. Because it was, after all, a baptism."

"I cried."

"As any sensible person would. You cried all the way back to the car, and then the minute we were moving again, you fell asleep."

"And that's the end," Jamal said.

"More or less. That's how this tired old thing you see before you became a godmother. Honey, the world is full of nothing if not surprises."

"That's the end," Jamal said.

"Well, yes and then again no," Cassandra answered.

Zoe was in the fever when they came home. She'd been out of it for a while, she'd been a woman in a room drinking a cup of chamomile tea, watching the snow tumble past her window, waiting for her son to return. Then the fever flared again and she was inside, she was only heat and sickness and odd sizzling thoughts that wanted to turn into dreams. The sickness was like a drug but it had a sharper edge, a meanness in it, and she fought to keep order, ordinary time in a room in the snow. It was New York, it was January. The faded roses on the armchair tried to move, to take on faces, but she said no and they remained roses, pink and purple, stationary. She was lying on her mattress watching the roses and then they were there, she'd been watching the roses too carefully to hear the door. Jamal climbed shyly and eagerly onto the mattress with her, emanating cold, his hair studded with perfect beads of clear water.

"Hey," she whispered. "You're back."

"I got a spaceship," he said. He showed it to her, a gray saucer with a clear bubble on top. He swooped it in a wide arc and she could smell it, the hard new plastic odor, the unliving sweetness.

"Just like you wanted," she said. She heard her voice, a watery thread that came from someplace near her but not in her. "Did you have a good time?"

"Yes," he said, though she knew he wasn't telling the truth. How did they learn to lie, so early, even when no one asked them to?

Her mother sat on the edge of the mattress, put her hand to Zoe's forehead. "You're still burning up," she said.

"I'm okay," Zoe answered. "I felt better for a while, this just came back about a half hour ago."

"I think you'd better go to the doctor," Will said. "If you won't call him, I will."

"No, I'm fine," Zoe told him. "It's the flu, people get the flu. Jamal had it last week, didn't you, honey?"

He nodded. He was lost, contemplating the spaceship, and she lost herself with him. Lamplight shone on the gray surface of the deck, on the white word *Enterprise*. Outer space was bright, not dark. You could go anywhere.

Cassandra said, "I'm going to heat up some soup for Jamal. Hon, do you feel like you could eat a little, too?"

"No," Zoe said. The deck of the ship was smooth and brilliant as granite, and briefly she believed that something fabulous lay hidden inside this simple toy. Then she didn't believe it, then she did again.

"I don't want any soup," Jamal said.

"Okay, fine," Cassandra answered. "I didn't want to risk my fingernails opening a can, anyway."

"He should eat something," Zoe's mother said. "Jamal, you haven't had anything all day but junk."

"He's had birthday cake, ice cream, and a considerable quantity of snow," Cassandra said. "Some days you feel like an all-white diet."

"Just a few bites of soup, Jamal," Zoe's mother said.

"No soup," Jamal said, but Zoe's mother went into the kitchen to heat soup because she had decided. Zoe felt Jamal's little chaos of fears and desires, his hunger, his need to have no hunger, his love of the spaceship. She reminded herself: You're his mother. Don't get too lost with him.

Will knelt beside the mattress, stroked her hair. "I'm worried about you," he said.

"Don't be," she told him. "Flu, what's the big deal?"

"Three times since September."

"I get it from Jamal, anybody who spends a lot of time with a child gets sick. He and I just trade germs back and forth."

"I still wish you'd go to the doctor."

"I don't need a doctor," she said. "I stay in bed for a couple of days, and it goes away."

Cassandra knelt beside Will. There they were in their nimbus of worry and love, their pride, their self-hatred, their complex dislike for each other. Cassandra said, "What I suspect you need is for all of us to go away and leave you the hell alone so you can get some sleep."

Zoe smiled, wreathed in heat. There was Will's face, handsomer now that he had invented a self, settled and sure as a garden devoted to just one crop. There was the frank defiant ugliness of Cassandra, the harsh shine. "You don't have to go," Zoe said, knowing that whatever she said, they'd go eventually, whether she wanted them to or not.

She'd been dreaming. A fever dream, roiling, shot through with anxious little jolts of terror that seemed to live in the world the way eels live in a rock. She woke up and lay breathing as the room came back, its uneven ceiling and old furniture, its blue window through which a single winter star shone feebly. Jamal had gotten into bed with her. She fought the urge to wake him up and then he woke up on his own, as if he'd heard her thinking. That happened sometimes. She couldn't decide whether it was a virtue or a failing of her motherhood. He opened his eyes and stared at her.

"Hi," she said. He didn't answer. He'd brought the spaceship with him.

"You okay?" she asked. He nodded. She pulled the quilt up over his chest. The one pale cold star shone through the window, and Zoe lived through a half-dream in which she and her son were hiding together in a ruin, in the blue shade of a decrepit monument, concealed among echoing marbles and wet tangles of vine while someone or something searched for them. It was so vivid that she put her finger to her lips, cautioning Jamal to keep quiet. Then the dream passed and she saw that she was just a woman in a room with her son, in New York, though the hunted feeling refused to quit. She told Jamal, in a whisper, to go back to sleep and he answered by taking the spaceship and holding it over his head.

"Beam us up," he said.

1 9 8 7 /   His mother wanted him. He lay under the bed breathing darkness as her voice put his name in the rooms, searching. "Ben? Ben? Benjamin?" He shrank inside his own silence. He wasn't ready to be seen, not now. He had old mistakes buzzing around in him, sour thoughts, a dank poverty of being. She wanted him in his shining condition. He couldn't shine, not now, so he disappeared and let her call his name into rooms that answered only with wallpaper and afternoon light, the mute feminine dignity of furniture. He waited; he felt her perfume as she passed. Please, he said, silently, and finally she went and said to his grandfather, "He's not here, maybe he went down to the beach." Right, he thought, the beach, and he could see himself there, the golden version, happy and strong, unafraid, holding a shell or the handle of a china cup or some other little gift he'd found. He waited, here, hidden in his sadder version, a boy under a bed who didn't answer his mother's call, and after a minute had passed he crawled out and peered up over the windowsill. There she was, walking toward the beach, looking for him, a thin determined figure in a pale pink skirt, moving with a fierce sense of ownership, as if she were the lost wife of the ocean, on her way back to reclaim her privileges. Mom, he called, silently, and watched as she strode away to find the son she needed, not sad or wrong, waiting with a gift for her.

When she'd gone he let himself climb up onto the bed and lie there, feeling his grandfather's house around him. He loved this house more than any other place. It threw a shadow over its own trees; all its secrets were new and clean. From the bedroom windows you saw the garden and from the garden you saw the firm blue line of the ocean, which seemed, when you stood in the garden, like something immense and simple and unimaginably expensive that had been placed where it was to show off the more complicated beauties of the house. The house had windows of blue and red glass. The house had chandeliers that shivered with precise colorless brilliance, a stone fireplace Ben could stand up in, a room he called the Ice Palace, with thick white carpets and white cloth flowers and white wicker chairs that waited in frozen silence for someone to sit on them so they could produce their hidden music of icy cracks and groans. Something bright and promising, something invisible, moved with unhurried certainty from room to room. It was not a ghost—the house was too immaculate for ghosts, too scoured by light. But something inhabited it along with his grandfather and Magda, a living non-human spirit Ben thought of as a white peacock, fabulous and proud and serene, strutting now up the curve of the staircase, now down the carpeted hall to the third-floor turret room, where the telescope turned its eye to the garden and the ocean and where the American flag snapped on the roof.

He lay on the bed he'd claimed for himself, in the small room that looked over the tree, where the chest of drawers had brass pulls shaped like scowling, indignant eagles. He let a minute pass, and another. Then he got up, briefly practiced a look of innocence in front of the mirror, and went out to find his grandfather.

His grandfather had gone downstairs, to the kitchen, where

he was arranging tomatoes on the windowsill. His grandfather was broad in a dark blue shirt, kind and soft-haired in a battered straw hat.

"Hi," Ben said, and thought his voice sounded properly ordinary. His grandfather turned. His grandfather had the meek generosity of old men, the blunted needs.

"Hey, buddy. Your mother was looking all over for you."

"I've been here," Ben said. He walked quickly to the windowsill and picked up a tomato, which shone, heavy and translucent, in his hand. There was the tomato and there was his grandfather's smell, the layers of his after-shave and his spicy, acrid flesh.

"She went down to the beach to look for you," his grandfather said.

Ben balanced the tomato on his palm. "Beefsteak," he said.

"The pride of New Jersey," his grandfather answered. "C'mon, let's go get your mother. Your dad'll be here any minute to pick you up."

Ben put the tomato back, reluctantly, and followed his grandfather out the kitchen door. As they walked toward the ocean his grandfather took his hand. Ben, at seven, was too old for a gesture like that but he permitted it, even desired it, from his grandfather, because his grandfather had secret knowledge and a truer, more satisfied life. Ben held his grandfather's hand and walked along the outer edge of the garden and he was filled with a flushed buoyancy, a large unfocused desire made of his grandfather's smell and the remembered heft of the tomato in his hand, its fullness and shine, the fat irregularities of its flesh. He knew a pure, tingling exultation—there was a fullness between his legs, the word *beefsteak* in his head—and then he fell immediately into shame. He was wrong, though he could not have said exactly how. He was his lesser self, the craven one, the one who hid, and soon, very soon, they'd find his mother, who would need him to be otherwise. As he and his grandfather passed the garden and started down the slope that led to the beach Ben imagined himself climbing inside his grandfather, riding in him like a soldier inside a tank, steering him toward the woman in the pink skirt who demanded righteousness. There she was, on the sand with the ocean behind her, searching.

"Hey, Susie," his grandfather called. "Look who I found."

She turned, and saw him. Ben was never sure how much she knew, how deep her eyes could go. He put his face in order, let go of his grandfather's hand. He ran to her and in running he began to catch up with himself, his own strength and purity. When he called, "Hi, Mom," his voice was solid as the waves.

"Hey, you," she said, and she was not angry or disappointed. Her face darkened with pleasure at the sight of him, the running fact. "I've been looking everywhere," she said.

"I was around," he told her. It was beginning to happen. He could feel it. He'd run right out of his fears and wrongness, he'd eluded everything, and here he was, a cheerful boy with nothing to hide. He ran to his mother, did a quick feinting little dance before her, picked up a stone and threw it into the blue water. He felt the strength of his arm, the heat of her pleasure in him.

"Come on," she said. "Your father'll be here any minute, and we're not even half ready."

Ben threw another stone, and another. He danced on the shore, a spastic jig in celebration of his own rightful life. "Come *on*," his mother said, but he knew his little disobediences, his rampant energy, were part of his charm. His grandfather tried to put a big brown hand on his mother's shoulder but she stepped away. She came and touched Ben, tenderly, with bottomless pride, on the back of his head.

"I couldn't find you anywhere," she said in a soft thrilling voice, as if it were a secret they shared and needed to keep from his grandfather. Ben picked up a stone, held it. The ocean was full of bright specks, a steady purpose. He stood with his mother, looking out. He held the stone.

"Better get moving," his grandfather said, and Ben felt what his grandfather's voice did along his mother's skin, the little scraping. He threw the last stone—it skipped once, twice—and ran back up the beach. He adored the air blowing over this skin of his, the late sun and the wind. As he ran he left small flashes behind, the opposite of shadows, little glintings he seemed to put out, like light bouncing off a knife. He ran to the house, knowing he'd be worth finding. He thought of going all the way to the turret room, pushing his mother's interest that far, but when he got to the foyer Magda was home, still settling her car keys inside her purse. She produced her little jinglings and sparks, the hard white glare of her attention. Magda looked at him. She aimed a searchlight; she knew the names of everything.

"Hello," she said. She looked from Ben back into her purse, where she saw a miniature world, one that gave her more satisfaction and ease than the larger one did.

"Hi," Ben said. Magda, alone among the adults he knew, did not feel compelled to say or do anything that would make him like her better. For that reason, along with several others, he loved her. She needed nothing, not from him or from anybody. She was rich and hard-spirited and defiantly, extravagantly fat.

"I was at the beach," he said in a tone of urgent conviction, as if he needed to expain something to her, to precisely locate himself. Magda had a huge, breathing chest and a square head; he thought of her sometimes as the prophetic spirit and voice of a volcano.

"That beach is full of broken glass," she said. "I don't know where it all comes from."

She snapped her purse shut, pulled up from her chest a rumbling sigh that seemed to excite the chandelier into a frantic, tinkling demonstration of its ability to refract and change. Magda left the pleasant little world of her purse for a world full of broken glass, a world that needed ferocious powers of judgment and restraint.

"I'm always careful," Ben said, in exactly the spirit he would toss a too-small offering—a hibiscus blossom, a pomegranate—into a crater.

"Are you hungry?" she asked, and her voice implied that hunger was intimately related to caution. It struck Ben as a riddle, with a right and a wrong answer.

"No," he said uncertainly, and she nodded. He'd chosen correctly. Magda wore big irregular pearls at her ears, the small opalescent cousins of Grandfather's tomatoes. A diamond lizard crouched, frozen, on the slope of her breast; diamonds on her fingers answered the nervous shine of the chandelier. Ben had gone with her to a jewelry store in New York once, and had seen that it gave her the same satisfaction she derived from the inside of her purse. The store had been sharp-edged and orderly, full of a cool, prosperous hush, and Ben imagined that Hungary, where Magda came from, was like the jewelry store and the inside of her purse. She was homesick for a world of perfect safety and glittering, velvet organization.

"It's hot today," she said.

"Uh-huh."

"I'm going to have a glass of soda. You want some?"

"Okay," he said, and she smiled wanly at him. Magda was complete. All her lacks had bottoms to them—she bought whatever she needed.

Then Ben's mother and grandfather came in, and everything changed. When Magda heard them entering through the kitchen door she looked at Ben as if he'd been withholding information from her, something she might have needed in her campaign against chaos and surprise. She set her purse, regretfully, on the gold half table and went to the kitchen to meet them. Ben followed in her wake.

In the kitchen, Grandpa was showing one of the tomatoes to Ben's mother. When Magda came in, Ben saw his mother look from the tomato to Magda and he saw that everything here was the cause of everything else, through invisible lines of blame and effect. Magda was somehow the tomato's fault.

"Hi," Ben's mother said cheerfully.

"Hello," Magda answered.

Grandpa came and kissed Magda's cool, powdered cheek. Ben's mother made a line with her mouth, a tight smiling spasm.

"Hey there," Grandpa said. "You buy out the stores?"

Magda's face shifted over into an attitude of impatience and disdain, like a car going from forward into reverse. The beach was full of broken glass; sea gulls were ruining the shingles on the roof. "I couldn't find a dress," she answered. "Everything was hideous."

"We're having another shindig here next week," Grandpa said proudly. "One of Magda's charities."

"Cancer," she said, and the satisfaction returned to her face.

"Mm," Ben's mother said.

"A big deal, this one," Grandpa said. "Tents, a band. Army of fairies with flowers and hors d'oeuvres."

Ben's mother looked at the clock and said, "I don't know what's keeping Todd." Magda was the tomato's fault and cancer was Magda's fault and everything, Madga and cancer and the broken glass that washed up on the beach, referred back to Grandpa, standing proud and happy in a battered straw hat. Grandpa was the one Ben loved above all others.

"Anna was trying to talk me into a *green* thing," Magda said. "Chiffon, with sequins. Hideous. There's nothing here, tomorrow I will have to go to New York."

"Yes, New York is *full* of dresses," Ben's mother said. "Oh, look, here he comes."

Ben's father's car was gliding up the driveway. Leaf shadows fell over its sleek maroon flanks, and Ben felt the tick in his belly. Soon he'd be alone again with his parents.

"Take the tomatoes," Grandpa said. He picked up a brown paper bag, shook it open with a quick competent snap of his wrist.

Grandpa always knew what he was doing. He was kinder than Magda but, like Magda, he could give himself whatever he needed. He loved his tomatoes, his house. He put the tomatoes into the bag, another and another and another. There was his strong brown hand, there was the fat fullness of the tomato he loved. Ben felt the rising sensation again, the shifting at his crotch, and knew he could slip over into the wrong condition, the lost place. He rescued himself by running out to meet his father's car.

Ben's father had parked and was getting out. He brought his stern self-sacrifice with him, his endless virtue. Ben ran to him and entered his father's goodness, the rigor and the daily work of him. For a moment Ben and his father were the same person. Then his father said, "Hi, pal, how goes it?" and the sound of his voice was enough to separate them. Ben's father lived a life of expectation. Ben was what he waited for.

"Okay," Ben said. He paused between the two conditions, the lost and the visible. With a surge of panicky love, he forced himself.

"I practiced my free shots," he said. "I sank seven out of ten."

"Good. That's very good."

His father was smooth-skinned and broad and anxious for happiness. Ben gave whatever he could find.

"I want Grandpa to raise the hoop," he said. "I want him to raise it all the way."

"Do you think you're ready?"

"Uh-huh."

Ben peppered the air around himself with punches. He danced for his mother; for his father he struck the air with his fists. His father had a handsome face, a body nervous and graceful as a boat. His father's eyes measured what they saw, made quick decisions.

"Simmer down, buddy," his father said, and his voice was so full of delight that Ben punched the air with a new determination, a fiercer mock fury. His father smiled, shed a thin beam of love for the future. He would run for senator. He would drive with a steady hand, be satisfied by food, find mercy in his work.

"Is your mother inside?" he said.

"Uh-huh."

"Are you both ready to go?"

"Yeah."

Ben's father touched his shoulder. His hand said that it was time to be calm, to move with precision and modesty. Ben imagined him that way at work, touching the people and the computers and the telephones, bidding them all to help him go forward, to make a sterner world that rewarded the good and annihilated the bad. Ben stopped hitting the air. He walked with his father into the house, where his mother was waiting.

She told his father she was happy to see him. She kissed his mouth, quickly, to be finished with kissing, and took her sunglasses out of her bag.

"Hey there, Todd," Grandpa said, and he and Ben's father shook hands in the way of men, advertising to one another their harmless intentions and their potency. Magda shook his hand also—she didn't kiss men or women—and Ben could see that she was thinking of jewelry stores and the inside of her purse, that perfection of quiet gold and black. She was lost in the placid contemplation of order. Tomorrow she would go to New York, which was full of dresses.

"We've got to run, honey," Ben's mother said to his father. "You're late."

Ben's father shrugged, elaborately, for Grandpa. They were both innocent workers trying to survive in a world of women. But Grandpa refused. He made the noise again, hwrack hwrack hwrack, and kissed Ben's mother, loudly, on the cheek.

"You got your tomatoes?" he asked her.

"Yes," she told him, and her voice crackled. Magda was the tomatoes' fault; cancer got Mrs. Marshall next door.

"Gimme a squeeze," Grandpa said to Ben, and Ben gave himself up to Grandpa's big bristling arms. There was his grandfather's perfume, the sweet sharp musk of his breath. Ben was unmade in his grandfather's embrace. He was free to be no one.

Then he was released again, back into the demands of the ordinary day. Magda gave him her dry kiss as she thought about dresses and cancer, the lost safety of other countries. He went with his parents to the car, got into the back seat and watched as his grandfather's house disappeared in the flat, watery shimmer of other houses and potato fields.

"How was it?" Ben's father asked his mother.

"Okay," she said. "The usual. I wish you wouldn't be late."

"I do my best."

"Magda's put on even *more* weight. She's big as a house."

"I guess your dad likes a little heft," Ben's father said.

"Please don't joke about it. Joke about anything else." Ben's mother took off her sunglasses, wiped them on her skirt, put them on again. She turned to Ben.

"Well, honey," she said. "We made it. What if we went to P.J.'s for dinner?"

"Sure," Ben said, and he could tell she was pleased with his own pleasure. The car moved forward through the leaf shade and the patches of sun. His mother was happy again, safe. She hummed something under her breath, a tune that was her gladness set to music.

"I am so relieved," she told Ben's father, "to be away from that place."

"You did your duty," Ben's father said.

"Do you know what they're adding now? A fountain. When you walk in the front door the first thing you're going to see is a plaster dolphin spitting water into a clamshell."

"Whatever turns you on."

"It's embarrassing. Who do they think they are, the king and queen of Sheba?"

Ben sat in the back seat with the bag of his grandfather's tomatoes on his lap. He slipped his hand inside the bag. He held a tomato, still warm from the sun, and permitted himself a brief lapse into the other way, the weak silent self who wanted only to be alone, and to sleep.

1 9 8 7 / The ladies' lunches had been Cassandra's idea. Mary put him off at first, saying always that she had another engagement or a sinus headache or just too much to do around the house. But Cassandra kept calling, with a grand and strangely innocent patience (couldn't he tell he was being put off?), and finally Mary gave in. Yes, fine, she'd drive up to the city and meet Cassandra for lunch. All right, a week from Monday at one-thirty, at an address somewhere in Greenwich Village. No, she felt sure she'd have no trouble finding it.

What else could she do? Cassandra was, really, Mary's best single point of access to Zoe. For some reason, Zoe seemed to trust this person. Zoe had made this person the godmother (her term) of her baby, though of course it hadn't been a real baptism and, of course, Zoe couldn't be persuaded to *give* the child a real baptism, in church. Mary had complicated feelings about that. On one hand, there was the question of the child's soul. On the other, there was, undeniably, a certain sense of relief at not having to go to Father McCauley at St. Paul's and discuss the particulars of baptizing an illegitimate half-black baby whose father was god knows where and whose mother wanted as godmother a man who might very well have shown up at the christening in a wig and a dress.

On Monday at eleven in the morning Mary stood in her bedroom trying to decide what to wear, and she thought, This is what's happening to me. The thought, in all its clenched simplicity, made her sit down, harder than she'd meant to, on the green silk bench of her dressing table. *This is what's happening.* Up until then her recent circumstances had existed in her mind as a shifting mass of no discernible shape or dimension, bright and silvery in some places, dark in others, made up of more or less random events: the minute slippage of the copper-colored toupee her lawyer wore when he drew up the divorce papers; a string of amber beads she'd bought for Susan but decided, suddenly, to keep for herself; a cloudy Wednesday morning sky full of promise and warning, as if the two states were intimately related. There had been only small incidents like those, sharp but hardly illuminating, moored to the particulars of cleaning and shopping and her new job, and to the surprisingly intense nightly pleasure she found in going to bed alone. Now, as she tried to dress herself for lunch, she thought with an almost scientific detachment, This is what's happening. I live by myself in a five-bedroom house. My oldest daughter hardly speaks to me. My son loves other men. I'm trying to decide what to wear to lunch with the "godmother" of my younger grandson and I have no idea what to wear because I don't know what kind of place I'm going to and I've never had lunch with a man who wears dresses. She picked up a bottle of nail polish, set it down again, and it occurred to her that Cassandra might, at that moment, be sitting in an apartment somewhere wondering what to wear to lunch with a woman like herself, wealthy and respectable, well-groomed. "I'm not," Mary said out loud, and was surprised by the sound of her own voice in the empty room. What had she meant by that? She was wealthy and respectable; she was undeniably well-groomed. What, exactly, was she *not*? She picked up the bottle of nail polish again, looked at it as if some kind of clue might be hidden in the pale, glossy beige liquid. I'm not sure, she said to herself.

The navy St. John suit, she decided. And then, abruptly, she started to laugh. This is what's happening, she said to herself, and she decided to think of it as funny. She decided to think of it as funny, and just that suddenly, it was. Lunch with a man who might outdress her. All right, then. The navy St. John suit. The Ferragamo pumps. A simple strand of pearls.

Cassandra had chosen a restaurant on a street called Charles Street, in a part of the city where Mary had never been. As a younger woman Mary had known—had insisted on knowing—only the New York of theaters and hotels, of turreted limestone rising above the calm green dangers of Central Park. Now, in later life, thanks to her children, she'd been to unspeakable sections. She'd passed among beggars and lunatics, ruined a Charles Jourdan flat on a broken beer bottle, walked up flights of dingy, reeking stairs. Once, on her way to visit Zoe, she'd had to step around a turd, human, that lay like stupidity and degradation itself in the exact center of an azure-tiled vestibule. If she'd survived all that, she could survive lunch in yet another unfamiliar part of town, in the sort of restaurant someone like Cassandra would choose. This was happening. It could be funny, if you let it be. If you didn't look at it too hard, or think too far ahead.

Neither Charles Street nor the restaurant, however, proved half as trying as Mary had expected them to be. Charles Street was actually very pretty, shaded by trees, lined with town houses Mary herself could imagine living in, substantial old buildings whose generous windows revealed bits of elaborate moldings, of fluted ceiling medallions and chandeliers. One of the houses was covered in wisteria vines, through which Mary could make out a stone panel engraved with leaves, arabesques, and a weathered face that seemed to advertise one of the harsher virtues, forbearance or strength or adamant virginity. She stood before the face, which was netted in its tangle of coarse brown vines, and felt an odd but not disagreeable sense of familiarity, as if she might have visited this street as a child. The face appeared to be female, though it was hard to tell absolutely, what with the vines and that old-fashioned style of carving in which everyone, men and women alike, looked somehow like self-possessed, slightly overweight young girls.

The restaurant, which stood at the corner and bore its name in discreet gold letters on its window, was the sort of little café Mary imagined in Paris: dusky but clean, dark-paneled, with snowy tablecloths that put out more light than did the amber wall sconces. As she paused at the door she knew an unexpected pang of regret: Now this lovely, mysterious street and this charming restaurant would remember her as someone who had business with someone like Cassandra. Someone whose life had gone this far. She told herself she'd fly to Paris; she'd put aside a little money every week.

Cassandra waved to her from a table near the window. Mary was relieved to see he'd chosen men's clothes, just a black turtleneck sweater and jeans. As Cassandra rose and extended his hand Mary was taken all over again by how undistinguished he looked, this thin, jug-eared specimen with patchy reddish hair and small, watery eyes. He might have been an aging salesclerk or waiter, one of the people you hardly noticed because they were neither succeeding nor spectacularly failing. They were just living lives of quiet service.

"Lovely to see you, Mary," Cassandra said.

"I'm happy to be here," she answered. She gave him her hand and he squeezed it with more power than she'd expected.

"Please. Sit down."

"Thank you."

She sat, and immediately took her napkin from the table and spread it on her lap.

"This is an adorable place," she added. It was easiest to be gracious. It was easiest to treat this as lunch, just lunch with a friend. If she abandoned courtesy she had no idea what she would say or do.

"It is, isn't it?" Cassandra said. "Very soothing. I come over here sometimes when my nerves can't take another moment of *joie de vivre*. You can sit by the window with a cup of tea for an hour if you want to."

"It makes me think of Paris, a little bit," Mary said.

"Oui. Ça pourrait être un bistro en plein Marais."

"You speak French?"

"God, that was unspeakably pretentious, wasn't it? Sorry, hon, it's just nerves. I'm not ordinarily a lady who lunches."

"Do you really speak French?" Mary asked.

"Oh, sure, I don't spend *all* my time trying out eye shadow. I've picked up French and Spanish and I can get by in German, but then all you can do with *that* is talk to Germans."

"Where did you learn your French?"

"In Paris, about a hundred and fifty years ago. I lived there for a while, this old scow has been to any number of ports. Cheesy little studio down by the Beaubourg, believe me, America is *not* the sole repository of the tacky or the vulgar."

"My husband and I were always meaning to go to Paris," Mary said.

"Oh, well, it's beautiful in spots, just like they say, but I don't know. Lately I've let my passport lapse. Travel started to seem . . . slightly pathetic, or something. You went someplace and then you went someplace else and then you went someplace else, and I know it was supposed to be marvelous, but frankly it was starting to make my teeth ache a little. I kept seeing people buying souvenirs and I kept thinking about how they'd turn up at rummage sales in the year 2000, how those Hermès scarves would outlast the people who bought them, and, well, never mind. Suffice to say that these days my idea of travel is going up to Central Park."

Briefly, Mary lost track of herself. She smoothed the napkin in her lap. Just say what you'd say to anyone, she thought.

"We always meant to travel," she offered. "But what with the kids and the business and everything—"

"So do it now," Cassandra said. "Believe me, if I was a stunning divorcée like you, I'd be on the next boat. Though frankly, honey, the men in France are pigs."

"I'm not thinking much about men these days."

"Well, whenever you're ready to *start* thinking about them, skip the French. Trust me."

"And I'm hardly a stunning divorcée," Mary said. "I'm a fifty-five-year-old woman and, honestly, I'm a little tired these days. I'm just, well, a little tired."

"Ridiculous," Cassandra said. "You're a great beauty, you know you are. You're only now coming into your mystery."

"That's sweet. But really."

"Don't *but really* me. How long's it been since you dumped that bastard? Five years? Honey, it's time for the Widow Stassos to cut loose a little."

Mary picked up her menu. "Shall we order?" she said. "I'm starving."

"What you need," Cassandra told her, "is a haircut. You need a *change*. What do you suppose would happen if you cut it right under your earlobes, just a simple blunt cut, and let it hang loose? No curls, no spray."

"It's fine like this, really," Mary answered. "I wouldn't know what to do with it any other way. Mm, chicken salad with papaya. That sounds good."

"Maybe you should stop coloring it, too. Let it go gray, I'll bet it's a beautiful silver gray."

"It's fine. Really. Thank you for your interest. Have you talked to Zoe lately?"

"This morning."

"How is she?"

"She's all right," Cassandra said. "Today is the day she works until seven, I'm picking Jamal up at kindergarten."

"Do you . . . Do you spend a lot of time with him?"

"Zoe needs help, it's too much raising a child all alone."

Mary sipped at her water. She believed she could survive this lunch just as she'd survived a wedding night and three births and a hard marriage and all the inexplicable little hatreds of her children. She could know someone like Cassandra. The peculiarity of all this could not harm her because she had lost her old hopes and she wasn't afraid anymore, not like she used to be. What else could happen? What more could be lost?

"I felt like I was alone when I raised my kids," Mary said. "My husband was hardly ever there."

"Well, then, you know."

"Yes. I know."

"Jamal is going through a gun thing right now," Cassandra said. "Suddenly the world is made up of two things, guns and useless objects."

"I guess that's normal."

"Oh, sure it is. Aggression, what could be more normal? Zoe doesn't like it, she keeps imagining herself being interviewed after he sprays a shopping mall with bullets, but I tell her it'll pass. A little boy is not Winnie the Pooh, however much you might want him to be."

"You sound like you've had experience," Mary said.

"I raised two brothers and a sister. Our mother forgot to come home sometimes, and frankly, I don't blame her. If I was a woman named Erna Butz trying to raise four children alone on no money in Table Grove, Illinois, *I'd* want to lose track of reality sometimes, too."

"She left you alone?"

"Please, don't start looking at me like I'm some kind of Dickens character. We were better off without her. I did a much better job with those children than she ever did."

"Well," Mary said. She was working for something further to say when the waiter came to take their orders. Mary ordered the chicken salad and, after a hesitation, a glass of white wine. Cassandra ordered the chicken salad and a cup of tea.

After the waiter had gone, Cassandra leaned forward and said in a low voice, "In case you were wondering, it's Bertram."

"I beg your pardon?"

"I was born Bertram Butz in Table Grove, Illinois. You think I blame my mother for taking off? Not for a minute, hon. I understand completely."

"Do you talk to her now?" Mary asked.

"Oh, no. She died."

"I'm sorry."

"Oh, I suppose I am, too. Not as sorry as I probably should be."

"What about your brothers and sister?"

"They don't know where I am."

"You're joking."

"No, it's better this way, believe me. They have very conventional lives. They all got married and had children and they live in Illinois. They don't want a visit from Auntie Mame."

"That's terrible."

"No, it's not," Cassandra said. "All it means is we don't have to suffer through Christmases together. Now, what about you? You're a New Yorker, aren't you?"

"Well. I was born in New Jersey."

"Italian, right? You've got those eyes and those cheekbones."

"I was Mary Cuccio. My parents never quite forgave me for marrying a Greek."

"Lord, the things people get worked up over. You married young, didn't you?"

"Seventeen. I wanted to get away."

"Honey, I hear that," Cassandra said. "Marriage wasn't exactly an option for me, so I went to college. I got a scholarship to the University of Wisconsin and I said to the kids, 'Here's how the washing machine works, here's how to put Momma to bed when she needs putting to bed. Now sayonara.' "

"I probably should have gone to college," Mary said. "I didn't really think of it, it didn't seem like something I could do."

"Well, I lasted a year into graduate school, but I didn't finish. I was a literature major but I couldn't seem to . . . let's just say something was missing. I couldn't seem to work up a head of steam about ending up as a skinny effeminate man teaching nineteenth- and twentieth-century literature on some remote little Midwestern campus where I'd probably have had a series of crushes on a series of students who'd flirt with me to make sure of their grades. In another era I'd probably have done it anyway, a flaming queen's choices are about as limited as a woman's, but, well, the times being what they were, I stood up one day in the middle of reading *The Wings of the Dove*, marked my place, took my three hundred dollars out of the bank, and moved to New York."

"Are you glad you did?"

"Yes, absolutely. I never really wanted to *teach* Anna Karenina and Madame Bovary, I wanted to *be* Anna Karenina and Madame Bovary. And really, when nature has elected to provide you with the soul of a tragic diva and the body of a scrawny man who started going bald at twenty-two, well . . ."

Mary said, "I was sixteen when I met my husband. My ex-husband. But, *sixteen*. Think of that."

"You were a Lolita. I'll bet you could work those hometown boys."

"Not really. I was pretty enough, I guess, but sixteen felt awfully young then. Not like today. Constantine was my first boyfriend, can you believe that?"

"You married your childhood sweetheart. It happens."

"I met him at a dance. A church dance in my neighborhood. He was assistant foreman of the crew my brother Joey worked on. He was my older brother's boss, and he seemed so important. He seemed like somebody. He was twenty-one. He showed up at this dismal little dance in a church basement wearing a red sport coat."

"Snappy."

"I'd just seen a picture of a boy in a magazine wearing a red sport coat like that. I think I fell in love with the jacket first, to tell you the truth. First the jacket, then the boy."

"It's one way of doing it."

"And I wanted to fall in love. I could hardly wait. You see, my parents, well, I was so terribly afraid of ending up like them. I wanted something—better. I thought I'd do just about anything."

"I guess that makes two of us, doesn't it?" Cassandra said.

That was the first of the ladies' lunches, as Cassandra insisted on calling them. After that, Mary met him every four or five weeks, always in the same restaurant. She began to feel a certain defiance in meeting Cassandra, a small thrill of illicit pleasure. Mary told herself she was meeting Cassandra to keep track of Zoe, and that wasn't untrue, but after six months or so, after five of the ladies' lunches, she had to admit that she also liked seeing Cassandra for the sake of seeing Cassandra. Within their range of shared topics she could say anything that entered her mind, and she knew Cassandra didn't feel superior to her. If anything, she felt superior to Cassandra, though she didn't like to think of it in those terms. So much in her life was difficult, and these lunches were surprisingly easy. They didn't count; they didn't matter. Cassandra could be relied upon to keep the conversation going, just as Mary's family had once relied on her to do. She was never boring (Mary had begun, somewhat queasily, to think of Cassandra as "she"), and she reminded Mary at regular intervals of Mary's beauty and of the contention, however doubtful, that at fifty-five she was just now entering the realm of true feminine mystery. After one of the lunches it occurred to Mary that Cassandra reminded her, in certain ways, of her childhood friends, the Italian girls from her old neighborhood to whom she hadn't spoken in over thirty-five years. Cassandra had a similar raucous extravagance; she seemed to take a similar pleasure in her own gaudy if limited prospects. Here she was, a friend who paid court and did not threaten, and Mary found that she liked having this secret friendship. She carried it with her in the shops of Garden City and at her club meetings, where the other women were unfailingly kind and courteous and not in any way truly interested in the divorced Italian wife of a Greek man who built shoddy subdivisions.

At the sixth of the lunches, Cassandra turned up with Jamal. Mary arrived and found the two of them, Jamal sitting in her own usual chair, propped up on a telephone book. He leaned forward across the table and spoke to Cassandra, softly but with great urgency, his small dark hands gripping the edge of the table so hard the cloth rippled and the saltshaker leaned, waiting to fall. As Mary stood at the door she lost whatever sense of familiarity she'd developed with Cassandra. In their shared attitude of intense, secretive conversation Cassandra and Jamal looked surreal and hyperbolic, freaks from a ragged traveling circus, full of perversities and little crimes and an insane, giggling wisdom. Mary was fighting an impulse to simply turn and leave when Cassandra spotted her. Jamal saw her an instant later, and sat back in his chair so quickly he might have been a parody of apprehended guilt.

"Surprise," Cassandra said, as Mary walked smiling to the table. "They had to close the whole kindergarten today, something lethal seems to have gotten into the pipes. It was too late to call you, so I just brought Jamal along."

"That's great," Mary said, though she was surprised to find

herself irritated by the notion of having Jamal all through lunch. He was her grandson, what was wrong with her?

"Hi, honey," she said to him. She bent to kiss him and he allowed himself to be kissed without indicating that he desired it in any way. He could be such a remote child, so silent and vague, although a second ago he'd seemed to have no reluctance about talking to Cassandra. Mary tried to care for him, to feel connected, and sometimes she managed it, but more often the feeling simply slipped away from her and she looked at Jamal as if he were anyone's child, balky and undemonstrative, a little dull. It might have helped, Mary thought, if he resembled her more. If he hadn't had such purplish lips, and all that woolly hair.

"We've been shooting at passersby," Cassandra said. "So far we've bagged an even dozen."

Mary took a chair from another table and sat down. This is a child, she admonished herself. He only wants the things all children want.

"So they closed the school, did they?" she said cheerfully to Jamal.

"They say it'll be open again tomorrow," Cassandra said. "Every now and then disaster strikes, and you get a day off."

"Well," Mary said. "Isn't it nice to have a day off?"

"We thought we'd go up to Central Park after lunch," Cassandra said. "Want to come?"

"We'll see," Mary said. "Jamal, what do you think you'd like for lunch?"

Jamal looked at Mary with such uncertainty, such naked absence of recognition, that she wondered, as she did periodically, if he was in fact of normal intelligence. Maybe they should take him in for tests.

"I'm having a cheeseburger," Cassandra said, "because I'm beyond caring."

"Cheeseburger," Jamal whispered.

"Two, then," Cassandra said. "Mary, a salad for you?"

"I suppose," she said.

Jamal turned to the window, pointed his finger at an elderly man passing by, and said, "Zzzip."

"Got him," Cassandra said. "Nice fat one." To Mary she added, "We take no prisoners."

"I see," Mary said.

Jamal shifted in his seat, aimed his finger at a couple sitting at the next table, and said, "Zzzip."

"Turn around, honey," Cassandra said. "And put that thing away, it's rude to shoot your luncheon companions."

Mary was surprised to see that Jamal obeyed. Suddenly his strangeness and all strangeness evaporated, and he and Cassandra could have been any ordinary parent and child, trying to get through the usual negotiations of leniency and demand, of adoration and propriety.

"Do you like playing cowboy?" Mary asked Jamal, who looked at her, once again, with an expression of utter incomprehension, as if not only her words but she herself were unprecedented, and quite possibly dangerous.

"Perfectly civil question, Jamal," Cassandra said. "Perhaps it would be an interesting conversational gambit to tell your grandmother about the Planet Sark."

"I beg your pardon?" Mary said.

Jamal looked down at the tabletop as if it, too, was unutterably foreign.

"The Planet Sark is where Jamal comes from," Cassandra said. "It's the medium-bright star just slightly to the left of Orion's belt. He isn't shooting bullets at these people, because on his planet murder isn't just forbidden, it's impossible. Sarkians can't kill any more than you or I could decide to stop breathing. It's involuntary. However, when confronted by a particularly irritating individual it *is* possible to zap them with a special gun that renders them invisible, and I don't mind telling you, the world is filling up fast with invisible citizens these days. They go on about their business, they go on being rude and mean and selfish and prejudiced, but no one can see them. Jamal, does that about sum it up?"

Jamal looked at his finger, looked at the floor.

"I guess that's better than shooting them," Mary said.

"Much, much better," Cassandra answered. "It keeps people's mothers happy, it doesn't entirely deny the aggressive impulse, it's really a highly satisfactory solution all around."

After lunch, Mary went with Cassandra and Jamal to Central Park. She didn't want to, not really, but if she'd invented an excuse she'd have been the kind of woman who pleads a hairdresser's appointment to escape her own grandson. When she offered to drive, Cassandra insisted that they take the subway. "Traffic's terrible by now," she said, "and there's no place to park up there." Mary agreed, it was easiest to agree, although as they walked the several blocks to the subway she couldn't help wondering if Cassandra was reluctant to be in her car—to sit in the cool prosperous hush she owned. Mary's car was serene, ordered, sound; the subway station when they entered it was full of harsh light and furtive, defeated characters. A low crackle emanating from a loudspeaker might have been the unconscious mutterings of the city itself, its restless, elderly dreams. Cassandra seemed at home there, standing on the platform, holding Jamal's hand and chattering to Mary about the new shorter hemlines that were predicted for fall. The air was full of rot and urine and food fried in sour oil. Mary thought, suddenly, of her own childhood, the oppressed future that had wanted her, and it seemed she couldn't breathe at all here, she'd have to run gasping back up to the surface. Instead, she smiled at Cassandra, and nodded, and breathed. She'd grown adept by then at managing suffocation without appearing to be anything but calm. She could get through it. And if it overwhelmed her, there were always the pills. Then she saw the lights of the approaching train, and Mary knew she could manage.

The park, when they reached it, was beautiful in a sketchy, nascent way. The early April sun had started to deepen, to take on the first of its warmth, and the dry brown grass had been dusted here and there with a tentative gloss of green. "How pretty," Mary said. The light that fell from the limpid sky seemed almost visibly to be thawing the earth, and it was possible to imagine, on a day like this, that a huge rolling kindness, soft and unremarkable, more closely resembling human sentimentality than the more scourging benevolence of God, did in fact prevail in the world.

"It's pretty if you like nature," Cassandra said. "To be frank, we come here because Jamal likes it. I get nervous in parks, all these branches could snatch the wig right off your head."

Jamal had run along the concrete path, checking back over his shoulder to be sure Cassandra and Mary were following. Mary could see that he was in fact a child, delighted in a child's way by freedom and open space, fearful in a child's way that he would become so free he'd never find his way back again. As she watched him running on his short skinny legs she vowed silently, I will do better with him. I'll remember this.

"Do you bring him here often?" she asked.

"Once or twice a week, now that the weather's changing. We cut back when it was snowy out, he didn't like it, but really, there are *limits*. I'm not very good in the cold."

"I love winter," Mary said. "I love a cold, crisp day."

"Then, honey, next winter *you* can bundle him into his snow-suit and take him up here to make snow angels."

"That'd be nice."

"Then *do* it. Dear."

It was the first remark Cassandra had made that wasn't wholly sweet-tempered and admiring, and it took Mary by surprise. She looked at Cassandra's face in profile and saw—of course, she had

always known—that she had a temper. She saw, too, here in the
soft spring light, that Cassandra was firm-featured and regally,
serenely damaged and probably older than Mary had imagined, well
past fifty. A faint but clear illumination, like the illumination of the
white tablecloths in the restaurant on Charles Street, seemed to
rise up off Cassandra's face and answer the yellower, more diffuse
light of the afternoon air.

"Maybe I will," Mary said. Where would someone like this have
gotten such bearing, such a fierce sense of purpose?

"Fine," Cassandra said.

A chill settled between them, and Mary understood for the first
time that Cassandra's feelings about her were not confined to admiration and a desire to please. The two of them walked in silence
for a while. The branches threw pale indistinct shadows on the
walk.

"I'd like you to spend more time with him," Cassandra said at
length, and Mary could not read the tone in her voice. It was not
angry, nor was it kind. It was, if anything, strong but blank, as if
she were reciting a set of important, indisputable facts.

"I should," Mary said. "I will."

How could someone like this presume to lecture her? Still, she
listened.

"I mean it," Cassandra said. "He should know you better, he
may need you someday."

"Mm-hm."

"This child leads a less than orthodox life, and believe me, I
don't have any illusions about the orthodox. Still. There are limits.
I don't want to think of him just bouncing around if anything
happens. I don't want him to have to go and live with anyone who
seems like a stranger to him."

Mary felt something. She couldn't name it but it was there, an
inner tug, like the lost memory of a dreadful sorrow. There was a
chill, an insistent inner tug. Two black women sped past on roller

skates, laughing, their wheels setting the pavement abuzz. Cassandra was pale and thin and full of obscure purpose, and Mary touched her arm with her fingertips.

"What is it?" she asked.

Cassandra put her own hand over Mary's.

"Nothing. It's exactly what I've just said."

"Well," Mary said, and she could think of nothing else to offer. A flock of pigeons flew by, so close Mary believed one of their wings would brush her face, though she didn't flinch. She thought she would welcome the flick of the bird's wing. That wild gentleness, that effortlessly beating life. She almost felt the feathers graze her. Up ahead Jamal bent over to pick up something, a coin or a glittering stone, which he held in his hand and came running to show to Cassandra.

1 9 8 8 /   The most terrible beauty came out at night. In daylight the world was full of facts; you could live in a swarm of errands. At night, late, there was only desire or its absence, after the other stories had been pulled in off the streets. It was Boston—most citizens were dreaming by midnight. During the deeper hours men owned the streets, at least in certain neighborhoods, and for those hours, on streets usually devoted to the most ordinary transactions—a pound of coffee, a haircut, fire and theft insurance—a defiant, muscular beauty was the only virtue.

Will filled his clothes now, he moved without apology. On a cold night in April he kissed his friends good night outside a movie theater and walked toward home. A winter smell, rainwater on bare branches, still hung over Boston, though Easter had come and gone.

On the sidewalk ahead of him, two boys whispered and laughed, shoved one another with the easy familiarity of brothers. They were big and young, underdressed in cheap leather jackets and bright scarves, painfully handsome in their size and their broad, unexceptional faces. By their heedless presence they told the street that sex was not a torment, not a doomed striving of the spirit. Sex was ordinary as grass—what's the big deal? Will tried to be un-obtrusive, to watch them without appearing to. He wanted . . . Not them, though he'd gladly have slept with either. It wasn't anything quite so simple as a yearning of the body. He wanted their certainty, the easy motion of them. He wanted whatever they were creating with their jokes and loud laughter, and he wanted what they made for themselves when they ran up the stairs of a brick apartment building, clattering in their boots, going home to bed together or to a party Will wouldn't know about because it was the province of young men like these, confident and affable, brand-new. Will fid-geted with his jacket, adjusted the cuffs. He'd be thirty-five in a little more than a month. He liked his life well enough—he couldn't think of another he'd prefer—but still he felt haunted by absence. Still the years felt featureless, for all their event, and still he waited to inhabit himself. He had no complaints about the details, the hard but satisfying work and the band of good-hearted, interesting friends and the series of affairs that lasted anywhere from three weeks to a year but always turned out to have contained the spe-cifics of their endings right at the start, in the first brittle conver-sations, the first nervous sex. Passions turned into needs; strong opinions devolved into peevishness or rage. Will didn't mind, not really. He told himself that anything could happen. Anything still could. He had affairs, and always held on to some kind of friendship after the sex and the hope were gone. He worked out at his gym, ran five miles every other day, spent hours shopping for the right pair of boots, and yes it was all vanity but he wanted something that lay beyond simple vanity and the small, sour satisfactions it offered. He was looking to fall into conviction, so he no longer needed to stare covertly and wistfully at strangers. So he no longer needed to envy foolish boys, or the muscles of men less muscular than he.

Because he wasn't tired he walked four blocks out of his way to have a beer and watch the women play pool. He stood gratefully in the dark yellow heat of the bar, watching them clear the table. This band of women was notorious; nobody could beat them. Hardly anyone tried. Men sipped their drinks and watched the women beat one another. On the far side of the bar, in another room, a few determined souls danced to "Smalltown Boy," though on a cold weeknight in April even the disc jockey didn't look like he believed in music.

A thin woman in black jeans banked the 2 ball, sent it spinning into the corner pocket like blameless competence being born. Will said something appreciative to a man standing near him, or the man said something appreciative to him. They'd never agree on who spoke first. It would never seem to matter who spoke.

"These women are good."

"Terrifying."

"I always wanted to be the kind of guy who's good at pool."

"I sometimes forget that I'm *not*. I walk around like somebody who's good at pool. I try to walk around that way."

"How exactly does a man who's good at pool walk?"

"You know. Confident. He struts. Maybe a little bowlegged."

"Ambitious. I mostly just try not to fall over."

"I fell on the way *here*. I tripped over nothing, this little bump in the sidewalk about a sixteenth of an inch high. While I was strutting along looking like a man who's good at pool."

"You *fell*?"

"I stumbled. There were people around. And you know, I'm never sure how to recover when something like that happens. I can never decide. Do you go on as if nothing had happened? Do you smile and shake your head? Do you look back at whatever it was you fell over?"

"You can always just sit down on the curb and weep."

"I guess so."

The woman in black jeans cracked the cue ball into the 6, which knocked the 10 ball into a side pocket.

"I'm out of clever things to say now," the man said.

"Me, too," Will answered.

His name was Harry. He was neither handsome nor homely. He had hard, thin arms and a cowlick. He had a quirky face, eyes with flecks of yellow in them, and lines bracketing his mouth. He was forty and he looked like forty. The name Harry fit him. Harry was the right name for his dishevelment, his black-rimmed glasses, the graceful shifting of his ass inside the baggy, wrinkled wool slacks he wore.

They finished their beers. They left the bar together, without having agreed on what they were doing. Will was tired of pretty boys and he was still in love with pretty boys and he wanted, in some numbed way, to rest. He walked along the wet black streets with Harry. He felt neither attracted nor repelled.

"This is where I turn," Harry said. They stood on the corner together. Droplets haloed the lights, scraps of neon shone on the asphalt. Harry took his glasses off, wiped them on his jacket.

"Do you think we should trade phone numbers or something?" Will said.

Maybe they'd be friends. Maybe they'd have sex, and become friends.

"Yes. I think we should."

"I don't have a pen."

"I don't think I do, either."

"Maybe we should just go home together."

"I don't know. I've pretty much decided to stop sleeping with guys right away."

"Actually, I'd more or less decided the same thing."

"It gets things off to a funny start, sleeping with somebody before you know if his parents are alive or dead. Not that I think anything is starting up."

"Uh-huh."

"I always think I'll be sort of smooth and butch and graceful. And I never am."

"Neither one of us has tripped yet."

"That's true."

"Maybe we should call each other up and go out on a date."

"That's really terrifying."

"I know."

"If I told you my phone number, would you remember it?"

"Sure."

"You won't remember it. Let's go to my place right now."

"You think it's a good idea?"

"No. But let's do it, anyway."

Harry lived on the second floor of a brownstone. He was a cardiologist, he played the saxophone. Naked, with one small lamp burning, he was small and chiseled, nearly hairless. He didn't exercise. He'd been a fast-moving, sinewy boy and now as a man he had the body of an aging acrobat, thin snakes of muscle on his arms and legs and an incipient belly, round and hard and economical under the smooth flat squares of his chest. Will knew right away that if anything happened beyond one night, he'd be the beauty and Harry the one who paid cool, humorous tribute. Will loved and hated the idea. It surprised him. Here in this expensive but haphazardly furnished apartment, he was the one with the body and no cash. It wasn't where he'd expected to go.

In bed, Harry kissed the muscles of Will's chest. He ran his tongue over Will's nipples, worked his way down. Will liked it well enough. The sensations, Harry's tongue and Harry's bed, were pleasant, just that. It was neither large nor dangerous. There was nothing to fail at. Will stroked Harry's shoulders, and did not worry. He let it happen. When Harry kissed his way back up to Will's face, they moved carefully together, as if they held an egg pillowed between their stomachs.

Harry, Will thought. Why does his name have to be Harry?

Afterward, they slept. Will started to leave, more out of politeness than desire, and Harry held his arm. "Just stay," Harry said. And he did. It seemed right to stay. He fell quickly, deeply asleep with his back touching Harry's back.

When he was still Billy he sat in the dark of his father's closet, exploring. He burrowed amid the wreckage of shoe-polish tins, brushes, lost coins. The closet floor was snug and blackly glittering as a storm drain. Things drifted down and settled there. He groped around on the floor until his hands touched something solid—a shoehorn, perfect as a floating keyhole. He put the shoehorn to his lips, tasted the slick rubbery non-taste of the new. He bit down hard, then held it in the strip of light that shone under the door. His toothmarks were surprisingly perfect, symmetrical.

His mother's closet, next door to this one, was a garden of color and sweet, flowery smells. He liked that closet, too, but found its lushness overpowering and its heavy, perfumed air difficult to breathe. In his father's closet, things were spare and disorderly. Things were the color of night. Overhead, the dangling sleeves and cuffs disappeared up into blackness. On the linoleum, his father's shoes waited silently. Billy put his face down close to one of his father's black dress-up shoes. It was titanic, nearly as long as Billy's arm, and even in the dark of the closet it put out a dull, brown-black shine. Billy inhaled. The shoe had a ripe but strangely compelling odor. It smelled of polish and it smelled in some unspeakable way of Billy's father's secret life. A strong, foul, fascinating smell. He was lost in the smell when his father opened the closet door.

In the morning, early, Harry got up to make coffee. Will lay in bed, half awake, returning from his dreams. Small incidents of gray, rainy light played on the keys and bell of a saxophone. There were shelves crowded with books, books piled in corners, books stacked on a rickety chair. There were daffodils dried to scabs in a drinking glass. Harry came back from the kitchen, bare-assed and sleepy in a white tank top. Just Hanes, the kind old men wore. He gave Will a mug of coffee, got back into bed.

"Could you sleep?" he asked.

"Yeah," Will said.

There was nothing unusual to say. They sipped their coffee. "I have to be at school in an hour and a half," Will said.

"I go in late on Fridays."

"Nice."

The coffee mugs were heavy and white, the kind waitresses slap down on diner counters. On the table beside the bed: a Kleenex box, a notebook, a scattering of pens, a solemn-faced stone angel, and a paperback copy of *Anna Karenina*.

"You're reading Tolstoy?" Will said.

"I read *Anna Karenina* every few years. I'm a Tolstoy slut."

"I love Tolstoy, too. George Eliot is the one I'm really a slut for, though."

"*Middlemarch* is incredible."

"I read *that* every few years. It practically gives me a nose-bleed."

There was nothing unusual to say. There was a sense of oc-casion, occasion made out of the simplest materials, and the passing seconds were apertures, clicking by. It occurred to Will that he could be to Harry what he'd always wanted pretty men to be to him. He could be kind and intelligent, present, with a world inside him. He could stay for a while and then, when he wanted his freedom again, he could go.

With mingled sensations of pride and sympathy, Will put his hand on the bony complications of Harry's thin, pale knee.

They had dinner together two nights later. They told their stories, or parts of them. Harry came from nine children, an im-mense cold house in Detroit, a father who believed in military discipline and a mother who searched between the rules so hard

she fell into religion. Harry's only regret, the only one he'd admit
to, was music. He treated heart patients and that was fine, he liked
doing it well enough, but it would never take the place of pulling
in chestfuls of air and giving it back to people as one long melody.

He said, "I didn't have the courage to be a musician." On the
restaurant walls, old posters announced ocean liners that hadn't
sailed in thirty years.

Will said, "It takes courage to be a doctor."

"Not really. Not the same kind. Once you start being a doctor
it just rolls you along, it has this momentum. It would take a lot
more courage to quit practicing medicine than it takes to do it."

"Do you want to quit?"

"No, I like what I do. I like playing the sax in my apartment
and fantasizing about playing in clubs. Some fantasies are better
as fantasies, don't you think?"

"I guess. I was going to be an architect and I've ended up
teaching fifth grade."

"Isn't it what you want to do?"

"It's *become* what I want to do. I think I did it at first to spite
my father."

"I've done much worse things to spite my father than teach
fifth grade."

"He had such grand hopes for me, he was so intent on my
becoming some kind of big deal, and one day I looked him in the
eye and said, 'Fuck you, I'm going to be an elementary school
teacher.' "

"I did a lot of drugs and played guitar all the time. I had to go
to medical school in Mexico."

"I got drunk and drove too fast. My friends and I wrecked three
cars before we graduated from high school."

"That must have shown him."

"I guess."

"Plus, it was fun."

"Hm?"

"It was fun to do drugs and play the guitar. I'm sure it was fun wrecking those cars. It hasn't all just been to get back at our fathers."

"Well, no. I guess it hasn't."

Harry smiled, ran his finger along the rim of his water glass. His fingers were tufted with golden hair. A loose thread hung from his cuff, tickling his wrist, and without thinking Will glanced at his own wrist, as if the thread had touched him, too.

He was not afraid of Harry. He wondered if he'd been a little bit afraid of every other man he'd ever known.

He and Harry made careful love. It was good sex, good enough, but it lay differently along Will's skin. Ordinarily he felt concealed by sex; he disappeared into the beauty of the other man. With Harry he was more visible. Sometimes he liked the sensation. Sometimes he thought he'd get up and leave, return to the comfort and the familiar unhappiness of his usual life.

They went to movies, they ate in restaurants. On the first sunny day they drove to Provincetown in Harry's car, walked shivering at the water's edge in sweaters and coats. Harry stood in a brown suede jacket, scraps of dark hair blowing against his eyeglasses, and a perfect beauty gathered around him, a beauty of circumstance, the bright cold sky and the fine golden stubble on his upper lip. Will and he made no declarations; it just unfolded. Another night and another, all day Sunday with coffee and the newspapers.

Sometimes Will believed he was falling in love.

Sometimes he told himself, I want more than this.

He'd been waiting so long for a dark-haired boy-man, a hero carrying all he'd learned about adventure and the body. He'd prepared himself for that; he'd turned into someone who could have it. Will had never pictured a thin, decent-looking man who disliked dancing and late nights. He'd never pictured questionable taste in clothes, rooms full of clutter, thin legs and a flat ass.

They talked, always. There was everything to say. Will found no limit to what he could tell. Lying in bed at night, he said, "I worry sometimes that I can't really fall in love. Not what other people mean by 'fall in love.' "

"What do other people mean?" Harry asked. His bare leg was hooked over Will's legs. Harry's jacket and pants had been draped on a chair and they sat in the dark like someone patient and elderly, keeping watch.

"I don't know. A loss of the self, I guess."

"Why would you want to lose yourself?"

"What I mean is, I worry that love calls for some kind of fundamental generosity I lack. I worry that I'm not generous, maybe that's it. I'm very vain."

"I know you're vain," Harry said. "It's not the worst failing."

"That's part of the trouble. It's not even a grand sin. It's one of the creepy minor sins. Better to be really, truly bad."

"Do you think it's time to tell me you love me? Do you feel like I'm waiting for you to do that?"

"No. I don't know. *Are* you?"

"I don't think so. Maybe I am. I don't need you to, though."

"It's been six months," Will said.

"Almost seven. Please don't turn this into something you could fail at."

"But you *can* fail. At love. You can pull back. You can get to a certain point, and then say no."

"I guess so. Do you feel like that's what you're doing?"

"I'm not sure. Maybe."

"Love gets a bad rap. Who wouldn't be afraid after all those movies?"

"Do you think you love me?"

"You just want me to say it first," Harry said.

"Do you?"

"Yes."

"Okay."

"Okay?"

"Okay."

"It doesn't kill me if you're not sure. I'm not nervous like that."

"You're really not, are you?" Will said.

"No. I'm really not."

They kissed, and made love again.

It happened to Will when he forgot his umbrella. He'd left
Harry's apartment in the morning and gotten to the street and then
gone back. The door was open. Harry was playing his saxophone
in the bedroom, a quick riff before he got ready for work. He didn't
hear Will come in. He stood in his shorts and a pair of white socks,
playing. Will didn't recognize the tune. He watched from the doorway. He'd seen Harry play plenty of times but never like this, never
when Harry didn't know he was being watched. Something
changed this way. Harry leaned over the saxophone, his eyes
squeezed shut and his face flushed. He was more lost than Will
had seen him, even during sex. A vein bulged fatly at his temple.
He played well, not brilliantly, but he was lost in it. He was a man
with the beginnings of a belly playing a saxophone in a disorderly
bedroom, wearing baggy white socks and blue striped boxer shorts
as rain spattered the windows. It was only that. But something rose
up in Will. He would never understand it. He believed he saw
Harry's childhood and Harry's old age, the whole curve of Harry's
life that was passing through this room, this moment. Briefly Will
left himself and joined Harry in the ongoing rush and clatter of
being Harry, and briefly he felt Harry's fears and hopes and something else. The sum of his days. The sensation of living inside his
body, blowing music through the horn. Will stood silently. He didn't
speak. He got his umbrella from the living room. He left.

He started living with satisfaction, a kind of satisfaction. The
satisfaction of bread and talk. The hours of his days took on a new

shape, squarer, more densely packed. He lived as himself and he lived as the younger man who was loved by Harry and he lived, obscurely, as Harry, too. The old floating feeling seemed to be going away, though it was subject to fits of return. When it went away Will found in its place a simple joy and a new disappointment. His disappointment fluttered around the edges of his contentment, persistent as a bee. Now he wouldn't be present for the perfect man, the one who stopped time with the powerful slumber of his muscles. If that man existed—that cheerful and bulky spirit—Will would not meet him because he'd found this one instead, a kind man with thinning hair. Something was marrying him; something was lashing itself to his flesh. He felt exultant and, less often, disconsolate. He slept several times with several of the beautiful, foolish boys he met in bars or at his gym. He bought jazz records for Harry, and a cashmere sweater, and cream-colored stationery from France. He worried over everything that could happen, all the accidents in the world, and he cried, sometimes, from a sorrow and a happiness he couldn't name.

1 9 8 9 / Zoe had felt all right for so long. She'd known about the virus. She'd imagined that she felt it inside her, a low sizzle of wires, little misfirings that flared somewhere between the skin and the bone. But she'd never felt sick, and it had been almost three years. She'd let herself imagine that she'd received the disease but was not harmed by it, the way a radio would safely receive transmissions from a broadcaster who demanded wider systems of persecution, better compensation for the rich, harsher penalties for everyone else. A radio could carry vicious messages and not suffer damage. Over the years Zoe had drifted into the idea of her body as a radio, glowing and humming but intact.

There were more colds and flus than usual, but they always ran their course and after they'd gone she felt victorious, wildly alive. When the headaches and the first true fever finally arrived, when she awoke at three in the morning with her sheets soaked, she was incredulous, almost as much so as she'd been upon learning about the infection for the first time. Or differently so, but with almost the same intensity. When she'd heard the news, three years earlier, she'd felt invaded, colonized. Now she felt betrayed not by the virus but by her body. It was supposed to have adapted, and learned to carry her. It was supposed to live in the infection the way a fish lives in water.

Had she believed she might be different, the unprecedented case?

She had.

She stayed out of bed as much as possible. She went to her clerical job at the Legal Aid Society, cleaned the apartment, talked on the phone. It seemed that if she acted in her usual way, normality itself might catch up with her. She didn't pray, but she offered a running thread of entreaty to whatever it might be that governed the movements of pattern and chance. Please, don't let pneumonia into her lungs. Thanks for having kept her son healthy. She sometimes praised herself for caring about her son more than she cared about herself. She sometimes reviled herself for what seemed like nothing more than delusion: her gratitude for Jamal's deliverance and her worries about his future disguised the fact that she wanted nothing, really, more than she wanted to live. Would she let him die in her place? No. Genuinely not. Would she offer a measure of his happiness and security in trade for her own survival? Yes. Up to a point, she'd sacrifice her son.

She found herself watching for omens: telephone numbers that were all even or all odd, the first word her eye went to in a newspaper. Once, on Second Avenue, when she saw a blind woman walking toward her, she said to herself, 'If she passes me on the left, I'll get better. If she passes me on the right, I'll get worse.' When the woman turned and entered a store, Zoe felt first blessed, then cursed. Even if omens and portents did exist, she found that she couldn't decide how to read them.

She'd waited to tell Jamal. He was only four when she'd gotten the news. She'd told herself there was time. But she'd wondered: Would he hate her more for protecting him, or for telling him the truth?

She knew he'd hate her for dying. Wasn't that the single unforgivable act? What seemed impossible was the idea that she might die before Jamal grew old enough to know her as someone who had been a child herself. If she died while he was still young she'd exist in his memory only as a mother. He'd remember kindnesses and faults. He'd work out his own myth and that would be what he carried of her. That was how she'd live after death, as an exaggeration and an abstraction. She hated the idea and, in a far region of herself, was fascinated by it. She, Zoe, would become a myth. She found a gray, horrific safety in it, a sense of haven.

He was seven when Cassandra's first lesions showed up. Zoe decided she couldn't wait any longer. She fixed him a sandwich, sat at the table with him. It was a cold white day that refused to snow. The sky outside the window, between the buildings, was fat and billowed, opaque.

She said, "Jamal, honey. You know what AIDS is, right?"

Jamal chewed his sandwich. He held the bread with both hands, like a child younger than seven. He needed a haircut. Loose corkscrews of shaggy black hair fell over his forehead and the back of his neck. She found herself staring at his eyelashes.

Wondering, would he like a bicycle for Christmas? Would he be safe on it?

He nodded.

"AIDS," Zoe said, "is a kind of sickness, right?"

He nodded again.

"It's called a virus. It's like a tiny bug, too small to see. It can get into people's blood. And it makes them get sick."

"Uh-huh."

"Well. I have it. It got into my blood, and I might get sick. I'll probably get sick."

"When?"

"I don't know. It could happen anytime. I thought I should tell you now."

"How did you get it?" he asked.

"I'm not sure." She paused. Don't stop, she told herself. Just let him know. He'll always remember every lie you tell.

"Probably from a man," she said. "I honestly don't know who. Or from a needle."

"Did you get it from my father?" he asked.

"No."

She didn't know that. But there were limits to what she could say to him.

"Will you die?" he asked.

"I don't know. I hope not. But I could."

"If you died, would I go live with my father?"

"No," she said.

"Good."

She stroked his hair. He took another bite of his sandwich, chewed, swallowed. A pipe in the ceiling thumped.

"If you died I'd live with Cassandra," he said.

"You love Cassandra. Don't you?"

"I don't have it. Do I?"

"No. I had you tested years ago, you probably don't remember. The doctor took some blood, you screamed for half an hour. But no, you're fine."

"Can I go up to Ernesto's?"

"Do you want to ask me any more questions?"

"No."

"You sure?"

"Yes."

"Is going to Ernesto's what you really want to do?" she said.

"Uh-huh."

He got up from the table, walked to the door.

"Jamal?" she said.

"What?"

"Be careful."

"Okay."

"Don't play around in the halls with Ernesto. Stay in his apartment."

"Okay."

"The other day, I saw, well, just a man who didn't look very nice, hanging around out front. I don't think you and Ernesto should play in the halls anymore. Okay?"

"Okay."

"Don't stay too long, okay?"

"*Okay.*"

"Okay. Bye."

He walked out the door and closed it behind himself. She could hear his feet ascending the stairs.

That had been the conversation during which she'd told her child that she would get sick and would probably die. What had she wanted, screams and accusations? A weeping collapse into her arms? This was probably better. But still she resented her son for being calm, and for wondering what would happen to him. She was relieved and she was furious and she was sad almost beyond tolerance. Would death itself be like this, so awkward and ordinary? She could see that it might. It might prove surprising mainly in its resemblance to every other event. It would not necessarily mean the end of unspoken emotions or self-concern; it might not even be the end of social embarrassment. Sitting at her kitchen table with a Mason jar full of hothouse tulips and her son's half-eaten sandwich, with the virus buzzing in her blood, she saw that she could leave her life worried only for herself, surrounded by people who would hold her hand and stroke her forehead and who would be wishing, under their grief, that she'd get through with her dying so they could continue their lives. Who'd be grateful it was her and not them.

This wasn't what she wanted, this bitterness and hollow fear. She wanted transcendence. She wanted bliss.

No. Not even that. She wanted to go on buying groceries and listening to music and reading the newspaper in bed. She was so present in those daily details, so attached to them, that she realized, suddenly, she was not going to die. She was not going to die. She was too entirely here in the room, in her skin.

She lifted her wrist to her face, smelled her own flesh. Then she reached over and picked up Jamal's half-eaten sandwich. It bore the imprint of his teeth. She sat at the table holding it.

"Well, hon," Cassandra said over the telephone, "what did you expect him to do?"

"I don't know," Zoe answered. "I honestly don't."

"Figuring out how he feels about you getting sick is going to be part of his life's work. Expecting him to know how he feels about it the first five minutes indicates, well, an admirably extravagant view of reality."

"How do you feel?" Zoe asked.

"Not bad, considering. I went out this morning and picked up six pairs of opaque black hose, I am *not* resorting to wearing makeup on my legs, there are limits."

"I didn't tell him about you yet."

"Probably wise. He doesn't need the whole dose all at once."

"But I honestly don't know who'd take care of him. If neither one of us could."

"I've been trying to break your mother in."

"I don't know if I'd want him living with my mother. She'd do her best—"

"But she's a suburban matron, and he's a wild boy raised by drag queens. I know. But think about it, hon. None of our friends is exactly the maternal type."

"Alice and Louise might do it."

"*Alice* would do it," Cassandra said. "Louise would *agree* to do it because Alice wanted to. She'd have every good intention, and within three weeks she'd be making his life hell. He'd leave the peanut butter out and she'd go for a wire hanger."

"Maybe you're right. What about Sam?"

"I don't want Jamal living with an alcoholic. Period."

"He's not an alcoholic," Zoe said.

"Drunk two nights out of three is close enough for my purposes."

"The twins?"

"The twins can barely take care of *themselves*. It would make more sense if Jamal adopted them."

"And Tim and Mark and Robert are all sick, too," Zoe said.

"Your mother's got money, and plenty of free time, and she isn't crazy. Well, no crazier than most people."

"I've been thinking about my brother," Zoe said.

"The Ken doll? Ugh."

"I don't know why you two can't get along. It's a mystery to me."

"Nothing mysterious about it. I'm a fabulous creation of my own subconscious and he's a muscle boy who believes in magazines. What's to get along about?"

"He's not like that. You're so unfair to him."

"Oh, well, maybe I am," Cassandra said. "I can't help it, he has all my least favorite qualities. He likes going to smart little bars and restaurants and he follows every fashion and he lives in *Boston*, for god's sake."

"He's a teacher, and he's in love with a doctor. You don't look at the whole person, you just decided to dislike him, and that's that."

"Maybe so, maybe so," Cassandra said. "It's a hobby of mine, disliking pretty boys who think the sun rises and sets out of their own assholes. Pardon the expression."

"He'd be good with Jamal. He likes kids."

"He'd dress Jamal in clone clothes, he'd teach him to enjoy

cocktail parties. He'd take him to live in Boston. Oh, all my years of work come to nothing."

"I'm going to call Will, anyway," Zoe said. "I have to tell my family about it now, I'm going to tell him first."

"Your mother's a better bet for Jamal. I'm sure of it."

"Well, he's my child. Isn't he?"

"Honey, he's *our* child. Don't try pulling rank on me."

"This is a decision I have to make, Cassandra."

"Now wait just a minute. Do you honestly think I spent all those years changing diapers and going to the zoo so that when the shit hit the fan I'd be shunted aside like some doddering old nursemaid whose services are no longer required?"

"Let's not fight. Okay?"

"Let's not boss one another around either, okay? The fact that you gave birth to him doesn't give you final veto power. I've given my soul to that little fucker just like you have. He's my child, too."

"I know. I just—"

"You just nothing," Cassandra said. "You know me better than this. Don't confuse me with some meek little thing who knows her place. I may be a fairy godmother but I can be Medea, too."

"I know."

"Well. We can take this up again later, I suppose. How are *you* feeling?"

"All right. A little tired."

"You feel like going shopping?"

"I don't think so," Zoe said. "There's nothing I need."

"Honey, if that kept people from shopping, the economy would be in ruins."

"I think I'm just going to stay home the rest of the afternoon. I think I'm just going to read."

"Suit yourself. I'm off to bag a few trinkets, maybe I'll work the mezzanine at Bloomingdale's. I haven't been there in so long, I'll bet they've forgotten all about me."

"Okay. Have fun."

"I will, there's nothing like an expedition to lift a girl's spirits. And, Zoe?"

"Mm-hm?"

"I just want what's best for Jamal."

"I know. We both do."

"Lord, can you believe this? I'm the voice of reason and respectability. Well, we just never know what's going to happen, do we?"

Zoe called Will in Boston. She left a message on his answering machine, and he called her back several hours later.

"Hi, Zo."

"Hello, Will. How are you?"

"Okay. Well, sort of okay. I had a real shit of a day."

"I'm sorry," she said.

"I've got this kid in my homeroom class, your basic fuck-up. I've kept him after school, not just as punishment but to go over the work with him in private, so that maybe he learns a little something. I don't get paid for this, right? I do it because I like the kid for some perverse reason or other. Everybody else around here would just hand him along until he's old enough to expel. He thinks he's stupid, and he thinks that if he can sabotage the whole class, if he can just derail the entire educative process, maybe nobody will find out. So I get his parents to come in and talk about how they could help encourage him at home. And they're nightmares. The mother's this tight-lipped little thing, like prim and trashy at the same time, one of those women who were slutty girls and got pregnant when they were fourteen or so and then got religious. And the father. Big fat guy, silent and mean-looking. They'd never read a book and they probably had a gun in every room of the house and about halfway through the conversation the father looks at me with this sly patronizing gleam in his eyes and says, 'You don't see a lot of men teachers.' It's the first thing he's said. And glances over at his wife in this knowing way, and she glances back. And it hits me—they can tell I'm gay, and they're going to tell their son to have nothing to do with me. I may be the one chance this kid's got, I can tell you no one else at that school is going to bother with him, and these assholes are going to turn him against me. They don't care how he does in school anyway, they want him to be just as stuck as they are. And it feels so fucking hopeless. I mean, there's this bottomless meanness and stupidity and it's so embedded and, I don't know, it seems to be *increasing*, it's like people are getting meaner and stupider and more and more proud of it."

Zoe said, "I know. I mean, it's terrible."

"Sorry to go on like that. You're always taking your chances when you call me on a weekday. What's up, Zo? How're tricks?"

"I have AIDS, Will."

"What?"

"I have AIDS."

"My god."

"I tested positive almost three years ago. I didn't tell anybody in the family, I'm sorry."

"Oh, my god."

"There's no excuse, really. I just—as long as a lot of people didn't know about it, it could still seem sort of unreal to me, I guess. If people didn't know, I wouldn't have to live as somebody with an illness."

"You've been to a doctor?"

"Of course I've been to a doctor."

"Somebody good?"

"Yes. Somebody good."

"What are your . . . Have you had symptoms?"

"Some night sweats, they just started. Headaches. That's why I realized I had to tell you."

"What's your T-cell count? Do you know?"

"*Yes*, I know. It's four hundred."

"I'm coming down there."

"You don't have to."

"The planes leave every hour."

"There's nothing you can do, Will."

"It'll take me two, maybe three hours."

Will arrived less than three hours later. Zoe was making tea. Jamal sat at the kitchen table eating his dinner. When Will appeared at the door he hesitated, uncertain about whether or not Jamal knew.

"Hi, Will," Zoe said. She kissed him as if it was an ordinary visit. She didn't look any different. Of course, no one did at first. Will had buried a half-dozen friends, he knew well enough how long the changes could take. When people first started getting sick their eyes still held the same liquid depths, their skin was still tautly wedded to muscle and bone. All the disease's early work was invisible, a network of meticulous stitches sewn on the inside. But this was his sister, and in spite of all he'd seen he let himself imagine, briefly, that nothing was wrong. It had been a trick, a mistake. Zoe's apartment was the same apartment, bright and shabby. Here was the big kitchen with its broad planked floor and its smells of cinnamon and coffee. Here were her chipped plates and unmatched cups stacked behind the glass cupboards, here the faded pictures of Mexican saints and the awful amateur paintings she collected in thrift stores (an angel with cascading Nancy Sinatra hair, a chihuahua, a smiling crewcut man with porcine, off-center eyes). The place didn't seem profound enough for mortal illness. It lacked solemnity and weight.

"Hi," Will said. "Hi, Jamal."

Jamal sat at the table, pretending to eat. "Hello," he said. Lately he'd abandoned his tendency to silence with people he didn't know well. In its place he offered a regal, slightly pained formality. He said 'Hello' and 'Thank you' and 'Do come again.'

"Are you hungry?" Zoe asked Will.

"No. Yes. A little."

"We're having rice and beans," she said. "Jamal has become a vegetarian."

"Really?" Will said to Jamal.

Jamal nodded. "Yes," he said.

"Not even fish?"

"Fish are alive. They have blood in them."

Zoe fixed a plate of rice and beans for Will. He sat at the table beside Jamal. Jamal speared a single bean with his fork, placed it carefully between his front teeth, sucked it in.

He didn't seem nervous or afraid. He didn't appear to wonder why his uncle had appeared suddenly from three hundred miles away.

Will asked, "How's school?"

"Enchanting," Jamal said. He did not seem to intend it ironically.

"Second grade, right?"

"Yes," Jamal answered.

"I could be your teacher in a few more years, if you lived in Boston. I teach fifth grade."

"I know."

Zoe poured herself a cup of tea, sat at the table. "I finished my dinner twenty minutes ago," she said. "Jamal is the slowest living eater."

Jamal smiled shyly, as if it had been a compliment. He impaled a single grain of rice on one tine of his fork.

"Better for the digestion, I suppose," Will said. Why did the presence of children so often feel like that of visiting politicians from obscure and remote countries?

"Cassandra never eats at all," Jamal said.

"Of course she does," Zoe said. "Everybody eats."

"Cassandra only drinks water and juice and coffee," Jamal said.

"Not true," Zoe told him. "Cassandra eats a lot, this one doesn't even *resemble* reality."

"Once a day, she eats an apple. One green apple."

"I won't debate this with you. You don't believe it yourself. I'll bet you've watched her eat a cheeseburger sometime within the last forty-eight hours."

"How is Cassandra?" Will asked.

"She's okay," Zoe said.

"Cassandra has quit eating cheeseburgers," Jamal said. "She finds them repulsive."

After Jamal and Will had finished eating, Zoe sent Jamal to his room to do his homework. She took the plates to the sink, and Will followed her. He put a hand on her thin back.

"Baby," he said.

She ran hot water over the plates. "Jamal knows," she said. "But thank you for not bringing it up in front of him."

"I'd never—"

"I don't want his face rubbed in it every five minutes. Sometimes I wonder if that's right, maybe he should hear about it all the time until it just blends in with every other regular thing."

She squeezed soap onto a sponge, the way their mother did. She kept the soap in an opaque plastic bottle, just as their mother had. She wore a black shirt, faded black jeans.

"I think this is probably the right decision," he said. "Or, well, who knows? Who has any idea what to do with children?"

"Thank you for coming down," she said.

"Don't thank me."

There was a pause, oddly social, as if they were new acquaintances who had run out of subjects but couldn't find a way to gracefully leave each other. It seemed they should fall into each other's arms and cry together. They didn't cry. They were adults in a kitchen, washing dishes while a child did his homework in another room.

"I feel a little embarrassed," she said. "Isn't that crazy? Of all things to feel at a time like this."

"Are you taking anything?"

"Not yet. Sharon, my doctor, wants to start me on AZT. But it makes me nervous, I hear terrible things about it. I told her I'd think about it."

"I think you should do the AZT. Or maybe not. I don't know. I've heard some terrible things about it, too. Is this Sharon a good doctor?"

"Yes, I told you she was. Don't worry so much."

"Sure, right. Why should I worry?"

"And please don't be sarcastic, either."

"If you take away worry and sarcasm, I don't have any responses left," he said. "You're not doing any kind of drugs at all?"

"Not yet. I'm taking a ton of vitamins. I'm eating well."

"That doesn't sound like enough."

"I'll probably start on some stuff for opportunistic infections soon," she said. "Bactrim, I think. I'd like to maybe think about aerosolized pentamidine, but it costs a fortune."

"Who cares what it costs?"

"Will, my insurance won't pay for everything. I'm lucky to have insurance at all. Why do you think I've been putting on a skirt and going downtown and sitting in front of a word processor every day all these years?"

"Don't worry about money," he said.

"I have to worry about money."

"I can help you."

"Thank you. But what do you make? Twenty-five thousand a year?"

"Harry's got money. Dad has money. Susan has money."

"All right. I won't worry about it."

"Speaking of drugs," he said, "I, well. I brought a joint. Do you want to smoke a joint?"

"Okay. Yes. I'd love to."

Will nodded in the direction of Jamal's bedroom, raised his brows.

"He's seen me get stoned before," Zoe said. "What can I say? I'm one of those mothers you read about."

"I think you're a good mother." He took the joint from his wallet.

"I don't know. I try. It's harder than you think it's going to be. No, that's not quite it. It's hard in different ways than what you expected. It's—more human than you expected. I'd always pictured clearer boundaries, like I'd know exactly what to say to a child."

Will lit the joint, inhaled, offered it to her. She dried her hands on a jungle-patterned dish towel.

"Mom wasn't all that human, do you think?" he said. "I don't mean she was some kind of ogre, but she never seemed exactly like a *person*, I mean somebody who's just alive and nervous here on the face of the earth. You know what I mean?"

Zoe hit on the joint, blew out a thick curl of smoke that hung stodgily in the lamplight. "Oh, Mom was scared," she said. "She was just so, well, *scared*."

"I guess. Have you, have you told her?"

"Not yet. I needed to try it out on you first."

Will took the joint from her, inhaled.

"I'm handling it all right," he said. "Don't you think?"

"Mm-hm. I knew you would."

Will lifted a small plastic man from the countertop.

"What's this?" he asked.

"One of Jamal's Star Trek people. That's the doctor, I forget his name."

"Bones. Captain Kirk called him Bones."

"Right," she said. "He wasn't one of the really major characters, was he?"

"Semi-major. He was always around. He was . . . helpful."

"Jamal has them all. Look, here's a Klingon."

"Nasty-looking character."

"He loves the aliens. He doesn't care if they're good or bad. Will?"

"Yeah?"

"Cassandra has it, too."

"Oh. God."

"She's had it longer than I have. She's got a Kaposi's lesion on her leg."

"Oh."

He held the little plastic doctor, the man called Bones. The doctor had tiny black eyes, skin the off-flesh color of a Band-Aid.

"Is Cassandra on AZT?" he asked.

"She tried. It made her so anemic she could barely stand up. That's part of why I'm not sure about doing it myself."

"I don't know what to say."

"You don't have to say anything," she told him. "I'm just glad you're here."

She went and sat at the table with singular determination, as if that was the obvious next thing to do. She still held the plastic alien. She stood him on the tabletop before her, looked at him with the appraising gravity of a jeweler considering a stone that might or might not be priced beyond its value.

"Dad is building a greenhouse," she said.

"I know."

Will filled a glass with cold water from the tap, brought it to the table with him. He took a sip, set the glass down beside the Klingon. Zoe took a sip.

"He wants to grow orchids," she said. "Isn't it funny to think of him growing orchids?"

"He and Magda are trying to be genteel. She's started doing all this charity work, have you heard about that?"

"Like Mom."

"Like the Beverly Hillbillies. She cruises around Bridgehampton in a fox coat, I can't believe some animal-rights activist hasn't thrown blood on her yet."

Zoe laughed.

Her eyes were unchanged.

"Mom is so lonely," she said. "She should sell the house."

"Would it bother you if she did?"

"No. I'm not really attached to it."

"Me, neither. It's supposed to be this classic traumatic incident, when your parents sell the house you grew up in, and all I can seem to think is, 'Mom, get a condo. Go, girl.' "

"We weren't very happy there."

"Sometimes we were. There were moments."

"Well, sure. There were moments."

She balanced the Klingon on the edge of the water glass.

"I haven't done all that much with my life," she said.

"Come on. Don't say things like that."

"It's the truth, that's all. When I think of myself, you know. Not being here anymore. I sometimes think about how, well, it's not like I'm in the middle of producing a great work of art or saving people's lives or anything. I've just got Jamal and my job and this apartment."

"That's enough," Will said. "You don't have to be a brain surgeon."

"The thing is, if this went away. If a miracle happened, and I wasn't sick anymore? I don't think I'd change all that much. I can't honestly say I'd become a doctor or work with the poor or anything like that. I mean, for a while I was having these kind of silent conversations with, like, some invisible power, and I'd try to convince whoever it was that if I had another chance I'd do everything differently. But even when I was saying it I knew it wasn't true."

"You've done plenty, sweetheart. I don't want you to worry about this."

"The really funny thing," she said, "is how I don't seem to feel any better about, you know. The idea of dying. The fact that it wouldn't interrupt some great work of mine."

"Mm-hm."

"Sometimes I feel like I'd like to be a bigger tragedy. It's ridiculous, isn't it? I feel like I want my absence to be this huge loss to the world, and I know it wouldn't be. The one person it'd be really devastating to is Jamal."

"Listen, Zo, this kind of talk is premature, don't you think?"

"If something happens to me, and if something happens to Cassandra, I think, I mean I was wondering."

"You look fine. These are only your first symptoms—"

"I was wondering if you'd think about maybe taking Jamal. I need to know he'd have somebody to take care of him."

"God, Zo," Will said. "I guess I would."

"Cassandra has this thing about Jamal going to live with Mom. And, I don't know. Mom is so, well. She's *Mom*. She and Jamal just aren't a match for each other, I'd rather think of him with you."

"I'd have to think about it. But, well. It'd probably be okay. I'd probably take him if you wanted me to."

"Thank you."

Will said, "Do you want to come up to Boston? I could help you find a place up there."

"No. This is our home, Jamal has friends here. And I couldn't separate him and Cassandra."

"Right."

"Cassandra is at least as good a parent as I am. You have no idea."

"Well, if you ever change your mind, if you want to come up north for a while, just let me know."

"Thank you."

"Don't thank me. Please."

She walked the Klingon across the tabletop, stood him in front of Will.

"Thank you, Will," she said in a deep voice.

"You're welcome," he said.

They sat at the table together until Jamal came into the kitchen to say that he had finished his homework and wanted to watch television. They watched television with him for an hour, then Zoe put him to bed. She and Will returned to the kitchen table and sat there for most of the night, talking. Sometimes Will moved the Klingon idly around on the tabletop, and sometimes Zoe did. As they talked, Will worked the tangles out of Zoe's hair.

1 9 8 9 / Mary got to Boston once or twice a year, to see her son and to be in a city that didn't recognize her. Or, rather, she went to see her son and as a side effect, an added and less complicated pleasure, she enjoyed being in Boston. Boston was a kind of miniature New York where she looked better than most of the women her age and where she had no history. She always stayed at the Ritz-Carlton, an extravagance under any circumstance and even more so now that she lived on her alimony checks and the money she made working at Anne Klein. Still, the Ritz was worth it. Walking through the lobby in a skirt and jacket, she could have been a discreet, prosperous businesswoman from San Francisco. She could have been the American wife of a wine importer who kept an apartment in Paris and a house in Tuscany. She saved her money for these trips, took no other vacations, and when she bought new clothes it was always with an eye toward wearing them in Boston. In Boston, walking on Newbury or Arlington Street, past the windows of expensive stores, she could have been almost anyone. In Boston, where the women in the better part of town tended toward the squat, puggish, disappointed look of old Anglican money; where Burberry raincoats appeared to be the height of fashion and women fifty pounds overweight didn't seem to know better than to wear plaids and bold checks—there Mary could love her own aura of exotic strangeness, her dusky Italian skin and sharp, large-featured face.

There she could lose track, occasionally, of the facts of her life. She was not the mother of a girl with a mortal illness. She had not spent her youth on a harsh-tempered, uneducated man who'd left her for a fat secretary with canary-colored hair. She did not live modestly in a vast, empty house. She did not wait on some of the women with whom she had once hoped, and failed, to become intimate.

When she went to Boston she was a woman in a good hotel. In her pocketbook she carried a slim golden pencil, a black enameled tube of lipstick from France. She was there to meet her son, a strapping man in jeans and a tweed jacket.

Billy (she'd learned to call him Will to his face) met her in restaurants or stores, or called for her at the Ritz. On many of her visits she didn't even see his apartment. A certain formality prevailed during her trips to Boston. She left her life to come to this city and, in a sense, Billy left his life, too. He put on a jacket and his most presentable shoes and rode the subway to a part of Boston almost as foreign to him as it was to her. They were tourists together. They walked the streets emanating a proud, defiant anonymity. Boston had its dappled brick and limestone, its self-centered fury of commerce, its windows full of merchandise. Mary placed her hand in the crook of Billy's elbow and spoke to him of pleasant, everyday things. So much lay undeclared between them. She knew about him, although he'd told her nothing and she'd never asked a direct question. She couldn't quite date her knowledge. She couldn't have said that in the spring of 1980 or the fall of 1982 or at Christmas the year he turned thirty, she'd realized her son was homosexual. She thought she could remember not knowing, but if she tried to take herself back to a time when she hadn't known, her memory reversed itself and she believed she had always known, even when he was a baby. Her recollection of innocence existed only on the periphery, like another person sensed but not yet seen. When she turned to look—when she tried precisely to locate a Mary who'd believed her son loved women and would someday take a wife—what she saw was infected with what she knew, and the very image of herself with a heterosexual son vanished as if that Mary had never existed at all.

She let it be a fact, remote and serene as Boston itself. She let it live quietly in her and did not contemplate the particulars. She and Billy had an unspoken arrangement. He called for her, arrived nicely dressed. He talked about his work, asked after his sisters, listened a good deal more than he spoke. He resembled, at times, a shy suitor. There were even moments when he reminded her of Constantine as a young man: Constantine the day laborer in the best clothes he could afford, his English less than fluent, treating her with courtly patience because he was dazzled and because he did not understand half of what she said and because he had surprises—his temper, the business between his legs—stored up for after they were married. She didn't think about Billy's surprises. She let him buzz from the lobby. She took him to stores and bought new clothes for him, firmly producing her charge card in answer to the protests they both knew he offered as ritual. She took him to dinner in nice restaurants, let him listen noncommittally to her own conversation. It seemed a form of respect, a way of showing their love for each other.

It had worked that way for years. As far as Mary was concerned it would continue for years into the future. She could picture herself as an old lady, precise and solemn in a dark suit, known to the staff at the Ritz, arriving every few months to be met by her son, gone gray himself, a handsome and solid man with a well-trimmed gray mustache and skin creased and burnished like fine leather. They would walk through the Public Gardens together. They would have dinner at quiet little restaurants where she would continue, with the serene, childish impertinence of age, to insist on paying.

It seemed a decent way to grow old alongside her son, and she silently congratulated herself for her openness. Not every mother would respect a child's choices this way, or honor his privacy. Some mothers were harridans. Some mothers begged and threatened. She, Mary, packed her best clothes and took a room at the Ritz.

It was on her spring visit that Billy leaned toward her in a restaurant and said: "Mom, I think I'm in love."

Just those words. She didn't realize, at first, how much they carried. She took a sip of her water and said, "Really?"

Neither of them spoke for almost a full minute. Mary was aware of how much gentle and contented noise the other diners were making with their silver and their coffee cups and their conversations. It was a lovely restaurant, one of her favorites in Boston, a formal place where the waiters were all handsome and where candles flickered before their own reflections in smoky mirrors. It was the kind of place Mary had hoped to go for lunch after Billy's commencement, all those years ago, when Constantine had been in charge and had taken her to an awful café done up in gingham and travel posters, with a single hothouse rose dying on every table. Now, as she sat across from her son and waited for him to continue speaking, she had an urge to leave. Not to walk off and abandon him—she wouldn't do that—but to merge with the restaurant, to abandon her own body and inhabit this room with its buzz of confident talk and its buttery damask-covered walls, the expensive and competent glow of it.

Billy said, "His name is Harry."

"Well," Mary said. She decided against pretending surprise. What would it earn her? "How long have you known him?" she asked.

"Almost a year." Billy picked up his knife, set it down again. Mary saw that he was proud and embarrassed. She saw that a part of him had not changed at all since the day when, at the age of ten, he'd brought home an elaborate beaded necklace he'd strung for her at summer camp. She'd known he was pleased with the necklace and she'd known that most of the other boys at camp must have chosen to make ashtrays or wallets for their mothers. She'd pictured her son sitting among the girls, stringing beads with a look of furious concentration, full of a profound abandonment to his own love of feminine industry. Now, at the age of thirty-six, he frowned shyly and sheepishly over his knife.

He said, "I figured you probably knew. About me."

Mary didn't speak. It seemed she would lose something she might need later if she admitted to her own knowledge. Billy waited, turning the knife over, and when he realized she was not going to say anything, he went on.

"I feel pretty stupid, coming out at this age," he said. "I should have told you years ago. I just knew you knew, and I always told myself I'd formally announce the fact when and if I fell in love. Because, well, I wanted to tell you about it with a real live person attached, not just as, you know, a *proclivity*. Which was probably just cowardice on my part. But anyway, here it is. Better late than never, right? I'm in love with a man named Harry."

"Well," Mary said.

"Does it shock you?" Billy looked up at her and she saw how much he wanted her not to be shocked. How much he needed— what? Not her forgiveness, not exactly that. Her recognition. He desperately wanted not to be strange to her. At this age, after almost twenty years of living on his own and doing exactly as he liked. For twenty years, all three of her children had lived far from the sphere of her opinions. They had mocked her with their politeness and their forbearance. They had done only what they wanted to do, and left her to her own shrinking life. And now, this late in the game, Billy was suddenly as available to damage at her hands as he'd been when he was a baby.

Her first impulse was to take advantage. She could tell him it turned her stomach to think of her only son in love with another man. She could say that all her hopes were squandered. Or, worse (she knew, somehow, it would be worse), she could simply change the subject. She could treat this love of his as a minor distraction, barely meriting comment.

She could repay him for every slight, every disappointment and act of disrespect. She thought of him whining at four. She thought of him wild at seventeen, more loyal to a band of stupid, brutal friends than he was to her. She thought of him going to the movies on his own graduation day, denying her a deep satisfaction that would have cost him almost nothing.

She was nearly overcome with anger and with a throbbing irritation, like a piece of gristle caught deep in a tooth. But what she said, almost against her conscious will, in a soft clear voice, was, "No. I'm not shocked."

"Good," he said.

"Tell me more about Harry."

Billy smiled, an involuntary little tic of a smile, and she could see—or she sensed more than she saw—that his eyes were hot with the possibility of grateful tears. Because she had expressed a calm and simple interest. Only that. Incipient tears in a boy, a man, who for so long had been remote as an almond inside its shell.

He said, "He's a cardiologist. He plays the saxophone. The main thing about Harry is, I feel like I could talk to him forever."

Mary nodded. She felt something inflate within her, a tough little bladder of air that seemed to reside under her ribs like a third lung. She was disappointed. She was angry. But she couldn't harm her child, though she wished she was powerful enough to do so. If she'd been the kind of woman who could lash out at her son, who could take revenge, who knew how different her life might have been? If she'd been that kind of woman, firm and ruthless, quick to anger, mightn't she have married better? Mightn't she have raised children who respected her, who accomplished much in the world because their mother was always behind them with her sword and her scales? Wasn't that the woman at the Ritz? Someone with teeth, with influence.

But here in this restaurant, faced with her son's ardor and fragility, his aging hands, she knew finally and forever that she was not that woman. She was herself. She carried the long tangle of her history. All she could do was listen to her son with love and fear and a low distant crackle of rage as he smiled shyly and spoke, in a tentative voice, about a man he loved.

"It's a little mysterious to me," Billy said. "He's not the best-looking guy I've ever met. He's very smart and kind, but he's not some fantasy come true. I just seem to love him. It's never happened to me before, not something like this. I just get more and more interested in him."

"It sounds serious," Mary said.

"It is," Billy answered. "I think it is. Would you like to meet him?"

Mary thought, suddenly, of herself walking through Central Park with Cassandra and Jamal over two years ago. That strange little boy who carried her blood mixed with the blood of a black man she'd never meet. She thought of Cassandra's face, the ancient and commanding look it had assumed as all pretense of girlish cordiality fell away.

What had Cassandra said? *He may need you one day.* Something like that. *I don't want him going to live with strangers.*

Mary thought of the wings that had almost touched her face. "Yes," she said. "Yes, of course I want to meet him."

1 9 9 2 / There was a green emptiness down beyond the houses. There was a depth of buzzing grasses. Ben went with Andrew and Trevor, singing bits of "Jeremy," blueing the air with cigarette smoke.

"I love Mary Kelly," Andrew said. "I mean, I love Mary Kelly." Andrew had the expanse, the romantic fearlessness. Trevor was smaller, more intricately balanced, more prone to caution and laughter.

Ben was the one with the silence. He held Andrew and Trevor with his eyes, promised quietly that somebody knew. Somebody knew about everything, and held them.

"You love Mary Kelly's tits," said Trevor. "You love exactly two and a half pounds worth of Mary Kelly, you fuck."

"They weigh more than two and a half pounds."

"You weighed 'em?"

"Trust me."

"*Right*. Trust *you*."

"Then eat me."

"You wish."

They walked deeper into the green. Andrew was the blond one with the loose stride. Trevor was broad, bunched up, pulled in around his strength and his habit of mockery.

Behind them, houses gave back squares of late sky from their window glass. Flowers whitened in the dusk. Water rose up in spirals, spun and hissed over lawns.

"Mary Kelly is a fucking goddess," Andrew said. "Mary Kelly can have me if she wants me."

Trevor laughed loud enough to flush a crow, which angled out of a spruce and flapped slowly away like a living illustration of the idea of black.

"Mary Kelly already had the football team," he said. "Varsity and junior varsity."

Ben walked behind, not speaking. He didn't look at his friends' backs, the strong innocent curves.

"Mary Kelly," Andrew said, "is a slut, it's true, but she never did the whole football team. She left out a lot of guys."

"The only guys in the junior and senior class Mary Kelly hasn't fucked are fags," Trevor said. "Hey, Ben?"

"What?"

"You got the cigarettes?"

"Yeah."

Trevor stopped, took a cigarette from the pack, lit up. He inhaled with his eyes closed, adoring the smoke.

Trevor asked Ben, "You think Andrew has a chance with Mary Kelly?"

"Mary Kelly's a senior," Ben said.

"I hate being fucking twelve," Andrew said.

"It won't last."

Ben lit a cigarette, handed it to Andrew, lit another for himself. Andrew took between his lips the cigarette that had been in Ben's mouth, and inhaled. He sighed out a ragged blue-gray stream.

He said, "I hate it. All the women I want are seventeen fucking years old."

"Want women you can have," Trevor told him.

"I can't want women I don't want."

"I want every woman," Trevor said. "I want the old ones and the young ones and the fat ones and the ones that've lost all their hair from chemotherapy."

"Uh-huh."

"What about you, Ben?"

"What?"

"You're being very goddamn quiet over there."

Ben said, "Yeah."

"We're not bothering you, are we?"

"You're not bothering me."

"Talking about women doesn't offend you. Does it?"

"No. It doesn't offend me."

"Good."

A silence passed. When they were little boys together, it had been enough to be present. It had been enough to take the chances, to have strength and a simple talent for games. Now, as changes started, you needed to speak as somebody new. You needed a galaxy of desires, and a language to tell them in.

Andrew said, "Ben's a cool customer. Ben's the guy who acts, he doesn't need to talk about it."

When it was time to start hating him, Ben thought, Andrew would be the last.

"Ben," Trevor said, "is a wiener."

"Shut up," Andrew told him.

"You a wiener, Ben?"

"No," Ben said.

"You a dork?"

"Come on, Trevor."

"You a princess?"

Andrew cuffed Trevor with the back of his hand, hard enough to send him staggering. Trevor nearly fell. He sprang back, blinking and squinting, getting his bearings. The air around him buzzed with confusion and he looked at Andrew as if Andrew had grown too small to see.

"Don't talk to your friends that way," Andrew said.

"It was a fucking joke."

"Nobody's laughing."

Trevor sucked it in, the sour shiftings and the outrage. He would hold it, save it.

He said, "Joke, man. You fuckers better lighten up."

"I don't like jokes like that," Andrew said.

He was large enough to be generous, to defend others. He could afford it. The future was written on him. He had a carved and stoic beauty, a perfect throwing arm.

"Let's get out of here," Trevor said.

But none of them moved. They cupped their cigarettes in the dimming green. Behind them were the houses, and ahead, a row of black trees ringed the lake. They watched the trees gather darkness around themselves.

At home, his mother served soup from the white tureen. Steam curled up and touched the tired beauty of her face. There was a yearning toward good in the world. It lived here in Ben's house, where every bowl and spoon was cherished. Where Ben himself, at all ages, smiled behind glass on the walls.

"I've been thinking," his mother said, "that maybe we should start a college fund for Zoe's son." She gave a bowl of soup to Ben, filled a bowl for his father.

"Hmm," Ben's father said.

"I'm worried about him. Nobody's made any kind of provisions, he's just growing up any which way."

"And whose fault is that?"

"It doesn't matter whose *fault* it is. We could help out a little, that's all that's important."

Ben ate a spoonful of soup.

"Sure we can," his father said. "Ben, what do you think about Jamal?"

The room went bleary from the heat inside Ben's head. He held his spoon. He looked at his father and said, "He's all right."

His father said, "You're his cousin, you're an older boy, and you're, well, you're the kind of example a kid like that needs. You're the closest thing he has to a big brother, really."

Ben kept his face usual. He concentrated on being who he was.

"Uh-huh."

"Maybe we should invite him up here more often," his father said. "Let him run around in the woods, blow off some steam. You'd have to take him under your wing a little, would that be okay with you?"

Ben's father was full of worried hope. So much depended on him. He had to be at the State Assembly from early morning until late at night. He had to pay for everything and drive carefully and know the troubles of the larger world. He had to perfectly duplicate himself every day as a patient man who would improve the workings of governments—now Connecticut's, soon the country's—by the steady force of his knowledge, his hatred of laziness and waste.

"Sure," Ben said. His voice sounded good. He sounded like himself.

"The city can't be good for him," Ben's father said. "There's plenty of human garbage down there that likes nothing better than to prey on innocent ten-year-old boys."

Ben was afraid the pound of blood in his head might be audible. The room was blurred, blazing. He sat in his chair, eating his soup.

"I think we should be investing some money for him, too," Ben's mother said. "He's going to be applying to college eventually."

"If any decent college will have him," Ben's father said.

Ben's mother touched her lips with her napkin. She had sacrificed everything. "Jamal is very intelligent," she said. "You know that. His tests are practically off the scale."

"And you know he goes to school about one day out of three. Good colleges don't base their decisions strictly on test scores. They want kids who look as if they give a damn."

"He's having a hard time right now. For obvious reasons. And he's only in the fifth grade."

"That's why I'm saying we should have him up here more often. Take him in a little, give him some family love."

"I suppose," Ben's mother said. "I'm not saying we shouldn't do that. But he'll need money, too."

"Throwing money at people doesn't necessarily help them."

"Please don't start."

"Besides," Ben's father said, "some college or other will give him a full scholarship even if he quits going to school altogether. I'm not talking Ivy League. But believe me, there are still places out there that are dying for kids like this. Lining up for them."

Ben's mother said, "Ben, honey, do you want some more soup?"

"I'm not sure about handing him a bank account," Ben's father said. "I'm not sure that'd be much of a favor to him, sending that kind of message. About something for nothing. I'd rather have Ben teach him a thing or two about values and hard work, while he's still young enough to learn."

"Honey? Soup?"

Ben's voice failed. It curled back in his throat. He flexed the muscles of his legs, thought about lawns and skies, the plock of a tennis ball struck squarely in the center of the racket.

"Yeah," he said. "More soup. Please."

That night, he awoke with his pajama bottoms sticky. The dream had already sunk into his bloodstream. Andrew had been in it. Andrew had been swimming. He'd risen up out of cold clear water, spangled, naked. There had been a roar, like wind but not wind. Andrew had stood naked and suddenly frightened in a platter of icy water and the roar had grown louder and without wanting to, without agreeing, Ben had come. He woke. He jumped out of bed, tore his pajama bottoms off, and went into the bathroom. He rinsed them under the tap. He put the wet pajamas in the back of his closet, got another pair from his dresser drawer. He tried to go back to sleep but he was too nervous for sleep.

How could he let this happen?

After nearly an hour, he went downstairs to the kitchen. He could feel his parents slumbering. He could hear the ticking of the hall clock. In the kitchen he took the pitcher from the refrigerator, drank a glass of water, and washed out the glass. He told himself that was what he had come for. But he stayed in the kitchen, in his pajama bottoms, looking around at it as if he had never been there before. Here were the varnished oak cabinets and shelves, here the tiles with pictures of herbs printed on them. Here were the clear glass canisters full of pasta and beans and sugar and salt.

He took a knife from the drawer, held it in his hands. Curiously, as if he wanted only to know what would happen, he drew the blade of the knife across his forearm, at the tender inner spot just below the elbow. It didn't hurt, not much. There was only the line the knife had made. Then the blood started. There was more than he'd expected. It welled up from the center of the cut, one bright drop, then came out along the full length. The blood briefly held a single line, gathering fatly. Then a drop from the lower edge meandered down his forearm and spread into the creases at his wrist. He watched the blood. He thought it might be possible that something was leaving him, and that once it was gone he'd be free. He was surprised at how little it hurt. He was surprised, too, at how much blood came out. A second drop trailed down his forearm, and a third. He realized it was going to fall to the floor and he quickly raised his arm to change the direction of the blood's flow but it was too late. A single spatter bloomed on the speckled white floor, and then another. He got a paper towel. He used it to wipe up the floor and then to wipe the blood off his arm. The blood kept coming and he kept wiping until the paper towel was entirely soaked with red. Holding the bloody paper towel in his good hand, he held his other arm under the faucet and let the water wash the blood away until it had stopped coming. He rinsed the sink out and scoured it with cleanser. He threw the bloody paper towel in the garbage, hid it under the dinner scraps and a half head of lettuce that had gone bad. But then he thought his mother might find it, anyway. It wasn't likely that she'd find it but if she did she'd ask him about it and he didn't know what he'd say. So he took the paper towel back out of the garbage can. Black flecks of coffee grounds had stuck to the blood, and a scrap of cellophane and a kernel of corn. He felt as if he might faint from the sight of garbage clinging to the blood. He didn't faint. Walking quietly, he took the paper towel into the downstairs bathroom. He thought he'd flush it down the toilet, but what if it stuck in the pipes? What if they called the plumber, and he came up with this wad of garbage and blood? Ben walked from room to room with it, in a mounting panic that made the rooms themselves stranger and stranger, with their comfortable chairs and needlepoint pillows, their vases full of flowers. What could he do with this rag of his blood? Where could he put it and feel certain it would not be found? It seemed his parents knew every moment of the house, every shadowed and concealed place. Finally, taking care to make as little noise as possible, Ben eased his way out the kitchen door and took the paper towel into the yard. It was a cool night, the grass was wet and icy under his bare feet. He walked quickly to the back fence, crouched, and dug a hole in the loose earth near the compost heap. He dug deep, almost to his elbow. The earth smelled cold and harsh, unfresh, like old clothes. He dug in a paroxysm of fear so intense it clouded his vision. At any time, one of his parents could turn on the outside light and look out the window, and if that happened he would have no explanation. He dropped the paper towel into the hole, filled and smoothed it with the palms of his hands. He jumped up again, relieved, but when he turned back toward the house it was changed. It was still a white house with a shingled roof and dark green shutters but it was not his house anymore and he ran to catch up with it, to get inside and back to his bed before it changed so much he could never get in again. Once he was in the kitchen, he felt better. The kitchen was immaculate. It was the kitchen he knew. He washed the dirt from his hands at the kitchen sink, then went quietly upstairs and bandaged the cut so it wouldn't leak onto his sheets. The bandage could be concealed, and by the following night he could claim to have cut himself in any number of ways. He got back into bed. He returned to himself; he mostly returned. He was able eventually to sleep, though before he fell asleep he was stricken with worry about the buried paper towel. He worried that it might be found, and he worried about something else, something crazy. He knew it was crazy, but he couldn't stop thinking about it. He pictured the paper towel rising up out of its little grave like the bloody ghost of somebody murdered. He imagined it floating around out there at the dark far end of the yard.

1 9 9 2 / What they wanted was to have the same day. Sometimes they got it. Sometimes Jamal went to school and hung with his friends and his mother went to work and they both came home. She made dinner. He did his homework. Cassandra called to talk trash, or stopped by for a cup of coffee before she got herself ready for the clubs. Jamal and his mother watched TV for a while, went to bed, let the night fold up around them with its pipes singing in the walls, its sirens and radios. Sometimes they got all that.

Sometimes she was too sick for work and she spent the day on the sofa, reading or not reading, slipping in and out of a pale unsatisfying sleep. She moaned along with the doves that perched on the fire escape. Sometimes he came home from school and lived with her in the heavy air. Sometimes he stayed on the front stoop until late. On those days he sat, neither home nor away from home, listening to the passing radios and watching the haircuts walk by. He sat while the lights came on and he sat through a long portion of their burning as the street passed in its regular time.

Sometimes when the old days thinned out he went to Cassandra's. He hoped to disappear there the way he used to, in with the mirrors and necklaces. He timed himself to the chatter of the sewing machine as she worked on her tulle and chiffon, her stitching of beads. But lately the air there was too close. There was no room for his long legs, the moves that wanted out. He got bored. When he was a little boy it was his favorite place, two small rooms so draped and layered there were no walls or floors, only the high white of the ceiling. On the walls and the floors were pearls and fake leopardskin and colored scarves and Oriental rugs and hats and old photographs and passages of yellowed lace. There was a blue velvet sofa and there were lamps with scenes painted on their shades and candlesticks and striped hatboxes and bouquets of dried roses in silver cups and spindly gold chairs and a tapestry where blue and brown people danced in ivory-colored wigs. There were shelves full of books and a tarnished trumpet and an old electric fan and satin boxes and carved wooden boxes and silver boxes and a smiling white Buddha with crackled skin and a framed painting of an ecstatic blond girl on a swing and two life-sized iron monkeys holding ashtrays on their heads. Jamal had loved it but now he didn't fit there, he'd grown too big. He'd joined a time that moved faster than Cassandra's sewing machine, all the brightly colored nothing that happened in her rooms.

Cassandra grew tireder, tighter. She got impatient at her machine. She started smoking again.

"You shouldn't do that," Jamal told her one afternoon. It was March, nothing had put out any green. The trees in Tompkins Square Park still looked like they were made of cement.

"I know, it's a filthy habit," Cassandra said. "But there are just some places you can't go without a cigarette." She sat sewing bugle beads on a black bodice, smoking big, with wrist and elbow, huge exhaled clouds in the spangled dimness. She was wearing her pink chenille robe. Beside her, one of the silent monkeys held up its ashtray.

"It's bad for you," Jamal said.

"Honey, I *know* it's bad for me, do you think I need a ten-year-old to tell me that?"

"Then don't do it."

She squinted at a bead. "With all due respect," she said, "mind your own goddamn business."

"It *is* my business," he said. "I'm breathing it, too."

"There's an easy solution to that problem," she said.

"What?"

"Guess."

"You mean, leave?"

"If the smoke is bothering you that much, there's a whole smoke-free world right on the other side of that door."

Jamal picked a scrap of white satin up from the floor, tore it in half. He liked the sound it made.

"You going out tonight?" he asked.

Cassandra wanted the same night over and over again but she believed in some hidden way that if she had the same night enough times it would all crack open, and something better than love would be revealed. Something better than music.

"I am if I get this gown finished on time," Cassandra said through a mouthful of pins. "I have to be more mindful of my customers these days, I don't have as many as I used to. It's nose to the grindstone, just like everybody else."

"I want to go out with you sometime," he said.

"The places I go are *not* for ten-year-old boys."

"What do you do when you go out?" Jamal asked.

"We've talked about this before."

"I want to know again."

"Dance on top of the bar and talk to fools. If I thought you were missing anything, I'd take you. Trust me."

"Then why do you go out all the time?"

"I have a talent for it. People should do whatever they're good at, don't you think?"

"I want to come sometime."

"Okay, fine. You can come with me to the Pyramid, I'll go to the fifth-grade dance with you."

"You could come to the dance with me," he said.

Cassandra sewed and smoked. She didn't pause in the long work of being herself, but she let a silence fall onto her face. She pulled herself in, and the room was less intricately inhabited. Smoke shifted in the heavy golden air.

"When's the next dance?" she asked in a voice that was not hers. This voice came from farther away, like a radio playing in the apartment next door.

"Easter," he said. "I don't think you'd like it."

"Don't worry, I don't want to come to the fifth-grade dance with you. I only wanted to know when the next one is."

"Easter. It's at Easter."

"Do you take a date?"

"*No*," he said.

"You're growing up, aren't you?"

"I don't know."

"Forgive me for being corny. You're growing up. You're turning into somebody."

"No," he said. "I'm not."

"Jamal?"

"What?"

"Nothing. Do me a favor, all right?"

"What?"

"Don't grow up to be an asshole."

"Uh-huh."

"I've been a good mother to you, haven't I? A reasonably good mother, considering?"

"I guess."

"Well, if you're going to grow up without me, that's about all the advice I've got for you. Try not to be an asshole."

"Okay."

Cassandra sucked at her cigarette, exhaled a dense, ragged plume. "Okay now, *out*," she said. "Zoe must have dinner ready by now, you shouldn't keep her waiting like this."

"I'm not ready to go," he said.

"Well, I'm ready for you to be gone."

She raised her head, spit a pin onto the rug. She was changing, growing smaller. Jamal wanted to snatch the cigarette out of her hand, tear the robe off her, push her naked out the door and into the yellow stink of the hallway, where the crack dealers talked their talk and women sang in other languages. He wanted to lock her out, get into her bed, and ignore her as she banged and pleaded.

"No," he said.

"You get that little butt of yours home, you're not doing me any good here and your mother's all alone."

Jamal touched the leg of his chair, touched the cold curve of the monkey's ear. He had an urge to touch everything in the apartment, just touch it.

"Well?" Cassandra said. Her skin blazed white. She had a skeletal grandeur, the aristocratic righteousness of a ghost.

Jamal touched his own forehead, the back of his neck. Cassandra reached over and touched the same places he had touched. She pulled her hand away quickly, as if she'd been burned by his skin.

When he first knew about it, Jamal had called it "eggs." My mother has eggs. That was how he pictured it: bad eggs she carried, rancid and sulfurous. The eggs hurt her, but if she dropped them it would be worse. When somebody had eggs they couldn't keep them but they couldn't drop them, either.

Now he knew the facts of blood. He wasn't stupid. But privately, inside his head, he still called it "eggs." He still thought of his mother and Cassandra as coming back from a chicken house with their arms full of tainted eggs.

He went home but he didn't go inside. It was one of the days he sat watching from the stoop. He sat on the concrete as the air turned blue, filled with particles of night. He watched men and women rushing toward whatever waited to happen to them. He watched dogs adoring the smells. He let into the building people who lived in the building, people he knew to be safe. He looked at the street and did not let his attention wander.

When he went inside, it was later than it had ever been. She was there, so much like he'd pictured her that he thought she wasn't there at all. She was too expected, on the sofa with her pillows and Kleenex box, her book, her half-filled glass of water.

"Do you know what time it is?" she asked.

"Yes."

"It's almost a quarter past ten."

"I know."

"Where've you been?"

"Just out."

He couldn't tell her anything. He couldn't take her with him.

"You can't stay out this late," she said.

He watched the room, its bright disorder. She'd started buying 100-watt bulbs for the lamps. There were shopping bags on the floor. A fishhook of hair lay sweat-plastered to her cheek.

"Did you hear what I said?" she asked.

"Yes."

"Then answer."

"What's the question?"

She took a breath, and another. "The question," she said. "The question is what makes you think it's okay at your age to stay out half the night like this."

"It isn't half the night."

"Do you know what it's like, sitting here since three in the afternoon, thinking you're on your way home from school? Seven hours ago. If Cassandra hadn't called me, I'd have had no idea where you were the whole seven hours, instead of just from six o'clock until now."

"I wasn't doing anything wrong," he said.

"You have to call me. You have to tell me where you are. Did you have any dinner? Did you do your homework?"

"Sure."

"Jamal—"

"What?" he said.

"Please don't do this. I can't—I need you to be a little bit helpful. I need you to come home from school in the afternoons. I need you to tell me where you are when you go out."

"Uh-huh."

She took a Kleenex from the box, didn't wipe her eyes or blow her nose. She tore it in half. She held the two pieces.

"I don't know what works with you," she said. "I'll do pretty much whatever I have to. Give me a hint, all right?"

He couldn't say anything to her. They both knew what they wanted, but when the old days wouldn't open for them they were trapped. She was wrong on the sofa. He was wrong everywhere.

"Jamal?" she said. Her eyes had the sickness, the plastic look. Wet but not wet. He tried to tell her that nothing would work, and the only way he could say it was by going into his room. He could feel her breathing in the living room. He lay in his bed, in the dark. He thought about himself, lying in the dark, thinking about himself. Not thinking about her.

The next day he came home and found his uncle and aunt there. His aunt had brought Ben. They sat around the living room with his mother, sipping water like it was delicious. Had they been waiting for him?

"Hi, Jamal," Uncle Will said. Uncle Will performed his business: skeptical half smile, modest nod, a whole earnest nervous knuckle-cracking demonstration of attention.

"Hi," Jamal said.

Aunt Susan kissed him. She was always sure. She moved in straight lines.

Ben shook his hand. He was a boy who shook hands. He had shame around him, little invisible rays of it. He had a strangled politeness.

Jamal figured it—he'd surprised them by coming home on time. They were here to help his mother through his absence. His presence made a problem.

"You've grown," Aunt Susan said. It wasn't true. He hadn't grown half an inch in the last year.

Ben had grown almost a foot. Something invisible and frightened was threaded through his muscles and manners, the clean broad blue of his polo shirt. There was something starved about him, for all his bulk.

"How's it going?" Uncle Will asked.

"Okay," Jamal answered. Quickly, he added, "Ben, you want to go play video games?"

Ben looked at his mother. Aunt Susan looked at Jamal's mother, who looked at Uncle Will.

"You just got here," Jamal's mother said.

"I know."

Ben said, "Okay." His voice came from the big blue swell of his chest, spoke through his mouth.

"Half an hour," Aunt Susan said. "No more."

Uncle Will said, "It'd be nice to spend some time with you, Jamal. I hardly ever get to see you."

"Uh-huh."

What he hated about other people's concern was how visible it made you. All he wanted was to be unseen, and to watch.

"You're just going to the place on Second Avenue?" his mother asked.

"We'll be back in half an hour," he said.

"Okay. Bye."

He got out the door, with Ben behind him. He took a quick look back at his mother and his aunt and uncle. He thought about the ocean, that cold green nowhere. He thought about his big cousin, nervous and strange as a horse.

Out on the street he asked Ben, "Do you really want to play video games?"

Ben let the question fall, looked down at the ground where it lay.

"I guess," he said. "You don't want to?"

He thought there was a right and a wrong answer. He wanted to get it right.

"We can play video games," Jamal said. "I don't care what we do, I needed to get out of there."

"Oh," Ben said.

They walked north on Avenue B, toward the park. It was a cold sunny day, the radios were out. The woman with the box on her head walked by, screaming about the plots of the Dutch and the Jews. She wore a blanket covered with rodeo riders, pale cowboys roping pale blue bulls.

"I guess she's crazy," Ben said.

"I guess so."

"Do you still hang around with that other crazy guy?"

"What guy?"

"The one who wears the dresses."

"Oh, Cassandra. She's not crazy."

Ben said, "He used to give me the creeps."

"You should call Cassandra 'she.' "

"Why?"

"It's polite," Jamal said.

Ben nodded. He believed in rules of every kind.

They walked through the park, past the homeless tents. An old man sat on a bench with his collection of dirty foam rubber, licking a sheet of tinfoil that sparked and dazzled in the sun like something precious. Strands of spaghetti quivered in the man's beard.

"Gross," Ben said.

"Shh," Jamal answered. "He can hear you."

They walked for a while without speaking. Jamal felt like he was leading a horse through the streets of his neighborhood. A white horse, beautiful but easily frightened and desperate to please.

"Let's not play video games," Jamal said.

"Okay."

"Let's just hide out for a while."

"What?"

"Come on."

Jamal led him to the abandoned building on Eleventh Street. The building was as crazy as the woman with the box on her head, as crumbled and empty. Its roof had fallen and a small tree had sprouted on its top floor, so that the building was crowned with twigs. The boards had all fallen from the windows and the windows still held, here and there, a triangle of glass.

"You want to go in there?" Ben said.

"Yes."

Ben balked at the front stoop. Snorted and pawed the concrete, whinnying nervously, getting ready to bolt. But Jamal liked the idea of leading his big frightened cousin into this risky-looking silence. It seemed like the right thing to do, taking him somewhere that wasn't part of the world. It seemed like what he wanted: to hide.

"I've got something to show you inside," Jamal said.

"I don't think I want to," Ben said.

"Come *on*."

Jamal ran up the cracked front steps, pulled aside the loose board that covered the doorway. He waited. And, after a moment, in an agony of anxious compliance, Ben followed.

"You think this is safe?" he asked.

"It's safe. I come here all the time."

He led Ben into the front hallway, with its smells of plaster and piss and rot. One last scrap of wallpaper, fat rust-colored flowers, curled on the wall. There was a wet quiet, crack vials on the floor. There was a smoky light.

"This way," Jamal said, and he started up the stairs. The banister had long been broken off for firewood, and half the treads were gone, but you could still climb up easily enough. Somewhere, in a back room on the second floor, a dove called.

"You *sure* this is safe?" Ben asked.

"Yes." It was probably safe. There might be a crackhead or two, but they were harmless. Mostly harmless. His mother and Cassandra would kill him if they knew he came here, but he needed it, a place that was private and not part of things.

He led Ben through the second-floor hallway, with its empty doorways opening into rooms that were empty except for the bottles and syringes people left behind, the soggy mattresses. In one room a pair of woman's platform shoes, bright pink, stood defiant and forlorn, as if they were clues to a mystery everyone had given up trying to solve.

"This is weird," Ben said.

"Just follow me."

Jamal led him past the third floor and up to the top, where the roof was missing and where the little ash-gray tree had managed to take root in whatever plaster dust and windblown earth lay under the broken floorboards. The walls, bare powdery brick, still stood, with empty windows looking down onto Eleventh Street. Jamal led Ben into the room where the tree grew.

"Look here," he said. He went to the window. The window faced across the street to the front of a church, level with the gold statue of a robed man with a beard. The man wore a solemn, slightly startled expression. He held a cross in one hand and pointed to it with the index finger of the other, though he appeared to be pointing to his own head. When Jamal was younger, he'd believed the man was miming a vital question about the connection between the cross and his head.

"I used to think this was God," Jamal said. "But it isn't. It's just St. Francis Xavier."

"St. Francis Xavier," Ben said.

They stood for a while at the window, looking out at the church and the street. A sparrow lighted on a branch of the spindly tree, shook itself, flew away.

"I hang out here sometimes," Jamal said. "Not as much as I used to. When I was a little kid, I called this my house. I used to think this room was my room. I used to think if I ran away I could come here and live."

"Rain would get in."

"I know."

Ben aimed his serious face into St. Francis Xavier's. A squadron of bikers roared up the street.

"Do you have a girlfriend?" he asked.

"No. Do you?"

"There's a girl I like," Ben said. "Her name is Anne. Anne Dempsey."

"Uh-huh."

"She's really cute."

"Uh-huh."

Ben picked up a nugget of old cement from the windowsill, weighed it in his hand. Jamal took a penny from his pocket. He threw it at the statue of St. Francis Xavier. The penny fell short, landed in the street.

"Why'd you do that?" Ben asked.

"For luck."

"I don't have any pennies."

"Here."

Jamal gave him a penny, and Ben threw it. The penny struck the statue on the chest, on the stiff golden folds of its robe.

"Yeah," Ben said. He raised his fist in a victory salute. He was simply and completely happy because he'd been able to hit a statue with a penny. Jamal pitied him and, for reasons he couldn't name, loved him a little. His life was so certain, so unharmed.

"So you've got good luck," Jamal said.

"You try again."

"No. I don't believe in luck."

"Then why'd you throw a penny the first time?"

"Do you still have that fort?" Jamal said.

"What?"

"That fort, at your house. Up in the tree."

"Oh, the tree house. Yeah, it's still there."

"When I was a little kid, I used to think I'd sneak up there and live in that fort."

"Why would you want to do that?" Ben said.

"I used to like that fort. I thought I'd go live in it, and steal food from your momma's kitchen at night."

"I still sit in it sometimes. The tree house."

"You used to not let me go up there," Jamal said.

"No, I didn't."

"Yeah, you did. When we were kids, you told me it was a private club. You said it was members only."

"I don't remember."

"I remember."

"We were little kids."

"I was crazy for that fort. I don't know what I thought was up there. Treasure, maybe. Something."

"There's nothing up there," Ben said.

"I know that. I know that now."

"Listen. If you ever, if you want to come up to Connecticut sometime, you could."

"Okay."

"I mean, we're cousins."

"Yeah."

St. Francis Xavier's face stared blind and golden through the empty window. Jamal and Ben stood together for a while in an aspect of hush, a creaturely stillness quieter than any ordinary quiet. Ben reached up to tuck a dark curl behind his ear, and Jamal saw what it was about him. How had he missed it all these years?

It was right there in everything he said and did but Jamal hadn't recognized it until now, until he saw Ben arrange a curl of his own hair as carefully and tenderly as he'd put a letter into an envelope. Afterward, Jamal would tell himself that the secret had been somehow revealed to him by St. Francis Xavier, of the cross and the questioning head.

Ben was like Cassandra.

Jamal had an urge to stroke his large head, to calm him and then climb on his back and ride him through the streets of the city. He would reassure Ben with his own competence. He would tell him, by the pressure of his thighs, that there was nothing to fear.

"We'd better get back," Ben said.

"Uh-huh."

They didn't move. They continued standing in the wide-open room where no one could find them. The golden man stood across Eleventh Street in his quizzical silence.

After a while, Ben said, "I like it up here."

"Yeah."

They didn't move. Something was happening, something without a name. Jamal didn't try to understand. He let it happen. It had to do with being blood kin, with being a horse and rider. It had to do with the statue's question and with the tree growing out of the floorboards. Jamal and Ben were standing in the secret room together, and Jamal wanted to give comfort. He wanted to disappear in the giving of comfort to a boy luckier than he. When Ben reached for him, fearfully, Jamal didn't back away. He offered comfort. He and Ben stayed in the room for a long time, and when they got back home again everyone was mad at them.

1 9 9 2 / The money had never been easy, and now, with Reagan gone and Bush on the way out, it had just about dried up completely. The construction business was a graveyard. First the fly-by-nights folded, and then the solider guys started to collapse. The young guys who'd bought Nick and Constantine's houses seemed to disappear, all those machinists and salesmen and lab technicians who worked like demons and who, with a little up-front money from their parents and a little from the wife's, could just manage the monthlies on a tarted-up three-bedroom sitting on a quarter acre of New Jersey or Long Island earth. They were gone now, those guys and their big-haired, slutty-looking wives. Now they rented apartments, or lived with their parents. Nobody felt secure anymore, not even the people with jobs. Nobody was taking any risks.

Constantine told Nick that if they wanted to stay in business it was time to dump the frills. No more picket fences, no more dormers, no little panes of stained glass set into front doors. The new tract was going to be about value, and he wanted to advertise it that way. No more copy promising affordable luxury, or charm on a budget. But Nick was in love with his flourishes, his breakfast bars and bay windows. Constantine was surprised by Nick's stubbornness, and eventually grew insulted by it. Clearly, even after more than twenty years of partnership, Nick considered himself the brains and Constantine the muscle.

"Con," he'd said at first, "people won't buy 'em all stripped down like that. I know things are tight, but if we keep building houses people want, people will buy. Trust me."

He'd spoken patiently, the way he'd explain a simple concept to a child.

"If anybody out there's still got money for a house," Constantine had answered, "he's not gonna spend any extra. Those days are over, we need to go dirt cheap. Our only chance is to offer the lowest goddamn prices in the region."

A few days later, when Nick's patience broke against Constantine's stony insistence, Nick had said, "These are just shit boxes, what you're talking about here."

"They've always been shit boxes," Constantine had said. "These are shit boxes that might not drive us out of business."

Nick had actually been hurt by that. For half a second, his eyes had gone glassy. Poor, dumb fuck. What had he thought they were building all those years, monuments that would live for centuries? Did he really believe brass-finish colonial hardware made some kind of difference?

"It's product, Nick. And product has to change with the marketplace."

Finally, in a voice unsteady with rage, Nick had said, "I been doing this fifty years. You think maybe I know what I'm talking about?"

"No," Constantine had answered. "Not anymore, I don't."

They'd decided finally on what they called a "trial separation." They hadn't dissolved the partnership, but agreed that the new project would be Constantine's alone, bankrolled by him, with sole responsibility for losses. Nick had refused to give up his dogma. He'd maintained, with the droning certainty of a priest, that the fancy touches were what made the houses sell. He'd considered it a proven formula, the secret of his success: for every dollar you spend putting in a whirlpool or a fireplace, you can tack another twenty onto the price. Poor, dumb fuck. It was the biggest purchase people made in their lives, he'd said, and it was the one least governed by reason. A prospective buyer looks at a lot of houses, he's knocked out by little comforts. He's looking to fall in love. He wants to picture himself and his family gathered around a fire at Christmastime. He wants to screw in a Jacuzzi. He wants marble-look vanities, he wants to impress his parents. Give these guys a little something to love, do it at a reasonable price, and they'll buy.

Constantine had known differently. Under Bush, the economy was turning to shit. Nothing was happening out there. Nick had been too old to understand—he'd thought the easy money of the Reagan years was the direct result of his own hard work. Constantine had known how far away that money had gone, but he suspected there might be a new kind of buyer loose in the new, pared-down version of the U.S. He wasn't thinking about real Americans, the hardworking, optimistic white people, third or fourth generation, for whom he and Nick had tacked on plaster moldings and aluminum eight-over-eights. He was thinking about immigrants. Not the trash but the voracious workers, hell-bent on self-improvement; the husband and wife who both worked twelve-hour days doing jobs real Americans refused to do, while the kids stayed with some old aunt who didn't speak a lick of English. He used to work with people like that, back when he was just a day laborer. Hell, he practically used to *be* one of them. These people, Constantine believed, were crazy to own, to invest, to have a little piece of the United States that was theirs. They wanted one thing— value. Their only romance was possession. They'd buy the cheapest house they could find.

So he took a chance and used his share of the bankroll to bang out seventy three-bedroom units in Rosedale. He offered competitive square footage—part of the reason these people *came* here was to stop feeling crowded—and cut everything else. The houses were trim and clean, sheathed in white stucco, so bereft of detail they looked like the ideas of houses, lined up, waiting to be called into their final form. Which, in a way, was the point. These houses were intended specifically for Juan and Vladimir and Shaheed, who'd grown up dreaming of a house in America. Buy it, and do what you want with it. Paint it pink or turquoise. Construct a shrine to an elephant god in the dirt out front. Or do it up like colonial fucking Williamsburg. Knock yourself out.

The Starter Special. We Pass the Savings On to You. You Change It to Fit Your Dream.

That had been three years and four tracts ago. It had gone even better than Constantine had hoped. Pull your prices down to a certain level, advertise in the ethnic papers, and a whole invisible population came to light. They drove out in used cars, not the sensible little Celicas and Chevy Novas of Constantine's former customers but hogs, Buick Rivieras and Chrysler Imperials, fifteen or twenty years old, well past the hundred-thousand-mile mark but better cared for than some of the kids crowded into the back seat along with an aunt or a grandparent or two or three. Black faces, brown faces. White faces, too, but those usually spoke halting English, looked like they'd be more comfortable driving an ox cart than an Olds 88. And a lot of these people actually preferred the cheesy stuff. They liked linoleum and fluorescent lights. They were the opposite of born Americans, who wanted you to spend a small fortune making the places look old-fashioned. These people could give a damn about oak veneer and simulated brick and plantation-style ceiling fans. They wanted their vinyl to look like vinyl. When they turned on the lights, they wanted to blind the neighbors three houses away.

Why Wait? Make Your Dream Come True Now.

While everyone else was going bust, Constantine became a millionaire. He had a million in the *bank*, plenty more sunk here and there. Nick was history, who needed him? Constantine had developed his own formula, and it was just two words: *Cut costs*. He knew that formula would never pass out of date, and with everybody hurting, it was easy to make special deals. He found a cement works in Scranton that was willing to push its water content past the legal limit, just to get his business. He found a guy in Teaneck—a frightening character, and Constantine didn't scare easily—who had a warehouse full of old insulation threaded with asbestos, just slightly less illegal than plutonium. The guy practically paid Constantine to take it off his hands.

He didn't let his habit of thrift infect his personal life, though. If anything, it worked in reverse. The more he saved on houses for other people, the more willing he felt to improve his own. It was a system of balances. He added a greenhouse and a sauna, had the foyer done in white marble. His place was turning into a palace, and sometimes when he walked through the rooms he felt a thump of satisfaction deep in his chest. He'd created this out of nothing. He'd had no help. It was all profoundly his, the four-poster bed and the deep velvet sofas and the hand-painted mural in the dining room, a Hungarian village scene Magda had worried and argued over for half a year or longer. He got Magda anything she wanted: fag decorators and mural painters, endless dresses, an emerald ring that cost more than a new car. It was all good, and satisfying.

Mostly satisfying. There were little things. His health, his goddamned tricky heart. One attack already, that awful seizing-up, a fist driven into his chest. He'd shrugged it off. He wasn't the kind of guy who coddled himself. He refused to consider an old age made of caution and special diets. But it did make him nervous sometimes. One minute you could be walking along thinking about dinner or a good hard fuck, you could be thinking about the water content in your concrete, and the next minute your heart could explode.

And, okay, there was a thing or two about Magda. Why couldn't she be more of a lady? Nothing prissy or shrill, he wasn't looking for some jeweled dowager who was all tired smiles and hard, untouchable hair. But a lady. A rare thing, electric, with perfumed mysteries and hard-won wisdom and an aura of rich, honey-colored sex. Constantine listened to Frank Sinatra singing "The Lady Is a Tramp," and thought, Yes. That's it. The lady is a tramp. She's tough but elegant and she makes most other women look like wilted gardenias. Magda was almost that, so close to it that sometimes Constantine felt elated just walking with her into an expensive store or restaurant. He felt like a colorful guy, his own man, who'd left a prim beautiful woman, a life of days and nights, and married into adventure. A guy brave enough for an abundant bosom and the music of a foreign accent, thrills in bed most men his age only fantasized about. He could drift along on that for a minute or two before he fell back again into uncertainty, an obscure but stinging embarrassment. Magda was fifty pounds or more past voluptuous, and she made a low sniffing noise when she ate, something adenoidal, as if when she chewed her sinuses fell out of alignment with her jaw and needed to be gently snorted back into place.

Sometimes he loved her for being big and strange. Sometimes he bitterly regretted all the beauty he was missing, the way a pair of slender shoulders could look in an evening gown.

He didn't mean to make her unhappy. He didn't mean to insult her. Right, he lost control sometimes. That was part of who he was. He always apologized afterward. Was it just unforgivable, what he called her at the Heart Fund dinner? A pig, all right, he'd been drunk. Yeah, he'd made snuffling noises, like a pig rooting in a trough. Joking, he'd been *joking*.

"What is it you *want*?" She'd tottered drunkenly through the front door, stumbled on the first stair, torn her dress, sunk slowly to the marble, holding the torn fabric in both hands and looking at it as if her skin had ripped open.

"I want to go to bed." He'd stood on the pure white marble tiles, none too sober himself, a little unsure about how he'd gotten them both home in the car.

"A pig. You think I'm a pig." She'd looked into the hole in her dress. She'd knelt on the hard floor.

"Joke, can't you take a joke? I had a few too many, call the cops."

"You did this to make a *joke* out of me. That's why." Her eyes were smudged, her hair squashed. Kneeling among the stiff folds of her dress, she'd looked like a giant, withered aquatic plant.

"I don't know what you're talking about." He'd started for the stairs. Let her bust her gut, he was too drunk and tired to care.

"This. All this." She'd flung her big arms out, fat but strong. She'd waved her hands in the air. "All this."

"I'm going to bed."

"You did this to humiliate me. You married me and built this house so you could take me to parties and call me a pig."

"You're crazy, is what you are."

But he'd thought, There's some kind of crazy truth here. Somebody insane spitting out the truth because she'd lost track of what wasn't possible.

He was just drunk. They both were.

"I'm your pig," she'd said. "This is my stall."

He'd stepped around her, started up the stairs. "It's called a sty," he'd said. "Why don't you learn to speak goddamned English?"

"You bastard. You bastard."

It had struck him funny, her calling him a bastard. Hey, he'd been drunk. And he'd known it came from the movies. She'd seen some glamour girl collapse at the foot of a big curved staircase and call her husband a bastard. She'd even lost her accent when she said it. So he'd laughed. And gone to bed.

He'd spent the next three days on his knees. She saved things like that. She stored them up. No apology, however tearful, and no gift, however lavish, seemed to restore the balance. She lived in an atmosphere of grudge and injury, a small invisible house she erected inside the larger house. She lived there alone. Three days worth of steady apology hadn't quite undone it. Or a new Cartier watch. It had faded, finally, the way things do, though when Magda came home with a new dress or a pair of shoes she still sometimes said, "Look what your pig bought now." He just smiled. It was already on its way toward becoming a kind of endearment, one of those sweet-sour sparrings that went on among couples.

At night, every now and then, he drove to one of his new tracts. At night they looked a little more normal. The occasional paint job of chartreuse or lemon yellow didn't stand out as much; the lawns decorated with pagodas or shrines to the Virgin Mother were softened by darkness. On his drives through the new tracts he smelled strange cooking, heard music that was barely recognizable as music at all. He did not hate or love these people. He only watched them until he grew tired, and then he drove home again.

One night, late, after ten, he parked his car and sat in it for a while before he realized that a little boy had been sitting on the curb across the street from him. The boy was so dark he blended with the night. It was a cool October night but he sat on the curb in shorts and a skimpy little undershirt, shivering, with his legs drawn up to his chest. He couldn't have been more than five or six.

Constantine rolled down his window. "Hey," he said.

The boy looked at him, did not speak. He wasn't black. Indian, maybe. But dark.

"Hey," Constantine said. "Shouldn't you be at home?"

The boy continued looking at him with mute incomprehension. Maybe he didn't speak English.

Constantine got out of his car. He walked across the street and stood before the boy.

"I'm talking to you," he said. "Understand? Do you know what I'm saying?"

The boy nodded solemnly.

"Do you live around here?" Constantine asked.

The boy nodded again.

"Don't your parents want to know where you are?"

This time, the boy did not nod. He just sat, watching Constantine.

"Go home," Constantine said. "It's late. It's cold out here."

The boy didn't move. A peculiar spice, pepper mixed up with something that reminded Constantine of a wet dog, drifted through the air. From far away, he thought he could hear a snatch of that Negro music that wasn't music at all, just a bunch of guys shouting insults at white people while somebody banged a drum in the background.

"Go home," he said again. The boy looked at him with puzzled kindness, as if Constantine was asking for an obscure favor the boy was willing but unable to grant.

Finally, Constantine got back into his car and started the engine. He put his face out through the open window and said, "I'll give you a ride home, if you want."

The boy continued shivering, continued staring.

"All right, if that's the way you want it," Constantine said.

He stepped on the accelerator and drove away. He wondered if he should call somebody, but decided against it. Who could know about people like this? Maybe they let their children run around all night, alone, without enough clothes on. Maybe that was one of those foreign traditions you needed to respect, the kind of thing Billy always carried on about. What did he call it? Something-centric. Don't be something-centric. Fine. When Constantine turned the corner he drove through a surge of music, those rhythmic Negro shouts, coming from a house that had been painted pink and brown, like a giant cake. At this distance he couldn't make out the words—probably telling other black guys to shoot cops, rape their wives, burn the whole world down. He was probably lucky the kid on the curb didn't pull out a gun and shoot him. He kept driving, out of the tract, out of the music, and he told himself he wouldn't go there at night anymore. When he got home he parked for a while in front of his own house, and found that he didn't feel like getting out of the car right away. He lit a last cigarette, sat in the car until he saw Magda, large and furious, pass by the bedroom window in her nightgown, carrying the German newspaper she insisted on subscribing to and eating what appeared to be a salami sandwich.

There was work and love, a kind of love. You ignored the little glitches.

And then there was Zoe. He couldn't let himself think too much about that.

He never asked how she got it. He didn't want to know. She looked okay, she didn't look any different, and half the time he almost forgot about it altogether. It wasn't always fatal. They were working on a cure. He did have her out to the house more often, and she was usually willing to come. To help with the garden, he said, and she hardly ever refused. He knew how much she missed a garden, stuck in the city like that. Sometimes she came out alone on the train, sometimes she brought the kid. What could you do about that? He wasn't bad, quiet, could entertain himself. Constantine wondered when he'd start listening to that murderous music, when he'd come home from school with a gun. He tried not to think too much about that, either. He and Zoe worked in the garden together all spring and summer and into the fall. It was a beautiful garden, sheltered behind a low grassy rise that fell away to the Atlantic. He'd had two tons of topsoil trucked in because you couldn't grow shit this close to the ocean. The garden thrived, partly because of the topsoil and partly because he sprayed it with chemical pesticides and fertilizers when Zoe wasn't around. She didn't approve of that, so why tell her? Let her believe the lettuce and beans and tomatoes were springing up all glossy and perfect because they were tended with love. It did something to him, working in the garden with her like that. It made him feel he'd done the right thing with his life. He had this garden for his sick daughter. He had this view of the ocean for her.

There was only one bad moment with Zoe, on an afternoon in September, when she picked a ripe tomato off one of the vines.

"Beautiful, isn't it?" she said. She crouched in the dirt, held it cupped in her palm, close to her breast, the way she'd hold a bird.

"You used to hate tomatoes," Constantine said.

"I grew up."

"Yeah. Hey, we've got a nice crop coming in here." He knelt beside his daughter. She wore jeans that were too big for her and an old striped T-shirt with the sleeves raggedly cut away, just the kind of clothes he hated to see her in, but right then she looked beautiful, as if every second of her life, every condition in which he'd ever seen her, had been leading to this, Zoe kneeling pale and calm in this garden in September with the Atlantic rolling just beyond and a ripe tomato cupped in her hands. Constantine's little girl. The youngest, the unplanned one, the one he'd insisted on naming after his grandmother, where Mary would have named her Joan or Barbara. He reached out a finger, flicked a speck of dirt from her cheek. He felt how big his finger was, how rough against her skin.

"Lately I feel like I don't want to eat anything I didn't help grow myself," she said. "The food in stores looks strange and, I don't know. Dangerous. You don't know *where* it's been."

She laughed. She raised the tomato to her mouth, and Constantine had an urge to yell, 'Don't, it's poisoned.' Which was ridiculous. It was no more poisoned than most of what people ate, and probably less. But as he watched her bite into the tomato, a chill shot through his heart.

"Mmm," she said. "This is one of the best tomatoes I've ever tasted."

He was full of terror, an icy dread that swayed inside his chest like something swinging on a cord. He could have taken her in his arms, begged her forgiveness. Then he pulled himself together. Forgiveness for what? For loving her, for being the best father he knew how to be? Next spring, he'd rent a house at the beach, big enough for everybody. A vacation house, not just his and Magda's place, maybe up on Cape Cod. She could bring the kid, let him blow off a little steam.

"Try it," she said. She held the tomato out to him, balanced on her thin white hand.

"Thanks, darling," he said. He accepted the tomato from her. He took a ravenous bite.

1 9 9 3 / Jamal lived in him. Ben thought about Jamal's eyes and lips, the dense crackle of his hair. When he thought about Jamal he was filled with an abject, weighted sensation like nothing he had known before, a hot wet ball of feeling, impenetrable, hissing with fear and hope and shame though the ball itself was not made of those emotions. It turned thickly inside his belly. It frightened him. It wasn't love, not what he'd imagined of love. It more closely resembled what he'd imagined as cancer, the cancer that got Mrs. Marshall next door, a ball of crazy cells that, as his mother said, had *eaten her up*. Like cancer it was him and not him. It ate him and replaced what it ate with more of itself.

1 9 9 3 / Connie wanted Ben to do what she told him to. She stood on the dock, pretty and mean, netted with watery light, hands fisted on her hips. She had an athlete's belief in discipline, the powers of orderly motion.

"Bring her about," she shouted.

Alone in the boat, thirty feet from the dock, Ben could feel how it wanted to stutter and stall. How it wanted to fail. It had taken less than two days for him to understand the boat's laziness, its bent toward a slumbering life spent nudging the dock. It needed to be bullied, it needed to be coaxed. It was a lapdog. He'd imagined wolfish strides over brilliant ink-blue water. Cleaving with one perfect claw.

"This thing's a sow," he called.

"Bring her *about*," Connie answered. The Sunfish's sail luffed, then filled, caught the light, and briefly Ben loved the boat for its modest but insistent little life. Even a lapdog had moments of animal certainty, a remorseless grace.

"Good," Connie called. "Now tack over to the buoy."

He tacked to the buoy, came about, tacked back again. He

leaned over the calm water, working the boom. In a boat, he found that he knew what to do. He could almost feel what the boat needed. He had an instinct for sailing, an automatic intelligence about the ways canvas could answer wind.

"Back to the buoy again," Connie shouted. He came about, tacked easily back toward the buoy. He glanced at the dock, the jumble of gray-shingled houses, the pale crescent of bay beach. There was Jamal, on the beach, waiting his turn. Jamal stood on the sand, skinny in loose white jeans, his brown hands wrapped around the back of his neck. He looked out at the water, at Ben in the boat. Ben forced himself to think about the wind bellying the sail. He forced himself to think about Connie, getting ready to shout her next order.

Then it was Jamal's turn. Ben stood on the dock, watching. Jamal had no talent for sailing, though even in his helplessness he had a dancer's precision of movement, a defiant authority. The sail shuddered, lost the wind. Connie cupped her strong stubby hands around her mouth, hollered at Jamal to bring her about. In the boat, Jamal looked serene and doomed as a young prince. Sun ignited the smooth honey-colored muscles of his back, the black wire of his hair.

"Bring her *about*," Connie shouted. Jamal tried. When the line slipped out of his hands he smiled in the shy and knowing way he had. The whole world was funny, and touching, and odd.

"Your cousin doesn't catch on as fast as you do," Connie said.

"He's just not as worried about doing what people tell him to," Ben said.

"That's a nice way of putting it. *Jamal.* Come *about*."

"He'll do whatever he wants to do," Ben told her.

"Not while I'm being paid good money to teach him how to sail."

"Good luck," Ben said.

After the lesson, as Connie was instructing Ben and Jamal about tying up the sail, their grandfather got out of his car and stood at the landward end of the dock, looking at the water and nodding as if the bay and the sky were turning out exactly as he'd intended them to. Ben left Connie and Jamal to finish tying up the sail, ran into the roil of his grandfather's approval.

"So, are you turning into a sailor?" his grandfather asked.

Ben knew the answer. "I want to try a bigger boat," he said.

"I'm sure you do." His grandfather's face clenched with pleasure. His grandfather's face was fissured and creviced, eroded in spots and powerfully massed elsewhere. He seemed, at times, to be transcending the human and becoming geological. He carried with him a mountain's sense of silent will and design, a life so old it's been scoured clean. Granite smooth as a newly swept floor, no trees, just bright patches of moss anchored to the rock. In his grandfather's presence Ben inhaled more deeply, as he would in mountain air.

"I know how to sail," Ben said. "I already know how, and this Sunfish is a pig."

The old man put a hand on Ben's shoulder. His fingers were thick as rope. "Finish up your lessons," he said. "Then we'll see about a bigger boat."

"I want to get out of the bay," Ben said. "I want to get onto the ocean."

"After two days of lessons." His grandfather smiled, squeezed Ben's shoulder. Wind picked up and then smoothed the steel-colored strands of his hair.

"I can do it," Ben said.

"I believe you, buddy. You can do anything."

Connie and Jamal, finished with the boat, came up the dock. Walking side by side, they looked complete, two beings so opposite they belonged together, the sturdy, dictatorial blond girl and the coffee-colored boy whose strength lay in silence and in never considering retreat. They looked like enemies whose battles had been going on so long they could no longer live apart.

"So, how're they doing, Connie?" Grandpa called.

She hesitated, smiling. Ben realized that she disliked Jamal not for being an unpromising sailor but for being what he was. For being small and dark and unembarrassed.

"They're doing fine, Mr. Stassos," Connie said.

"This one here says he wants a bigger boat," his grandfather said. He clapped Ben's shoulder with the palm of his hand. "Thinks he knows how to sail already."

Connie's eyes deepened. A welter of pale freckles disappeared into the top of her bathing suit.

Ben told himself to want that. He thought of the stories he could tell Andrew and Trevor, at home.

"He's got a knack for it," Connie said. "He could be a really good sailor."

"I thought he would be. That's part of why I dragged us all up here this summer. Time to get this boy out on the water."

"He's just got to finish in the Sunfish," Connie said. "He's got to log his hours, three more days. Then he can graduate to a faster boat."

"This one never wants to wait," his grandfather said. His grandfather swarmed with pride the way a tree swarms with bees. "Bigger and faster, that's his motto."

Jamal stood proud and quiet, semi-visible. He looked down at the dock, waiting for this to end and the next thing to happen. His eyes were his own. His shadow touched Ben's.

The evening was cool and blue. Shards of cloud, sharp-edged and fragmentary, like pieces of something shattered, held the last orange light from the vanished sun and laid a shimmering slick of it on the tidal flats. Ben and Jamal walked barefoot among tangles of green-black kelp, rocks fat and fetid as sleeping walruses. In pools of trapped seawater, shadows of minnows darted under the rippled, orange-streaked surface.

"There are porpoises out here," Jamal said.

"There aren't."

"They come in after the fishing boats. They jump around in the bay at night."

"You're crazy."

"*You* are."

"This is too far north for porpoises."

Jamal paused, considering. "I saw one last night," he said. "I saw it jump out there."

"You're nuts."

"Will is coming," Jamal said.

"No he's not. He was invited and he said no."

"He changed his mind. I heard my mother talking to him on the phone."

"Uncle Will gives me the creeps," Ben said.

"Why?"

"He just does. Grandpa doesn't like him, either."

"He's Grandpa's son."

"That doesn't mean they have to like each other."

"I like Will."

"You like everybody."

"Not everybody," Jamal said.

Heat rose to Ben's ears, a high buzz of blood.

"You like *me*," he said.

Jamal bent over and picked something out of the sand. "Look," he said. He held up a little plastic head, hairless and eyeless, bleached white.

"Hey," Ben said. Jamal always found things: animal bones, money, single playing cards, a thin gold bracelet. He just seemed to see them, to pluck them out of empty landscapes.

"A doll's head," Jamal said. The head was black-socketed, sedately smiling. Jamal held it up for Ben to see and then stooped and put it back, carefully, as if it needed to be returned precisely to where he'd found it. As if it was part of some huge, precarious purpose.

"Aren't you going to keep it?" Ben asked.

"No. Why would I want to?"

"It's probably old, it might be worth money."

"I think it should stay here," Jamal said. "I'd rather think of it in the bay."

Ben picked up the doll's head, put it in his pocket. "If you don't want it, I'll keep it," he said.

"Sure. If you want it."

The light turned violet. The clouds gave up their orange stain and blanched to silver. A minute before, it had been the last of the day; now it had begun to be night. Lights shone on the dock and in the windows of houses and on the boats moored out in deep water.

"We should go back," Ben said.

"In a minute."

He never obeyed. He did what he wanted to.

Ben threw stones that vanished in the dimness, sent back the sound of soft invisible splashes. A commotion of gulls flapped and fought over something they'd found, a dead fish or a juicy piece of garbage. The gulls beat the air violently. One flew straight up, too white against the sky, holding a ribbon of something foul in its beak.

"I think Will is coming tomorrow morning," Jamal said.

"Fuck Uncle Will," Ben said.

He would turn into himself. He would want a girl like Connie. He touched the little head in his pocket.

Back at the rented house the windows were steamed, the paneled walls orange in the lamplight. There were the smells of mildew and old cooking, of cold ashes in the fireplace. In the kitchen, Ben's mother laughed and then Jamal's mother laughed too.

"I can't do it. It's up to you." Ben's mother had had a drink or two. Ben's father was at home, living his life of work. He didn't mind the pleasures of others but considered pleasure too small for his own use.

"Okay. Here goes." Jamal's mother had AIDS but everybody treated her as if she was just herself, crazy and fragile, with a history of bad behavior.

Ben's grandfather and Magda sat watching the news in the living room, in the salt-dampened bamboo chairs upholstered in orange starfish and shells the mottled yellow-green of limes. Magda filled her chair, filled her dress, which crawled with thumbnail-sized yellow butterflies. The television showed a fire somewhere. Animals were dying. A horse ran, blazing, through a neighborhood of neat prosperous houses. Magda scowled, interested.

"Hello, guys," their grandfather said. "We were wondering where you were."

"Some fool with a match," Magda said to the television. "Some idiot, and look. They should shoot him when they catch him."

Magda believed in shooting people who were careless. She believed in protecting animals, who could not make mistakes because they lived in a state of inspired ignorance. Ben still loved Magda but had come to fear her, too. She'd begun treating him with more than her usual suspicion.

"Shooting's too good," his grandfather said. "They should set him on fire."

Magda nodded. She and Grandfather sat in a frowning ecstasy of judgment. On television a column of smoke rose, gray and yellow as a bruise, bearing the souls of dead animals.

"Hey," his mother called from the kitchen. "Is that the boys?"

"Yeah, Mom," Ben called. His voice sounded fine. Probably.

He went to the kitchen, stood in the doorway. "Hi, honey," his mother said. She kissed him, while Aunt Zoe slid a lobster into the pot.

"Murder," Ben said.

"I know," Aunt Zoe answered. "But it's the food chain, what can I say? Nature isn't pretty." She wore black jeans, a shirt with the purple face of Chairman Mao. Ben's mother had on a white blouse, plaid shorts. The gin and tonic in her hand rang softly with ice.

She smoothed his hair, put out a soft phosphorescence of perfume and gin, a low hum of interest in him. Ben imagined that she started every day counting, silently counted all day long, starting from one. She was calm because she knew the number of every minute.

"Have a nice walk?" she asked.

"It was okay. The tide's all the way out, you can go way past the dock."

"I can smell it on you," she said, sniffing his hair. "The salt."

She had all the beauty in the room. Outside of her it was just this old kitchen, scarred salmon-colored Formica and pine cabinets with big black whorls and knots, like someone had put cigars out on the wood. Outside of her it was just Aunt Zoe, sick and crazy, skin white and patchy as a plaster saint's, tossing lobsters into boiling water.

Jamal came and stood beside Ben.

"Hello, Jamal," Ben's mother said.

Jamal nodded, smiled shyly, as if they'd just met.

"Jamal is a vegetarian," Aunt Zoe said.

"We know that, honey," Ben's mother said.

"I was a vegetarian, too," Aunt Zoe said. "For fifteen years. And then one day I walked into a McDonald's and had a Quarter Pounder. Just like that."

"I know," Jamal said. He stood in his coiled way, as if he were gathering himself up, getting ready to leap. He was himself, neither masculine nor feminine. He was Jamal, brave and unconcerned, quiet, with living eyes and spirals of heavy black hair.

"I'll make the salad," Ben's mother said. She kissed Ben's forehead. She went and broke a head of lettuce with her hands.

"I went deeper and deeper into it," Aunt Zoe said. "I got so I couldn't stand the idea of ripping carrots out of the ground, or pulling tomatoes off a vine, or cutting wheat. It seemed like even vegetable life had some kind of consciousness. Like a tomato plant suffered. I got so that I'd only eat things that had fallen off on their own. Windfall fruit, nuts. My diet got tinier and tinier. I couldn't slap mosquitoes or swat flies. Then one day I walked into that McDonald's, almost without thinking, and ordered a Quarter Pounder. It made me sick. But the next day I went and had another one. And that was the beginning of my downfall."

"A Quarter Pounder has, like, seventy grams of fat in it," Ben said.

"Well, fat is part of life, I guess," Aunt Zoe said. "Death and fat and, you know. All kinds of things."

"We eat a lot more grains these days," Ben's mother said. "I've tried to cut our fat intake by at least half."

Aunt Zoe looked at the boiling lobsters with an expression of appetite and regret.

"Lately I've been on a couscous kick," Ben's mother said. "It's easy, and you can do a lot of different things with it."

"I know," Aunt Zoe said. "Proper nutrition is a good thing, I know that. I just had to—I don't know. Release myself from the obsession, I guess."

"You don't have to turn everything into an obsession, you know," Ben's mother said.

Aunt Zoe laughed. "Balance," she said. "It's the hardest thing."

She looked at Jamal, humorously, helplessly. She was getting ready to let him be the one who worried and measured and said,

Just this much and no more. Eleven years of motherhood had been enough for her. She wanted to be a child again.

Jamal didn't let anything happen on his face. He left the room, walked out the screen door onto the porch. Ben could see him through the window, stretching his long thin arms, looking up at the sky.

His mother followed his eyes, saw Jamal, winked at Ben. Had she felt the movement of his thoughts when she smoothed his hair?

"Ben, honey," she said. "Maybe you could set the table."

"Sure, Mom." He got plates and silverware, went into the dining room. The dining room had a long blue table, flying fish painted on its bare wood walls. From the living room, an announcer talked about a wall of fire marching to the ocean. As Ben set the table, he made sure the knives and forks and spoons were perfectly straight.

Uncle Will arrived the next morning, with his boyfriend. Ben's stomach heaved at the thought. He watched from an upstairs window. He chipped away scabs of paint with his fingernail.

They came in the boyfriend's car, an old MG Ben wouldn't have minded taking out himself. But he wouldn't get in their car, he wouldn't want his ass on their upholstery. He watched as they got out, were met in the yard by his mother and Aunt Zoe. Hugs, kisses. Uncle Will was tall, rabbit-faced, too clever, wearing cutoffs and a white muscle shirt to show that he owned one of those cut-up unathletic bodies guys could hack out with free weights. An invented body, hefty without being fit. He looked like he'd trained for the decathlon and probably couldn't run ten yards. His boyfriend was a professor type, with a boxy head and a distracted attitude, as if music he hadn't chosen was playing inside his head. His skinny legs ended in a pair of high-top sneakers, which he wore without socks.

Ben's mother and Aunt Zoe loved Uncle Will with the hypnotized steadiness of feminine blood. They were sisters and they were women. They had no choice. Men were the ones who decided; women could only say yes or no to the love that lived inside them. Men were responsible for their devotions. Women were pulled through the world. Only the most powerful disappointment could make them stop loving, and once they'd stopped they couldn't decide to love again. Inner valves would close. Their body chemistry would change. It wouldn't be what they wanted.

"—thought you weren't coming," he heard his mother say through the glass.

"Hate to miss all the fun," Uncle Will answered. He spoke in wit, a private language. Everything meant something else.

Ben watched them walk up the porch stairs. Uncle Will carried two suitcases, and Ben's mother and Aunt Zoe crowded around him. They let the boyfriend straggle behind, listening to his silent, unfamiliar music.

Ben heard them come in the front door. He heard his grandfather trying to navigate between courtesy and outrage.

"Hello, Billy," his grandfather said. The voice came up the stairwell, patient and powerful as the house itself, this wooden fortress that had stood here looking at the bay for almost a hundred years.

"Hello, Dad. You remember Harry."

Uncle Will's voice was skittish, piping, delighted with itself. A flute of a voice. Ben got up, ran downstairs. He didn't want to stay in the house anymore. He didn't want to listen.

He'd have to see them on his way out.

They were in the living room, all of them except Jamal, who had a talent for being elsewhere. As Ben came down the stairs, Uncle Will looked up, arranged his face into a witty parody of surprise.

"Ben?" he said.

Ben said a soft hello, got himself down to floor level.

"Good god, you've grown, like, three feet."

Ben shrugged. His size was his own, his right, not something he'd invented. Not something to be clever about.

"These days you've got to check in at least once a week if you want to keep up," Ben's mother said.

Don't help him. Don't give him anything.

Uncle Will came over, put out his soft hand. Ben let him perform a parody of a manly shake.

"How've you been?" Uncle Will asked. "What's up?"

"Nothing," Ben said.

"You look good."

Don't touch it. Just leave me alone, don't look at me.

"Hey, Ben," Uncle Will said, "this is Harry."

Ben didn't know where to look. He looked down at his side, where sunlight stretched over the rag rug. Then he looked at his grandfather. His grandfather's face was clouded as a mountain's.

The boyfriend shook his hand. The boyfriend's hand was harder than he'd expected it to be, dryer. The boyfriend had a talcumed smell, not flowery, more like chalk.

"Hello, Ben," the boyfriend said.

For his own sake and because his grandfather was watching, Ben didn't look at the boyfriend's face. He let his hand be shaken, took it back.

"I'm going out," he said to his mother.

"Don't you want to stick around for a little while?" his mother asked.

"No," he told her. And he left, knowing his grandfather would respect him for not being polite.

Outside, the light hung languidly, heavy white in the August air. It was a dead-calm day, close as a held breath, no good for sailing, though Connie wouldn't be coming around for a few more hours and things could pick up by then. Ben walked down to the bay along the short stretch of road that was graveled in pulverized clamshells, bone-white in the whitened air. The water of the bay glowed green. It foamed listlessly around the domed heads of the rocks.

He found Jamal lying on the dock, face down on the boards. Jamal wore loose purple trunks. Ben stood for a moment, watching him. He didn't think about beauty. He walked onto the dock.

"What's going on?" he asked.

"There's a big fish under here," Jamal said.

"Where?"

Ben lay beside Jamal, put his eye to the gap between the boards.

"You have to wait for him to move," Jamal said.

Ben saw only still green water that reflected, unsteadily, the boards of the dock, like a rope ladder fluttered by the wind. He was aware of Jamal's body beside his own, the innocent pressure of Jamal's elbow against his elbow and of Jamal's bare knee against his thigh. He looked for the fish. He thought of nothing else.

"He's down there," Jamal said. "He's a really big one."

"I don't see any fish," Ben said.

"There. There he goes."

Ben saw the sweep of a fin, spined and flat, broad as his hand. Then an eye. One staring yellow eye, big as a poker chip. Rising toward the surface. Ben sat up quickly. His heart pounded.

"Shit," he said.

"What's the matter?" Jamal asked.

"It's huge," he said.

"Pretty big. I bet he's two or three feet long."

"Bigger than that," Ben said.

"No."

"It's *huge*."

"Are you afraid of it?" Jamal asked.

"No."

But his heart still pounded. He fought an urge to run back to land, scramble up the road to a high place.

"It's just a fish," Jamal said. "It can't hurt you. It's just a fish."

1 9 9 3 / Zoe lived in the sickness now. She could speak as herself, she could make the usual jokes. But she was going somewhere else. She felt herself changing away even as the dinners were cooked, as stars appeared in the windows and the television played its familiar music. She watched from a place she'd never been.

Will ran up the porch stairs, shining. Harry sat with the newspaper in a metal chair shaped like a clamshell.

"Right," Harry said. "Run ten miles in August. On your vacation."

"I love it," Will said. His chest heaved. He wore a do-rag on his head. He was cheerful and smelly and he carried with him a small, barely visible angel of hope. Zoe remembered his nipples from when he was a boy.

"And Zoe and I have enjoyed watching you," Harry said. He laid his hand on the back of Zoe's chair. He propped his feet, sockless in dirty white high-tops, on the railing.

"Hey, Zo," Will said. He stood behind Zoe and Harry. He bent over to kiss the top of Harry's head.

"You're dripping on my newspaper," Harry told him.

"I'm gonna drip on more than that. How's it going, Zoe?"

"Okay," she said. "It's so pretty out here."

"Yeah."

They were surrounded by bees and a scoured blue sky, the bright unsteady water of the bay. It seemed that nothing would happen because this existed, bees browsing among beach roses in the August light.

"How would you feel about a swim?" Will asked.

"I'd go for a swim," Harry said. "How about you, Zoe?"

"Hm?"

"Do you feel like swimming?"

"Oh. I don't know. How about if I just sat on the beach and watched the two of you?"

"Whatever you like," Will said.

Zoe took a strand of her hair in her hand. She couldn't tell whether she was leaving time or entering it more deeply. She held her hair as if for balance.

"What I'd like is to sit on a beach," she said, "and watch you boys swim."

"We're not boys," Harry said. "Only in our dreams."

"I think of you that way," she told him. "That's what I call you, to myself. The boys."

"I don't mind us being thought of as boys," Will said.

"You wouldn't," Harry said.

"Give me a break."

"Right. The oldest living boy."

They fell into a false slugging match. Will feinted and parried exaggeratedly, like a boxing kangaroo. Harry slapped his fists away.

"Don't mess with me," Harry said to Will's fists. "I'm in no mood."

"I haven't even started messing with you," Will said.

A bee buzzed onto the porch, hovered over the floorboards.

Zoe watched it in its lush, suspended heaviness of body, the transparent shadow it cast. She watched her brother and his lover move together. Was their affection for each other related to the flight of the bee? No, that was just her habit of seeking connections.

Will said something to her, and she only smiled. These days, she didn't always worry about the words.

"Earth to Zoe," Harry said.

"I'm here," she told them. "Don't worry, I'm right here."

Ben and Jamal came up the porch stairs, paused together at the top. The bee made its decision. It angled off the porch and flew east, over Ben's and Jamal's heads. Zoe saw—had she known?—that Ben and Jamal were a couple, too. They were a kind of couple. Will and Harry were another couple. The bee had desires of its own. She held on to her hair.

"Hey, guys," Will said. "What's up?"

"We saw a fish," Jamal said.

"Really?"

Ben stood silently in his wounded virtue, all the love he wanted and didn't want.

"A pretty big one," Jamal said. "Under the pier."

"You guys feel like going swimming?" Will said.

"Okay," Jamal answered.

Ben didn't speak. He went into the house, banged the screen door behind him. He sent out onto the porch a stale breeze full of the smells of the house. Will looked at Harry. Funny kid, huh?

Jamal came and stood near Zoe. He waited for her to speak or not speak, waited for the next minute of her life.

"So let's hit the beach," Harry said.

"Mom?" Jamal said.

"You three go," Zoe said. "I've changed my mind, I'm happy right here."

"You sure?"

"Absolutely."

When Jamal didn't move she gently swatted his behind. "Go on," she said.

"Do you want me to go swimming?"

"Yes. I want you to go swimming."

"Okay."

"Okay."

She sat in her chair as Will and Harry and Jamal went inside the house to change into their bathing suits. There were tiny shifts in the air, intervals of greater and lesser incandescence. Something was gathering, something golden and blue and old. When Jamal and Will and Harry came back out Ben was with them, sleekly muscled in his baggy orange trunks. Will kissed her, and the others said goodbye, even though they'd return in less than an hour. These days, people always said goodbye. She watched them walk toward the bay. As her son and her nephew and her brother and his lover walked away together, Zoe saw that an equipoise had arrived. Here it was, right now: the heart of summer. For months, forces of ripeness and decay had been rising together toward this, an enormous stillness, a slumbering depth of gold and blue that contained no changes or contradictions.

Then she saw it pass. She saw the first descending light arrive, the first infinitesimal click of autumn. She realized she had been holding her hair all this time. When her son and her brother and his lover had passed out of sight, she let go of her hair.

"Are you warm enough?" a voice said. For a moment she thought it was the voice of the air itself, deep, with a hint of oboe and kettledrum. Bees could float in a voice like that, little electric sparks flying through the music.

"Yes," she said.

Her father came and stood beside her. It was his voice. It was his sweet, rank smell.

"You okay?" he asked. "Just sitting by yourself?"

"Everybody was here," she said. "They all went swimming."

"Who?"

"Will and Harry and Jamal and Ben."

He walked to the railing. He frowned out into the day that had begun its long cooling, its descent. Tomorrow would be the first day of autumn, though the calendar wouldn't acknowledge it for another three weeks. Tomorrow the light would be fatter, more prone to blue.

"Ben and Jamal have a sailing lesson at two," her father said.

He had love and hatred turning inside him, a system of tides. His hair was going transparent. His skin was freckling with age.

"It's all right," Zoe told him.

"Huh?"

"They'll be back in time."

"Right."

He left the railing, reluctantly. He bent over Zoe, put his face next to hers.

"You're okay here?" he said. "Warm enough?"

"Yes. I'm fine."

He nodded. He sucked on his teeth, pulled in a quarter note of air, and Zoe thought he might have tasted the day, the fading promise of it.

"I'm fine," she said again. "It's good to just sit here."

"My darling," he whispered. "My little girl."

That night, because there weren't enough bedrooms, Will and Harry pitched a tent in the patch of scrubby grass that lay behind the house. They'd bought a tent epecially for the trip, red nylon, bright as candy. Zoe watched them laugh and argue about setting it up. She watched Will's arms and back as he sunk pegs in the sandy earth. The night was alive with fireflies and mosquitoes, with rustlings of leaves and the restless, invisible presence of the bay. She heard Susan and smelled her and then Susan touched her shoulder.

"How are they doing out there?" Susan asked.

"Hm?"

"How. Are. They. Doing?" Slowly and loudly, as if she was speaking to a foreigner.

"Abbott and Costello go camping," Zoe said.

Susan massaged Zoe's shoulder. Her fingers were stronger than anybody knew. "You feeling okay?" she asked.

"Mm-hm."

"Hey." Susan called past Zoe, into the night. "If you guys can't manage it, Zoe and I will pitch the tent for you."

Susan's voice was the engine of the family. Her unhappiness only deepened her well-oiled shine.

"We're doing fine, thank you," Will answered. His skin was burnished in the darkness. A quarter moon had risen.

"Let's go help them out," Susan said to Zoe.

"Okay," Zoe said.

"Let's. Go. Help. Them. Out."

"I heard you, Susie. I'm here."

Zoe and Susan stepped out of the rectangle of kitchen light, off the small wooden stoop and into the grass. Zoe felt as if she was wading into warm water. She could feel the hidden eyes of animals, watching from the bushes. Susan held Zoe's elbow, the way she'd guide an old woman.

Harry said, "Thank God, the National Guard is here."

"We've *got* it," Will said. "Look. All done."

He stood up. There was the tent, saggy but upright. In its red triangular simplicity it might have been a child's drawing of a tent.

"Are you sure you'll be all right out here?" Susan asked.

"Sure we're sure," Will said. "We love the outdoors."

"We think we love the outdoors," Harry said. "Neither one of us has ever slept outside before."

"That's not true," Will said. "I went camping once, with my best friend's family, when I was twelve."

Zoe said, "I want to see what it's like in there."

"Be my guest," Will said.

She parted the nylon flaps and crawled in. The inside of the tent was a slick red-black world, surprisingly separate from the larger world, full of a warm plastic smell.

"It's nice in here," Zoe said. "Cozy."

Will crawled in and crouched beside her. "Not bad, huh?" he said.

"I want to sleep in here, too," Zoe said.

"Can't. It's for men only."

Susan parted the flaps, knelt in a triangle of black grass and stars. "This looks like it'll be fine," she said.

Then Jamal was in the triangle with her. Zoe saw his hair, the indistinct glitter of his eyes.

"Cool," he said.

"Come on in," Will told him.

Jamal hesitated, and climbed in. Zoe saw how much like an animal he could be. She thought of a raccoon sneaking into the tent, the sense of ownership it would bring.

"Cool," Jamal said. He sat close to her. She took a corner of his T-shirt between her fingers.

"Maybe," she said, "the boys will let you sleep out here with them."

Will said, "Sure, if you want to. I think there's room for three of us."

Jamal looked at Zoe. She felt his desire and his fear. She knew about his need to stay with her and his need to go away.

"Go on," she said. "It'd be fun, you've never slept in a tent before."

He pulled his knees up to his chin. He made the smallest possible package of himself, sat silently before Zoe and Will.

"You don't snore, do you?" Will asked.

"No," Jamal said.

"Well, you're invited. You can protect Harry and me if we get scared."

"That's stupid."

"Right. It is. You can stay out here if you want to. If you don't want to, nobody's going to be offended."

"Okay," Jamal said. "I'll stay with you."

Later, in the house, Jamal changed into yellow pajama bottoms. He still wore his Jesus and Mary Chain T-shirt. Zoe stood in the bathroom doorway as he brushed his teeth. "This will be fun," she said.

Jamal watched his reflection in the speckled mirror. A moth whirred dryly against the painted tin lampshade.

"You like Will and Harry, don't you?" she said.

He nodded. He might have liked Will and Harry. He might only have wanted to please her.

She said, "Do you want to take something out there with you? One of the Star Trek people?"

"*No*," he said impatiently, through toothpaste. His love of the Star Trek figures had become a secret vice. He believed he was too old for toys. Zoe thought, A mother knows too many secrets. That's why she has to die.

Jamal spit toothpaste in the sink, rinsed his mouth. Here was the steadiness of his being, as he cupped water in his hands and took it to his mouth. Here were the years to come, a night and another and another.

"Come on," Zoe said. "I'll walk out there with you."

When she and Jamal went outside, she could see that something was wrong. Her father stood near the tent in his fighting posture, feet planted wide apart and hands fisted on his hips. Zoe wondered if he knew how feminine he looked in that position, how much like an indignant queen. Will was talking to him and Harry stood behind Will, neither present nor apart.

"—fucking believe this," Will said to their father's angry face.

"Calm down," their father said. "Just keep cool, here."

Zoe and Jamal walked through the grass to where her father and Will and Harry stood.

"Zoe," their father said. His face changed. His face stopped, paused, pulled back a quarter inch.

"Is everything okay?" she asked.

Will said, "Dad doesn't want Jamal to sleep with us."

Their father did not move. If somebody tipped him over, he'd have fallen with his hands still on his hips and his feet still wide. He'd lie in the grass like a toppled statue of Queen Victoria wearing men's clothes.

"What?"

"Take Jamal back to the house, Zo," their father said.

Will said, "No, oh no you don't. Jamal should hear this, it's part of his education."

"You don't have any shame, do you?" their father said.

"You ready for this one?" Will said to Zoe. "Dad's afraid Harry and I will molest Jamal if he stays in the tent with us."

"Don't you tell her that. I didn't say that."

"Go ahead, deny it."

"Jamal's got his own bed in the house," their father said. "He's too young for this, that's all I said."

"Right," Will said. "He's too young to sleep out in the back yard. Dad, you are a piece of work, you know that? You are one fucking piece of work."

"Watch your language, mister. Zoe, you and Jamal go back in, now."

"Don't move," Will said. "Don't you move."

"Dad," Zoe said. "Please."

"You evil bastard," Will said. "You really think—"

"Stop this, now," their father said.

"Or what? Or you'll beat me up? I've got news, Dad. You can't do it anymore."

"Be quiet," Zoe said. "Both of you."

"I take a lot from you," their father said to Will. "You show up here with your boyfriend, parade around in front of the kids, I don't mind. I keep my mouth shut. But when you tell me you're planning on having an eleven-year-old boy sleeping between you all night, that's where I put my foot down. That's where I have to step in."

"I'm your son, goddammit," Will said. "However much you hate me. And you really think, you honestly think . . . I can't even say it. You're the fucking pervert."

"This kid's grown up with enough bad influences," their father said. "You expect him to grow up twisted just so you don't have to feel guilty?"

"Guilty? You think *I've* got things to feel guilty about?"

"I didn't say that."

"After all you've done. Look at Susan. Look at Zoe."

"What do Susan and Zoe have to do with any of this? What are you talking about?"

Will was going to kill their father. Zoe saw it. It rose off him in waves. Will had taken on a murderous clarity, and he was going to fall on their father and batter his head until his head stopped. Zoe saw that Will had been preparing himself for this. He was a man physically powerful enough to murder their father with the raw strength of his body. That was the true purpose. That was what men were doing in gyms.

"Will," she said.

Harry put his hand on Will's shoulder and said, "Come on now, let's just go."

Will hesitated. At the touch of Harry's hand the rage faltered, and began to turn. Slowly, with an immense and weary patience, Will shook his head.

"Fine," Will said. "I'd like nothing more than to get out of here and never have to look at this asshole's face again."

"You don't talk to me like that," their father said. He stood in a cold fury of righteous, fading strength.

"I don't talk to you at all from now on," Will said. "Ever."

He turned to Zoe and Jamal. His face was dark with anger and something else, something that lay on anger's other side. It looked like a kind of terrible inspiration.

"We're going to go," he said softly to Zoe and Jamal. "Sorry. I'll call you when you get back to the city."

She nodded. He and Harry kissed her, and Will shook Jamal's hand.

"The tent's all yours, buddy," he said. "Our parting gift."

They walked through the kitchen door, past Susan and Magda and Ben. In less than ten minutes they'd packed their suitcases and gotten into the car. Susan and Zoe walked to the car with them.

"This is crazy," Susan said. "Don't leave."

"We can't stay," Will told her. "I'm sorry. We shouldn't have come in the first place, I should have known something like this would happen."

"Why don't you give it one more try? Let me talk to him first."

Will took both Susan's hands in his. He pulled her close to him.

"Remember," he said, "how I told you once I was going to kill him?"

"No," she said.

"I remember it perfectly. We were in the back yard together, we were kids. I told you I was going to kill him one day, and you know, tonight I almost did. I really almost did."

"You're exaggerating."

"Maybe. Maybe not. I think I might have done it."

"Billy," Susan said. "I mean, Will—"

He kissed her quickly. "I'll see you later, Sooz," he said. "I'll come to Connecticut. Bye, Zoe."

"Bye."

Will kissed her, and Harry kissed her. She took Will's hand to her face, pressed her lips to the backs of his fingers.

"Be careful," she said.

Harry told her, "Don't worry. I'll watch out for him."

Harry fired the ignition, and they drove away. Zoe thought she saw Will bury his face in his hands. She thought she saw Harry stroke his head. She stood in the road with Susan.

"Well," Susan said.

That was all she said. They stood in the road, in darkness, until the red lozenges of Harry's taillights were gone.

Back in the living room, their father sat heavily on the sofa. Magda had gone upstairs to bed. Their father shook his head. "Sorry you had to see that," he said. "I just felt like I had to put my foot down."

Susan said, "You should be ashamed of yourself."

"Now, Susie, don't you start in on me, too."

"What's the matter with you?" she said. She was bigger than herself. She was bright in the dimly lit room. "What business is it of yours where Jamal sleeps?"

"He's my grandson. I try to do what's right."

"Oh, you do, do you?"

"Yeah. I do."

Susan groaned.

"Please," Zoe said. "Stop, everybody."

"It's okay, Susie," their father said. "He'll get over it."

A silence passed. When Susan could speak, she said, "He won't get over it. People don't."

Zoe could not be in the room any longer. She couldn't find her own shape. She felt herself disappearing. She walked through the kitchen, out the back door. She thought she would go into the tent for a while. She'd hide there until she returned to herself. She waded into the grass but when she got close to the tent she heard them, Ben and Jamal, whispering. They were already inside.

1 9 9 4 /   Mary squeezed a final rose onto the cake, stepped back and squinted at it with a cold, hopeful eye. Yes, it looked all right. Happy Birthday Zoe, framed by butter-cream roses and lilies, leaves she had molded out of almond paste. The class in cake decorating had been a good idea. She knew what she was doing now. She had the solace of competence. The cake sat on the kitchen counter offering its petals and leaves, its pale blue scrollwork message, to the silence of the room. The sight of it filled Mary with a satisfaction so simple it seemed, fleetingly, that satisfaction was the fundamental human state, and all extremes of loss and emptiness aberrations.

She walked into the dining room, adjusted a tulip in the centerpiece. As Mary stood surveying her efforts—the napkins tightly rolled in their silver rings and the candles erect in their silver holders—her sense of satisfaction rose and then dropped away into a more complex but equally familiar muddle of happiness and dread. Here among the waiting flatware and crystal was a beauty all the more moving and frightening for its impermanence. It would have no life if the guests weren't due to arrive shortly, and yet the guests, when they arrived, would spoil it. She had no complaints, nothing specific, about the people who would come at any time now. She regretted only the disorder, the using-up. In its pristine condition the table was a devotion, a flawless gesture. Mary had created a perfect party, and it was about to be spoiled by the guests.

Will and Harry arrived first, in Harry's sports car. Will jumped out like a teenager, lifted Mary off her feet.

"Hi, gorgeous," he said. His hair was beginning to gray.

Harry followed with a buff-colored canvas suitcase. "Hello, Mary," he said. He kissed her cheek. He was a handsome man, deliberate in his movements, with a quirky and competent face and an aspect of potent, generous calm. At odd moments, Mary understood completely. She had imagined someone like this for herself.

"Come on in, you two," she said. "You made good time."

"No traffic at all," Will told her. "Hey, the place looks great."

"I try," Mary said. She ignored the little panic, the urge to show them the dining room and then usher them out again with the admonition that it must be left untouched for the company. They *are* the company, she reminded herself. "I've got you both upstairs," she said, "in Will's old room. I hope Ben and Jamal will be all right down here in sleeping bags. We're going to be a full house."

"Do you need help with anything?" Will asked.

"No, thank you. It's all set. Would you boys like something to drink?"

"I'm going to make some coffee, okay?" Will said. "We got up early, we could both use a little shot of caffeine."

"I'll get it," Mary said.

"Relax. I know where everything is. I used to live here, remember?"

"Fine," she said. She would let it be fine. Will seemed to like these little demonstrations of his claim, all the powers of territory and domestic critique his childhood had bought for him. All right, then. She would try to relinquish her own habits of propriety, at least for the weekend. She'd been alone in this big house too long.

She said, "Harry, why don't I show you up to the room?"

"Mom," Will said, "Harry's been here before. He knows exactly where the room is. Sit down, relax. I know what you've been doing. You made three birthday cakes, and threw the first two away. You went to seventy-five different stores looking for Zoe's presents. Am I right?"

"Oh, I've given all that up in my old age," she said. "These days, people just have to take me as they find me."

"Right," Will said. "Go. Sit. Make conversation."

Mary paused, full of love and a steady, relentless anger that made her think of ants invading a house. Here was her grown son; here was all he'd become. Here he was with his mate, beginning to treat her like a childish and eccentric figure, someone too old to fear. By accepting him she had lost much of her power, and she saw that she would not be able to get it back even if she wanted to. He'd moved beyond the reach of her disapproval. She had released him. She was in a sense no longer quite his parent. Since his infancy she'd been able to follow the logic of his emotions, more easily than she could follow Susan's or Zoe's, and she could follow him here. She knew about the urge to be free of a mother. She knew about the love of men. She recognized her son, did not hate him, though she was periodically invaded by this low-grade anger, this stream of ants. She loved him both more and less for what he'd proven to be. She felt related to him in ways she did not feel with either of her daughters.

"Let's go sit in the living room, Harry," she said. "Will, honey, you're in charge."

She led Harry into the living room, gestured him toward the wing chair. She sat near him, on the sofa, with her hands folded over one knee.

"So," she said. "How's everything?"

"Pretty good," he said. "Everything's more or less all right. Busy."

"I can just imagine. Heart patients, what a terrible responsibility it must be."

"To tell you the truth, most of it's pretty undramatic. Every now and then, you save somebody who would have died if it hadn't been for you. We all like to play that angle up. But mostly, people are going to live or they're not going to live, and you're a mechanic, and as long as you don't make any really stupid mistakes, the people who were going to live anyway live, and the people who were going to die, die."

"Well, it still sounds pretty dramatic to me," Mary said. "Speaking as a housekeeper and a saleslady."

"How's work?"

"Not bad. I'm actually a pretty *good* saleslady, I know what women are afraid of when they go shopping."

"Afraid?"

"They're afraid of looking dowdy and they're afraid of looking like fools, and there's just a narrow little space between the two. I sort of help them find their balance."

"Sounds tricky," Harry said.

"It is, a little. Frankly I wish I'd had somebody like me to wait on me when I was younger. Someone sort of, I don't know, *sisterly*. I grew up in a house full of boys."

"Hard, huh? Being the only girl."

"Well, it has its advantages, too. But when you grow up, and you're trying to put yourself together, it's hard to know, because you can't really *see* yourself no matter how long and hard you look in the mirror. And I think sometimes about how much I'd have appreciated a saleslady who wouldn't lie to me. Because, you know, women sabatoge one another, and you can get so nervous. Just trying not to look like a clown. This must sound awfully silly to you."

"Actually, no," he said. "I don't worry much about clothes myself, but I think I understand it."

"Women are judged differently."

"I know. Gay guys are, too. People suddenly think they can take you less seriously."

"I suppose that's true," Mary said.

Harry stretched his legs. Mary could hear the cracking of his knee joints. "Sorry," he said. "It's a long drive in that little car."

He was gray-eyed, clear-skinned, beginning to wrinkle. He did not dislike Mary but did not need to be loved by her. Sometimes, with unexpected intensity, she regretted the absence of a daughter-in-law. One of the reasons a woman raises a son, she thought, is to see what kind of woman he'll choose. Harry was charming but he was another son. She could not take any credit for him. She could not conquer him.

"I think your little car is adorable," Mary said.

"You've never been in it, have you?"

"No. I don't think so."

"I'll take you for a spin later, if you want. You can drive."

"Oh, no, I'd love to go for a ride with you, but I couldn't drive a car like that."

"Sure you could. There's nothing to it."

"You know," Mary said, "I forgot to tell Will about this new coffeemaker I bought, if you fill it too full it leaks all over the counter. Excuse me a minute, all right?"

"Sure," he said.

He seemed to listen to her, to take her seriously. She wasn't sure how she felt about that.

In the kitchen, Will stood looking at the cake. When Mary came in he turned to her with a startled, apologetic expression, as if she'd caught him at some minor indiscretion.

"The cake's beautiful," he said.

"Thank you. And I didn't throw two of them away."

One. She'd thrown one away.

"Zoe's thirty-eight," Will said.

"I know."

"Little Zoe. She was always so, I don't know. She always seemed so young. She still does."

"Mm-hm."

Then nothing happened. Mary stood beside Will. They were alone together with the cake.

Susan pulled up two hours later. Mary stood in the doorway watching them all disembark, and the sight carried her, briefly, into a waking dream. From Susan's cream-colored Volvo came Susan herself, pretty and smiling and rancorous in jeans and her beige linen jacket. Then came silent, handsome Ben. Then came Jamal, heavy-lipped, bristling. Then Cassandra, even thinner than Mary remembered, and finally Zoe, helped by Cassandra, her skin white and opaque as paper. It seemed to Mary that she had seen this procession before, or one like it, though it was familiar in the inchoate way of dreams, simultaneously known and profoundly, vertiginously foreign.

Mary did not hesitate long. She stepped out onto the lawn in her sandals, welcomed everyone in.

"Hi, gang. How was the drive?"

"Hi, Mom," Susan said. "It was fine. We got here."

Susan kissed Mary, and then Ben kissed her. Jamal, standing close to Ben, performed a singular snap of a dance, one quick snakelike movement that seemed to rise out of the driveway and shoot up into him through the soles of his feet.

"Zoe," Mary said. "Happy birthday, darling."

Zoe smiled distractedly. Cassandra held her hand.

"Nice place, Mary," Cassandra said.

"Thank you, dear."

"It's Sleeping Beauty's castle, isn't it?" Cassandra said.

"It's too big. I've been telling myself I should sell for years now."

"I wouldn't," Cassandra said. "All this space, I can't think of anything I'd like better."

"It feels very empty at night sometimes," Mary said. "I'll be in the kitchen with just the kitchen lights on and I'll feel like I'm sitting at a campfire deep in the woods somewhere."

"But with no bugs," Cassandra said. "Sounds like heaven to me."

Zoe stood silently beside Cassandra. For months Zoe had been quieting down, taking on the contemplative, dazed remove of the elderly. Like an old woman of a certain type, she was courteous and cautious and secretive. She conserved herself.

"Zoe," Mary said. "Happy birthday. Oops, did I say that already?"

"Yes," Zoe said. "But thank you, Momma."

She had not called Mary 'Momma' since she was a little girl. She shifted her weight toward Cassandra.

"Shall we go in?" Mary said.

Zoe nodded, and did not move. Her eyes were full of a dark, astonished light.

She said, "Happy birthday to you, too, Momma."

The afternoon passed. Harry gave Ben and Jamal driving lessons in the driveway. Will and Zoe sat on the front lawn, watching. Susan had invented an errand for herself in the basement, looking through old papers of hers for a journal she'd kept in high school. Cassandra, more subdued than Mary had ever seen her, had wrapped herself in a sheet and stretched out on the chaise on the back patio, her sharp, pale face exposed to the sun like that of an ancient society woman incubating at a spa. It was a warm afternoon in May, full of lush green rustlings and the smell of lilacs in their final days.

Mary kept busy in the kitchen, alone with her dinner preparations, a solitude she had insisted on and which she treasured and obscurely resented. She sautéed onions, set the potatoes to boil. It was her usual kitchen. She took a stick of butter from the refrigerator and glanced at the cake, which she'd set on the bottom shelf so Zoe wouldn't see it. It was a lovely cake. It would be a nice dinner. She closed the refrigerator door and stood, just stood, with the stick of butter in her hand. The cake was in the refrigerator, perfect in the cold darkness. Mary found that she could not perform the next action; she could not touch anything in the kitchen. She watched it as if it were a replica of a kitchen on display behind glass in a museum. There was the wallpaper with its sheaves of wheat. There were the copper molds and the three-tiered wire basket full of Bartlett pears and Granny Smith apples. There were the potatoes hissing in the pan. It was a flawless representation of her kitchen and she felt as if something unspeakable would happen if she touched anything. She stood in the room but she was not of it. Carefully, she set the butter down on the countertop. From outside, Harry's motor revved in the driveway and Jamal shouted, "Let *me*."

Mary went upstairs to her bedroom. She would wait this out. She would freshen her makeup and come back downstairs and finish dinner. In her room she paced for a while, uncertain about where to settle. Everything was impossible. Leaf shadows fell from the window onto the snowy flowers of her bedspread. The bed stood again, bisected, at an oblique angle, in her dressing-table mirror.

Mary sat at her dressing table. There was her face in the mirror. She watched herself and she thought of how it would feel to not finish dinner, to remain here in her room. To refuse all comfort. On the glass-topped table before her, perfume bottles and a white leather jewelry box were precise, solitary, permanent. She watched those things. She did nothing else.

She could not decide how much time had passed before someone knocked at the door. Go away, Mary thought. She waited. There was another knock, and Cassandra's voice.

"Mary?" Cassandra said. "Are you in there?"

Mary did not answer. She did not move.

Cassandra knocked again. "Honey, I'm going to come in, all right?"

No, Mary thought.

Cassandra opened the door.

"You all right?" she said. "Sorry to barge in like this."

Mary nodded. "I'm fine," she said.

"I went into the kitchen for a glass of water," Cassandra said, "and I saw the potatoes just about boiled dry. And I thought, Mary Stassos is not the kind of woman who neglects her potatoes unless something really big comes up. So I came looking for you."

"I'm all right," Mary said. "Thank you."

She assumed Cassandra would murmur something polite, and close the door.

Cassandra came into the room and sat down on the edge of the bed.

"It sucks, doesn't it?" she said.

Mary didn't answer. She turned back to the mirror, saw herself and Cassandra there. Cassandra was nearly bald now. As her hair and her flesh diminished, her eyes seemed to increase. Mary could see that Cassandra's eyes were set in the sockets of her skull; she could see that Cassandra spoke to her from inside a skull.

Cassandra sighed, and looked around the room with the mild curiosity of a tourist. "This is a nice bedroom," she said.

"Thank you," Mary answered.

"I used to dream about a house like this."

"Please don't make fun of me," Mary said. "Not right now."

"I'm not. I couldn't be more serious. When I was a little boy I used to fantasize about getting married and having a house with a big bedroom like this. It wasn't an especially practical fantasy, but why would you want a practical fantasy?"

"I should sell the house," Mary said. "It's too big, I just rattle around in here."

"Mm."

"You see," Mary told her. "It's just that. I can't."

"Can't what?"

"This," she said. "Any of it. I don't think I can have this party."

"Of course you can. It's a nice little party. Easiest thing in the world to have, a party like this one."

"I've worked so hard," Mary said. "I don't want to spoil it."

"A quick little nervous breakdown isn't going to spoil it. I have them all the time."

"It seemed. It seemed like we could, I don't know. Before everybody came I was just here, by myself, and everything seemed so perfect."

"I know all about that," Cassandra said.

"Maybe it would be better if I was alone for a little while."

Cassandra said, "I don't want to tell you how many hours I spend putting my drag together. What with shopping and, well, other forms of procurement, and doing my makeup, and my hair, and putting it all together. I sit in my apartment for hours and then finally, *ta-da*, there I am. You haven't seen me at my best, I can be quite a splendid sight. Or *could* be, back in my prime. I once wrapped a wig around a birdcage and wore a live canary on my head, it was my homage to Madame Pompadour. And you know, there's always a moment, when I'm all finished and I've exceeded even my own expectations, and I'm alone in my apartment, well, there's always a moment when I feel unbelievably good. Invincible, like a member of a new, improved species. And of course I'm looking forward like crazy to getting out there and showing it off, that's the point, imagine how depressing it would be to put all that stuff on, stand around in front of the mirror, then take it all off again and go to bed. No, I adore strutting around in front of the multitudes, but there's something about standing there by myself, about to go out, that's perfect, in its way. I don't know if I'd say it's *better* than going out and showing off, because, honey, I was born for display. But I do know about how fabulous your drag can feel right before anybody sees it."

"It's funny," Mary said.

"What is?"

"I don't know. It's funny to think of me arranging a party like this and you, you know."

"Dressing up like the Christmas tree in Rockefeller Center," Cassandra said. "In a parallel dimension, I'm the housewife and you're the drag queen."

"It's funny."

"It's a riot," Cassandra said.

"I should get back downstairs."

"I turned the potatoes off, don't worry."

"Oh, right. The potatoes."

Cassandra said, "It's hard to live. It's hard to keep walking around and change into new outfits all the time and not just collapse."

Mary thought she would stand up. She didn't stand up. She continued looking into her own eyes and Cassandra's eyes. Something opened in her. She put her palms down on the cool glass of the tabletop.

She said, "There is nothing more unthinkable than losing a child."

"I know."

She turned. Cassandra was there.

"Honey, I know," Cassandra said.

"Are you all right?" Mary asked her.

"I'm dying, dear."

"I didn't mean that."

"Do you mean, am I scared?"

"Not that exactly, either."

"Sometimes I'm scared," Cassandra said. "Not of dying itself, it just doesn't seem to scare me all that much. I mean, when you've gotten on a subway at four in the morning dressed as Jackie Kennedy, well . . . No, I'm scared of being enfeebled. All my life I've relied on my ferocity, my how do you say queenly bearing, and, honey, it works. It's my power. I'm tall and I'm more than a little crazy and when somebody even *thinks* about fucking with me I draw myself up to my full six three and I look at them as if to say, Don't mess with me because I've got nothing to lose and I will mess with you worse. You'd be amazed, the scrapes I've gotten out of by attitude alone. But I do worry that if I start looking weak, if I don't have it in me to look like I'm too mean and too nuts to be worth bothering with, the wolves'll be on my ass. They can smell weakness. And frankly, there are a few characters in my *building* who'd just as soon kill you as look at you."

"I guess I can't imagine," Mary said.

"I envy you, living in a big house in the suburbs like this. You seem so safe here."

"I don't feel particularly safe."

"Oh, well, I probably can't imagine, either."

Mary was aware of the quiet of her bedroom, its perfumed ease and its starched ruffles. Cassandra sat in the middle of it like a wild creature, pale and hawk-nosed, ill and rouged, and yet it seemed, fleetingly, that Cassandra belonged there more than Mary herself did.

"You've been wonderful with Zoe," she said. "And Jamal. I hope you know how much I appreciate it."

"Don't thank me," Cassandra said. "Don't you dare. Zoe is my daughter. Jamal is my godson. I haven't done anything for you."

Mary looked into Cassandra's harsh, dying face.

"No," she said. "I guess you haven't. Sorry."

"It's all right," Cassandra said. "These are difficult times, a girl can lose track of herself."

"That's true."

"Well, now," Cassandra said, and she rose with a small, brittle wince from the edge of the bed. "Shall we go down to our guests?"

"All right," Mary said. "Yes, we should go back down."

"Better fix your face a little first."

Mary turned back to the mirror. "Oh, my, yes," she said.

Cassandra stood beside her. "Honey, have you tried a water-proof mascara?"

"Once," Mary said. "It was too thick."

"Well, they've improved them. Technology has come through for us once again."

"Maybe I'll try one."

"In these times," Cassandra said, "it's more or less a necessity."

"I suppose so."

"No question about it. Oh my lord, is this Opium?"

"Mm-hm. Do you want to try a little?"

"Maybe just a dab. There is nothing like really good perfume to cut the stink of mortality."

"Cassandra."

"Joke, dear. Honestly, how have you managed all this time without waterproof mascara or a sense of humor?"

"Well, it hasn't been easy," Mary said.

"No. It isn't really very easy for anybody, is it? Not even Sleeping Beauty in her castle."

"I'm not half as secure as you think I am."

"*Secure?*" Cassandra said. "Honey, I think you're a *mess*. But you have a decent heart. Come on, now, get to work on that mascara."

1 9 9 4 / Constantine lay in the king-sized bed watching Magda undress. Everything was friendly now, more or less friendly. All right, it wasn't exactly what he'd wanted. It wasn't the kind of glamour he'd thought about, that whole Gabor sisters thing. But he had a piece here. He had a big house and a beautiful plot of land and a wife who cut a figure, hey she wasn't Mamie Van Doren but she had stature and conviction, she scared the hell out of other guys' wives. For sex he could always drive into town and grab a whore, not much more complicated than picking up a six-pack. It was better this way, really. His sex life kept changing, some of these girls knew their business, and he still, at his age, got a jolt when a new girl climbed into his car. A young man's mix of lust and nerve. He had that still, a sixty-seven-year-old guy whose heart had already failed him once. He had the newness of whores and he had the defiant Viking starchiness of his wife and he had a thriving garden and he had grandchildren. He had the sailboat he'd just bought for Ben. This perfect boy, this kid who could do anything, who had nothing holding him back. Nothing. He was handsome and strong and smart and rich. Constantine was still flying from going out with Ben to buy the sailboat, a nineteen-foot Rhodes, fast, a lot of boat for a kid who was still only fourteen but he'd handle it, he liked to be stretched. Magda took off her bra as if her tits were secret weapons in a war against men. Who cared? This was happiness. It was a kind of happiness. This was how you lived into the future. You stopped thinking so much about *you*, all those ambitions, the urge to sing in the loudest voice. You slacked off on that and started getting your satisfaction from being a man your grandchildren could love and respect. Your children were too close to you, they'd picked up too many of the mistakes you made when you were young yourself. But grandchildren. You gave the best of everything to your kids' kids. You talked to them, encouraged them. You groomed their hearts the way you'd raise a jungle bird that could live a hundred years. You bought them a sailboat, pointed it toward the horizon, and climbed in. Come on, you said. Let's move. Let's take the old man away. He pictured himself cutting through the water.

Ben loved what the boat meant. He loved what it said about his capabilities, the rise of his future. He thought of his grandfather's house raising its lights against the ocean and he thought of the marina on the bay where the boat swayed in black water, waiting. He saw the ocean stretching away until it met the stars and he saw the constellations with their inhabited planets, a system of worlds so immense that on one of them a boy like himself must exist, a boy with his voice and body and thoughts but without the other thing. It seemed he could get in the boat and sail to that other world, meet himself. He was a natural sailor. He could grow and change, set a transatlantic speed record before he turned seventeen. He'd be in *National Geographic*. There would be a glossy two-page picture of him, his bare chest glistening with spray, his face severe and certain as the profile on a coin, and once that picture was published he'd be his own twin. Lying on his bed, he was taken by a conviction of happiness. This was his past, right now. He was shedding it. Everything could happen, he could feel himself changing. Then he heard Uncle Will's voice from downstairs, followed by Uncle Will's high-pitched, breathy laughter. A moment later, when the door to Ben's room opened, his joy turned immediately to terror, as if he were about to be caught at something shameful.

Susan had forgotten to knock. She tried to remember. He was almost fifteen, he needed privacy. It was hard for her to remember because he seemed to have no secrets, none of the petulant shadows she'd expected from an adolescent son. His life still seemed soft and unblemished as his skin. "Hey," she said. "Sorry I didn't knock, I was worried about you. Are you feeling okay?" He didn't look quite right. He'd left the dinner table so quickly. It wasn't like him. He told her he was fine. She nodded, standing in the doorway with her hand still on the knob. Sometimes she just needed to look at him. She was increasingly astonished and relieved that she'd helped produce this boy, this luminous presence in the world who got straight A's without grinding for them and who understood sports the way a bird understands flight and who, most miraculous of all, never bullied other children, most of whom were his inferiors in one way or another. It felt like deliverance. If she'd been religious she'd have considered it a sign of God's approbation, his approval of our efforts and his willingness to overlook our failure-prone flesh. Together she and Todd had raised a boy who animated the house with his kindness and his modest, utter competence. He was their forgiveness; he was the reason for everything. She asked him, "Are you sure you're all right?" And reluctantly—because he was who he was, a boy visibly pained by his own occasional angers and jealousies—reluctantly he told her he didn't like Uncle Will all that much. She sucked in her lower lip. Oh, Billy. She refused to turn on him, she'd known him too small and too helpless. She knew too well the net of harms woven by their father and mother. But at the same time she understood her son's objections. With an inner flush that pained her, she even applauded them. Her son lived in a world of simple virtue, there was no room for the life Billy had made. She was surprised to find that she could adore her son and she could love Billy and she could vaguely admire her son for disliking Billy. She reminded Ben that it was important to be tolerant of all kinds of people. She told him his Uncle Will was a good man, and we can be generous toward other people even if we don't completely approve of their choices. She had to counterbalance Todd's fine-ground morality, his growing hatred of difference. Ben agreed with her, as she'd known he would, even if she didn't quite fully agree with herself. She asked him to come back down for dessert. She promised that after he'd had dessert he could say good night and go back to his room.

Todd was relieved when Susan came back with Ben. He didn't like being alone with her brother. Not that he was nervous about that kind of thing. It was a social embarrassment, not a discomfort of the body. Funny, a funny feeling. Not even strictly social, really, because there was always education for them to talk about. Luckily, the guy was a teacher. Whenever Todd and Will were left alone together one of them brought up the sorry state of the American educational system, and they could work it until Susan came back to rescue them. So it wasn't purely social. There was something too loose about the brother's presence. It was like having a bird get into the house. His presence inspired that same feeling of crazy threat. You'd never show it but you'd be afraid of a lark or a jay, even a sparrow, if it was buzzing around in your house. It would get to you. That disregard, the life that wasn't where it belonged. When Susan and Ben walked in, he felt as if the bird had been caught.

Will was always surprised by Susan, even when she'd only been away a few minutes. She was aging, and it surprised him.

Not the fact of aging itself, but the fact that she was turning into one of those stringy, lacquered women about whom it was said, 'She used to be a beauty.' He was surprised that Susan *used to be* beautiful, that she had embarked upon her decline. She said, as her son dropped sullenly back into his chair, "He's been working too hard on that science project, I'm going to feed him a little dessert and then I'm going to send him back up to bed." It was perverse, really, that Susan had started taking on an exhausted look when Zoe looked better than she ever had. Zoe who was sick and who lived on no money with a kid in the East Village. Zoe was pale and precise as a rose these days. Well, Susan had bought the package, hadn't she? She'd married a lawyer and a columned house in Connecticut; she'd taken on the obligation to be a treasure. And the strain was starting to show. People paid a price for this kind of orderly existence, all this obedience. Will loved Susan and pitied her and he searched scrupulously for every sign of her unhappiness. It made sense that she should owe a debt of grief for all she'd received. He felt guilty, but couldn't seem to stop himself from wishing some form of chastisement on all this Republican good fortune, this faux farmhouse interior and this dim-witted husband whose politics were only slightly left of Hitler's and this son of theirs who was being raised in such unquestioning wealth that he might grow up and do real damage in the world. Will survived these visits to his sister's place but he didn't enjoy them. He told Harry he felt like an anthropologist trying to record the rites and rituals of an ancient culture that was beginning to collapse under the weight of its own accumulated history, its insistence that it was possible to live and not change. At the thought of Harry, Will excused himself and went to use the telephone in the den. He said he'd forgotten to call Harry to tell him he'd arrived in Connecticut, though in fact he just wanted to hear Harry's voice amid the pine cupboards and ancient mirrors, the Amish quilts and the copper pots and the old chintz pillows and the fact, never acknowledged, that if he were not Susan's brother neither her husband nor her son would feel entirely comfortable about having him in their home. He wanted Harry to remind him that these people were not necessarily winning.

"Hello?"

"Hi. I'm here. I got here."

"Are you all right?"

"Sure. More or less."

"Are they driving you crazy already?"

"Yes. Definitely."

"You can't talk?"

"Not really."

"It'll be over soon. Weekends are only two days long, and there's a bottle of Scotch right here, waiting."

"Good."

"And me. I'm waiting."

"Better."

"Now go back and speak kindly to the Republicans. Take pity on them. They lost the election, things aren't going their way anymore."

"Do you really believe that?"

"No. I'm just trying to make you feel better. Call me tomorrow, if you want to."

Zoe inhaled through the plastic. She wondered if she was smiling. She watched Will and Susan watching her. She'd gone somewhere new. Where she was now there was the same sickness, the weight in her lungs, the fatigue that held her down like tiny ropes looped around her body. There was pain and a limit of breath, there was the same fear but she lived inside it now. She had begun to join her illness and she watched her sister and brother from a distance, as if she were on a train and they stood on a platform watching it pull away. And, as if she were on a train, she felt sadness mingled with relief, a surprising and perverse contentment at the sheer fact of going somewhere while others stayed behind. She began to see that dying might not be as hard as she'd expected it to be. She began to see that she could just leave. She could join the illness and not worry anymore; she could stop holding herself. She could let it have her. Her sister was speaking. Zoe lifted her hand, which required that she strain against the invisible ropes. She laid her hand over Susan's. Susan needed comforting. Zoe was happy to have that to do because she knew how to do it; it was a simple, usual thing. Then her mother came back with Jamal and stood helpless, well dressed, with her hands on Jamal's shoulders. When Zoe saw Jamal she left the illness and came back into the room because she felt no pleasure, not even a secret hint of it, in leaving her son. He hung back. He looked at her with an angry glint of non-recognition. She tried to stay in the room for him. She tried to smell like herself. Was she smiling? She lifted her hand off Susan's hand and held it out to Jamal. He stepped back and for the first time Zoe heard a voice that was not a voice, that did not speak in words but rolled through her like a stone. Give him his terror and his hatred and whatever he chooses to remember of love and let him be. She thought she'd do it, and she knew a blissful release deeper and more profound than any sleep. But then she decided to refuse. She stayed in the room, breathing, until Will finally understood the effort and made everybody go away.

Jamal couldn't be anywhere. He couldn't be alone and he couldn't be at home and he couldn't be at Cassandra's, ever, now that the sickness was there, too. He could be with Delores. There was that one place. Delores was rough and semi-ugly and she didn't care about anything. He could be with her. "Hey, baby," she whispered. "Hey, do me right here." He did her in the abandoned building on Eleventh Street and he did her in her sister's kitchen and he did her at the far end of the E train platform. Delores had big breasts for thirteen. She had strong narrow thighs and a lush

slightly cross-eyed face and all that wet heat between her legs. He
pushed in and lost himself there. He could be no one with her, just
the heat and the pillows of her breasts and the smell of lip gloss
and vanilla perfume. He didn't love her, not the details of her being,
not the movie things, but he loved losing himself. He loved going
inside. They did it everywhere. They did it on rooftops and on the
Christopher Street pier and in the doorway of the Ukrainian church.
She bit him, whispered his name. She took his ass in her hands
and pushed him harder, wanting him nowhere but in. He thought
about nothing else. When he wasn't with her he was beating off
or planning where and when he'd beat off next. The idea of her
moved him through the days. Once as he sat beside his sleeping
mother in the hospital, at a time when everyone else was out of
the room, he beat off there. He worked himself through the pocket
of his jeans as she took one breath through the tube, and another.
He was helpless. He lived in this desire now. Only once did a
thought stop him. He and Delores were walking up Avenue B, it
was dark enough to do it in the bushes of Tompkins Square Park
and Delores had led him there but he stopped her. He said it wasn't
safe. "Right," she said. "And doing it on the church steps was." He
insisted. He got away from her, walked out of the park. She followed
him. She complained, and he had no apology for her. He didn't tell
her that from the park you could see the windows of Cassandra's
apartment, and he couldn't do it there. He couldn't do it there.

Cassandra didn't bother turning on the lights. She sat in the
dark, smoking, listening to music. When Mary rang the bell she
buzzed her in, and turned on the lamp that sat on the claw-footed
table. Now the darkness had a cast to it, a honey color behind the
dark floating spots. Cassandra unlatched the door, waited. She
could hear Mary's footsteps and she could smell Mary's perfume.
Joy today, three thirty an ounce.

"Hi," Mary said.

"Hi, hon," Cassandra said. "Come on in, take off your coat. How's Zoe?"

"A little better, I think. They gave her something to help her sleep."

"I want to get her out of that hospital as soon as we can," Cassandra said. "Hospitals are dangerous."

"Well, they seem to be taking pretty good care of her."

"They're terrible places, don't be fooled."

"Well," Mary said. "There's not much choice at the moment. Is there?"

"No. There's not."

"Have you eaten?" Mary asked.

"Mm-hm."

"What did you eat?"

"I had a little soup," Cassandra said.

"Just that?"

"It was all I wanted. Don't push it, dear."

"Do you feel like reading?" Mary asked.

"Just a minute, there's something I want to give you."

Cassandra walked to the vanity, groped until she found the string of pearls.

"Here," she said, holding them out toward the place where she believed Mary to be standing.

"Oh, I couldn't take them."

"Please do, I hardly ever wear them, and frankly, they were one of my greatest heists. I never cracked Tiffany's or Cartier's, they're just too careful in those places, but believe me, even getting these out of a place like Bergdorf's was no small trick. Most of my devotions have been to trash, this necklace is one of the few things of mine I can imagine you wearing."

"No, really," Mary said.

"Humor me. Accept a few pearls from an old drag queen. At least try them on."

"Well. All right."

Mary took the pearls. Cassandra could hear the sound of the clasp being fastened.

"How do they look?" she asked.

"They're beautiful."

"You might as well take them now, I'm leaving them to you anyway. And frankly, honey, when the time comes, there may just be a free-for-all around here. I know queens who can strip a room faster than you can strip a bed."

"Well," Mary said. There was a pause.

"Are you all right?" Cassandra asked.

"I'm fine."

"Good."

"You know, I never told you this—" Mary said.

"Don't get sentimental, please. I'm not in the mood right now."

"I'm not being sentimental. I was going to tell you that I used to take things, too."

"What was that?"

"Shoplifting. I used to do it, too."

"Well, what do you know," Cassandra said.

"I don't know why I did it. I never took anything very big."

"There's nothing so mysterious about it. You want things, everybody does. It's a great big world full of stuff and you want some of it."

"But I could have afforded these things so easily."

"So, you were a thrill seeker. You had a criminal streak. Just think, in another version of our lives, we might have been cell mates."

"I did get arrested once," Mary said.

"I've been arrested, oh, let me think. Five or six times, I guess. Jail fantasies, none of the really good ones ever come true, though."

"I've never told this to anyone. My husband knew, but our kids don't."

"And now you've confessed. Do you feel any different?"

"Not really."

"Confession is highly overrated, in my opinion."

"I got the book you wanted," Mary said.

"Did you boost it, honey?"

"*No*. I paid for it. I haven't taken anything in years. I just stopped doing it, I don't really know why I started and I don't know why I stopped."

"We're mysterious creatures."

"Yes. I suppose we are. For a long time I had these fits of breathlessness too, I took Valium for them, and then gradually they just seemed to go away. Well, mostly they've gone away. I don't have them often enough to need the pills anymore."

"I've always maintained you can either cure your neuroses or you can just outwait them."

"Maybe so."

Cassandra said, "How are you feeling?"

"*Me*? I'm fine. How arc *you* feeling?"

"I'm fine, too, honey."

Mary took Cassandra's hand. "It'll be all right," she said.

"Please."

"I mean, Jamal will be all right. I'll help take care of him."

"Good."

"He's a sweet boy."

"He's a *wild* boy," Cassandra said. "And he has a great heart. Please don't try to rein him in too much, you won't win, and you'll just make yourself miserable trying."

"I'll do the best I can."

"That's all we can do, isn't it?"

Mary touched the pearls at her neck. "These are lovely," she said.

"Hm? Oh, the pearls. Yes."

"Why don't you sit down? You must be tired."

"I am, a little."

Mary guided Cassandra to a spindle-legged love seat uphol-stered in pale blue velvet. Cassandra said, "I stole this out of the ladies' room at Bonwit Teller."

"This love seat? How did you do that?"

"It wasn't easy, dear, believe me. I'll bet you never managed anything half this big."

"No," Mary said. "I didn't."

Cassandra arranged herself with a pillow at her head. Mary sat beside her on a high-backed chair.

"Do you want anything?" Mary asked. "A glass of water? A cup of tea?"

"No. Nothing. Begin."

Mary opened the book.

" 'I had a farm in Africa, at the foot of the Ngong Hills.' "

1 9 9 4 / Aunt Zoe had decided to let her body die but to live, anyway. That was what she said, sitting wrapped in a blanket on Ben's grandfather's terrace. Aunt Zoe put out a cold white glow, a brilliant dead non-color. She wore sunglasses in the October light and she shivered slightly under the blanket on a warm, clear day.

Zoe could hear the trees. They were restless with all they remembered. They lived in real time, they looked like they were standing still. Zoe didn't speak their language but she knew about their witnessing. What had her father told her? These are my yew trees. Like he owned them.

Aunt Zoe laughed for no reason. Ben's mother sat beside her on one of the canvas chairs, illustrating the difference between health and death. Ben's mother gleamed. She sat thin and straight as a sunflower stalk in her red blouse. Her hair was so stiffly alive it threw tiny sparks, an effervescence, into the soft, gold-washed air.

Ben's mother said, "Zoe, honey, look at what a beautiful day it is."

"Yes," Aunt Zoe answered. Ben's mother put her hand on the rise of Aunt Zoe's blanketed knee. She was nervous and she loved Aunt Zoe and she was tired of her, too. She wanted a big broom with steel bristles that would clean better than any broom had ever cleaned.

Susan was the harmed one. She had the most perfection in her, the truest and greediest heart. All the accidents of fortune happened to her, Will and I could sneak away. We had lives in the world; she gave herself to duty. In every story about a man who asks the witch or the beast or the fish for too many wishes, isn't there a daughter whose job it is to die?

"Susan," Aunt Zoe said. "Susan."

"Shh," Ben's mother said. "Just rest now, don't get all worked up."

Aunt Zoe looked through her dark glasses at the empty air. She nodded as if agreeing to something she saw written there. Ben's mother kept stroking her knee, smoothing it as if it were deeply wrinkled. Ben stood at the far edge of the terrace. He was surprised at how long death took, and how ordinary it was. He'd pictured dramatic momentum, a gathering of event that would suck everybody straight into the moment of loss, which would be terrible and large and satisfying. He'd never imagined all these awkward silences, the way hours could bleed into hours with the television on.

Ben had the twitch in him, the crazy passion. It was his secret and his rescue. It was his doom. Zoe spoke in her other voice. She told Ben to survive, though children never listened to advice.

She turned her crazy head, slowly, and stared at him. He prayed to her to look somewhere else.

Ben's grandfather and Uncle Will came out onto the terrace, full of silence. Aunt Zoe's craziness had canceled all the arguments, frozen them, and Grandpa and Uncle Will could come out of the house together like any father and son. Uncle Will dressed like a son, like somebody harmless. He wore jeans and a plaid flannel shirt.

"Hey, girls," Ben's grandfather said. Ben could imagine him as a father. He would have been kind and generous, full of fun. He would have come home at night with gifts. He would have stood just inside the front door with his arms full, calling, 'Hey, girls.'

Aunt Zoe kept looking at the air. She kept nodding.

It was too full. There was too much old desire, too many purposes. Zoe listened to the trees her father thought he owned. They spoke in a language too old to know. Zoe saw herself wearing pajamas, trying to smile into a moment of blinding white light. She saw her father and Susan dressed in the patience of whiteness. In every story, there's a daughter whose job it is to die.

"It's not a good idea," Aunt Zoe said. "Trust me."

Uncle Will crouched beside Aunt Zoe. Ben watched from the far corner, by the potted evergreens. Uncle Will whispered to Aunt Zoe, who kept looking at whatever she saw.

"The sun is nice out here," Ben's mother said. "I think it's good for her, sitting in the sun like this."

"Please don't talk about Zoe in the third person," Uncle Will said. "She's right here. Aren't you, kid?"

Aunt Zoe went on nodding. She said, "I'm never anywhere but here."

"Sure, baby," Uncle Will said. "Are you tired?"

"Yes. And no."

"It'd be good to take a rest, wouldn't it?"

"Yes," she said. "And then again, no. Do you know what I mean?"

"Uh-huh. As a matter of fact, I think I do. Hard to stay and hard to go, right?"

"Well, right," she said. "And then again, wrong."

Under his skin, Will was surviving. Something in him had lived, a pellet of clean light that burned inside all the mistakes and foolish habits. Zoe touched his chest, not with her body. He smoothed her hair. He did it with his real hands.

Ben's grandfather went and stood behind Aunt Zoe's chair. He laid his hands on the back of her chair, looked down at the top of her head. He stood over her as if she were a fire.

"I'm going to take the boys out in the boat," he said in Aunt Zoe's direction, over her head. "It's a great day for a sail."

"You don't think it's too windy?" Ben's mother asked.

His grandfather looked up at Ben. His grandfather was tanned and white-haired, the center of everything. Ben thought of what his grandfather saw: the planks of the terrace, Ben himself, the broad slope of dune grass that made an unsteady line across the ocean. Ben tried to be part of that, part of the terrace and the ocean and the sky, all the things that gave his grandfather pleasure.

"What do you think, Ben?" his grandfather called. "Too windy for you?"

"No," Ben answered, and he saw himself on his grandfather's face, what his courage did to it.

"Let's go, then," his grandfather said.

"Yeah. Let's go."

"Where's Jamal?" Uncle Will asked.

"Right," said Ben's grandfather. "Where's Jamal?"

"I'll find him," Ben said.

He jumped over the terrace railing, happy with his own demonstration of grace. He knew where Jamal would be. At their grandfather's, Jamal always found his way down to the miniature forest at the farthest corner, the little stand of pine trees that had been stunted and deformed by the winds that blew in off the ocean. It was where he and Ben had been going together for the past year, huddling down among the scrub to share their quick secret as pine needles whisked over their heads and their parents drank beer on the terrace. Ben was flattered by the fact that Jamal went there alone, for solitude, when the perfection of their grandfather's house overwhelmed him. As he crossed the dune grass, conscious of being watched from the terrace, he was filled with pride and a rinsing, agreeable sense of penitence. He would tell Jamal that they had to stop. They had to take responsibility; they had to think of other people. It would be difficult and gratifying, telling him that. It would be a clean kind of death. Ben would claim his own righteousness. He thought Jamal would understand. Afterward he and Jamal and their grandfather would go sailing. Maybe he'd teach Jamal what Connie hadn't been able to last summer. They'd work the tiller like brothers. As Ben descended the slope that led to the trees he was taken by happiness, a sense of rejoicing he hadn't felt in a year or longer. The ocean spread before him, dazzling, flecked here and there with foam. Behind him stood the shadowed rectitude of the house and the eyes of his family.

His exaltation withered when he reached the little forest and found it empty. He'd been so sure of finding Jamal there, sitting alone, dreamily, on the ground, weighing a pinecone in his hands with his back propped against one of the scaly brown trunks. Everything had turned on the idea of standing beside Jamal in that position, speaking tenderly but firmly into his upturned, lonely face. Ben was overcome by a sudden and wrenching solitude, a desolation, as if by entering the place Jamal was supposed to occupy he'd stepped accidentally into feelings that more rightfully belonged to Jamal. He thought of finding Jamal and dragging him back to the trees, throwing him to the ground and saying—what? Demanding an explanation. Some kind of explanation.

He went to the far edge of the trees, the ocean side. He looked angrily out at the ocean and was thinking of running back to the house, telling everyone that Jamal had disappeared again and that he and his grandfather would have to go out in the boat without him. Then he saw Jamal down on the beach. Jamal stood at the edge of the water, letting the waves splash over his ankles, picking up stones and throwing them in. He picked them up and threw them, over and over, methodically, as if he'd been hired to rid the beach of stones. Ben ran onto the beach. He did not call Jamal's name. He did not put it into the air like that.

Jamal didn't hear Ben approaching, and Ben had to stop himself from grabbing Jamal's baggy yellow shirt and turning him forcibly around. He stood several paces behind Jamal. He said loudly, "Hey."

Jamal turned, and everything changed again. There was his face, frightened in ways only Ben knew. There were his eyes.

"What?" Jamal said.

A new rush of sentiment rose so quickly in Ben that it collided with his anger, exploded into it. He was so full of rage and tenderness he thought he wouldn't survive.

Jamal said, "Look what I found." He bent and picked up a gull's wing. The wing was searingly white, nearly two feet long from the stiff, serrated feathers at its tip to the circle of yellowed bone that had been neatly sheared, as if with a cleaver. The wing had been bleached, hardened, cleaned of its flesh. It was only bone and feathers.

"Gross," Ben said.

"Sort of gross," Jamal said. "And sort of great, huh?"

He stood with the wing in his hands.

"Do you want to go sailing?" Ben said.

"I don't know."

"What else have you got to do?"

"Nothing."

"That's right."

"There's nothing to do here."

"Sailing's something to do."

Jamal held the severed wing in both hands, frowning over it as if it were a treasure and, more obscurely, a burden.

"Okay," he said. "I'll go."

They started up the beach together. Ben said, "You're not bringing that, are you?"

Jamal said, "I think I want to keep it. I want to take it back to the city with me."

Ben knew what their grandfather would think: The crazy son of crazy Aunt Zoe, dragging home parts of dead animals.

"Maybe you should leave it here," Ben said.

"No. I want to keep this. I want to put it on the wall in my room."

"You're really weird."

"Maybe I am."

"It'll *smell.*"

"I don't care."

Jamal carried the wing with him as they walked up the sloping sand and into the miniature forest. The wing in his hands looked strangely correct, as if he had gone out into the world and brought back something that was required of him, something awful and fabulous. When they were hidden among the trees Ben stopped walking and said, "Wait a minute."

"What?"

"I want to talk to you."

"Okay."

Jamal stood carelessly, waiting. He examined the wing, poked a fingertip between the feathers. He was in love with this piece of garbage, this horror. Stupid, so stupid. This stupid boy, but all Ben's plans had involved finding Jamal sitting here, and now he was faced with Jamal's complexities of being, his drifting, unconcerned beauty. Ben was overcome with desire, a nagging and insistent love. He dropped to his knees, pulled at the hem of Jamal's shirt.

"Come on," Ben whispered. "They can't see us."

Jamal remained standing. His shirt stretched tightly over his chest and belly as Ben pulled at it. The tips of the feathers starchily tickled Ben's hair.

"Come *on,*" he said. He wanted to hold Jamal, to feel his defiant head against his chest. He wanted to win him, to comfort him and own his affections. He was lost to rightness, he couldn't make it matter.

"No," Jamal said.

Ben knelt in the dirt, breathing. He didn't say anything. He didn't let go of Jamal's shirt.

"I don't want to do it anymore," Jamal said. "I'm sorry."

"I don't, either," Ben answered.

"Let go."

Ben didn't let go. He didn't speak.

"I have a girlfriend," Jamal said.

"So do I."

"We should stop, okay?"

"This'll be the last time."

"No."

"Please," Ben said.

Jamal looked down at him. The lower half of his face was raggedly framed by the wing.

"Man," he said. "I'm not gay."

Ben didn't speak.

"It's not because I don't love you," Jamal said.

"I don't love you, either. What do you think I am? Your *boyfriend* or something?"

"No," Jamal said. His eyes were black and opaque as coffee. "I don't think you're my boyfriend."

Ben unsnapped the fly of Jamal's jeans. He would lose himself, he would make Jamal stop talking. He would go somewhere else. He wanted only to be lost. "Ben," Jamal said. Ben had Jamal's cock out. He'd never done this before. With a queasy sense of release, like diving from a great height, he took Jamal's cock into his mouth.

It had a slightly salty non-taste. It was Jamal; it was the most secret part of his gentle but decisive beauty. Ben put his hands on Jamal's skinny butt, holding him firmly, and he let himself be lost. He could feel it happening. The golden innocent part was leaving him but he didn't care, he wanted only to be alive in this way, as a vast unreasoning hunger that adored.

"Stop," Jamal said.

Ben didn't stop. He only wanted. He didn't stop until Jamal pulled his hair and looked down hard at him. "I think I hear somebody coming," Jamal said.

Ben listened. He didn't hear anything. He was surprised to feel a single tear sliding down the side of his face. He was lost. He was only desire. He reached again for Jamal but Jamal pulled away and tucked himself back into his pants. Ben throbbed with shame and ardor. He got to his feet. He had just stood up when his grandfather parted the bushes and said, in a voice loud as cracking wood, "Hey, guys, what's holding us up here?"

Ben turned to his grandfather before he remembered the tear. He swiped impatiently at it, as he would at a fly, but he knew his grandfather had seen. Ben's face burned. He said, "Hi, Grandpa," and it came out in his small voice, the one that wanted girlish pleasures.

His grandfather could see the remnants of what had happened. Ben felt certain of it. His grandfather might have become a photograph of himself taken at the precise moment of his death, when the soul had begun its first infinitesimal rise but was still too mired in the cooling flesh to know anything beyond the fact that it was rising, either to glory or torments or just the frigid unthinking fire of the stars.

He knew. He might not yet know that he knew, but the fact had entered him. He had seen Ben in his other condition, red-faced, guilty, stained with a tear.

When Ben's grandfather said, "Let's go, boys," his voice had given up its cheerful, vigorous roll.

Jamal came and stood beside Ben. He slipped his arm over Ben's shoulders. Ben could feel the heave of his own breathing, the pressure of Jamal's arm.

He knocked Jamal's arm away.

"Get away from me," he hissed.

Jamal hesitated, blinking, uncertain.

Ben said, "Get out of here. You fucking little fairy." He said it loud enough for his grandfather to hear.

Jamal appeared to grow smaller and darker, as if a measure of air had seeped out of him. His eyes shrank.

"Leave me alone," Ben said. "Get out of here."

Jamal turned, slowly, and walked back to the beach. Ben watched him go. If Jamal had run, Ben might have felt some scrap of vindication. If he'd shouted or wept or called Ben any of the obvious names. But he only walked, without speaking, as if he had the rest of his life to digest what had happened. He returned, it seemed, to the same spot Ben had found him. He started picking up rocks and throwing them into the water again as if it were his true, fathomless work.

He had left the wing on the ground. It lay curled like a bow, its dry articulate tip and circle of bone pointing up.

Ben turned to his grandfather. There was silence stitched by the distant sound of a bell. There was the smell of pine sap.

His grandfather said, "What's going on?"

"Nothing," Ben answered.

He knew his grandfather would not believe him. The secret hung in the air like gunpowder.

"Jamal isn't coming?" his grandfather said. His voice was measured, illegible.

"No. I don't want him to come."

"You sure?"

"Yes. Let's just you and me go for a sail."

"Okay."

They crossed the field of dune grass together in silence. Sun still picked out each blade, threw its infinitude of sketchy shadows. The house still glowed, its stucco slightly pink, irradiated-looking, in the full light of the ocean. Birds still clattered raucously among the pines.

On the terrace, Aunt Zoe sat between Ben's mother and Uncle Will. She smiled at Ben and his grandfather as if she'd never seen them before.

"Where's Jamal?" Uncle Will asked.

His grandfather said, "Couldn't tear him away from the beach."

Ben took a breath. His grandfather meant to keep the secret, at least for a while. He would respect Aunt Zoe's craziness, her death.

He would tell Ben's mother later, in private. He would tell her something was wrong, and they'd begin the long process of finding out.

"So, I guess it's just Ben and me," his grandfather said. "Unless anybody else wants to come."

"Not me," Ben's mother said. "I'm a land mammal, you know that."

"I'll stick around here, too," Uncle Will said. "The three of us can start dinner."

Aunt Zoe smiled. She looked straight ahead.

There was a watery green light. There was the ordinary business of living and dying, but trees had no words in their language for that. It wasn't something a tree would understand. She would have herself put under a tree, so its roots could wrap themselves around her, enter her body. She wouldn't disappear. She would go up into the branches.

Ben and his grandfather drove to the marina in his grandfather's Mercedes. They did not speak. The day was littered with brightness. As they pulled into the marina's parking lot, sun sparked coolly on the asphalt and on the white masts of the boats. Colored flags snapped. Ben sat in the front seat of his grandfather's car so deeply sunk in misery and shame he knew he would never return.

He was tainted by shame, so marked by it he thought he might be leaving a shadow behind on the upholstery, something dark that would not wash out.

His grandfather turned off the ignition but remained seated at the wheel. Neither of them moved. Presently his grandfather said, "You having some problems with your cousin?"

"I don't know," Ben answered.

"That boy," his grandfather said. The word *boy* caught in his throat like a sliver of bone. "That *boy*"—he coughed the word up—"has had a lot of problems, he's grown up with a bunch of screwballs."

Ben didn't speak. A pressure was growing inside his head, like a fist of hot ice, pushing at his eyes and his ears from inside. What he saw through the windshield—the parked cars, the flags, the masts bobbing with the waves—looked inspired and desolate, like a distant corner of heaven that could not be visited.

"That boy," his grandfather said, "is a little screwy himself. I worry about him."

"Uh-huh," Ben said.

"Did you two have a fight or something?"

"Not really."

His grandfather nodded. He continued to hold the wheel and look straight ahead, as if he were still driving.

Ben understood. He could blame Jamal. He could accuse Jamal of seducing him, and be saved.

"I can straighten a few people out," his grandfather said. "If Jamal is bothering you, I can help take care of it."

Ben nodded.

"I'm not going to let you get screwed up. Not by anybody, not even certain members of your own family. Got that?"

"I've got it."

Ben would accuse Jamal, if he needed to. He would let Jamal be the stranger.

"Let's go for that sail," his grandfather said.

"Okay."

The boat waited for them, serene in its costly perfection, sleek and cool as marble. Ben rigged the mainsail and the jib and thought of Jamal carrying the severed wing. The mainsail, when Ben raised it, was full of a clean, accusatory light.

His grandfather was too large for him. His mother and father were too large. He would allow them to understand that Jamal had tried for sex, and that he had refused. He would let the lie take wind and light the way the mainsail did, and he would be believed.

He would ruin Jamal. He would save himself.

He helped his grandfather into the boat. He cast off, and seated himself at the tiller.

Zoe looked up and saw that Jamal was sitting with her, holding her hand. He was going into time. She had made him and loved him and here he was, the living boy. Here was everything that would still happen. Zoe's lungs filled with fire and she reached for him. She was burning, she was not afraid. She would stay here, watching from the branches of a tree.

Ben's grandfather sat at the prow, solid as an emperor, full of an emperor's massive resolve. Ben piloted the boat easily out of the marina and into the bay. It was a windy day, more of a blow than he was used to but nothing he couldn't handle. He was surprised to find a bitter comfort in his talent for sailing.

"Windy day," his grandfather said. His sparse hair fluttered. It was a good boat, a fast one, and for a moment Ben felt better. A little better. The wind and the boat held each other in a fat luxurious tension Ben commanded. He was able to feel better because here, on the water, he knew exactly what to do. He could pilot his grandfather safely through a slightly difficult afternoon's sailing and he could, if he wanted to, run hard into the wind and dump both of them in the water. It was strong enough today, fifteen or twenty knots, the kind of wind that could capsize you if you didn't treat it with respect. A chop had risen. The swells brewed frothy topknots that sent drops up into the air. Ben took the boat straight out, toward the horizon, toward the deep water. It was a good, fast sailing day. He turned the boat firmly into the wind, looking for as much speed as he could find.

"We'll just make it a short one," his grandfather said. "Half an hour or so, and we'll go home."

Ben lost his small, precarious happiness at the sound of the word *home*. Jamal's strangeness would soon be confirmed, his dangerousness. He would receive no love or comfort after his mother died.

Ben would ruin him.

Water slapped the sides of the boat. A strand of kelp snaked past, its rubbery amber-colored pods floating like a string of miniature bowling pins. Ben turned the boat more directly into the wind, and it heeled so hard to port that his grandfather grabbed the railing for balance.

"We're going pretty fast," his grandfather said.

"Yes, sir," Ben answered.

"You're in charge, buddy. You're the sailor."

"I know."

Ben steered straight out, away from shore. Behind him, windowpanes flashed from rows of diminishing houses. His own hair whipped at his face and it seemed as if his compromised spirit was lashing him, irritating and weak. He brushed the hair angrily out of his face. The wind was getting stronger. It was probably time to take down the jib but Ben left. it up, he wanted more wind and more speed. He wanted to lose himself, to sail so hard and fast he would be nothing but that, a claw cleaving the water. He turned more squarely into the wind. The mainsail and the jib had gone taut as balloons, the boat was heeling so far to port that water splashed up over the side. His grandfather looked back at him. Ben could see the fear on his old, weary face. For now, for a little while, his grandfather had left his world and entered another, a world Ben commanded. The boat was clipping along so fast the wind half blinded him, and he turned still another degree into it. His grandfather said, "Son, aren't we going a little fast?" Son, he'd called Ben son. He couldn't bear it, the love or the shame, and in a last spasm of love and shame he turned the boat too far and it capsized. Ben saw that it was happening. He saw water boil up over the side and he saw his grandfather's face, the pale confused rising of his soul from his body, and then the boat flipped over and spilled them both into the water.

She saw time passing. She saw that fear would be foolish, like wearing an extravagant hat on a windy day and cursing at the wind. Jamal spoke to her in a language she had once known. She was on fire and she felt fine.

The water felt wonderful. It was cold and utterly clean, alive with froth and the sting of salt. Ben lingered underwater, looking from the brightly wrinkled skin of the surface down into the green darkness below him. When he finally surfaced he saw his grandfather's sputtering head less than ten feet away.

"Are you okay?" his grandfather asked.

"Yeah. Are you?"

"What in the hell happened?"

"We capsized."

"I know that."

"We're okay," Ben said. "We're not in any trouble."

"How could this happen?"

"It happened."

"Can we tip the boat up again?"

The boat lay on its side, its hull rising like the back of a small white whale, its sails floating gracefully. Ben looked at the boat and he looked at his grandfather's angry head.

This was the end of the little journey. Now it was time to right the boat, get in, and return to everything that waited on shore.

"It may be hard to do," Ben said.

He wanted only to stay in the water, to join the cold nowhere of it.

"Salesman told me it wouldn't be a problem," his grandfather said, paddling with his strong, thick arms and breathing heavily.

He was right. It would be easy to take hold of the gunnel and bring the boat back up out of the water.

Ben said, "I better go get help."

"What are you talking about, get help? We don't need help."

But Ben started swimming away. He wasn't ready to go yet, so he swam away. His grandfather shouted, "Where are you going?" Ben had no answer beyond the fact that he was swimming away. He wasn't going toward another boat. He wasn't going toward shore. He was going away and with each stroke of his arms he felt freer. Salt water slapped his face and he swam as hard and fast as he could. Ahead there was only more water, water and the blaze of the sky. He swam away from the boat and his grandfather. He only swam. He didn't think. He heard his grandfather calling his name but he was swimming away from that, too. He didn't stop. He didn't slow down.

Zoe laughed at the strangeness of it, the strangeness and the unexpected simplicity. She heard the sound of her own laughter. It was easy, after all. Who'd ever expected it to be easy? She knew how to die; she'd known how all her life. It was as strange and ordinary, as perfect, as a naked man singing a hymn on a fire escape at dawn. You gave it your name. It didn't give back. She remembered the joke she'd told herself, years ago: Other tenants could look out across the cemetery at the source of the music and think, well, shit, it's judgment day, guess I don't have to go to work. Here it is, immaculate music and a hard-on in the new light. Funny to think that the naked angels were as lost as their mortal sisters and brothers, searching the hours in fear and wonder. Nobody knew, and everybody knew. After light there was another light,

and another. Only that. She held her son's hand. She dreamed that
he gave her a wing to hold.

Ben swam for a long time before he allowed himself to pause
and look back. His grandfather and the boat were gone. There was
only water and, surprisingly, a paper cup floating some distance
away. Dixie cup, he said to himself. Sunlight bounced on the water
like an enormous school of jumping, electrified fish. He was afraid
but the fear felt solid in his blood, a large sensation that was not
entirely bad. As long as he stayed in the water, as long as he kept
swimming, nothing had to happen. He couldn't swim forever but
he could swim a little longer. He swam toward the line where the
water met the serene, fiery sky. He swam for a long while. He was
strong. It did not seem possible that no one would find him. Helicopters would come for him soon, Coast Guard cutters, competent
sunburned men with life jackets and bullhorns, whose job it was
to know and to rescue. He let himself swim until they found him.
He swam hard, to exhaust himself, to drain off the wrongness of
his being. When he began to be seriously tired he stopped swimming but when he stopped swimming he returned to himself. He
was not tired enough yet; he was not gone. A swell rose behind
him, broke over his head, and he sucked water in through his mouth
and nose. He coughed. He heard how small the sound of his cough-
ing was in the middle of all this brilliant, restless silence. He became
aware of something in the water, something huge, and he lived
through a paralyzing terror at the thought of sharks. Then the terror
moved beyond him and he knew there were no sharks here. It
wasn't that kind of hunger. It was bigger than that. He was alone
with something enormous that lived in the water, something patient
that heaved and murmured under the daylight sky and watched as
the lights appeared on shore at night, unmoved even by their minor
beauty. He could feel it, the spirit of the water, though *spirit* wasn't
quite right. He could feel the vast, slumbering being of the water
itself. Here, in the water, time was generous, flat, featureless. He

saw that the constellations were present in the afternoon sky. He saw that water lived in another way.

There were no helicopters whirring in the sky, no sleek gray Coast Guard boats slicing through the water. He realized—how could he have forgotten?—that his grandfather didn't know how to sail. His grandfather had probably managed to right the boat but he wouldn't know how to get it moving. He'd be sitting there, helpless, calling Ben's name out over the water.

Suddenly Ben wanted to return to the land and live there with his name. He wanted every humiliation, every regret, all of it. He wanted to swim back but he could see only water, and he'd lost track of the direction in which land lay. There, probably. Or maybe not. If he swam in that direction he might only be swimming farther out. To his right, in roughly the direction he thought of as landward, he saw two sails, pale as quarter moons. They were a long way off but he swam in their direction. He forced himself to swim hard. He swam until his arms and legs started to burn and his breathing grew shallow. His body demanded that he stop but he refused to stop. He needed to reach the boats just as urgently as he had needed to swim away from his name. He needed to be pulled out of the water by strangers' hands, and taken back. As he swam he realized he had started to shiver. It surprised him with its violence, and it seemed to have been going on for a while, though he could not remember when it had started. His teeth were clattering loudly. He told himself he had to reach the boats and he swam with a steady push of his will until suddenly his arms would not move. It had never happened to him before and he assumed it to be temporary. His arms always moved when he wanted them to. His legs could still kick and he continued kicking while he waited for his arms to return. His body refused to stop shivering. His arms hung heavily in the water and he made his legs kick. He looked for the boats. He couldn't see them. His head slipped underwater and briefly his arms returned, paddled him back up to the air. He looked for the boats. He told his body to swim and it did, jerkily, in froglike movements. Was he in trouble? Maybe. Maybe he was in trouble. He swam. He thought he would be all right. He was tired. Without having meant to, he slipped into a dream. In the dream he stood on a field of grass. Beyond the field there were hills, and in the hills was a town. He didn't go to the town, but he knew it was there. A bird flew over, and he returned. He fought his way back. There was something in the water, an immense, silent being. Gulls dipped down to the surface, skreaking, looking for fish, and he thought he couldn't be in serious trouble if there were birds present. He swam but he was shivering and his arms didn't work very well. He saw one of his hands floating by and for a moment he believed there was someone with him, swimming alongside. No, it was his own hand. He looked at his hand. He saw how it shook. He went into a dream again, and in this dream he was held like a baby. He was rocked, and he had his red car, the one he loved so much, with the cream-colored seats and the doors that opened. The dream ended but a part of him stayed inside it. He saw that there was a place inside the dream. He could let himself be rocked. He could hold the car, spin its wheels with his fingers. Or he could keep swimming. He knew he could find the ability to do so, but he knew he could also stop and if he stopped he would be here, in the silence, outside of time and his name. It struck him as a guilty pleasure, a marvelous and forbidden thing. He let out a voluptuous sigh. He had a song running through his head, something stupid he'd never meant to remember. He let himself dream about little rubber wheels and a wing and a tree. They were radiant. He was surprised to find that he was not dreaming of other people. He was dreaming of wheels and a wing. Green transparencies opened before him, a lush field scattered with stars. He saw himself going down into a cold granular darkness, though he seemed to bring a quantity of pale, unsteady light with him. He watched, fascinated. The water below looked dark but when he got to where it had been dark he found it to be light, faintly light, like the air of his bedroom at home when the light from the hall seeped in under the door. He spun the wheels of the car with his fingers. He looked up. The surface was far above him, illuminated like living glass. Surprising, how far away. He realized where he was, he realized what was happening, and with a spasm of terror his body bucked and he rose toward the surface. It grew closer, his arms and legs burned and his chest burned. He would be all right. The surface was far away and he had no sensation of reaching it but he must have reached it because his lungs filled with air, painfully. He looked around for the birds and the boats but saw only the grainy jade of the water. He saw light hanging in the water. He saw bubbles perfect as stars. It was then that he realized he could leave himself and breathe the water. He could go or he could stay. The water was spacious; it was he; it would hold him. He let himself breathe. The pain vanished. The coldness of the water came into him, an icy relief. He was rising and he left himself, he let the water have him. He let it have him.

The current carried Ben's body with a steady insistence south-west, back toward the shore. Minnows browsed over his face, and occasionally one darted halfway into his open mouth, hung there with its gills twitching, and sped away again. As Ben moved through the water the bottom rose, grew lighter and more distinct. Strips of watery sunlight played over him, caught the translucent shine of his eyes. Then the sunlight began to fade. His body didn't reach the beach at Shelter Island until after sundown, and by then the beach was empty. The waves kept pushing his body onto the sand, pushed it and pulled it back and pushed it that much farther forward again, until finally at high tide, just before midnight, a wave laid him on the sand and retreated and did not return. Ben's body lay face up on the sand, one arm flung back over his head and the other angled awkwardly over his chest in a contorted position particular to the dead. It was a clear night. The Crab and the Seven

Sisters were out. Ben's body rested undisturbed on the beach for several hours, facing up. He was spangled, ominous, full of a dark and abandoned beauty. A sprinkling of small shells had caught in his hair and a circle of translucent white glass, worn smooth as an opal by the water, lay in his open mouth.

1 9 9 4 / If he'd come home earlier.
If he'd visited Cassandra more.
If he'd loved the way he should have.
If he'd been less selfish.
If he'd gone in the boat.
If he hadn't said no.

1 9 9 4 / Susan thought she would steal him. She was awake. She hadn't taken the pills. She lay in bed, thinking about what she'd do.

She needed to see him. She'd had no time.

She lay in bed thinking about where he was. The embalming would be finished by now and everyone would have gone home. He'd be there in the strange building with green imitation-leather chairs and white-wigged porcelain figures silently bowing in the curio cabinet.

She knew what was coming tomorrow. The gifts of food, the friends with condolences. There would not be a second, not a second, for her to be alone with Ben. Even if she demanded privacy at the funeral parlor it would be a contained privacy, with friends and family on the other side of the door, waiting generously but with mounting impatience for her to finish up so they could all get on with the business at hand. And she'd have Todd to take care of. He lay in bed beside her, breathing under the sleeping pills she herself had only pretended to swallow. She didn't want sleep, not now. She wanted every minute.

It wouldn't help her, a stolen hour at the funeral parlor with Ben lying quietly in his navy-blue suit while the wristwatches ticked down the hall. It wouldn't help to sit with him in a room amid the hush of flowers, the shifting particulars of colored light.

She wanted no one to know where they were, not even Todd. She wanted to carry him out onto the grass and sit with him while his body was still his body, before the changes started. She wanted to comb his hair and she wanted to sing the songs of his childhood into his cold, familiar ear. If she could do that, she might be ready to relinquish him to mourning, to the realm of the dead. If she could do that, she might continue to live as someone she recognized.

She got quietly out of bed. Todd murmured, slept on. To avoid waking him, she didn't get dressed. She went downstairs in her nightgown, took a coat from the hall closet. She walked barefoot out onto the cold stones of the porch.

She drove to the mortuary and parked behind the building, in a space reserved for staff. She turned off the ignition, turned off the headlights. She sat in her car watching the clapboard wall, the single window in which a potted geranium bloomed. She wasn't sure why she'd come. She hadn't meant to break into the mortuary, not really, although the thought had been somewhere in her head. Even if she got in, if she broke a window, what would she do? Would she search among the caskets for Ben's body? Would she drag his body out and put it in the car? She wasn't crazy, not crazy like that. But she needed to be here. She imagined taking Ben in her arms, the supple chill of his body. She saw her fingers raking through his hair. She sang, softly, under her breath. She sat in her car for several hours, keeping watch, sometimes singing and sometimes only sitting. Shortly before the sun rose she fired the ignition and turned on the headlights, which cast a watery, lunar light on the brightening clapboard wall of the mortuary. She drove home again. She hung her coat in the closet, walked carefully upstairs, and got back into bed without awakening Todd. She waited for the alarm to ring.

The viewing room slightly resembled the house she grew up in. It had that air of carefully assembled normality. There were armchairs upholstered in imitation leather and love seats done in a fabric meant to resemble embroidery. There were glass-topped oval tables and brass lamps with stiffly pleated shades and a spotless fireplace with three birch logs stacked on the grate. Ben's casket lay like a piece of furniture before a mute gathering of bronze-toned metal chairs with white cushions, on an expanse of deep-pile carpeting the color of limes coated with dust.

Susan had insisted on keeping the casket closed. She now regretted that decision. She found that she wanted to break the glassy spirit of the room, its lime-and-brass insistence on domestic order. She thought of telling the director to raise the lid but she worried that her son's body, his rouged face and still hands, would too closely match the room's other furnishings. The lid remained closed. She spoke to visitors as they entered, and thought only once or twice during the afternoon of how a room like this, all cleanliness and chemical hush, was the true representation of grieving. As children we imagine tilted stones, a shifting darkness, clouds cutting across the moon, and think we're entertaining our deepest fears. We are wrong. The true horror that waits, she believed, are these Scotchgarded love seats printed with pale green and blue needlepoint, these shelves with their porcelain figures. This well-kept, empty room. The dead disappear into it.

Susan acted like a woman at the funeral of her only son. She couldn't break through it, not quite. She couldn't not perform. There were so many people who needed her courage. She told herself, as the time passed in front of her, that she was glad to have these limits. She thought it probably saved her to hold Todd as he shuddered dryly, racked by a grief that took him beyond tears, and it saved her to comfort her mother and Will and Todd's parents, to cry with them and hold them reassuringly. It saved her to be kind to Jamal, who stood blank and frozen in a corner.

"Hi," she said, bending slightly into him and speaking distinctly, as if in his silence he had lost a measure of hearing and sight.

He smiled weakly at her.

"I'm glad you came," she said.

He nodded.

"Do you want anything?" she asked. "A glass of water?"

"No, thank you."

She straightened herself, withdrew from him. Maybe he needed to be left alone, this strange boy. Maybe something showed on her face, however polite she made herself. She tried not to think about it: He was still alive. This boy who was not a bad boy but was not remarkable in any way was alive, and her son had died.

"There are more comfortable chairs over there," she said, "if you feel like sitting down."

"No, thank you."

"All right," she said, and left him.

Her father sat in the first row of seats, with Magda beside him. He had been weeping, though he was not weeping now. He sat bent over, with his elbows planted on his knees and his hands covering his nose and mouth, as if he feared what he might smell or what he might say.

Susan sat on the empty chair to his right. She nodded to Magda, who returned her nod with an expression that might have been grief and might have been impatience with the whole stately business of mourning. Susan thought she would put her arm over her father's shoulders, but she hesitated and then folded her hands in her lap.

"Susie," her father said. His voice was clotted and indistinct.

"Yes, Dad?"

She could not seem to lose this sense of herself as a hostess. She sat erect on the metal chair. Her father breathed wetly beside her and in front of her her son lay inside a casket. She saw, suddenly, how much the casket she had chosen for him resembled the stereo cabinet in the house her parents had bought and furnished when she was thirteen. It had the same chestnut luster; it had the same curved bevel along the lid. When she and Todd had had to make the selection, she'd gone immediately to this one without quite knowing why.

"Susie," her father said. He reached for her. He wrapped his arm around her shoulders and drew her close. She could smell his familiar cologne, the old musk of his skin. She felt herself being taken by him. She knew what he needed from her, how much love and forgiveness.

"Get your hands off me," she said. She had not meant to say anything. She had not meant to speak as loudly as she did.

Her father clasped her more closely. Her lips touched the grainy slope of his cheek and she believed she could taste him, a combination of lint and age and rank, perfumed sex.

"Shh," he said. "Shush, now."

She pulled out of his embrace and said, more loudly, "Get your hands off me."

She stood up. A part of her acted and a part of her watched herself act. Her father raised his hands to his chest, palms out, as if to protect himself. Magda looked at Susan with an expression of pity more dreadful than any rage.

"Susie," her father said.

"I don't want you here," she said. She was aware of her voice, how loud it was among the love seats and the dusted shelves.

"Susan. Honey. Please."

"Get out," she said. "You've paid your respects, you've seen what you came to see. Now go. I can't look at you anymore, I don't want you touching me."

She could feel the silence around her, all the stunned horror. Unthinkingly, she smoothed her hair with her fingertips.

Her father glanced at the back of the room, searching for help. Magda stood up and walked toward Susan. She said, "Sit down, dear, you don't know what you're saying."

Susan stepped backward. "I do know," she said. "I know exactly what I'm saying. Magda, I want you to take him home. I want you to get him out of here. Do it and I'll never ask you for anything again."

A hand touched her shoulder. It was Billy.

"It's okay," he said, close to her ear.

"No it isn't," she told him.

"Let's go for a walk. Just leave him here and come for a walk with me, will you do that?"

"No," she said. "I can't leave."

"We'll come back. Come on, now."

He took her hand and she found that she followed him. She hadn't meant to. They walked together down the aisle that had been left between the rows of chairs. Todd came to her, tried to speak. Billy waved him away.

"She and I need to be alone together," he said. "I'll bring her right back."

"Susan?" Todd said.

"It's okay," she said. "I want to go with Billy."

They left the mortuary and walked along the flagstone path to the sidewalk. The mortuary stood in a neighborhood of prosperous old houses, on a street lined with trees that had begun, tentatively, to go yellow. Billy held her hand and led her up the sidewalk, which was honeycombed with cracks in which emerald veins of moss fatly grew.

She found that she could be with her brother. Of all people, she could stand to be with him. She could let him hold her hand. She could walk beside him.

"You really let the bastard have it," Billy said.

"I can't talk."

"You don't have to. I just want you to walk with me until you feel calm enough to get through the service. It would be better to get through the service, if you think you can do that."

"I'm not sure," she said.

"Wait and see. Just walk a little, and see what happens."

She walked with her brother. There was nothing else for her to do. She let him hold her hand and lead her past the houses with their lawns and porches, their flower beds. After a while she said, "I can't stand having him there."

"You'll kill him if you make him leave," Billy said. "He already feels so guilty."

"He's never felt guilty about anything in his life."

"He feels guilty about this. Believe me."

"You don't know. You have no idea."

"I was the one who used to want to kill him," he said. "You used to defend him to me."

"We were children then."

They walked for a while in silence. Susan was filled with a white-hot, dispassionate fury unlike anything she had known. She wished ruin on the people who owned these comfortable houses, the people who tended these yards or who paid others to tend them. She wished bankruptcy on these people, disease, unspeakable losses. She touched the trunk of a tree and thought of floodwaters roiling down this innocent street, a wall of churning mud that would break through the doors of the houses and carry off their clocks and books and chairs. She wanted to race the flood back to the mortuary, throw herself on her son's casket and ride with it as the water swept it out into the ruined world. She imagined the living drowned and the dead floated up out of their graves, a battalion of coffins racing past the mute, shattered faces of houses and stores.

"Are you feeling any better?" Billy asked her.

"I don't know. Maybe a little."

"Can you face the service?"

"I suppose."

They turned and started back toward the mortuary. Billy said, "He's just an old man. Try and remember that."

She said. "Remember how he used to beat you up?"

"And remember how you used to tell me he didn't know what he was doing?"

"Yes."

"That was all a long time ago," Billy said.

"It was, wasn't it?"

"He's an old man now, and whether or not he knew what he was doing when we were kids, he's just about out of his mind with guilt about what happened. We can probably let him off the hook a little, don't you think?"

"I suppose."

"It would be better for you, too. I don't want to seem like I'm giving advice, or anything."

"No. I know what you're saying."

They walked back to the mortuary, up the flagstone path, past the discreet iron sign with the owners' names—two brothers—done in scrolled lettering. Inside, the foyer and the green lobby had not changed. They would be like this forever. Billy escorted her into the viewing room, and when they entered, a wave of hushed recognition ran through the crowd of mourners. She could feel it. She thought of her wedding day, the moment when the march had started and she'd stepped down the aisle in her dress and veil. Todd came immediately to her, as did her mother.

"Are you all right?" Todd asked, and at the same time her mother said, "Honey, what's going on?"

"I'm okay," she answered. "I just needed some air."

"Sit down," Todd said. "Over here."

"No. I'm all right, really."

She reassured them as best she could, though her true attention was fixed on her father, who waited for her at the head of the aisle, near Ben's casket. She disengaged herself from Billy and Todd and her mother. She walked down the aisle to her father.

"Susie?" he said. His face was worn and expectant, full of ravaged hope. He was dense and shame-faced in his somber suit, haggard under his suntan, jowled. He had never looked so old.

"Hello, Dad," she said.

"Is everything okay?"

"What do you think?"

"I don't know. I don't know what to think."

She stepped up to him, took his jaw firmly in her hands. She knew how crazy she must look, how vengeful, by the panic she saw skate across his eyes.

"Susan?" he said in a small voice.

She decided. Still holding his jaw, she put her mouth on his. She kept her eyes open. Soon he tried to pull away but she kept her mouth on his. She held her mouth in place and she continued looking into his eyes until she saw that the knowledge had entered him. Then she held her mouth over his a little longer, until she felt sure he knew he was not forgiven.

1 9 9 4 / He had the pictures, but he never looked at them. He had them. That was enough.

He had the house and he had the pictures. He had land with a garden on it. He stood at the edge of his garden. He watched the constellations turning over the bare vines and the black scraps of the leaves. A winter moon had risen.

Ben was buried. Zoe was buried. His youngest and strangest child. His most familiar child. She had knelt here, right here, and held a tomato she'd believed to be clean. She'd worn a dark silk dress into the ground.

He had failed. He hadn't loved enough, or had loved too much. He couldn't follow it, not quite. He could list his failings but they didn't add up to this, the empty earth and the sky filled with bright little points of ice.

The house rose behind him. Inside were the pictures. He thought of the house as containing the pictures. That was its purpose now. That was why its boards lay solidly, one upon another, and its windows were kept closed and its curtains drawn.

West of here, Mary lived her life of order. She'd wanted to

name their youngest child Joan. She'd wanted to name her Barbara.

She'd wanted safety for her, ordinary beauty, and now Constantine wondered: Had Mary dreamed of this garden at night, this cold moon? Had she hoped Zoe would live more certainly under another name?

He said their names, quietly, over the garden. He said, "Mary. Susan. Billy. Zoe."

"Constantine?"

He turned. It was Magda, standing pale and stern as a second moon.

"Hello," he said.

"Come in," she said. "It's cold out here."

He shrugged. He gestured with his hands at the moon and the frozen garden.

"Never mind about that," she told him. "Come on, now."

"I'm not ready," he said. "Not yet."

"Don't be foolish."

"All the stars are out tonight. You can see the Seven Sisters."

She frowned up at the sky. "It's freezing," she said. "Come in the house."

"Soon."

"Now."

"Now?"

"Yes. Now."

She stood with her arms folded over her breasts. "Now," she said again.

"All right," he answered.

"That's a good boy," she said.

"Right. A good boy."

"Come on. Let's put you to bed."

"I'm not ready to go to bed."

"Yes, you are."

"I am?"

"Yes."

"All right."

"All right?" she said.

"Yes," he answered. "Let's put me to bed."

"Come on, then."

"I'm coming."

She held out her arm and he took it. He walked carefully back with her toward the darkness of the house, where the pictures were and his bed lay in a square of moonlight.

"Magda?" he said.

"Yes?"

"Do you love me, baby?"

"Shh."

"Do you? Do you love me?"

"Be quiet," she said. He obeyed her.

1 9 9 5 / Fat waves rolled lazily up against the Battery, broke blue-black and glittering, with a faint sound of exhalation. The sky over Manhattan held an immense and agitated light, here gray threaded with yellow, there an unsteady, aquatic green. In the harbor the Statue of Liberty held its book as tiny people stood inside its head, looking out.

Mary sat on the bench with Jamal and Harry, facing the harbor and the statue. Jamal wore his Walkman, nodded to the music. The bass line leaked out, a staticky thump/thump/quarter-thump.

"It's nice here," she said. "I've never been to the Battery before, isn't that funny? In all these years."

"I've been making Jamal and Will show me the sights," Harry told her. "Since I'm not from New York, I don't have to obey the rules about corny tourist attractions. Last week we went to the Empire State Building, right, Jamal?"

"What?"

"We went to the Empire State Building last weekend."

"Uh-huh."

Harry knew nothing but to speak and act. His life was too

unexpected, he couldn't let himself worry. If he'd started wondering, he'd have lost his nerve. He'd have lashed himself to his old habits; he'd have said no. He didn't want to say no. So he didn't wonder, he didn't worry. He got the new job in New York, rented the apartment. He insisted on being shown the sights.

"That's Ellis Island out there, isn't it?" Mary said.

"Yeah," said Harry. "That's it."

"Constantine didn't go through there," Mary said. "By the time he came to the States, Ellis Island was closed. He just landed at a dock somewhere on the West Side, I've never been sure where. We never talked all that much about his life before he came here."

"They've fixed it up," Harry said.

"I know."

"It's a tourist attraction now. You can walk through the rooms where all those people were inspected to see if they were healthy enough to be allowed in here to work as day laborers for money no native-born American would accept. Then you can go have lunch in the restaurant."

"I'd like to see it someday. Ellis Island."

"We can go today if you want. We have all afternoon."

Mary said, "What do you think, Jamal? Do you want to see Ellis Island?"

"What?"

"Do you want to go see Ellis Island?"

Jamal shrugged, jiggled his feet to the music. He looked at his feet as if they might, at any moment, do something marvelous and unexpected.

"Maybe Ellis Island is a little too tame," Harry said. "Maybe we should go shopping in the East Village, and then have a pizza."

"Okay," Jamal said.

"You spoil him," Mary said.

"I know," Harry answered. "There's nothing I can do about it."

Mary was seized by emotion, and she did not speak. She sat with Jamal and Harry. She knew herself as a woman of sixty-three, wearing slacks and a cotton sweater and a strand of pearls given to her by someone impossible whom she had loved. So little remained. Jamal's music thumped, and she could feel his agitation along the slats of the bench. She watched gulls careen through the cloudy air. She saw Will coming back, carrying soda in paper cups. There was a sky full of shifting light and there were these people, this boy who was as closed to her, as impenetrable, as either of her daughters had been. There were drinks in red cups.

So much remained.

"Here comes Will," Harry said.

"Mm-hm."

Mary thought, I can love this. I can try. I can try to love it. There's nothing else for me to do.

"Okay," Will said. "Coke, Diet Coke, Diet Coke."

"Thanks, honey," Mary said.

"Thanks, Dad," said Harry.

Jamal accepted his drink without speaking, without leaving the music.

"You're welcome, Jamal," Will said.

Boats churned through the water. Pillows of air blown in off the harbor turned the leaves of the trees.

Harry said, "We've decided to abandon all notions of going out to the Statue of Liberty or Ellis Island. We've decided to go shopping in the East Village, and then get a pizza."

"You spoil him," Will said.

"I know."

Will reached over and ran his fingers through Jamal's hair. Jamal pulled his head away, pretending an attack of rhythm.

"So," Will said. "Shall we go up to the East Village?"

"Okay," Jamal said.

"Spoiled, spoiled," Will murmured.

Jamal stood up and shifted from leg to leg, in sunglasses and a pair of pants so enormous Will wondered how he kept them up. Jamal asked, "What are those big blocks over there?"

"A memorial," Harry told him. "I don't know what war."

"Want to go take a look?" Will asked.

"I don't know," Jamal said.

"Let's look," Will said. "That'll be our nod to education and general self-improvement for today, all right?"

"I think it's World War II," Mary said.

"What?"

"Those stones. I think they're a memorial to the men who died in World War II."

"And the women?" Jamal asked.

"Well, yes. I suppose there must have been some women, too."

They walked up the esplanade toward the stone tablets. Trees shivered with their new leaves, silver green in the cloudy light. They climbed a bank of stairs to a broad plaza flanked by two rows of tall, concrete-colored marble slabs incised with thousands of names. At the landward end an immense bronze eagle spread its heavy wings. They walked quietly among the stones. Jamal ran his hand over a roster of names, feeling the squeak his hand made. He swayed to the music.

In another year, Constantine will lie in a hospital bed watching the white summer sky through the window as he begins to die from the stroke he's suffered. He will be aware of his feet under a white blanket, and of a gray feather blowing by beyond the glass. Magda will sit beside him. She won't say anything when he whispers, "Momma." She won't contradict him and she won't answer. She will let him take her hand, and will listen as he repeats the word. She will sit in silence, waiting.

Soon after Constantine dies, Susan will leave her husband. She will find a job in the sales department of a printing company, and will eventually marry one of the men who own the company, a man much older than herself. Her new husband, a widower with grown sons, will take his sons out the night before the wedding and tell them, in a voice he is scarcely able to control, that he had believed his life would hold no new pleasures, nothing beyond the daily particulars of ink and paper, until he met this woman.

The sons will wish him well, and secretly despise him for betraying their dead mother. He will love Susan with a quiet tenacity that does not end, and Susan will give birth, at the age of forty-nine, to a girl. She will insist on naming the baby Zoe.

Will and Harry and Jamal will live in New York together until Jamal leaves for Berkeley at eighteen. While Jamal is still young, Mary will sell her house and buy an apartment in the city. She will wait for him in her apartment when he gets out of school and will try, not often successfully, to keep him there until Will and Harry are home from their jobs. After Jamal leaves for college, she will live another twenty-two years in intermittent spells of contentment and loneliness. She will know, at moments, a perfect joy made of simple things: a teacup throwing its shadow on a windowsill, a book she takes to the park on a warm September afternoon.

Will and Harry will stay together, not always easily, for the rest of their lives. Will will have an affair, be forgiven, and then have another. He and Harry will part for almost a year, in their early fifties, and then begin dating again. As Will's muscles soften and his skin goes opaque with age, he will remain faithful.

Harry will die first, at seventy-eight. When he falls ill, Jamal will fly east from California with his wife and his son to be with him. They'll stay for a few days and then Will will tell them to go back, return to their lives, they've said goodbye to Harry and there's nothing else they can do. Will will kiss Jamal, who is weeping. He'll tell Jamal he was a good son, and that Harry knew he loved him, it didn't matter about visits. After Jamal and his family have gone, Will, nearly deaf, will sit another several days with Harry. He'll whisper to him, lay his spotted hand over Harry's wasted one. At the end, when Harry is shivering from an inner cold the heat of the room can't touch, Will will carefully ease his own body into bed beside Harry's and hold him, trying to give whatever warmth he can. He won't be certain if Harry knows he's there. He will tell Harry, softly, speaking close to his ear, that it's all right now, he can go. It would be a good time to go. There will be no telling whether Harry can hear him. Harry will live another twelve hours, and slip away late at night, while Will sleeps nearby in the other bed.

Will will live another seven years. As he dies, Jamal will return to stay with him. Jamal won't hire a nurse. He'll feed Will himself, wipe his chin, change the foul linens. He'll grow impatient with Will's helplessness. He'll curse, inwardly, but he'll do everything that's needed. He'll feed and wash Will and when Will is able to talk he'll talk to him. He'll talk to Will about the fears he feels for his children. The boy from his first marriage runs wild, has no ambition. The little girl, born when Jamal himself faces the close of middle age, exhausts him with her fits of temperament, the magnitude of her will. Jamal will talk about his second wife, whom he loves with a desperation that wounds him, exalts him, drains him of energy. Will will nod, listening and not listening. He'll be thinking of Jamal, not the facts Jamal restlessly narrates but the living fact of him, here in the room. He'll think of the living presences of Jamal and Harry, who has not been much affected by his body's death. He'll be visited by everyone he's known and he'll see that they've been burned clean of their traits, all the meannesses and failures, all the virtues. There will be company, a certain satisfaction. There will be a trembling, as if the room itself is shedding its qualities—bed, table, picture on the wall—and melting into a ferocious light that has no name.

Now, right now, Jamal performs a loose-limbed, solitary dance among the stone tablets. When he fills his head with music he doesn't think about his mother and Cassandra. He doesn't think about Ben. He goes to another place. Will and Harry stand together, silently reading the names of strangers. They try to absorb themselves in the list because neither of them can imagine how he'll get through this afternoon or the next day. Mary runs her finger into the corners of a stranger's name, looks out at the harbor. If she read every name she would probably recognize somebody, a son of a friend of her mother's or a slightly older boy she'd longed for in high school. She drinks from the cup her son has brought her. She fingers the pearls at her throat.

Will squeezes Harry's hand. He has lived to this point, and he feels grateful. He's lived to be a forty-two-year-old man who loves and is loved by another and who must pose, somehow, as father to a shocked, grieving thirteen-year-old boy. Here they are together, he and Harry, feigning interest in a roster of deceased strangers, about to spend a few hours going from store to store. Will knows how much Jamal wants a new pair of white Nikes. He knows Mary will buy them for him. He knows that, for Jamal, much suffering pales beside the vision of new white Nikes. A new pair of shoes will save him. In the right shoes he can jump out of harm's way, walk an immaculate walk.

Will reads a few names, silently. George E. Swink, Leonard J. Szulc, William E. Talley. Men half his age, most likely—young men who fell burning from the sky or were shot or drowned or crushed in a war that has already lost its edges and become a fact of history. He imagines the names of his own dead, carved into the face of a stone, and he thinks of buying shoes for Jamal. This is what the living do, he tells himself. We perform the little errands, and visit the stones.

He beckons to his mother, who is standing between him and the harbor. She is outlined in light.

"Let's go," he calls.

She nods, and walks toward him.

Harry says, "Jamal? You ready?"

Jamal is nodding to the music. He performs a shimmy, half in and half out of the shadow of a stone.

Will speaks.

Jamal watches from inside the music.

2 0 3 5 /   "Where are you going?"

"I told you."

"Where?"

"I'm going down to the bay. I won't be too long."

"What's in that box?"

"I've told you this five times."

"What?"

"It's your grandfathers' ashes. Do you remember your Grandfather Will?"

"No."

"We went to see him, oh, more than a year ago. You were very
small then. We flew to New York and we stayed in his house with
him. He was very old."

"I know that."

"These are his ashes. His and Harry's. I'm going to go put
them in the bay and then I'm going to come home and we can start
the garden together, all right?"

"I want to come."

"You can't come. I've told you and told you this."

"Why not?"

"Because I need to go alone."

"Why?"

"Well. Because I lived with Harry and Will a long, long time ago."

"When you were a little boy."

"That's right. So now I need to be by myself when I put their ashes in the bay. I need you to stay here with your momma, and when I come back we'll plant the garden. Okay?"

"I want to come."

"You can't."

"I want to take the box to the car."

"Okay. Will it make you happy if I let you carry the box to the car? Here."

"It makes a noise."

"What?"

"It makes a *noise*."

"Well, sure, if you shake it like that. Be just a little bit careful, okay?"

"What's inside?"

"Ashes. I told you. Just some ashes."

"They make a noise."

"It's ashes and little bits of bone. It's nothing to be scared of."

"I'm not scared."

"Don't I know that? You're not afraid of anything, are you?"

"I can hear them."